A TICKET TO HELL
HELL CAN WAIT
Harry Whittington
Introduction by Tom Simon

Stark House Press • Eureka California

A TICKET TO HELL / HELL CAN WAIT

Published by Stark House Press
1315 H Street
Eureka, CA 95501
griffinskye3@sbcglobal.net
www.starkhousepress.com

A TICKET TO HELL
Copyright © 1959 by Fawcett Publications, Inc., and published
by Gold Medal Books. Copyright © renewed January 7, 1987
by Harry Whittington.

HELL CAN WAIT
Copyright © 1960 by Fawcett Publications, Inc., and published
by Gold Medal Books. Copyright © renewed February 22, 1988
by Harry Whittington.

Permission to reprint granted by the Kathryn L Whittington Trust.
All rights reserved under International and Pan-American Copyright
Conventions.

"Investigating Harry" copyright © 2022 by Tom Simon

ISBN-13: 978-1-951473-66-2

Text design and layout by Mark Shepard, shepgraphics.com
Cover design by Jeff Vorzimmer, ¡caliente!design, Austin, Texas
Cover art by Victor Olson
Proofreading by Bill Kelly

PUBLISHER'S NOTE:
This is a work of fiction. Names, characters, places and incidents are
either the products of the author's imagination or used fictionally, and
any resemblance to actual persons, living or dead, events or locales, is
entirely coincidental. Without limiting the rights under copyright
reserved above, no part of this publication may be reproduced, stored, or
introduced into a retrieval system or transmitted in any form or by any
means (electronic, mechanical, photocopying, recording or otherwise)
without the prior written permission of both the copyright owner and the
above publisher of the book.

First Stark House Press Edition: April 2022

A TICKET TO HELL

When Ric pulls into the New Mexico motel, he isn't looking for company. He's supposed to meet someone. He doesn't know who, or when, but he knows that he can't afford to get involved with anyone else's problems. But while he waits, he watches the couple across the court. The husband is too handsome for his own good, and the woman's pretty easy on the eyes as well. When Ric sees the man step outside his room, turn off the gas, turn it on again, then leave, he knows that something is not right. He discovers the wife unconscious, her body staged to look like a suicide. Ric doesn't want to get involved, but now he's got a desperate woman on his hands, and more trouble than he needs.

HELL CAN WAIT

Greg Morris is twisted up with hate. He and his new wife and been driving to Rainbow Lake when they are hit by another car. And not just any car, but one driven by rich and powerful Saul Koons. His wife dead, Morris lies in his hospital bed, expecting justice to prevail. Clearly Koons was in the wrong. A local lawyer wants to prove it. But by the end of the trial, Koons has turned it around so that the accident appears to be entirely Morris' fault, and Koons the injured party. Now Morris is back in town, sick with hate and plotting his revenge. But how to you hurt a man who owns the whole town and everyone in it? You find his one weak spot... his wife.

7
Investigating Harry
By Tom Simon

13
A Ticket to Hell
By Harry Whittington

121
Hell Can Wait
By Harry Whittington

243
Harry Whittington
Bibliography

INVESTIGATING HARRY
by Tom Simon

"Have you ever heard of an author named Harry Whittington?" I asked the used bookstore lady.

I was in Ocala, Florida trying to dig up information that might be helpful for the introduction to this Harry Whittington twofer. Smarter guys than me have written introductions for previous Harry Whittington reprints. I needed an angle, so I was sniffing around Harry's childhood hometown looking for leads.

I should probably explain that I'm a recently-retired FBI Special Agent who spent the last five years investigating federal crimes in Northern Florida. I worked a handful of cases in Ocala, but this was my first time back since I retired and opened my own private eye firm. However, it wasn't my sleuthing that landed me this writing gig. Stark House hit me up because of my side-hustle, a blog and podcast called Paperback Warrior where I cover pulp fiction with my buddy Eric. We host the largest collection of Harry Whittington book reviews on the internet, so Stark House figured I might have something to say about Harry's work that hadn't already been said—a tall order.

Facing the problem of what to write that hadn't already been covered, I recalled a saying: "When all you have is a hammer, every problem looks like a nail." I'm an investigator, so I drove down to Ocala to knock on some doors.

A *Ticket to Hell* was the first of Harry's books I read and remains my favorite. I reviewed *Hell Can Wait* much later and enjoyed it quite a bit. I could go on and on about the stuff I liked about each paperback, but I don't want to spoil either novel for you. I hate it when introductions do that, and I don't want to be that guy. You should read both, and I promise you'll like them. If you only have one week to live and must choose, go with *A Ticket to Hell*. It's the stronger of the pair.

Ocala is pretty far inland, so erase from your mind images of the sandy beaches of Miami or Daytona. This is non-coastal Florida marshland. Harry clearly drew upon this lush and humid ecosystem for many of his swamp-noir novels— *Cracker Girl*, *Swamp Kill*, *Backwoods Hussy*, and *Backwoods Shack* among them. If that sub-genre is your jam, the best is *Backwoods Tramp*, also released as *A Moment To Prey*. Driving through the sand pines and magnolia trees of the Ocala National Forest, I understood why this setting was so alluring for many of Harry's early paperbacks. It's a vivid and earthy place thick with Spanish moss dripping from the branches—a perfect setting for a rural noir tale.

When Harry was growing up, Ocala was a one-horse town. Nowadays, there are thousands of horses. In fact, breeding and training horses is Ocala's main industry. The city leaders call it "The Horse Capital of the World," and Marion County is home to more than 600 thoroughbred farms. Back in Harry's day, Ocala farmers were mostly raising citrus, cotton and tobacco.

Fun Fact: The town's only real celebrity today is John Travolta, who owns a giant compound in a subdivision with its own runway. I wanted to ask him if he's heard of Harry Whittington, so I drove out to his gated neighborhood to snoop. I made it through a haphazardly-opened gate and toured for about ten minutes marveling at the mansions—each with its own airplane hangar. There was no sign of Mr. Travolta when I was pulled over by neighborhood security and swiftly shown the exit gate.

I continued my field investigation at Ocala's best used bookstore. There are only two remaining, and the other one is a lousy firetrap. The good one is called A Novel Idea, and it's in a strip mall near a movie theater. I always made it a point to swing by the place whenever I was working a case in the area. I had long since bought all their vintage crime paperbacks, but I still liked visiting—mostly to see the store's two in-house cats: Lord Byron and F. Scott Fitzgerald. In my absence, Fitzy had died. Now there's only Lord Byron on the lookout for paperback shoplifters.

The store's proprietor is Lori. Her daughter is the owner, but Lori runs the joint. She's from Ocala but had never heard of Harry Whittington. Meanwhile, the store carried none of his books.

"He was born and raised here as a kid," I explained. "He later moved to St. Petersburg and authored over 170 novels during the mid-20th century. They called him The King of Paperbacks because he was so prolific. He wrote books in a bunch of different genres under his own name and a giant list of pseudonyms."

She listened politely to my Wikipedia speech and acted about as interested as retail politeness would dictate. Honestly, I wasn't sure what I was expecting. Excitement? Tears? A discount?

I swung by the Ocala Public Library and asked the same question with similar results. The lady at the information desk had never heard of Harry, and the library carried none of his books. I hadn't struck out this much with women since I was dating. Small towns are supposed to lionize their native sons, but Harry had been seemingly wiped from everyone's memory here.

I needed an informant with good intel, so I contacted the Marion County Genealogical Society and asked for some help. A fellow named Arnold Davis turned up some good dirt using historical records.

Harry's parents (Harry Sr. & Rosa Hardee) were married on June 12, 1912 at the home of Rosa's parents on South Magnolia Street. The happy couple settled into a house on Pond Street, and Harry was born on February 4, 1915. His dad ran Staple & Fancy Groceries on Main Street, and the family was somewhat wealthy compared to the farmers residing in the area.

Arnold the Informant uncovered a mosaic of family stories from Harry's childhood—family trips to the beach in Daytona and a wayward nail that almost blinded his mom. One foggy night in 1922, Harry Sr. crashed his truck into a "dummy cop" statue erected in the middle of Main Street. The city had strategically placed these dummies to slow traffic, and the accident resulted in a lofty fine of $11.10 to cover repairs to the inert lawman.

I went by the locations of Harry's three childhood homes in Ocala. I was pleased to find that there were many places in the Historical District remaining from Harry's era, but none of his houses remained. I had lunch at an old-fashioned diner that used to be Elliott's Drive-In back in the day. The food was excellent, but the waitress had never heard of Harry.

After World War I in 1918, Ocala was a hot spot for tourists from the north visiting by way of the Orange Blossom Trail, now Highway 27. This was before the development of America's interstate highway system, and Model-T tourism sparked the golden age of roadside attractions. Ocala's contribution to this culture was Silver Springs. It's now a state park, and I paid two bucks to walk through the paths surrounding the waters. Signs warned me to beware of both alligators and monkeys (feed neither, please). When Harry was 14, a guy named Ross Allen used to wrestle alligators there to the delight of both locals and tourists. From 1958 to 1961, Lloyd Bridges filmed the underwater adventure scenes for *Sea Hunt* in the spring's crystal clear waters.

I hit up my friend Ben Boulden. He's a great author living in Utah and a solid guy. I remembered his introduction to a Stark House double by Lionel White and how much I enjoyed it. Ben is a whiz at researching old census records, so I solicited his help.

Ben hooked me up with a good timeline of Harry's life using census and other historical records that I overlaid with the intel from Arnold to create a coherent timeline. Sometime around 1924, the Whittington clan moved 100 miles away to Tampa on the Gulf of Mexico, and Harry's dad landed a job as a salesman for C.B. Witt Company, a wholesale grocer. For unclear reasons, Harry returned to Ocala in September 1930 as a transfer student from St. Petersburg to complete his final two years of high school. I'm guessing he lived with grandparents or extended family until he graduated from Ocala High School on June 3, 1932.

I wanted to head over to Harry's alma mater to regale the students vaping in the parking lot with stories about "The King of Paperbacks." It became Forest High School in 1969 and is now Marion Technical Institute, a place for kids looking to get into the trades. I went by the school but didn't see the upside of hassling these future welders, cooks, and first responders with dumb questions about a long-dead author.

Harry returned to the family home in St. Petersburg after graduating high school in Ocala. By 1935, Harry's dad was employed as a driver for Florida Milk Company. I recalled that a milkman was the main character in *Like Mink, Like Murder*, a Whittington oddity also reprinted by Stark House. For his part, Harry landed a job as a mail carrier for the U.S. Postal Service.

On February 6, 1936, 21-year-old Harry married Kathryn Odom, and the couple settled down in Saint Petersburg with Harry continuing his mailman gig until he was drafted in 1940. This military service was followed by a voluntary enlistment in the U.S. Navy from April 1945 to March 1946.

Shortly after his release from the Navy, Harry sold his first novel, a western titled *Vengeance Valley*. In 1947, he sold a hardcover called *Her Sin* about a pleasure-loving girl named Iris. Demand for paperback original novels exploded in 1950, and Harry met that demand becoming one of the most prolific writers of paperback potboilers in the world. By 1957, Harry had 50 novels published under his own name and a cadre of pseudonyms. That same year, he was identified as a professional author in a St. Petersburg citizen's directory uncovered by Informant Ben.

In 1979, Harry settled in Indian Rocks Beach, just south of Clearwater. I saw his house, a modest ranch-style home built in 1951 two blocks from the gulf. Harry paid $45,000 for the place the same year he sold a mainstream flop called *Sicilian Woman*—the last novel published under his own name. It was in this house that he wrote six entries in the Longarm adult western series as Tabor Evans and 12 plantation gothic titles as Ashley Carter. Evidently, the market for paperbacks in the king's own name had dried up by that point.

My manhunt concluded at Royal Palm South Cemetery in St. Petersburg where Harry was laid to rest in 1989—later to be joined by his wife and daughter. His tombstone reads, "Master of the Roman Noir: One Of The Greats Among American Novelists." An internet search explained that "Roman Noir" is a French term for a mystery or thriller, literally a "Dark Novel."

Indeed, Harry's best work was noir fiction, and you are holding in your hands two excellent examples of an American author at the top of his dark novel game. Still, I found his tombstone epigraph a bit reductive. Harry excelled at so many different genres: Westerns, Espionage, TV Tie-Ins, Historical Gothics, Erotica, Nursing Dramas and on and on. Some were good and others were not—but the guy's cross-genre productivity was staggering and unmatched among his peers.

I left his gravesite thinking that even on his own tombstone, Harry didn't get the credit he deserves. In any case, I'm glad you cared enough about his writing to pick up this Whittington double-shot.

After all, Harry is a guy who deserves to be remembered.

—December 2022

Tom Simon is a former FBI Special Agent and current private investigator in Jacksonville, Florida. His firm is Simon Worldwide Investigations LLC (www.simoninvestigations.com). The vintage paperback blog and podcast he co-hosts is Paperback Warrior (www.paperbackwarrior.com). He can be often be found driving around Florida asking strangers if they know about Harry Whittington.

A TICKET TO HELL
Harry Whittington

Chapter One

Except for layers of dust, piled on across nine states, the Porsche was as new as it looked. Through his hands he could feel its headlong strength and untouched power reserve. It darted, low-slung, on the narrow roadway like a frightened beetle. The hum of power and smell of expensive newness gave him a sensual kind of pleasure. He let the sense of pleasure flood through him and drove without thinking of any of the rest of it.

On both sides of the highway the forlorn wasteland stretched as far as he could see, under the white, metallic glare of desert sun, to distant ash-blue hills.

The kid beside him had been mumbling steadily but Ric had stopped listening within five minutes after he'd picked him up at the LAST CHANCE FOR GAS signboard. There had been something faintly amusing about the skinny kid standing with his suitcase beside this sign when there was nothing else alive in that whole countryside.

He wished now he'd left the kid where he saw him back there. The monotone muttering was bad enough; it was meaningless, covering the jazzing that was rattling around in the kid's head. Ric was even less interested in the hitchhiker's inner tensions than in his diarrhea of the tonsils.

He kept his gaze straight ahead. There was no sense in letting the kid read in his eyes that he dug him loud and clear. Nothing moved in that desolation out there except the heat waves on the black road top.

The kid said it again. "I asked you, how far you going, mister?"

Ric shrugged. "What difference does it make? Anywhere ought to be better than that signboard back there."

"Yeah. That was a jazzing all right. I didn't even see the road there until the guy stopped and said he was turning off."

"Stow it, kid."

"Say. What do you mean? What kind of talk is that?"

"Son, I miss nothing. Don't you forget it. There wasn't any turn-off road back there."

The kid laughed. His hands were trembling. "Man. That's pretty good, man. I just flew there, out in the middle of that highway, huh? Like a man from Mars, huh?"

"If you say so."

Ric sensed the kid squirming in the bucket seat. He stepped harder on the gas, feeling the hot wind lick at his face.

Finally the kid made a slight sobbing sound in his throat, slumped deeper, looked at the dashboard.

"Yeah, yeah. Nice car. Let's see you touch a hundred and twenty."

Ric didn't answer. The speedometer needle didn't even tremble at eighty-five.

"Oh, man. You're tough, guy. You don't say nothing. You do like you want. Man. Funny, you don't look that tough."

A smile pulled at Ric's mouth. He heard the kid catch his breath. After a moment the kid said, "Mind if I look at that newspaper back there?"

"No. Help yourself."

The hitchhiker twisted in the seat. He was sweated and dusty with road-grime, and there was a smell about him, an odor of fear. He pulled the newspaper off the luxurious leather suitcase.

"Man. You buy real leather, man. Man, you live like you got it all."

"Shut up and read the paper."

The kid tensed, straightening slightly, then shook it off. He shook out the paper, stared at the headlines.

Ric pulled his gaze from the road long enough to glance at the black band of type: DEMAND QUARTER MILLION IN IRON-FIELD CHILD SNATCH.

"Say, man, you kidding me? This paper's too old for wrapping fish. Man, this here paper's five days old."

"You didn't ask me how old it was. You asked me if you could read it."

"Man, you ever bite yourself in the morning when you're shaving?"

"I'll tell you this, kid. Don't hold that paper while you try to get your gun out of your belt. I saw that gun when you got in the car."

"That ought to make it easy. I don't have to tell you what I want."

"You still going to make a play?"

"You saw the gun when I got in. Why didn't you leave me there?"

Ric smiled again, and the smile gave his lean face a somber sad expression. "Well, kid, I'll tell you. There was no side road, nobody in sight. That could have meant you'd pulled off a job on some sucker headed east. In that case, you just wanted a ride to a town."

"Man, you lay on it chilled, don't you? You knew I might of held up somebody—and you didn't cut out?"

"That was between you and your parole board, sonny. You fold up that paper, put it in the back, behave yourself, and it'll lie that way."

"Sonny, man. You lecture like a right joe, but you could be readin' the slides. Them shoes you're wearing cost sixty bucks anyhow. I've owned six suits in my life and combined they didn't cost what that jacket set you back. Man, they stitched that shirt to size. Me, I ain't asking much. Seems to me you got a load, I ain't got nothing—and that ain't the way

I like it."

"Sonny, that sad story won't buy you nothing but six feet of dirt with a hole in it."

The boy screamed suddenly. "Stop ridin' me. Damn it, stop ridin' me. You know what I want, man. You know I got my hand on my gun right now. You know you can make me real mad."

The car did not slow. Ric's voice had tightened; this was the only apparent change. "You want to get out here, kid? I mean all in one piece?"

"You talk big. You think I won't put a bullet in you."

"At eighty-five a bullet in me won't buy either one of us anything." Ric sighed. "Son, I'm going to slow down to thirty-five. When I do, I'm going to throw you out of here."

The hitchhiker jerked the gun free from his belt. His hand trembled. "Man, you talk. You gonna talk yourself to death."

"I told you not to pull that gun. Now, kid, by the time you pick yourself up off this highway, you're going to be one hell of a lot wiser. But it might be some time before it'll do you any good."

"Stop this car." The boy's eyes were distended. He sat forward in the seat, twisting toward Ric, jabbing the gun into his side.

Without seeming to move, Ric stepped hard on the brake. The car seemed to jackknife. Brakes screeched and the smell of rubber was acrid in the car.

Thrown forward, the boy struck his head against the front windshield. He made a gasping sound and tried to brace himself. In one movement, Ric lifted his foot from the brake, touched the accelerator, and caught the boy's wrist in his hand. He twisted, the sound of torn tendons sharp against the boy's scream.

Ric tossed the gun out his window. It smashed on the highway, bits and parts dancing and scattering in all directions.

Ric reached beyond the boy, slapped the door handle. The door opened just slightly against the wind pressure. As the car slowed to an exact thirty-five, the door swung out more. The kid glanced at the speedometer, screamed again and clawed at the car seat.

Ric put his hand against the boy's chest and shoved, half-lifting him across the door facing. The screaming boy grasped at the door and it swung wide under his weight, carrying him with it. For a moment he hung on to it until his feet touched the road. Then he was jerked free, rolling and bouncing along the pavement.

Ric hefted the cheap suitcase, pushed it out the door. It struck on its end and leaped straight up, snapping open and spilling its contents as it rolled slower and slower after the Porsche.

Ric reached over then, caught the door, slammed it. He did not look in the rearview mirror. Lines were pulled around his nostrils and down the sides of his mouth. There were a hundred old agonies roiling in his eyes. His knuckles turned white on the steering wheel. "Damn it," Ric said. "Oh, God damn it."

Chapter Two

He lifted his foot from the accelerator, glancing at the two oblong signs stabbed in the highway shoulder. The first read, LOS SOLANOS, NEW MEXICO'S FRIENDLIEST CITY, 8 MILES. He felt a faint sinking in his solar plexus. This was the town. This was what it all had led to. The other sign read, speed limit, 45 mph. He slowed, observing the speed regulation exactly.

He closed his eyes tightly for an instant against the glare and dryness of the sun. The air seemed to poke in the car window like hot lances through his eyeballs. The land was flat and empty and even patches of shadow were a bilious green. Cactus twisted as if withdrawing from the sun; the boulders reflected it; it glittered on the bald ranges.

He felt a sense of loneliness for a moment, an empty need for something he'd never put into words, and never would. The desolation of the vast country was like a symbolic painting of his own life—the boulders, the dry heat—without another soul as far as he could see. His mouth twisted. When he tried to be kindly, give a kid a lift out of the sun, he ended up with a gun poked in his ribs and another memory of violence that would grab at him in the night.

He shook his head. He did not allow himself to think about the violence or the few moments of pleasure.

He stared at the country, memorizing it, because all of it, its very deceiving sense of being changeless and unchanging, was important to him now. What had happened to him in the past, what was ahead—if anything—had no meaning. There was only one meaning to anything—Los Solanos was before him on Highway 58.

He glanced in the rear-view mirror. There was nothing back there, only the vanishing point of the road in surrealistic nothingness. He tried to tell himself that there was nothing behind him—no ships he'd longed to sail, no women he could have had, not even the woman who was always just ahead in the crowd. But she wasn't really there when he tried to catch her. And the funny part of it was, the woman hadn't really looked like Anne at all. One nice thing about being out here—he wouldn't forever be mistaking the way Anne walked in a crowd.

The town lunged into view suddenly. Los Solanos had less than a thousand citizens and almost none were out in the noon heat. The town wasn't much. It really looked as though whoever laid out towns had spilled this one into a crater between desert and mountain by mistake. He did not see why people would live here by choice, unless it was just too hot to move.

He stopped for the only traffic signal, a faded red in the sun's glare. Heat flared into the car, almost stifling him. On his left was a Texaco station with a pick-up truck baking on an untended oil-lift. Through a window on his right he saw a few people sitting in a café. It looked small and cool, and looking at it made him thirsty.

When the traffic signal changed, he moved forward slowly, looking the town over. Thirty or forty cars were parked the entire length of the wide street. A drug store, bank, Indian curio shop, a white two-storied hotel and other assorted shops lined the street. Nothing was happening in any of them. Then suddenly he found himself in a residential section dotted with cottonwood trees.

Ahead of him he saw the airport. Its metallic buildings and narrow runways were glittering. Beyond it was the jackrabbit and sage country.

He almost passed the motel before he saw it. A neon sign glowed palely in the sunlight illuminating its name—La Pueblo. *Swank*, he thought, *almost as swank as the Porsche.*

He pulled the car into the pebbled drive, parked beside a factory-fresh Cadillac and sat for a moment. He looked the place over, pleased with it.

To his right was the air-conditioned office. A man and woman sat inside. They stared at him but did not move. Outside the plate-glass window was a planting box of cacti and a stand of yucca beyond the entrance.

The small motel cottages were separate units, lined along a grass-plotted patio shaded with palms and a single cottonwood. Bright sun umbrellas were opened beside a swimming pool as blue as washwater. A lot of color, he thought, in this drab place. He admired all of it before he got out of the Porsche. When he unwound himself and stood beside the car, his face was expressionless. There was no sense in letting these people see how much better all this was than he was accustomed to.

He reached over into the rear of the Porche, lifted out the expensive leather suitcase that had impressed the hitchhiker. Hell, Ric thought, *it impresses me.* He rolled up the car windows, locked it. He gave it one last glance, admiring it even under its coating of dust that made it look as sweated and tired as he felt. *Don't worry, baby*, he silently told the Porsche. *You look at home in these swank surroundings, even if I don't.*

Ric walked slowly across the pebbled drive, the only sound the crunching of pebbles under his shoes. He was a tall slender man in his early thirties with a bitter hungriness in his face. He did not look like a gentle man; he was faintly ugly, and there was a toughness about him that the tailored jacket could not conceal or soften. He knew all this. He paused before he pushed open the office door, thinking about it. Anybody could see what he was. He was equally sure almost anyone could see he wasn't what he wanted to be, just as he had none of the things he'd started out wanting.

He stepped out of the sunlight into the cool office, blinking. The air conditioning grasped at him and shook itself downward through his skin.

"Got a vacancy?" he said. His voice was low and even faintly apologetic. There were vacancies. Only one other car was parked outside. But in his time he'd been turned away from crummier joints than this.

"Sure."

The man in the wicker chair was round, and his body was tilted so it fit the cool upholstery of the wicker chair. He did not move. His gaze went over Ric, to his suitcase and shoes.

"Come far today?"

Ric stood there with the suitcase. "Yes. Could I have a cottage, please?"

"Sure." The man let his pink head roll slightly on the chair back. "Peggy. Let him sign. Give him number eight."

"Which one is that?" Ric said. He glanced through the tinted window along the green patio.

"Last one down there on the right," the man said. "It'll be quiet down there. Real quiet. You look tired. Look like you could really use the rest."

"Thanks."

Ric pulled his gaze back to the room, batted it against the woman's for a moment. When he saw what was in her eyes—the naked look in them—he looked away sharply though he knew she was amused because he did.

She was in her late thirties, well-built, slightly overweight with most of it in her breasts and hips. She wore neither bra nor girdle—she didn't even control the look in her eyes.

"Sign this," she said.

She pushed a white card across the glass top of the case, leaned against it, her arms pressing her breasts.

"That's a slick car you're driving," the man said.

"Thanks."

"Always wanted one of them little bugs. Really travel, won't they?"

"Yes."

"Saw you locking it before you came in."
Ric's head jerked up. "Yes?"
He glanced over his shoulder, gray eyes cold.
The man shrugged. "Nothing to me, but closed up in that sun—be like a blast furnace when you open it."
"I guess so."
"Am I right, Peggy?"
"It's his car."
"I'm just trying to tell him."
"Thanks," Ric said.
"Don't have to lock anything around here," the man said. "Friendly people. Friendliest people I ever met. Peggy and me, we came from southern Illinois. Never met people friendly like they are out here. Never lock a door."

Ric looked up at the woman, pulled his gaze from her dress front. "That license number," he said. "I don't remember it. Never could remember license numbers."

The man said, "It's all right. We'll fill all that in for you."

Ric took a deep breath, signed his name. For a moment he stood looking at it. Ric Durazo. He turned the card slowly, watched the woman read it. Nothing happened. He exhaled. They had been right about this much anyhow. It was a long way from New York, longer even than he'd hoped.

"Want me to show you down to your cottage, Mr. Durazo?" Peggy said. It was naked in her voice now. He wondered how husbands could be so blind and deaf, and then decided maybe they got that way on purpose. Ten, twelve, fifteen years—it was a long time. Most women tired and bored him in three weeks, all except one, and that whole affair had been nothing but a joke on Ric Durazo right from the start.

He glanced at Peggy, saw the nakedness she wanted him to see. He shook his head, then took the key from her.

"No," he said. "I can find it."

Chapter Three

He stepped out of the office, feeling their gazes on his back and knowing what was in their faces without turning to look at them.

He looked both ways along the street. To the east was the shaded avenue of homes, west was the airport and the barren country. He stared at the airport for a moment, at the hills writhing faintly in the haze. Then he took another quick look around the motel grounds.

The car outside was a Cad with a California license plate. He read its number, and then read the number on the Porsche license, forgetting them instantly.

He turned and then followed the right walk along the patio. Ground sprinklers dribbled water on the plotted grass. It was cool and he felt slightly refreshed as he walked. He could forget the hundreds of cups of black coffee that had floated him from New York. Still, he held himself tautly, angered because he'd never learned to relax.

He inserted the key in cottage eight and stepped inside, feeling the kiss of air conditioning, the faint fresh odor of soap and disinfectant. He closed the door behind him and looked at the room—two deep easy chairs, a thick-mattressed bed, television set, gas wall furnace and a cool-looking tiled bath. He yawned despite the tensions in him and looked longingly at the bed.

He opened the Venetian blinds just enough to allow him a view of the patio and grounds. The cottage directly across from him was occupied. At the far side of it, he saw where the grass and landscaping ended and the brown of the desert began. Beside the other cottage was a round storage tank on a metal frame, bottled gas for the heating furnaces.

He smiled grimly, looking at the storage tank, the sagging clothes line beyond and the ugliness of the barren land beyond it. *Why do I have to see the back of everything?* he wondered turning away.

A shadow flickered along the walk and he stepped close to the window, watching it.

"Oh, hell," he said aloud.

The knock on the door was almost coy.

He said, "Come in."

Peggy came in and closed the door, cutting off the white blast of sunlight. "Ice cubes," she said. "Mr. Davis thought you might want some."

"Thanks." He nodded toward the glass-topped dresser.

She walked by him, warm-scented, and set the container on the dresser. Then she turned, leaning against it.

"Anything you want, Mr. Durazo, you let me know."

He watched her. "Yeah."

She gave him a faint smile and a sidelong glance.

"Are you afraid of me?"

"Why?"

"You act like it."

His voice went cold. "Does it go with the price of the room? Or is it extra?"

"Damn you." She lunged away from the dresser, her breasts bobbling against her dress front. "Where do you get off, talking to me like that?"

"Sorry. I'm tired and hot. I'd like to clean up."

Her eyes did not soften. "Why'n't you say so?"

She did not move to leave. Ric sighed. "You've got a nice place here, Mrs. Davis."

"Yeah." She shrugged. "Takes a lot of work, all right. You ever try to make flowers grow in the desert?"

"Not in the last week."

"You're not friendly at all, are you?"

"No."

"Nobody could accuse you of being friendly, all right."

"No."

"What's the matter with you? You don't like women?"

He exhaled, staring at her.

"Or is it you don't like me? I'm not pretty enough for you? Women throw themselves all over you—and I'm not good enough?"

"You trying to get yourself talked about?"

"What the hell does that mean?"

"Hanging around here? What will people think? What'll your husband say?"

"Who the hell cares? You try living in this god-forsaken desert three years and see if you care. Who'd talk? Who'd they talk to?"

"I don't know. I just don't want to make any trouble."

She laughed. "Trouble. I'd welcome a little trouble. Stir things up."

"Yeah." He walked to the door, turned the knob. "But I don't want any trouble. Not with anybody."

She looked at him a long time, letting her puzzled gaze go over him slowly.

She walked to the door. "Where'd a guy like you ever get a Porsche?"

"I won it in a church raffle."

She stared at him. "Didn't you though?"

She closed the door behind her, a sharp final sound.

After she was gone he stood there for a moment without moving. Then he set the suitcase on the baggage stand but did not empty it into the dresser drawers. He dug around in it for a moment, came up with a laundered white shirt, undershirt and shorts. He found a pair of socks and tossed them on the bed.

He stared at himself in the mirror, unbuttoned his collar and loosened his tie. His face was streaked with dust, and there were beads of sweat under his eyes. He pulled his gaze away from himself, shrugging out of his coat. He tossed it over a chair. Then he sat on the bed, yawning.

A small smile of pleasure tugged at his mouth. He moved, bouncing on the bed. He lay back, feeling the mattress give, supporting him. He stared at the ceiling. His head rolled. Then almost as if afraid he would go to sleep, he sprang up from the bed, moving with the taut muscled grace of a panther.

He walked about the room, touching the furniture, the pictures on the walls. He sat in the easy chair, sinking into it and stretching his legs before him. He nodded, pleased, and began unbuttoning his shirt.

He pulled off his shoes and socks, loosened his trousers. He sat for a moment wriggling his toes, scratching his ribs. He thought about Peggy Davis, allowing his thoughts to wander, but to go no further than Peggy, into the past, or into the future.

After he undressed, he stood for a moment, listening. There were no sounds from outside the cottage; inside the only sound was his own breathing.

He walked into the bathroom, the tile cold and pleasant against his feet. He ran the tub full of water while he shaved. Then he lay in the tub until he almost fell asleep. He came fully awake with a start.

He got out of the tub then, rubbed ice cubes on his face and across the back of his neck. He dressed, staring at the silent patio through the Venetian blinds.

He checked his watch, wound it, went back to the easy chair. From the chair he could see only the front of the cottage across the patio. Somebody had tossed a brief green bathing suit across one of the lounge chairs over there.

He got up, snapped on the television set. He watched it only a moment. He tuned out the volume, left a woman sobbing silently on the picture tube. He watched the flashing movements for a few minutes but the silent pictures could not hold his interest for long.

He checked his watch again, his face tightening. He turned the selector of the air-conditioning unit. It was cool in the room, but he was sweating. A faint stain showed on his shirt at the armpits.

He walked back to the window.

A Buick had parked out in front near his Porsche. The Buick was three or four years old, shaded with road film. He hoped there was something in it for Peggy.

He pulled the back of his hand across his forehead and then stared at the sweat he'd collected on it.

The green bathing suit was gone. After a moment the door of the cottage opened and a woman came out. She wore a green bathing cap and the green suit. It was even briefer than he'd thought, or there was more of her than the bathing suit people had bargained on.

She was tanned the color of desert clay. She might have been an

Indian, but he knew she wasn't.

She said something over her shoulder... A man taller than Ric showed in the cottage door. He had a fifth of whisky in his hand. He made a downward gesture at her and drank deeply. *That's the way*, Ric thought. *Those that have 'em don't know what in hell to do with 'em.*

He saw the sadness flicker in the girl's face. But she did not say anything else. She spread a large towel beside the pool, loosened the straps on her bathing suit and lay down. She had no idea he was watching her, Ric knew, but there was a look about her that said she wouldn't have cared if she'd known. She looked like money and breeding even in that bathing suit—even spilling out of it. Her tan was the color of old gold.

He watched her for a long time. She put on dark glasses, turned on her back, crinkling the suit back to her nipples. Ric yawned, the weariness like agony going through him. He was glad she was there. If she couldn't keep him awake, nothing could.

Their cottage door opened. The handsome one came out, carrying an iced highball. Looking at it, Ric licked his lips. Handsome said something to the girl, but she shook her head.

Handsome knelt beside her, caught her arm, twisting until she sat up, catching her bathing suit across her breasts with her free arm.

They stared at each other for a long time. Ric saw that they were speaking tensely. Finally the girl took the highball and turned up the glass. She drank it off fast, without taking the glass from her lips. Then he pulled her to her feet and they went into the cottage. The door closed and Ric yawned.

He walked slowly to the bed, toppled across it. He was asleep in five minutes, whether he wanted to be or not.

Chapter Four

Ric woke up sweating. He was bleary from sleep and for a moment he didn't remember where he was. He sat up, cursing under his breath. He put out his hand, touched the table. It was chilled under his fingers. The whole room was frosty, but he was sweating. He checked his watch. It was ten past seven.

His gaze jerked to the window. Had he slept all night? The quality of the darkness beyond the shades told him nothing. There was light enough to read his watch, that was all. Calming down slightly, he exhaled. It had to be night. Seven A.M. out here in the desert was like noon back East.

For a moment longer he sat on the side of the bed. He reached out to turn on the light, then changed his mind. He frowned, feeling the impatience building in him. He was beginning to feel caged waiting here, and God knew that was a sensation he knew and hated.

He stared at the telephone on the night table, willing it to ring. All calls had to come through the office up front. Had they considered that angle? There was no doubt about that. They'd considered all the angles. What was the matter with them then? Why didn't they call?

He got up, paced the room.

He walked to the window, stood beside it watching the silent patio. Darkness was settling down over the gaudy cottage rooftops.

The motel was enjoying a profitable evening. All the cottages across the patio were lighted. For a moment chilled loneliness flooded through him. What were they doing, these ordinary people who had what they wanted, loved and were loved?

He shook out a cigarette, put it in his mouth. The hell with them. He got his lighter from his pocket and then did not fire up the cigarette. Instead he dropped the lighter back into his pocket, caught the cigarette in his fist and crushed it.

He dropped the wadded paper and tobacco in an ash tray. He had known all along that he was playing according to their rules. They would get in touch with him when it pleased them.

His face darkened. He stared at the gaping leather suitcase on the rack. He walked to it, shoved his hand inside and came up with a thirty-five caliber Smith and Wesson. He held it in his hand, hefting it. Then he ejected the cartridge case, checked it and socked it back into the gun.

He placed the gun under his pillow.

Ric paced the room, staring at the telephone at every turn in the narrowing circle. A flash of light snagged his attention. He returned to the window.

He sighed. It was only the front door of the cottage across the patio. He thought for a moment about the girl in the green bathing suit—the way she was stacked, the way she had spilled from the suit, the gold color of her. Had they spent the afternoon drinking?

Handsome stepped outside the cottage door alone, stood staring casually at the sky.

Ric smiled bitterly. There was a man he could really envy. This boy was not out of place in a swank motel. The cut of his clothes, the casual way he wore them and the insolence in his face all were part of one package. There was the boy with the deal. No wonder Green Suit was nuts about him. Here was the kind of boy a woman went nuts about at least once in her lifetime—and sometimes if she never matured, fell for over and over.

He'd known men as pretty as Handsome. They grew out of the gutter. Most of them had dark wavy hair, black eyes, rich olive complexion, the tall, muscled body—too much of everything.

In all the men like Handsome that Ric had known, it was inside where the trouble was, where all the strength had been spoiled. *Sure,* Ric told himself, *try to hate him. Tell yourself he's queer. It'll make you feel better.*

Standing there by the window in his unlighted room, Ric watched Handsome, sensing something wrong. Handsome was casual, but it was a casualness that was uncalled for and out of focus. He looked both ways along the patio, seeming pleased that he was the only person out there. He stared directly at Ric's cottage. Ric knew he could not be seen, but stepped back into the shadows anyway.

Handsome glanced back toward his cottage. If they'd been drinking since early afternoon, Handsome should have been nearly potted by now anyhow.

Ric had never seen a man appear more coldly sober.

Handsome turned and walked toward the end of the patio, toward the scarred unkempt grounds. He moved lazily, as though unhurried, a man with all the time in the world. Yet Ric knew that Handsome was wound tighter than a dollar watch.

Handsome reached the side of his own cottage and Ric moved across his window where he could watch him.

Handsome went to the bottled gas container on its metal rack beside the building. He stood there for what seemed a long time to Ric. Then he reached over and turned the outside gas valve.

Then he quickly straightened up, looking around guiltily.

Ric watched him kick at a stone, stroll back to the edge of his own cottage, glance along the patio again.

Handsome stepped back into the deepening shadows at the side of the cottage. He walked back to the gas valve, turned it again. Ric stared at him. The first time Handsome had turned off the valve it had stopped the gas inside that cottage, killing the pilot light. The second he turned it, raw gas seeped into the room through the wall heater. *Some men are born sons of bitches,* Ric thought. *Others learn it, like a trade.*

He stood, not breathing, watching Handsome. *This boy should have been a movie star,* he thought. He was like a man playing a game. That was what he wanted it to look like if he were observed, a man out for a breath of fresh air.

Handsome walked calmly around the corner of the cottage. He did not hesitate at its door. He walked past, not hurrying, taking leisurely strides that increased in pace as he neared the front parking area.

Handsome glanced toward the office, then stepped around the Cad that had been parked there when Ric arrived. Handsome got into the car. He reversed the car, spewing pebbles all the way across the drive, sliding his rear wheels into the planting area across it.

Ric saw Peggy run out of the front door of the office and stand there as the Cad burned out of the drive. The car spun west on Highway 58, immediately gone. Ric knew that Peggy was too accustomed to seeing people leave the motel ever to run out the door like that. Handsome must have created quite a racket—quite a show.

Ric nodded. Wasn't Handsome still playing the game? Didn't he need an audience now to see him depart in anger? What better way to get one than to back into the owner's planting area with engine roaring?

Ric's gaze came back to the gas container outside the other cottage. He could hear the hiss of escaping gas. *Now that's as crazy as all the rest of my imaginings,* he told himself.

He turned away from the window, staring at the telephone, hating it because it did not ring.

Chapter Five

He could not see into the other cottage because their Venetian blinds were drawn. He could tell only that the lights were burning, glowing brighter as the desert night darkened.

He walked away from the window, telling himself to forget it. Suppose there was gas seeping into that cottage? Suppose Handsome was trying to kill the doll? Except for the fact that nobody had the right to destroy anything that lush, it was nothing to Ric Durazo—nothing but trouble.

He wiped the back of his hand across his mouth. So there was a murder happening over there that Handsome wanted to look like suicide. It was clever in that it was simple and had been worked only God knew how many times in how many places. So what was Ric Durazo supposed to do? Call the cops? Oh, fine.

He had never seen that girl before this afternoon out there beside the pool. Sure it was a pity for anything that lovely to die, but Ric Durazo had troubles of his own.

He heeled toward the window, then stopped. He could not afford to get involved in even an attempted murder. He had been afraid that Peggy would stay in his room long enough to attract attention to him this afternoon. If he had not been able to take that kind of trouble, he had to forget the doll in the green suit.

His gaze struck against the grate of the wall furnace. The pilot light burned so faintly inside it that he barely could detect its glow in his darkened room. That much unburned gas could—

He spun on his heel and walked to the door.

The telephone rang.

He stopped as though someone had chopped him across the neck. That nerve-shattering sound stunned him.

He turned, walked back to the night table, picked up the phone.

"Hello."

"Mr. Durazo? Ric?"

It was Peggy Davis.

"For God's sake. What do you want?"

"I just thought you might be hungry. We forgot to tell you this afternoon. We have a café next to the office. It's very nice."

"Thanks. If I get hungry..."

"We just want you to enjoy your stay here."

"All right."

"I mean, it worries me when somebody don't like me, and I can't think why. You know, you worry me, Mr. Durazo."

"I'm sorry. Like I told you, I'm tired."

"No man I ever knew ever got that tired, Mr. Durazo."

"Good-by, Mrs. Davis."

"Mr. Davis has gone into town. He plays pool every night. As soon as the sun goes down, he goes into town and plays pool."

"We all got our problems, Mrs. Davis."

She laughed. "That's no problem. My God, I don't know how I'd stand it if he didn't play pool. Why, he acts like we been married less than a week, you know?"

"That's fine, Mrs. Davis."

"Maybe later, if you get lonely."

"All right." He replaced the receiver.

He wiped his hand across his mouth, strode across the room. He stepped outside, pushing his door wide open.

He walked across the grass, hearing it crunch like corn flakes under his shoes. The ground sprinklers were still running. Somewhere he could hear a radio—rock and roll. *Darling, they're killing our song.*

He moved as casually as Handsome had. He would do what he could, but God help him if he attracted any attention.

He stood before the door, looked both ways along the patio. The darkness was complete now and beginning to fade out. The empty sky glowed with the first stars.

He rapped sharply against the panel. He waited, but there was no answer, no movement inside that cottage.

Light glowed at the front of the motel and he heeled around to walk away from the cottage. The light passed and he exhaled.

He could hear it now, the steady hissing of gas from within the cottage. He strode around the cottage, turned the valve. The hissing died slowly.

He walked around to the door again, knocked. He studied the knob, took it in both hands. Bracing himself, he put his shoulder against the door close against the jamb, lifting and pressing. He heard the lock snap.

The door swung open, spilling light around him when he released the knob. The smell of gas was strong. He thrust the door wide open and entered the cottage. It was furnished precisely as his was, but was in greater disarray. The man and woman had been here for some time or were extraordinarily messy. Make-up and lotions littered the dresser top, both men's and women's clothing were strewn all over the chairs. The green bathing suit was wadded on the rug. Near it, in a wide-open expensive housecoat, the girl was sprawled.

He glanced at her only long enough to see that she looked even better out of the green suit, and that her body was that same golden color all over. Her dark hair was loose across the rug, and her face was barely inches from the grate of the wall heater.

Ric's mouth twisted. Here was the work of an amateur, beyond any doubt. This girl had passed out somewhere in the room, possibly the bed, and then he'd dragged her here to this exact spot so that she would get the full impact of the gas. The police were supposed to believe she had fallen here in a drunken stupor. His lifting gaze found the empty fifth bottles just as Handsome had left them to be found. Near the girl on a chair was a tray full of cigarettes, all of them red-tipped from her lip rouge. He could see Handsome telling himself how clever this phony setup looked. Here was a despondent woman who smoked and drank her way into a suicidal mood.

He cursed, grabbing her roughly by her ankles and dragging her across the room to the door. No wonder the cops solved as many crimes as they did. When they were committed by brains like Handsome's, the phony look of them screamed all the way to the D.A.'s office.

He stood looking along the motel patio. He had attracted no one yet. He exhaled slowly, realizing it was the first time he'd breathed since he'd entered the cottage; and it wasn't fear of gas. He was afraid of trouble—and trouble hounded him.

Ric knelt beside her, slipped his arms under her body. He lifted her and walked slowly across the patio. He entered his cottage and kicked the door shut.

He laid her down across his bed, and for a moment paused to look at her. He felt his nails bite into the palms of his hands.

He bent over her, lifting her left breast slightly in the cup of his hand as he felt for her heartbeat. It was there through the texture of her breast. He pulled her housecoat across her rounded stomach and buttoned it almost roughly.

He left her there and went out of his cottage. He crossed the patio again. Inside her cottage, he stood for a moment, looking around. He selected a shirt and skirt, deciding these would be easiest to put on her if he had to dress her before she regained consciousness. One thing was certain; if there were any chance that she was to be found in his motel room, he wanted her fully dressed. And with Peggy running up and down the motel walks trying to cool off her hot pants, there was a chance she'd be found in his cottage.

He turned to leave the cottage; then, face set, he moved quickly, straightening up the room, ruining all the stage dressing Handsome had so carefully laid out. He dropped the empty bottles in the disposal, emptied ash trays into the toilet. He threw her loose clothing in the closet along with Handsome's and closed the door. He scooped up the dirty glasses and put them in the sink. He glanced around then, deciding the room looked almost respectable.

At the front door, he found that the lock catch had been sprung from the wall. He pressed it back into place, pushed the lock off the door and closed it gently so it held. There was no way he could keep an observant person from knowing something had happened in there, but at least it no longer looked like the room in which a despondent woman committed suicide.

Carrying her skirt and shirt, he returned to his own cottage. He turned on the light, drew the blind closed and locked the door securely.

She was lying as he had left her on his bed, the housecoat parted across one long golden column of her leg. He was going to be tormented by the looks of her for a long time.

It was pretty certain that she had passed out from the drinks Handsome had fed her, and that the gas had not touched her yet. Black coffee would be ideal for bringing her around. The trouble with black coffee was that he might run into Peggy trying to get it.

He got a glass from his dresser, went into the bathroom. He peeled open a bar of soap, dropped it in the glass, ran water in it and stirred until the mixture was gray and soapy. Then he removed the soap. He lifted the girl then, brought her into the bathroom.

He laid her down on the bathmat, leaning her body against the tub. Holding her head back, he forced the soapy water down her mouth. He pinched her nostrils closed, forcing her to swallow. It didn't take much of the water.

He half lifted her so she was hanging over the tub, and he turned the water on full force.

Wetting a towel, he washed her face and carried her back to the bed. She was whimpering and writhing back and forth.

He loosened the button on her housecoat. It fell away down her arms when he lifted her. He pushed her arms through her shirt, buttoned it.

She was still fighting him, her eyes closed and her mouth twisted pettishly when he pulled the skirt down over her shoulders. He turned her on her side, zipped and buttoned it.

He stepped back, watching her roll her head back and forth on the bed.

"Martin?" She whispered.

He did not answer. Her eyes opened slowly, seeming to focus even more slowly, as though she were unwilling to come back to whatever hell she had drunk her way out of.

When she saw him, her eyes widened. A shiver passed through her body. She sat up, moving in slow motion, never taking her distended gaze from his face. Then she let her gaze slide down to her wrinkled clothing.

Her mouth pulled. For a second Ric was afraid she was going to scream, and he set himself to leap forward and clap his hand across her mouth.

He saw the terror working into her eyes.

His voice was cold. "What's that for?"

"Who are you?"

"Well, I'm not Martin," he said. "That's for sure. I'm not pretty enough."

Her mouth trembled. "Where is Martin?"

"My God. You mean you still care?" He shook his head and turning, walked away from her. He stared at the television set. Gray pictures were still leaping silently on its picture tube. A woman was sobbing. For a moment he thought it was the same woman he'd seen there this afternoon.

Chapter Six

"Who are you?" Her voice had so much more in it than simple fear that Ric turned, almost pitying her.

She had not moved. She was still sitting crouched forward on his bed. Her head was tilted slightly to one side as though she were poised to run, as though she would have run except that she could not move at all.

Her skirt was still twisted across her golden thighs and a long shadow reached softly to her knee. He tried to forget the dimpled knees, the golden color of her, the kind of woman she could be if she were happy. *Hell*, he thought, *maybe he could have dimples in his knees, too, with a little happiness.*

She stared at him as if she were seeing a ghost. The blood had seeped out of her face, leaving it chalky, so even her lips were colorless and slack. The terror swirled in shadows through her eyes and though she did not speak, Ric knew she was screaming silently. He saw that she was filled with agonizing memories of the last moments over there with Handsome before she passed out. She was trying to work him somewhere into that pattern of terror.

Ric walked to the television set and snapped off the leaping picture, watching the eye contract and glow.

"Please. Where's Martin? Who are you?"

"Is Martin the tall handsome one?"

She nodded.

"He burned out of here in his Caddy."

"Who are you?"

"Nobody. I'm just the character that watched Martin try to gas you—and make it look like suicide."

She slumped, putting out her arm to support herself on the bed. She did not cry out or make any sound. For a moment she looked as though he'd struck her, but she was not astonished. She massaged at her throat.

Though he knew she did not, he said, "You doubt what I say?"

She did not move. A shudder ran across her and Ric saw she was thinking about Handsome now. He had tried to kill her and yet she was not going to say anything that might condemn him or incriminate him.

"A friend of yours?" Ric said.

She dampened her lips.

"My husband."

Ric shrugged. It figured. She wiped her hand across her eyes, then pulled at her skirt. She could not budge it and lost interest. She was numb, incapable of caring about anything. She began to stroke her arms as though she were chilled.

Ric turned down the air conditioner, but she did not notice. The chill came from within her.

He walked over to the easy chair and sat down, facing her. No use trying to rush her. She was suffering from shock and she was not going to recover easily.

He shook out a cigarette, patted his pocket, found his lighter. He extended the pack toward her, but she shook her head without really seeing him or the cigarette. He lighted up, drew in deeply, exhaling the smoke. He watched her through it.

Ric did not speak for a long time. He ground out the cigarette butt in an ash tray. He waited for her to come out of her shock and leave. But she stayed there, huddled on his bed, staring at nothing. Finally, when she looked around, he saw for the first time that she realized she was not in her own cottage.

She said, whispering. "Are you the police?"

He laughed shortly. "No. Are you all right now?"

"How did you find me?"

He told her again, watching the terror and the hurt make an ugly mask of her face.

"What am I going to do?" she whispered. Ric's head jerked up. Then he realized that she was not talking to him. She spoke the words the way one says "God help me" without really expecting any help.

"I know what I'd do if I were you."

She looked up. Some of the shadows of fear had faded in her eyes. But she did not change her position.

"What?"

"I'd run."

Her mouth trembled. "Where would I go? What would I do?"

"You've got folks haven't you? Parents?"

Her slack mouth pulled into the semblance of a bitter smile. "Oh yes."

"Go back to them. Now. Before Handsome comes back to discover you dead—"

"Comes back?" Her face was white again, the blood drained out.

"Sure. He's playing a little game. And you're it. He'll come back in a little while. Then he'll find your body in that cottage over there. And the people up front will agree that he raced out of here as though you two had had a fight—"

"Oh, we did. All afternoon."

"Sure you did. So Handsome has it all figured out. You were despondent when he walked out, you drank too much, turned on the gas. He's got it all worked out."

Her mouth quivered and only the way she held her jaw kept her teeth from chattering. "Martin wouldn't do that. No one would—"

He shrugged. "Okay. You feel better now so you run along back over there. The gas ought to be cleared out by now."

She made a sobbing sound of protest.

"What's the matter?" he said.

"I can't go back over there. I'm too afraid."

"Of Handsome? You just said he wouldn't leave you in a gas-filled room. You love him so much—"

"I married him."

"Not the same thing at all. There's some reason why he wanted to kill you. Why? You don't have to answer aloud. It's none of my business. I got my own woes. But answer it for yourself. It might help you decide what you've got to do."

She pressed her hands against her face.

"Martin wants to be rid of me. I know that. But he wouldn't try to kill me."

"Sure. If he wanted to be rid of you he'd just get a divorce, wouldn't he?"

She pressed her hands more tightly against her face. It was as if she was trying to burrow into them, to hide from him and from herself and from the truth she was going to have to face sooner or later.

"He wouldn't try to kill me."

His voice was flat. "Like I said, it's none of my business, but if you're going to stay alive and healthy, you better stop kidding yourself. I dragged you out of that room. It was full of gas. I saw him turn the outside valve off and on. If he was playing a joke on you, he plays rough."

She straightened finally, but did not look at him. Her voice was odd, taut. "I'm sorry. It's just that I can't believe it."

"You don't want to believe it. That's up to you. I know if somebody did that to me, I'd sick the cops on him."

"Why would he want to kill me?"

"Ask yourself. I came in late."

"I know what he wants. But I've lived with him for three years. Why would he kill me?"

He exhaled. "I don't know. When he comes back over there, you ask him."

She looked up at him, eyes distended. She shook her head back and forth. "I can't go back over there."

"But you love him. He wouldn't hurt you."

She lifted her head. Her eyes were filled with tears. She did not meet his eyes.

"All right. I love him." She shook her head and pressed her knotted hand against her mouth. "But I don't want to see him again. I don't ever want to see him again." The tears spilled down her cheeks.

"The first smart thing I've heard you say."

"You don't get over loving someone just like that."

"No."

"You try to go on trusting them, even when you know better."

"Now's the time to call a screaming halt. You don't want to see him any more, get on that phone there and call your father. Tell him to come and get you."

"I can't do that. Believe me, I can't do that. Father hates Martin—he always has hated him. He told me before Martin married me what he wanted. But I thought I was pretty, I thought I was as exciting as any other woman. I couldn't believe that Father was anything but prejudiced. No woman likes to admit she's being married for her money."

"You're past the point where pride matters a damn, baby. You're trying to stay alive. Have you stopped to think what Martin will do when he comes back here—and you're not dead? He'll know for sure that you know he tried to kill you."

She slumped back on the bed. Her shoulders sagged. Some of the color had returned to her cheeks, but it faded again. Ric spoke sharply, "I'm trying to help you. Looks like the only way I can help you is to scare you. Now if you're scared enough you'll get on that phone and tell Papa he was right. Only don't let him waste any time crowing about it. Let him come and get you."

"He's thousands of miles away—in California."

"So? Tell him about airplanes. Tell him where you'll be. Tell him you'll wait for him in town at the hotel—anywhere Martin can't find you. Then I'll walk over there with you while you pack a few things and get out of here. It's really simple."

"Oh, no. It isn't simple. I don't know what Father would do about Martin. He might make it worse."

Ric laughed. "When they try to kill you, baby, that's about as bad as things can get."

She looked up, her eyes lost, staring at him. She licked her colorless lips with her tongue.

"Can't I stay here, with you—just a little while? Just until I think what I'm going to do?"

"You don't know who I am. You don't know anything about me."

"You saved my life."

"All right. So I'll get my merit badge. That ends it. I don't owe you anything else."

"You can't just send me back. You said it yourself. He might try to kill me again."

"Maybe. Maybe not." He walked back and forth before the bed. Her eyes followed him. "Depends on whether he thinks you suspect him."

"You know he'll be afraid to take a chance."

"No. I don't know much about Handsome—except the type. Now, the murder he attempted over there was something he had evidently planned very carefully—"

He saw her shudder. He continued talking, his voice cold. "Yes, and you might as well face all of it. All the time he was holding you in his arms, making love to you, he was thinking about that pilot light, and that gas valve—"

"Oh, my God. Oh, God."

"Yes. It isn't pretty. That's why I can see it so clearly. It's my eternal view on life. I always get to see the ugly side of everything."

His voice was so bitter that she looked up, seeing him as a person for the first time.

He laughed. "Never mind me. Let's talk about why your husband tried to kill you. First, it wasn't just that he wanted you dead, wanted to be rid of you. You've already hinted that he wanted something."

"Money."

"Ah, yes. Money. You have money. Pretty Boy doesn't. He couldn't get his hands on enough of it, quickly enough, so he wanted you to die. Am I right so far?"

She lowered her head, nodding.

"So, that rules out any crimes of passion with Martin. He wants you to die, but he doesn't want it messy. He wants to get away with it. He wants to get all your money. There's just one thing—if your father hates Martin so terribly, how does he expect to collect, even if you're dead? Looks like Father would see he never got a dime."

"Inheritance." She whispered it. "Oh, I see now. How right Father was, how wrong I was—and what a fool. I see what Martin has wanted all along. I was bitter against Father. I wanted to show him. I wanted to prove to him how much I loved Martin and how much Martin loved me. Mother had left me half a million dollars. I made a will, leaving all of it to Martin."

"Was that Martin's idea? Or yours?"

Her mouth twisted. "I know now. It was Martin's idea. At the time, it sounded like mine. I remember Martin kept telling me I didn't have to do it."

"And all the time leading you to the lawyer's office?"

"I suppose so. Yes. It doesn't leave me very much, does it?"

"It leaves you lucky to be alive. And it brings us right back to whether Martin would try to kill you. Looks to me like he's got to have a plan that looks clever—at least to him—since I could point out at least twenty points in his last plan that weren't clever at all. For instance, did you leave Martin any insurance?"

"No."

"He wouldn't let you? Well, he was smart enough to stay away from the insurance angle, anyhow. So it looks like the surest way for you to stay alive is to get back to your lawyers and change your will again. Leave your money to a home for needy cats."

"But how will I get there? What will I do?"

"It's easy. Get in touch with Father. Move out of here. Leave no address. Wire your lawyer. Tell him to kill that will, as of this minute. Run."

"But I would be alone."

"That happens."

She burst into tears. "But I can't stand to be alone. I was always so lonely. I married Martin because I was so alone. I can't stand to be lonely." Her voice hardened. "I may as well tell you the truth. I knew all along I was wrong. I knew from the first. Martin never loved anyone but himself. But I couldn't stand to be alone. I had nobody but Martin. You know what I thought? I thought if I did everything Martin wanted, everything he asked, he'd love me—and never leave me."

"Well, now you know."

"Yes. Now I know."

"You're wasting time. Get over there, get some clothes and clear out."

She shook her head. "I'm afraid. Please. In the name of God. I'll pay you anything—"

"I'm not as pretty as Martin. I don't put a cash value on myself."

"Oh, God. I'm sorry. I didn't mean it to sound like that. But—what else have I got but money."

Ric smiled. His voice softened. "Look. You're low now. But what the hell? Just because a foul ball couldn't see you for the money. Plenty of guys would take you if you didn't have a dime—"

"Then let me stay with you. Just for a little while. Just until Martin comes back—and goes away. Please. I'll do anything if you'll let me stay with you."

Ric exhaled heavily, shrugged his coat up on his shoulders. He shook his head, his voice was cold and final.

"I'm sorry. Even if I wanted to, I couldn't let you stay here."

"You've got to help me. In God's name, I'm in trouble."

"Honey, you can pick up that phone, call Papa and all your troubles will be over. You don't know anything about trouble. I'm telling you real nice—but for the last time. Get out."

He picked up her housecoat, felt the soft rich texture of it for a moment, then he wadded it up and tossed it into her lap.

Chapter Seven

She clutched the housecoat in her hand and moved slightly on the bed. He thought she was going to leave. She was clinging to the housecoat as though it offered some strength, as though it were a boulder or a straw.

There was no sound. In the distance he could hear the faint swish of tires as cars raced by on the highway. She remained on his bed, barely breathing, staring at him.

He turned and walked toward the door. A single sob escaped her mouth. He turned and looked at her.

It was a mistake to look at her, because when he looked at her he had to see her eyes—her frightened and desolate eyes.

"Look," he said. "I know how you feel."

"The hell you do."

"I know how you feel. But there's nothing I can do about it. Nothing—not even if I wanted to."

He had felt lost and alone many times in his life. There was never a moment he could remember when it wasn't a struggle to exist, a lonely struggle. But for the first time he was looking at someone else who was lost.

"It's not as though you are alone. Nothing stands between you and safety except your pride. Call your father."

"If he helped me—he couldn't keep Martin away from me."

"What makes you think I can?"

She didn't answer that. She stared at the housecoat clutched in her fist.

"And he's so far away. There's a chance he would think I was drinking—he might not believe me. Don't you see how it is? Father and I have been separated a long time. Three years—by Martin. I've stood against Father with Martin on every score. Father was hurt and bitter. Suddenly, I call and tell him Martin is trying to kill me—"

"It's the truth."

"And Father would either have Martin hunted down and killed, or he'd tell me—" she did not finish it.

"You made your bed."

She slumped there. "It's a chance I'm afraid to take."

"Hell, you're still not alone. Call the State Police. Tell them what Martin did to you."

She shook her head. "You can help me. I look at you and I know it.

You're not afraid. You're big and you've never been afraid."

His mouth twisted, but he did not set her straight.

"That's out. I told you. Even I wanted to, it's still out. I don't even want you found in here. I've all the trouble I can take."

"If you'll help me, get me out of here, get me to my father and help me explain it all to him, I'll make him help you— no matter what it is."

He smiled, shook his head. "I don't know who your father is. But he can't help me."

Her mouth trembled. Her eyes were blurred with tears. "Why did you pull me out of that room?"

He breathed heavily, then answered softly. "I thought you were too pretty to die."

She looked at the housecoat, at her wrinkled skirt and at her loosely buttoned shirt.

"Did you think I was pretty?" She lifted her head.

She stared up at him, her breasts pressing against the fabric of her shirt, forming there and then fading slightly. He could not pull his gaze away. The tears dried in her eyes and something else replaced them. Her voice was very low. "You liked to look at me," she said.

She leaned back, straightening her shoulders, her breasts pulling taut. Her lips parted slightly. He saw in her what he had seen in the afternoon when she'd lain beside the pool. There was the same firm, soft-textured beauty and something else that went deeper—the hungry and unsatisfied part of her that Handsome had never plumbed, never reached, never even known. What a woman she would be for the man who really woke her up. He had thought a lot about dying before, because he lived precariously with death at his shoulder. But this was the pleasantest way he could imagine to die.

"Look at me," she whispered. "Look at me. Nobody's ever had me— nobody but Martin."

His eyes touched the bold stare. He smiled. "Oh, you're practically factory-fresh all right."

"You know I am. Don't you?"

He waited.

"You looked at me. You dressed me, and you touched me—and you wanted me."

She sprang forward from the bed. She came off it so the springs sighed, and her feet touched the carpet. She threw herself against him.

Her face was turned up against his face. He felt the warmth of her breath against his chin, against his mouth.

"You like me? You like my body? You liked looking at it. Did you like to touch my body?"

The sounds outside the room were gone, and all the memories and plans he had brought into it with him were gone. There was nothing but her body pressing against his body, the way her legs trembled as though she could hardly stand straight.

"Touch me. Touch my breasts. Hold them. You can touch them. You can hold them. You can do anything to me. Anything."

His hands closed on her waist. His fingers almost met. He felt a pulse throb at the base of his throat. He thought about her lying on the edge of the pool, lying on his bed, the way she would lie there now, the way she would open her arms and give herself to him, the way he would take her.

"You can have anything you want. Anything. You know you can."

It was as though she had thrown a handful of cold water from the pool into his face. He wanted her no less. He could not remember when he'd wanted a woman so terribly. She was offering him her body, but it was on a cash value.

He stepped back from her. "You've got your clothes on," he said. "You'd better get out of here. I might tear them off you."

She swayed toward him. "I want you to."

His voice was cold. "If I did, I'd have you and I still wouldn't help you. It's nice merchandise you're offering to sell. I'm just not buying."

Something flared in her eyes, but quickly died. She was fighting for her life, and there was no time for anger. But she was smart enough to see she could not buy him.

Her shoulders sagged. She looked around, not knowing where to go.

"I told you what to do. Call the State Police. Tell them what Martin did. They'll pick him up. You'll be safe."

Her mouth twisted. She looked at him coldly. "It doesn't matter to you."

"You'll be safe."

"Will I? You think I don't know Martin is too smart, too charming, too smooth, too clever for me. He's too gifted a liar. He'd have them laughing at me. Even if"—she paused. "Even if you were my witness."

He stopped her. "I can't be a witness. No matter what happens I can't be a witness. I'll swear I didn't see a thing. I'd have to—if I appear, and I wouldn't appear. I couldn't."

Eyes brimming, she looked at him, looked about the room. She spread her hands, completely lost and alone. "You see?" she said. "You see how it is?"

Chapter Eight

Ric walked to the window, glanced through a slit he made in the blinds. People sat in the lounge chairs out there, talking and laughing. They were enjoying the only part of the desert night that was going to be bearable. Earlier it was hotter than hell, later it would be colder than the inside of an iceberg.

"You can't stay here," he said. He did not look at her again. "There are people around. Too many people. Pretty Boy wouldn't try anything."

Her bitter laugh was the only answer.

"All right. He tried to kill you. You've got to face that. But maybe he doesn't intend to come back. Maybe he thinks it would be cleverer to let the maid find you."

He knew that she shivered, but he did not look at her.

"He's tried to kill you once. Not very likely he'll fool around here any more."

"You don't believe that. You know better."

He exhaled. "He was fool enough to try to kill you. Maybe he's smart enough to stay away."

Her bitter laugh clawed at him. "Anyhow, you're too busy. If you were going to let him kill me, why didn't you just leave me over there the first time?"

He spun around. "God almighty. I didn't know I'd have to adopt you."

She stared at him. Her lips were taut and her face starkly white. It was clear enough that she wanted to tell him where to go. She wanted to walk out and take her chances and spit on him. But she couldn't do it yet; the shock was too real, too near, the danger too close. She wanted to walk out on him but she couldn't walk at all.

He watched the people along the walk across the lighted court. They were sprawled in the cool night air, letting it eat the heat that had stored in them all day.

He released the blind, turned around.

The telephone rang and the sound was like something hurled into their faces. The girl cringed away from it on the bed and for a moment Ric stared at the instrument numbly. This was it. He could stop fooling around. It didn't matter what in hell happened to her, she had to get out now. For him, she and her woes no longer existed.

The phone rang again before he could reach it.

He felt his face creased with a frown, pulled taut. He stared at the girl on the bed, but didn't really see her. His hand gripped the receiver so tightly sweat squeezed from his palms.

He said, "Hello."

There was a hum, the sound of tension that went all through him, making him part of the phone, part of the wires. The line was open.

"Hello."

What hellish kind of game was this now? What they did to his nerves could not be important to them. How could they know they were connected with him? They didn't know the sound of his voice.

"Hello. Hello."

He remembered then. The call would come through the switchboard at the front office. They could call and ask to be connected to Mr. Ric Durazo's room. Sure. And when he answered, they didn't have to recognize his voice. They would know all they needed to know at the moment. He was there, waiting.

"Hello."

There was the soft click as though the receiver at the other end of the line had been replaced quietly, the caller satisfied. He went on standing there with the phone buzzing in his ear and then at last dropped it back in its cradle.

"What's the matter?"

Ric's head jerked up and he looked at her as though surprised to see her still in his room.

"There's nothing the matter."

A frown line indented her forehead between her eyebrows. She tried to keep her voice light.

"You sweat like that every time your phone rings?"

He hardly heard her. He glanced at the phone, slowly drew the back of his hand across his mouth.

"Who are you?" Her voice was soft, faintly worried. "Something is wrong. Tell me."

"You ain't got your own woes?"

"What's the matter?"

His voice sharpened.

"You run a lonely-hearts forum?"

"I don't run anything. You should see your face."

"Listen, baby. If you'd get out of here, you wouldn't have to see my face. And I wouldn't have to listen to you."

"I only want to help, if I can."

"You can. You can get out."

She caught her underlip between her teeth, staring at him. After a long time, she pushed herself up from the bed.

He stood tensely, watching her, thinking about that phone call.

She staggered slightly, walking toward the door. From the court he heard a sudden burst of laughter, and nearer, the uneven way she breathed. He did not move.

She was still as unsteady on her feet as she had been when she threw herself against him. He was afraid her knees would buckle under her.

She opened the door, dragging her housecoat behind her. The sounds of subdued laughter and talk flooded into the room.

She did not close the door after her. She left it ajar and walked in that benumbed way across the grass court. He stood there watching her.

She stopped outside her door. She reached for her door knob. For a moment she could not force herself to touch it. He saw her shoulders move in a shudder.

He strode to the door and closed it. The sound of the lock clicking was loud and final.

Chapter Nine

He had closed the door but the tension remained in the room like the air in an electric storm. It had been bad enough with her in the room. It was worse alone with the phone.

He paced the room, stopping beside the window. He wanted to open the blinds, but instead he jerked the cord, shutting them tighter. The sounds, whatever else happened out there, were of no concern to him. That girl meant no more to him than any other of the women stopping overnight in the motel.

He tried to sit down, but could not stay in the chair. He kept thinking about her lying on the bed, her arms spread, her legs parted, soft and golden and shadowed. *Fine. Drive yourself nuts now about a woman you'll never have. They're the only kind who ever really charm you, eh, Durazo? You simple-minded bastard.*

He walked back and forth before the telephone, unable to escape himself or his thoughts. Funny, a woman like the Davis bag could shake them all day; offer everything she had, a quick roll, quickly forgotten, but he could throw her out. What was the matter with him? Why didn't he pick up that phone and call Peggy? The old man waited until the sun went down and then he ran into town to shoot pool—probably the only rest the poor devil got. No wonder he never got out of that padded wicker chair. And there she was, her lips damp and her eyes naked—and he couldn't make himself care.

The phone rang again.

The breath exhaled from him in a long sigh. This was what he needed;

the long drive out here, the endless cups of coffee, the building tension, had tired him. Now his body craved action.

He picked up the receiver before it could ring again.

He opened his lips, then caught himself. He held the receiver against his ear, waiting, feeling the emptiness in the pit of his belly. But he did not speak.

The hum vibrated in his ear. He heard the distinct whisper as someone caught his breath across the wire.

A smile pulled Ric's mouth into a bitter line. Speak, you son of a bitch, or we'll stand here all night.

The line went dead.

Ric replaced the receiver, somehow feeling better. The emptiness remained in his stomach, but his whole body was set now. There would be another move, but it would be up to them.

He went over to the bed, got his gun from beneath the pillow. For an instant he glanced at the indentation her body had left there. He laughed sharply and thrust the gun into a shoulder holster.

He looked around the room, unable to escape the sense of emptiness. He checked the room, dropped the cottage keys in his pocket, snapped off the lights. He stepped out into the softly lighted night, aware of people in the lounge chairs glancing up disinterestedly the way strangers do. He did not look toward the girl's cottage.

He walked slowly along the court trying to appear the relaxed young man with nothing on his mind. He wondered bitterly if anyone were deceived.

He paused outside the office, dropped a nickel in the slotted container, took a Santa Fe paper from the rack.

"Hello there."

Peggy was leaning against the doorway. She was wearing a peasant blouse and loose skirt. He was sure she wore nothing under them.

He grinned at her, looking her over because she wanted him to. He said, "Hi."

She did not smile. Her eyes struck against his, held.

"See you had company," she said.

He felt himself tighten. He kept the grin on straight.

"Why Mother Hawk," he said.

"I don't miss much."

"You have a swell place for it. A motel like this."

She flushed. "I never watch anybody—unless I like them—or unless I hate them."

"I can't think why you'd like me. And I know you wouldn't waste a beautiful evening like this hating me."

"Wouldn't I?"

"*Seems* unlikely."

"You just don't know me very well. I could speak to Mrs. Kimball's husband. Just a word and he'd fix your wagon."

Oh, hell, he thought. If they hadn't picked this place, I'd walk out of here now. Maybe I better anyhow. Women. God knew if they'd realize what they were good for and stick to that, it would cure half the ills of the earth.

He kept the smile in place, teasing her.

"Mrs. Kimball?" he said.

Her laugh was cold. "You did not even know her name?"

He met her gaze. "She didn't bother to tell me. It didn't seem important."

Her face stiffened. "Oh, you feel fine now, don't you?"

He glanced toward the café beyond her office. "A little hungry."

"Go eat." She spat the word at him between her teeth.

He grinned at her, walked away from her, thinking that it was one of those things. A fool woman who didn't even know what she was doing could blow the whole damned thing higher than Explorer I.

He pushed open the door and entered the café, thinking he would clear out. The next time the phone rang, he'd say this motel stank and he was going to another one. When the waitress came he'd ask the name of another one close by.

Two waitresses were seated at a rear table near the kitchen doors, talking quietly over coffee cups. There were no other patrons. The café was brightly new, with gleaming white tablecloths, with polished chrome and shining terrazzo floors.

Ric sat down at a table near the wall. He sat and watched the cars pass on the highway until the waitress brought iced water and a menu. She was a tall thin girl with small breasts and tightly curled hair.

"Is there another nice motel near here beside the one next door?"

"What's the matter? Peggy all full for the night?"

"Just about."

"There's the Cactus Ranchero. About a mile down the road."

He thanked her, checked the menu, then ordered. "I don't suppose I could get a drink while I'm waiting?"

"I'm sorry."

He shrugged and she went away. The front door was pushed open and a tall man stepped inside. He let the door close behind him and for a moment looked the place over. The way he stood there made Ric go alert, and he felt his heart pound faster. There was a chance this was the man looking for him. It was unlikely they would just walk in like this, but on the other hand sometimes unless you were bold you lost everything.

They had set up Ric as a young man with plenty of money, plenty of clothes and a swank foreign sports car. A gray-haired gentleman could approach him in a motel or a café without arousing too much interest.

The man let his gaze pause on Ric for a moment. There was a set of warning signals going off inside him. This boy was too casual, his casualness cloaked an interest. Ric couldn't put his finger on it, but he smelled a wrong. And he was convinced when the tall gray-haired man crossed the room without looking at Ric and sat down at the next table.

Ric took a drink of water, looking the man over. He saw the lines of weariness about his chilled blue eyes, the fatigue on his face. His features were sharp-hewn, straight. His mouth was set in a hard line.

"Been a hot one."

The voice was casual, but it was tense, too, and there was power in it. Here was the kind of man who ordered other men around.

Ric traced his fingers along the chilled glass. He did not answer.

"I say, it's been hot. I really crossed some hot country. Had my Buick boiling. You have any trouble?"

"I live here," Ric said.

The man recoiled at this and Ric expected him to call him a liar. But the waitress came then, stood between them to take the man's order.

When the waitress was gone, the gray-haired man picked up his knife and drew it along the tablecloth in long straight lines.

"I ordered a steak," he said. "Wonder if it's any good. You take a restaurant, unless you know the restaurant— They have good steaks around here?"

"I don't know."

"Thought you said you lived around here?"

Ric shook out the newspaper before him, did not answer. He read about the latest exchange of notes with Russia. He slowly read the story about the Ironfield child kidnaping. The FBI had moved in, the newspaper said, and refused to talk for publication beyond saying that they were near a solution of the case.

"Anything new?" The man said. "In the paper."

Ric's voice was sharp. "You like to read it?"

He saw the man's eyes chill, head tilt. He was unaccustomed to being talked to like that. He watched the anger fade, the smile replace it. Here was a boy who wanted something.

"No. I don't mean to intrude, mister. Just I been traveling the last few days. Drove out from the East. Haven't had much time to stop and just gab, you know."

"I'm not much for talking."

"Funny. Woman who runs the place said this was a friendly town. I got in this afternoon. Guess I was about the third one. Sports car and a Caddy there ahead of me. You didn't look like a native to me. Surprised me to hear you say you lived around here."

Ric rattled the paper again, turning the pages.

The waitress brought his meal. The steak looked good, but Ric's appetite had faded. He laid the paper aside and began to eat. He did not glance toward the man again.

He could feel the man's gaze on him.

The man's voice was rueful. "Funny thing. I always prided myself I could tell a lot about people. Kind of work they did. Where they were from. You look—hope you don't mind me saying this—you look kind of pale for a native. This sun would burn anybody. And also, you don't wear one of them big hats."

Ric slashed off a large hunk of steak and jabbed it into his mouth so the man could not expect him to answer. He ate steadily, bolting his food. He looked at the pie when the waitress brought it, but left it untouched.

He finished off his coffee, tossed some money on the table, folded the newspaper under his arm and walked out. He glanced once in the plate-glass window. The tall gray-haired man was watching him.

He walked back past the office. Peggy was in at the telephone switchboard. He lengthened his stride. *Friendliest town in New Mexico.* Hell, he thought, people won't let you alone even when you want them to.

He entered his room and locked the night catch after him. He turned on the TV, watched the cowboys for a few moments and then killed the sound. He sat down in the easy chair, snapped on the lamp over his head. He turned the pages of the newspaper, reading slowly. His horoscope made him grin wryly: "Today everything is propitious for you. You have only to reach out and take what you want. You are the kind of person who takes what he wants and all the stars are with you today."

Whoever wrote that should go back to hawking fish. He let the paper slip out of his hands and laid his head back, staring at the ceiling. A man who took what he wanted. In a way that was true. The first trouble he'd ever got into was when he'd taken a car he'd wanted. But they'd caught him.

He lay there and thought about that, about the car and himself, the color of the car, and the depth of his yearning. You couldn't keep a kid from wanting nice things just by telling him he could not afford them. You could spend your life telling him, but something in him makes him want and need, and the only way open is to take.

He was not trying to make excuses. There were no alibis. He had lived thirty years and he had learned. Oh, he had learned—the hard way. He had to lose everything that mattered. He had held Anne in his arms and he had slept with her, only not very much—not much sleep, that is. He had been to bed with her and in cars with her. He had loved her with himself and with his hand and with his mouth and with every way there was to love, but mostly with all his heart.

He stirred in the chair, thinking, Oh, fine. Cry about the past, the loss. You spend all your lonely life needing somebody and you try to go straight for her. But they frame you, and you spend three of a five year term in prison. And when you come back she is gone, she is lost to you, and it is as though you never loved her with your hand, or with yourself, never touched her or lay beside her in a bed, or in a car. She is gone from you, and you can't touch her, any more than you can forget her.

He broke off the thoughts, hotly, angrily. He thought about the girl in the green suit, in the housecoat, in nothing but sun-golden flesh. He did not think about her because he wanted to, but because it was better than thinking back to Anne. He wondered if perhaps there had been something about her that reminded him of Anne, and that made him want her terribly. Was it the heap of her rounded stomach, the way her hip bones showed in pleasant ridges, or was it knowing she was untouched and ripe and waiting the way Anne had been? He did not know. He did not care. He just wanted to get out of there.

He stood up. They had no right to do this to him, to send him here, and leave him here with his loneliness.

He stared at the phone. Ring, damn you. Ring and say the words.

He removed the gun from his holster, checking it, thinking about the permit to carry it. There was a laugh. He had been in jail twice when he was a punk kid before he even knew they issued permits to carry guns. It had always seemed a joke to him. This man is licensed to kill. This man is not.

He laid the gun on the table beside the telephone. He liked it better there. It had been a long time and he could not forget it when he carried it under his shoulder.

He heard the fists against his door. They were not knocking, they were beating. They were begging him to open it.

He heard the terrified whisper. "Let me in. God, please let me in."

He did not stop to think. If he had stopped to think he would not have gone to the door. Or perhaps he was lying to himself. Perhaps he was waiting, had been waiting, breathing shallowly, knowing Handsome would come back and that she would run to him, beating on his door.

He threw the night catch, turned the knob, felt the door thrust hard against him. He stepped back under its momentum and she ran by him, clutching at him with her hands, as though he were a boulder—or a straw.

Chapter Ten

Ric felt her press close against his back, so tautly he could feel her trembling against him.

He pushed the door to close it and it was slapped out of his hand. The knob struck against the wall, making a loud snapping sound in the silent room. Martin Kimball half fell past him, carried by the momentum of his running.

Ric caught the rebounding door and shut it quietly. When he turned the girl was still behind him, still pressed against his back as though they'd executed some intricate dance step.

He faced Kimball in the silent room. Kimball was crouched slightly, arms apart. For the moment there was only the silence, in the cottage and in the courtyard. Ric didn't know how many had seen them burst into his place, but trouble was piling up. He could always be sure of that.

Kimball's gaze raked across his wife, pulled to Ric, measuring him.

Finally Kimball said, voice chilled and only faintly breathless, "I don't know who you are. I got no fight with you." He gave Ric the semblance of a charming smile. "As you can see, just a little trouble with my wife."

"I know."

He saw Martin Kimball react. It was the matter of less than a second but it showed in his face. He jerked his eyes toward Ric's window, realizing that he could have been seen from there in the afternoon. He recovered quickly, and his mouth pulled into a twisted grin.

"What you mean, you know?"

"Just what I said."

"You got a wife you got troubles with, too?"

"No. I got no wife."

Martin Kimball exhaled. He pulled his gaze from Ric's, spoke to his wife. "All right, Eve, fun's fun. We can't run around parading our troubles in front of strangers."

"I won't go, Martin."

"Oh, for God's sake, Eve. Be reasonable." Martin sounded as though he were speaking to a child.

"I won't go."

"Now, Eve, there's nothing we can't talk out."

"Then say it, Martin, and get out. I'm not going back with you."

Martin shook his head, his laugh exasperated. He spoke to Ric again.

"You ever see a woman act like that? This is nothing, friend, just a little domestic quarrel. Sorry she is carrying on like this in front of you. But

I'll take her along and—"

"I'm not going."

Ric said, "Maybe you better talk to me."

"What the hell is this? Friend, you ought to have enough sense to stay out of domestic quarrels. This doesn't concern you."

Ric kept his voice low. "Well, let's say it does. Let's say I'm talking for your wife for the moment."

"You're asking for trouble."

"You brought it in here. I'm just trying to keep it quiet."

"Then get out of the way, and stay out of this. Anything I've got to say, I'll say to Eve."

Her voice shook. "I'm not going back with you, Martin. I'm never going to see you again. I meant that."

Martin made one last effort at nonchalance. "How'd you like your wife talking to you like that, friend? I'm telling you, it hurts. In front of a stranger. How would you like it?"

"Maybe if I'd tried to kill her, I'd expect her to act just about like this."

Martin's face sagged again. He stared at Ric, mouth slack.

"Who are you?"

"Nobody. I stood here and saw you turn off the gas out there this afternoon, killing the pilot light, and then turn it on again."

"You're crazy. You're nuts."

"So far as I know, that has nothing to do with it. I'm not blind."

"I never heard such fool talk. No wonder Eve was upset when I got back from town. Did you go over there and tell her a crazy story like that?"

Ric's smile was cold. "After I dragged her out of that room and revived her, I told her."

Martin looked at Eve, back at Ric. "Sure. I left her in a drunken stupor. Why do you think we fought? She stays crocked all the time. I was sick and fed up. Maybe she tried to gas herself. I don't know."

Ric just looked at him. "Why don't you save that talk for the police? They might believe it."

"They will believe it. It's the truth. Listen, pal, before you get mixed up in something you'll wish to God you never heard of, you better hear this. I've got witnesses. Not one or two—twenty. They all say that Eve's a lush and has been ever since I married her. She spreads all kinds of stories when she's drinking. You better stay out of it. Anything she told you, you can chalk up to her drinking."

Ric said, chilled. "All she told me was that you were trying to kill her for her money."

Martin laughed. If Ric had not seen all he had, that laugh might have swayed him. He saw what Eve had meant. This man was clever; he had traded on his charm for so long that he relied on it to get him out of trouble.

"For her money. That's good. She begged me to marry her. She offered me a big cash settlement. Hell, ask her. She offered me plenty, and I wouldn't take it. Ask her."

Ric didn't have to ask her. She sagged against him slightly. It would be true anyway. Martin was after the big stakes, all of it. Why take peanuts, why be half secure?

"Still you had her make a will leaving everything to you."

Martin laughed as though this were comic. "Sure. After she begged me. She told me something might happen to her and her old man would never let me have a cent. I told her I was a big boy, could take care of myself. But she carried on—she was bitter against her old man. Finally I told her to go ahead. But her own lawyer will tell you I was against it from the first."

Ric's laugh matched Martin's. He saw the handsome man scowl at the imitation of his laughter. "All that would be fine. It would sound good in a court. It's phony as hell with just the three of us here."

"I'm warning you. Get out of this. Come on, Eve, we're getting out of here."

"No." She pressed harder against Ric.

Ric said, "Like you say, Kimball, this is no business of mine. But I've gambled in my time. I'm sure you have. I'm telling you—you played a hand and you lost. Why don't you clear out of here?"

Martin laughed at him. "Sure. I'll go. As soon as you get out of my way and my wife goes with me."

"She says she doesn't want to go."

"That's between us."

"Maybe it was before you tried to kill her."

Martin's voice hardened. "You'll never make a fantastic story like that stick."

"I won't have to. The reading of the will would take care of you."

"No. You see, I've stood all the trouble with Eve I'm going to stand. Sorry to drag you into it, but you insist. Things like this are happening all the time. All she thinks about is that damned money. I told her before she blasted over here that she was going to change that will or she and I have had it. When we leave here, we're clearing out, driving back to Sherman Oaks and she's going to have that God-damned will changed."

There was sweated sincerity in Martin's voice. But in his mind Ric could see the casual way he'd reached out, turned the gas valve once and then turned it back again. He stared at Martin, wondering if Eve

Kimball would trust herself alone in any car with him now.

"No." The word was ripped out of Eve.

Ric shrugged. "You heard her, Kimball. Why don't you get out? When she has changed the will, maybe she'll come back to you. If you're so honest, you can wait."

"If I want your advice, I'll pay you for it. That's my wife. Open that door and get out of the way."

Ric stared at him. "Why don't you open it?"

Martin hunched his wide shoulders. His gaze wavered a moment, then he stared around the room like a caged animal.

Their gazes struck the gun beside the telephone at the same instant. Ric lifted his arms, heaving Eve away from him. She fell against the wall, crying out. Then Ric moved up on the balls of his feet, lunged forward.

Martin dived for the gun. His hand closed on it as Ric chopped down across the side of his neck. The gun squirted forward and Martin landed across the table. The table legs crumpled—the splitting sound loud—and the table folded under Martin's body.

Martin sprawled full length across the floor. His right hand was still reaching for the gun, fingers extended. Ric stepped beyond him, snatched up the gun and stood against the wall, watching Kimball.

Ric shoved the gun back in its shoulder holster. He was aware that Eve had not moved. It was as though she were paralyzed, leaning against the wall.

Martin sat up, groggy and shaking his head to clear it. He rocked for an instant on his knees, then lunged upward at Ric, his hands clawing at Ric's throat.

Ric set himself to drive his left into Kimball's pretty face. He had fought in enough alley brawls to be on the alert, but Kimball's prettiness had thrown him off. Kimball came in close as though reaching for his throat, feinted away from Ric's left and brought up his knee into Ric's groin.

The room skidded and spun out from under Ric. The ceiling was the floor, and the walls were the floor and Kimball was spinning around in front of him.

Ric felt as though he were going to lose his insides; not only that he was going to, that he must. It was all that would save him.

He felt his back touch the wall. He rested for a moment with the good feeling of the wall against his back. Through the spinning fire flashes he saw Martin Kimball's grimacing face coming nearer, growing larger. He saw his fist smash into his face, but he did not feel it. There was only the red fire, flashing brighter, and then the taste of blood.

His hands went out. It was automatic. He had to stay alive. He kept his hands hitting at that face until it gave way. He did not close his fists. He slapped back and forth, cutting and chopping—the Adams apple, the side of the neck, across the temple.

His vision cleared. Martin's face was flush red and showed the marks of Ric's hands. Martin was backing up because those open hands did not give him an opportunity to set himself.

Ric paused, breathing through his mouth. He stared at Martin, weaving slightly, suckering him in. Martin grinned and set himself, lunging again at Ric's throat. But Ric sidestepped him this time and drove his left fist into Martin's face, feeling it crush and give under his knuckles. The impact jarred him to his shoulder socket.

He stepped away and Martin began to crumble. He was a tall man and his knees buckled first, then he fell to his knees. He did not reach for support. His arms were inert, hanging at his sides. He did not even try to break his fall. He struck face-first and did not move.

Ric stepped away, cursing under his breath. He wiped the back of his hand across his mouth. Then he turned and stared at Eve Kimball.

She had not moved. Her mouth was pulled slack, and she chewed at her underlip.

His voice was a hoarse whisper. "Now if you're smart," he said, "you'll do what you should have done this afternoon. You'll get to hell out of here."

Chapter Eleven

"No," she said.

"Why in hell not?"

She walked away from the wall, moving stiffly. She looked at Martin Kimball and for an instant the agony and hurt showed bare in her naked gaze. Then her head tilted. She went to an easy chair, sat down.

"I'm afraid."

"Too afraid to get to hell out of here and save your life?"

"He'd find me. He'd follow me. You know that. You want me out of here."

"You're damn right I do. I want both of you out of here. You're driving me nuts and Pretty Boy is bleeding all over my rug."

Her eyes filled with tears. "Don't you think I've thought of how to get away since I left here? I haven't thought of anything else. I can't go until I can get away from Martin."

"You mind hinting when you think that'll be—this side of hell?"

She looked up, her mouth damp. "I don't know. This side of hell."

"I can tell you. Call the cops. I'll cart him back across the court to your place. File a complaint against him—any complaint so they hold him overnight—then you get in that Cadillac and make tracks for Los Angeles."

She shivered. "He'd stop me. He'd even use the cops to stop me. You know he would."

Ric exhaled. He walked to the broken table, set it up straight and leaned it against the wall for support. He set the phone back on it. *The story of my life*, he thought, looking at the battered table with the phone perched precariously on it.

Ric sat down on the side of the bed. It was quiet in the motel court. He had the strange feeling that everybody was holding his breath out there, waiting to see what would happen next in cottage eight.

Neither of them spoke. Eve wiped at the tears that welled over her eyelids. He heard her sniffle, but did not look at her. He saw Martin's leg twitch.

Martin clawed at the rug, pushing himself up. He sprawled with his weight on his hands, shaking his head, drops of blood splattering his shirt.

After a moment, Martin got up on his knees. He stared at both of them, his mouth slack and his eyes not focusing. Gradually he remembered and Ric saw the wild shadows swirl in his eyes.

He jumped to his feet. His breathing was the loudest sound in the court. He spread his legs, wiped the back of his hand across his bloodied mouth.

"You're going to pay for this, you God-damned dirty son of a bitch. You think you can go around assaulting people, you dirty son of a bitch. But you're going to find out, you dirty damned son of a bitch. You tried to kill me. By God, you're going to jail for that. If it's the last thing I ever do, I'll get you for jumping me."

Eve got up. "Shut up, Martin. Get out of here."

Martin stared at her for a moment as though he'd never seen her before on the face of this earth.

"You slut." Blood trickled from the corner of his mouth and he smashed at it with the back of his hand. He stood staring at his blood on his shirt. Suddenly he lunged forward and backhanded Eve across the face.

She spun, toppling against the bed.

Martin yelled, laughing at her. "There you are, slut—in bed with your lover. You think I don't know? You think I am so stupid I haven't figured it? You and your boy friend, trying to set me up, trying to get rid of me, cooking up this murder thing. Well, I can tell you, slut, it won't work. You won't get away with it."

Eve sat awkwardly on the side of the bed, staring up at Martin. It was as though she had never seen him before now. No matter what he had done to her, forced her to do, how deeply he'd hurt her, she'd never seen him quite like this.

She whispered at him. "You're insane—you're crazy."

"Why wouldn't I be crazy? You tell me why I wouldn't be crazy? I followed you over here, just like you set it up. You run screaming to your lover—try to frame me for an attempted murder—you two lovely bastards. You think you can kill me and get away with it."

"No, Martin—"

"What the hell's the sense trying to talk to him?" Ric said.

"Yeah, Lover Boy. Yeah. You tell her. What's the sense in trying to talk to me? You two think you've got all the angles. You're going to find out. You think I won't get the State Police in here on you two, that's where you're crazy. You two god-damn lovely bastards—going to bed behind my back—trying to kill me."

He stood there staring at them, laughter wild in his bloodied face, angry insane tears streaming down his cheeks. He spun around then and ran to the door. He slammed it behind him.

"He's crazy," she whispered again.

"Most people who try to murder somebody else are nuts," Ric said, voice cold.

He got up from the bed, walked to the baggage rack. He threw his belongings in his expensive leather suitcase, snapped it shut.

"What are you doing?" Her whispered voice reached at him.

"What you should do. I'm getting out of here."

"You're running? Why?"

"Because I've got sense enough to run, baby, and if you've got good sense, you'll run, too."

"Why?"

"Baby, you heard him. Just like I did. Only maybe you think he won't do it. Me, I know better. He said he was going to the State Police. I know he's just nuts enough to do it."

She got up, caught his arm.

"He will go to them," she said. "But that's no reason for you to run."

"Maybe it's not, but that's why I'm running."

"Why are you afraid?"

"Because he's nuts and I've thought it over for one whole minute."

Her voice rose. "But you haven't done anything wrong. Why are you running? Martin attacked you. This is your cottage. You've nothing to be afraid of."

His laugh was a chilled sound.

"Maybe not. Maybe all you say is true. But maybe there's something more. I told you, you don't know me, you don't know who I am, anything about me. Maybe your loony husband has played his ace. Maybe he's done the one thing I can't sit around and wait for—gone for the police."

He picked up the leather case, patted the gun in his shoulder holster, looked around the room once more.

"Why are you afraid of the police?"

He laughed again and spoke over his shoulder, going toward the door. "There has to be a reason?"

She ran after him, caught his arm again. "You know there has to be a reason."

"Okay. Once I overparked. I've lived in terror ever since. Whether I have a reason or not, baby, I haven't got time to go into it with you now. Good-by, and I don't want you to think it hasn't been exciting."

He opened the door, moved through it, and closed it sharply after him. He did not look back. The cottages along the court were silent, with that breathless sense of silence. He paused at the office door, set down his bag.

He opened the office door, stepped inside. Peggy was sitting behind the counter reading a confession magazine. She looked up, gave him an odd smile. He had intended telling her to inform any callers, in person or via phone, that he was at the Cactus Ranchero. That unexplained smile stopped him. He would never have trusted the Mona Lisa, either.

"Well." She looked him over. "Kind of mussed up. I see you finally met Mr. Kimball."

"Something like that. I'm going out. I may be gone overnight. If there are any calls for me, any messages, keep them, will you?"

"Sure. I saw Mr. Kimball race out of here a few minutes ago. He looked terrible."

"You shouldn't have sicked him on me."

She caught her breath. "Why, I didn't. I never said a word. If you'd rather have that skinny little thing than—"

"Okay, if anybody asks for me, tell them I'll be back."

She smiled again. "Even Mr. Rehan?"

He stopped. The chilled feeling spread in his stomach again. "Rehan?"

"Sure. Your friend. Said he was a friend of yours. Said he was sure he knew you from somewhere. Said he wanted in the worst way to be sure. Asked all about you, where you're from, when you got here, anything I knew about you. I didn't tell him about little Mrs. Kimball, either."

His heart was slugging erratically. He tried to keep his voice level. "Oh, you're so good to me."

"Well. I could be anyway—if you'd let me."

"Who's this guy Rehan?"

She shrugged. "I don't know any more about him than I do you. Gave his home address as Washington, D.C. That ring any bells? Saul Rehan."

"No." He swallowed at the tightness in his throat.

She smiled again. "He's a tall, gray-haired man, very distinguished. Arrived this afternoon, about an hour after you did. Said he had picked up some poor kid out on the highway east of here. Kid was all battered—said somebody had thrown him out of a car."

Ric turned toward the door. His shoulders sagged.

"You remember Saul Rehan," Peggy's voice clawed after him. "Why, he said he ate supper with you."

"Oh," Ric said. He looked over his shoulder from the door. He met her gaze levelly. "Probably some insurance salesman."

"If you're going to fool around women like Kimball, you better pal up with Saul," Peggy said. He closed the door. He did not look back. He hefted his suitcase, strode across the graveled drive past the other cars to the Porsche.

When he set the bag down and got his keys from his pocket, his hands were trembling. He swore under his breath.

He unlocked the door, rolled down the window, leaned over and tossed his suitcase into the rear. He slid into the bucket seat then, still not sure what he would do except move long enough to keep Martin and the cops off his tail.

He started the motor, listening to its sluggish roar and then its ragged settling. He shoved it into reverse, leaped out of the parking place.

He glanced once toward the office. He did not see Peggy. He changed gears and the little car lunged forward. As he turned his head there was a flicker of shadow directly in front of the car less than two feet in front of the bumper.

He stepped hard on the brake. His hands gripped the steering wheel and he sat there for a moment staring straight ahead, seeing nothing. He was shaking all over.

Chapter Twelve

Ric sat there, breathing heavily. For a couple of minutes he experienced a bad time. Terrible enough to hit any one anywhere, anytime, but right now that was all he needed—to be dragged in and questioned in an accident case.

His hands tightened on the wheel. He stared through the windshield at her. She stood only inches in front of the hood staring back at him.

She did not move. She could have been an apparition, only he knew better. That would be too easy.

He slapped open the door, swung out of the car. His knees were so weak they would barely support him.

He strode around the front of the car, fists knotted and all the tensions in him clutched there. The desert wind was chill against his sweated face.

Ric's voice shook. "What in hell do you think you're doing now?"

She looked at him, eyes flat. Her voice was dull, there was no fear in it, or any reaction to her narrow brush with death. "I'd as soon you killed me as Martin—"

"Maybe I'd rather he did it."

"That's what will happen if Martin ever gets me alone and you know it."

"I got my own troubles."

"All I need is a little help."

"Then, sister, you get a little help. Go to the police."

"How can I? Martin's already gone to them. Remember, that's why you're running away."

"I only thought it was. I'm running away from you."

"Take me with you. I've got to get away from him. You know he's going to kill me. Maybe not today—but as soon as he gets a chance, and you know it."

"I'm not as opposed to the idea, baby, as I was at first."

Her head moved back and forth, her eyes were wide in the light from the motel sign.

"Damn you," he said. That was all there was to say. She could foul up everything, probably she already had. Success depended on so many factors, mostly on his living unobtrusively at the swank motel they'd chosen for him. He'd screwed that part of it.

The siren was a whisper in the dark distance, but he reacted as though it was the rattle of a coiled snake. He glanced around in the darkness, at the other cars, the highway, the silent wastes beyond, and the woman standing in the office window watching them. Peggy's smile was knowing and twisted.

"Get in." He snarled it at Eve. "Let's get out of here."

She ran by him, opened the door of the Porsche and slid into the bucket seat. He walked back to the driver's side, got in, put the car in gear and stomped on the accelerator.

The little car bucked slightly and then lunged forward, spewing pebbles. As they hit the highway, Ric glanced back over his shoulder at the motel. He did not see Peggy. She was no longer standing in the window. But just beyond the office, in a rectangle of light from its window stood the tall gray-haired man, silently watching.

Saul Rehan.

Whoever in the hell he was.

"You'll never be sorry," she said.

"I'm already sorry."

"Yes. But you're not through. You don't know how I can help you."

His laugh was as cold as the wind in the windows. "Look, I'm up to my ears in alligators without any help from you. Spare me. I'm going to lose this Porsche in some of the wild country out here until morning. By then you'd better have made up your mind what you're going to do."

"Tell me about it."

"About what?"

"Who are you? Where you're from? Who hurt you? Who made you bitter? Why are you afraid?"

"We're only going to be out here overnight. We haven't time for all that."

They raced west beyond the airport. Most of the buildings were dark. The administration building was vaguely lighted, and the tower gave off a blue glow, one of the runways was dotted with red and white signal lights.

"What's your name? You can tell me that, can't you?"

"Ric."

"That's nice. What else?"

"Durazo. Ric Durazo." He said the name coldly and waited.

After a moment, she said. "Is that name supposed to mean something to me?"

"Doesn't it?"

"No."

"Do you know this back country?"

"How in hell should I know it?"

She glanced out the window at the racing darkness that seemed to close down upon them like a star-patched shroud. Her voice was low.

"You act like you know it."

"I was never out here before."

"Shouldn't you stay on the highway?"

"Martin went to the State Police, they'd pick us up on the highway—fast."

"You can get lost in this country. Just hopelessly. Even I know better than to get off the highway on these side roads without knowing something about them."

"Any time you want to get out—"
"I'm just trying to help."

He drove swiftly, the speedometer needle sitting at sixty. They struck potholes in the narrow road, and the car skittered and wavered. Once it danced on the shoulder, struck it and lurched drunkenly for a moment in the darkness so the headlights rocked crazily against the blackness. Eve cried out.

"What's the matter? I thought you'd as soon I killed you as Pretty Boy."

"You don't even know where you're going and you drive like you can't wait to get there."

"I'm buying distance."

"It won't do you much good if you turn this thing over on its head—not unless you're strong enough to set it up right again."

He laughed coldly. "You promised to help me," he said sardonically. "Besides, this little car has a low center of gravity. They're hard to turn over."

She did not answer but slid down slightly in the bucket seat and braced her legs against the floorboard.

"You put a lot of faith in strangers," he said. He glanced at her legs, the roundness straining against the skirt.

"Sometimes you have to."

"Sometimes you're a fool to."

"You keep threatening me in that veiled way. Either tell me what's the matter, or admit it. You're a nice guy even though it would kill you to think so."

"I'm no nice guy, I can tell you that."

"Maybe you've just got a stricter conscience than most people."

"Think what you want to."

"No. I'd rather have you tell me. As you say, I've got to trust you—with my life. I want to. You haven't been a stranger to me—not since I woke up in your cottage back at the motel."

"No, but I've wanted to be."

"How tough you talk."

"We're strangers, baby, in every way in the world, and don't you forget it."

"Two strangers who sleep side by side in a motel and never meet. Isn't that a pretty thought? Only we met."

"Wires got crossed somewhere. You, born with half a million dollars. My old man ran away and left us, my mother died. I grew up in orphanages until I was old enough for the reformatories."

"Oh, Ric. I'm sorry."

"The hell with it."

She tried to smile. She traced her hand across the Porsche dashboard. "You're doing all right now."

"Am I?"

He stepped hard on the brakes, reached out and caught her roughly, dragging her against him. The car hopped to a stop, its headlights fixed on the eyes of a wild steer. The horns glittered in the lights.

Ric pressed on the horn. The sound sprang outward, struck against the steer and scattered into the nothingness on both sides of the road. The steer's eyes got round and wild. It turned suddenly and leaped like a mountain goat, going along the road and then leaping out of the light into the darkness.

Ric breathed out. He realized he was still holding Eve against him. She had not moved. He felt the softness of her hair against his face. He pulled his arm from around her.

"Sorry," he said. "Afraid you'd burst your head against the windshield."

"Are you?"

"Sorry?" He smiled. "Sure. I said I was."

"You should smile more often. You've a very nice smile. It lights your face all up. It shows what a nice person you are—under all that bitterness."

"All that in a smile. Do you read tea leaves, too?"

She did not answer. He put the car in gear, but now he moved forward more slowly. He had gone more than a mile when he realized she was still there, lying with her head on his shoulder.

"You can get yourself in a lot of trouble like that," he said.

"Trouble?" She laughed briefly and sat straight in the bucket seat. "What's trouble? I've never even heard of it."

"If you think you've got to pay me for bringing you away from that motel, you can forget it."

She exhaled sharply. He glanced toward her, found the lights from the dash pulling chilled shadows in the set planes of her face.

Her voice matched the bitterness in his.

"I hadn't thought about paying," she said. "But I'll tell you this. You try to touch me now and I'll kill you."

He grinned at her. "Two strangers who sleep side by side in a motel and never meet."

She was staring ahead. He saw her brace herself, grabbing the doorframe and the side of the bucket seat. He reacted by lifting his foot from the gas. She screamed.

He stepped hard on the brake. The car rolled a few feet and came to a stop on the jagged brink of Stygian darkness. He pulled up hard on the emergency, cut the engine and for some moments they sat there in the eternity of silence and did not speak.

Chapter Thirteen

Ric opened the car door. He had not realized that he was barely breathing. The headlamps were futile beams poking out into the blackness ahead. He reached behind his seat and found a flashlight. "Be careful," she said. He stood up and closed the door behind him. He did not answer her. It was cold out of the car, a bitter bone-chilling cold that closed in with the darkness. He snapped on the flashlight and walked to the jagged road edge.

He played the light down the incline which was covered with rocks and a few small sprigs of dry plants. He lifted the light and saw a broken pillar a few feet across the black space.

"What is it, Ric?" she said from inside the car.

"Bridge washed out. I can see one of the supports."

"Is it completely gone?"

"Yes. Sometimes it happens. A flash flood will take a bridge out."

He heard the Porsche door slam and then she was standing beside him, her arms tight across her breasts. She shivered in the cold wind that made an empty sound in the dry creek bed.

"But there was no sign. There was no warning."

"Who ever uses this road? An Indian, maybe, and some of those wild steers."

"We could have been killed."

"One way is as good as another."

"I want to stay alive. I'm stubborn."

"Yes. You're stubborn."

He walked away from her, flashing the light along the ground at the side of the road.

"What will you do?" she said. "Will we turn around and go back?"

"No. If they are looking for us, they will have roadblocks on the highway by now. Soon they will know that we did not stay on the highway. Then they will search the side roads. It's no good to stay here."

He walked along the road for forty feet. He did not find any ruts. Then he walked down the incline to the river bed.

She called after him. "I'm cold."

"Get back in the car."

"I don't like you to leave me. It's too dark. I'm scared."

"Be glad it's dark. Martin won't find you in the dark. Get back in the car before you freeze."

She did not speak again. He walked along the hard-packed ground to the river bed.

He returned to the car and started the engine.

"I'm going to try the right side," he said. "The ground is rock-hard. We can cross the creek bed and go up the other side."

She did not answer. She moved nearer to him in the bucket seat, kept her hands clenched in her lap.

He put the car in reverse, moved slowly. He turned it to the right and they side-slipped slightly going down the embankment. He heard her sharp intake of breath, but she did not speak. The car righted itself and they went down the incline. There were stones and broken hunks of pillars near the bridge. The stones and broken supports loomed suddenly in the car lights.

Still moving the car cautiously forward, he turned to the right. The car moved only its own length when the rear wheels cracked through the crusted earth, bogged down.

He exhaled slowly. "Oh, fine."

"Ric."

"If we're stuck," he said, "I'm as helpless as you are."

He stepped on the accelerator, spun the wheels only once. He could feel them sinking deeper.

He cut the engine, turned off the lights. The darkness closed down around them, seeming to press through the closed windows.

He said, "Well, here we are. Looks like a good place to spend the night, eh?"

"I can't see anything."

"That's what I mean. We can't do anything until morning. We might as well be comfortable."

"I'm cold."

He reached behind the front seat, brought out the tailored topcoat he had worn only once since buying it in Manhattan. "Put this over you. It's all we've got."

"It gets terribly cold out here before morning."

"Try to think of something else."

He reached down beside her, touched a control. The seat reclined. "How nice," she said.

"Oh, yes. We're fine."

He let his own seat down and lay beside her staring at the darkness beyond his window. Distantly, a coyote wailed. It was a lonely sound and added to the sense of cold in the car.

He buttoned his coat, turned up the collar. He felt the cold rising from the car floor, moving up his legs.

"You'll be cold," Eve said.

"Try to get some sleep." He thrust his hands into his pockets.

She turned toward him, moved as near as she could. She reached out, touched his arm. "Come closer. At least we can share the coat."

Ric rolled on his side. She spread the coat over both of them. Then he remembered the newspaper. He got it from the rear compartment. He unfolded it and spread it out. He pushed it around her legs, across her thighs and put another section across her upper body.

"That is nice," she said. "It's fine."

He spread the remaining papers across his own legs.

"The closer we are together," she said, "the warmer."

He slid his arm under her head and she burrowed against his throat. He smelled the faint warm fragrance of her hair. He remembered Anne's hair and the way he had buried his face in it, the way he had dreamed about the scent of it, even after he had heard she was lost to him.

"I wore braces," she said. "I was lonely, and I thought I was terribly homely. I guess I wasn't—terribly homely, I mean. I was just homely, and it made it worse because I was lonely."

"You changed."

"Yes. But I think it was too late. I never had any friends. Not even other girls. Father was afraid of all of them. He always told me they wanted something—none of them were good enough. Nobody was ever lonelier than I was."

His voice was low. "You should try a prison sometime."

"Were you ever in prison, Ric?"

"Yes."

"I'm sorry."

"It doesn't matter."

"It made you bitter."

"No. I was already bitter."

"Were you guilty?"

"Of what?"

"Whatever they sent you to prison for?"

"It doesn't matter, but I wasn't. You see, by then I didn't have to be guilty of anything. I had a bad rep. I was guilty unless I could prove I was innocent. I couldn't prove that." He laughed suddenly. "The story of my life."

"I want to hear it."

"Well, I don't want to tell it."

"But if you weren't guilty—"

"I told you, it didn't matter. The funny thing was that I was really trying to be honest—and that was when the roof fell in."

"Was she pretty, Ric?"

"Who?"

"The girl you loved. The one you lost when you were sent to jail."

"Is it that plain?"

"You're hurt, Ric. That's plain."

"She was pretty. I loved her. I was crazy about her. I was nuts about her. I thought about her all day, every day. I loved her truly. I didn't look at anybody else. I didn't know anybody else existed."

"And she married somebody else?"

"Sure. You see, there was this judge. You see, she was with me the night I was arrested. She didn't have anything to do with what I was arrested for any more than I did. But the cops—the lousy, stinking—well, so she was mixed up in it. She had to report to this judge. Every two weeks. God knows, he was old enough to be her father."

"She married him?"

"Why not? Hell, that was five years ago. I got over it. Look at me. I'm fine now."

"Oh, Ric. I am so sorry."

"Forget it. Go to sleep. It wasn't her fault. Hell, she was all mixed up. The guy was fine to her—and I was up for five years."

She tried to talk but he would not say anything else. The silence and the cold wind beat against the car so that it rocked slightly in the river bed. Under the coat and the papers they were warm as long as they pressed close together. They lay on the cold seats with their legs pressed hard against each other. Her head was on his shoulder and her hair spread across his throat. He closed his eyes and tried to forget the way her hair lay across his throat and the pressure of her breasts on his chest.

She lay quietly and did not move except to breathe. Her body stirred faintly against him when she breathed and her breath was warm against his throat. He felt the excitement building in him, felt himself grow hard against her warm thighs. He tried to put her out of his mind and think of nothing, the way he'd had to force himself to think of nothing a hundred other lonely times. But it would not work. It was no good now because it was too late.

Her hand lay against his belt buckle. He could feel the heat of her hand through his clothing. He covered her hand with his left hand, pushed her hand down until she was covering him and her hand closed on him. He heard her sharp intake of breath. For an instant she pressed closer, breathless, and her hand tightened on him. Suddenly she pulled away, turning on the seat with her face away from him.

She was out from under his coat, with only the newspapers to cover her. He heard the newspapers crinkle. She burrowed against the seat.

He said, voice flat, "You better come back under the coat. It's all right. I never make the same mistake but once in a lifetime."

He heard her ragged breathing for a moment, then she moved back near him, but not touching him. He spread the coat over her.

He stared into the darkness. All the chill of the night had congealed in the pit of his stomach. He tried to think of Anne, tried to remember her. Except that she was so lovely you ached looking at her, he could no longer see her in his mind. He closed his eyes tightly trying to see her, but it was no good. He could only smell Eve's hair. He had to get her out of his mind, too. Damn her. Why hadn't she stayed in Los Solanos? Why hadn't she stayed in California?

His mouth pulled bitterly. The hell of it was, he was too honest with himself. He could see her face in the darkness, see the needing and the hunger and the unfulfilled wanting. It was pleasant having her beside him in the darkness. He admitted it was better than loneliness.

It was like hitting yourself on the head with a hammer.

He thought about Martin Kimball and Peggy Davis and the character named Saul Rehan. He tried to place Rehan someplace in his past, but he could not.

The first faint cracks of daylight touched at his eyes. The light was painful and he closed his eyes to escape it.

And that was when he fell asleep.

Chapter Fourteen

The heat of the morning sun burned through the window and wakened Ric. He had no idea what time it was. It was not long after daybreak and yet the car would soon become an oven unless they rolled down a window.

He lay there a moment and stared at Eve. She was easy to look at, in a pleasantly painful way. The terrible desire he'd felt last night washed back over him, and he sweated. The sweat had nothing to do with the heat of the sun against the windows.

He opened the car door quietly and stepped out. He walked around the car, his shoes crunching on the crust of the creek bed.

He stared at the rear of the car and caught his breath. It had sunk to the bumper during the night. He broke through the crust with his heel and then stepped quickly back, staring.

"What's the matter, Ric?" Eve said. She leaned her head out of the car window.

"Stay in the car."

"What's the matter?"

"Quicksand. This damned river bed is quicksand. Now do what I tell you and stay in the car."

"Oh, Ric. What a mess I've made."

"What are you talking about?"

"About me. It's all my fault."

"What the hell. You didn't know about the quicksand."

"I should have. Everything I touch, that's what it turns out to be—quicksand."

"All very dramatic. Stay in the car and keep still."

Her head disappeared. He walked away from the car, looking both ways along the creek. It was deeply eroded between the two levels of the wasteland. As far as he could see there was only the crooked path of the creek, with sage and mesquite growing on both sides all the way to distant ranges that looked like foothills, but were not because their peaks were capped with snow.

He stood staring at the car. In the creek they were sitting ducks. They were lucky only the left rear wheel had broken through the crust. A heavier car would have been lost by now. Only God knew what would happen when he spun the other wheel.

He went back to the car, opened the door. Eve had folded the topcoat, replaced it on top of his suitcase. She was carefully refolding the newspaper. She looked up, met his gaze. Faint color touched her cheeks. She looked away. He felt better; he was not the only one with a functioning memory.

He reached in the back of the seat, opened a compartment. He removed a coiled rope.

"Thought you'd never been out here," she said.

"Friend of mine had. I came prepared."

He held the coiled rope, returned to the rear of the car. He secured an end of the rope about the axle just inside the rear tire, made two forward loops of the rope and then tossed it to the front of the car.

He pulled the rope out under the front bumper and then stood looking around. Behind them, the way they had come, he saw a far plume of dust. Except for a high circling buzzard nothing else moved.

There was a boulder on the incline but he was afraid to trust it. On the lip of the embankment was a stunted piñon. He walked to it. He was doubtful that it would hold once pressure was applied, but there was nothing else, no other hope. He secured the rope on the piñon and returned to the car.

He got in, started the engine, let it warm up.

"You ever prayed?" he said.

"Yes. Very often lately. I'm Mrs. Martin Kimball, you know."

"Yes. I remember."

"Can we get out, Ric?"

"How do I know?"

"I'll get out. It'll be less weight."

"All right."

She got out, walked to the edge of the creek bed.

Cautiously he put the car in gear, let the clutch out slowly so the rear wheels turned. The rope slapped against the bottom of the car, the piñon bent down the side of the creek.

"Ric!"

Eve ran to the car, caught the window. Her face was starkly white.

"Ric, there are two cars coming down the road from the highway."

"Yes. I saw the dust."

"I can see the cars, Ric. They're that near. One of them is a police car. I see the searchlight on its roof. The other is my Cadillac. Martin's in it. I know."

"Stand back. I'm going to try again."

He released the clutch, listening to the crackle of the thin crust. The car was inching forward, being pulled by the rope wound on the rear axle.

"Ric. You're moving."

"Just you pray that tree isn't uprooted."

"They're coming, Ric. We're not going to get away."

He did not answer. She ran along beside the little car as it was pulled painfully forward on the winding rope. Suddenly it bumped out of the quicksand bed.

"Ric. I think they see us."

Ric jumped out of the car. He ran to the tree, loosened the rope. He did not stop to unwind it from the rear axle.

"Get in the car," he yelled at her.

He could see her Cadillac now. It was ahead of the police cruiser and was speeding as though the bridge was ahead of it.

He got in the car, stepped on the gas, going at an angle up the incline. "Center of gravity," he kept saying over and over. "That's all we've got that they haven't got."

The car tilted, shaking like an awkward bug and then bumped over the edge of the embankment. Stones and earth crunched under its rear wheels. The tires spun for a moment and then caught.

The wailing of horns and sirens speared at them. Ric did not even look over his shoulder. He stepped hard on the gas, bumping over the rocks to the roadway. He saw that the bridge had been washed out a long time. The roadway on this side was full of holes and was eroded away in places.

They bounced along the roadway.

"This doesn't lead anywhere," Eve cried out.

There was the crack of gunfire behind them.

"You want to go back?"

"Why are they shooting at us?"

"You said it yourself. Your Martin is a smart boy. He must have laid it on thick. They've been searching for us all night. I guess they're out of patience."

"But shooting at us—"

"You're a fugitive from the law, baby, whether you are used to the idea or not. You have been, ever since you ran away from that motel last night."

"But we haven't done anything that gives them the right to shoot at us."

"According to Martin we have. I'd say we're wanted for assault with attempt to murder."

"Attempted murder." She shook her head.

"That's what Martin said he'd charge us with, and it looks like that's what he's done."

The rope was wound around the axle now and was slapping against the underside of the car.

Ric slowed, looking over his shoulder. They were out of range of the police guns. He saw that the men back there were scurrying around on the far bank trying to find a place where they could cross the creek.

He stopped the car, got out and unwound the rope. When he got back in the car he saw that the cars were moving slowly to the left side of the bridge structure.

"They've found a place to cross," he said. "Looks like the cops know more about the quicksand than I do."

"It's no good," she said.

"Now what are you talking about?" He put the car in gear. They moved forward again. He kept his hands on the wheel and stared ahead for deep washouts.

"Let's go back. The more we run, the worse it will be."

"You go back if you want to. I've got to stay free of the cops, that's all I'm thinking about. But you'll be safe with them. You want to get out?"

"No." She tried to smile. "I'm with you."

His mouth pulled into a grin. He handed her the rope. "Okay. Put this in that compartment back there. A boy's best friend is his rope. They may need it later to hang us with."

She took the rope, turned on her knees on the bucket seat. He glanced at the trim lines of her hips, felt the sudden pounding of his heart.

She stayed like that, staring at something. He turned, looked over the seat. She was still holding the rope. She had opened the wrong compartment.

His voice rasped at her. "Not that one, damn it. The other one."

He reached back, slapped the compartment lid closed. Meekly she opened the other compartment, put the rope away and turned around in the seat.

"All that money," she whispered. "Stacks of it."

"A quarter of a million dollars," he told her. His voice was hard. "I told you in the beginning—keep away from me."

"Yes." She whispered it. "Yes. You told me."

Chapter Fifteen

The next few minutes were stretched long and taut. Ten minutes seemed more like ten hours. Ric saw that Eve was sitting there, drawn tense, thinking a hundred things and waiting for him to make some explanation. The hell with her. She'd fouled him up enough.

He glanced back down the flat road. At first he saw nothing down there. The police car and the Caddy were down in the creek bed, but unless they hit a quicksand area as he had, they'd be coming up the other side any minute. After that it would be a matter of outrunning them on a road chewed out and eroded—or at least outlasting them in a country that the cops would know and that he did not know at all.

He let his gaze touch the mountain ranges that lay in the distance, maybe a hundred miles away. In this atmosphere distances didn't mean much. He decided he'd feel better driving through mountain trails. He'd have a chance of losing them, and he thought bitterly, the same chance of losing himself. Unless they had extra gas he could stay longer in this country because he would get at least twice the mileage of the police cars.

He searched ahead for a cut-off road that might point even in the general direction of the foothills. He was no longer looking for a hard-surfaced road. He'd learned that much by now. If there was a trail at all, he would gamble on it. This car would cross the desert trails better than the bigger ones.

He looked at the speedometer. They were going less than thirty miles an hour. But if he speeded up they bounced crazily against the roof and sides.

He checked the rear-view mirror. The two cars had found a rise and were coming up out of the creek bed. *You just have to know the country*, he thought. He saw that the police did.

Then he saw something else. The Caddy stuck to the road, and had to slow as he had, but the police car stayed just off the road and was soon racing through a cloud of dust that obscured the Caddy.

"The hell with this," Ric said aloud. "If they can do it, I can."

He saw the faint outlines of tire tracks to his right ahead. He whipped the car off the roadway and stepped hard on the gas. He heard the tires crackling over the dry alkali crusts.

He drove silently, checking the smoking dust cloud behind him and the foothills ahead. They drove for some minutes, but the country had not changed, the foothills were no nearer.

The police car and the Caddy had left the roadway now, following the same faint tracks he'd followed.

"Ric."

"Yeah?"

"Look. Behind the cars, back there coming toward us."

He turned and stared out his window. The wind against his head was hot and dry, clogged with dust. He felt his lips drying out, and he remembered what they'd told him: never get suckered into that waste country without water. The hell with it. It was no good remembering that. His first lesson had been not to get fouled up with a woman, and he'd disregarded that. Everything else that happened was just in order. He had been a damned fool to leave that motel with Kimball's wife. But for the hell of it, he didn't see how he could have done anything else.

"You see it?" Eve said.

"No. What?"

"Above the dust."

He lifted his gaze, stared into the stark pale sky. There was a shadow, and then he saw it was not a shadow. It was a helicopter. It was bearing in on them like a listing bird, windmill grinding.

He turned back, watching the country ahead of them. The land rose gently, and the patches of sage and brush were more sparse. They were crossing an outcropping of stones and they shook inside the car.

"Sure," he said. There was no astonishment. "Cops use them."

"Why don't we stop, Ric?"

"I told you. You can get out any time you want."

"It's only going to make it worse. I was afraid of Martin. I admit that.

All I could think was to run. But they're going to stop us. The longer we run, the worse it will be. You can see that. They'll search your car."

"They'd search it anyway, if they stopped me."

She was watching the helicopter. "I'm sorry for what I've done to you, Ric. You tried to warn me. I was a fool. But we're not going to get away from them. Even if you outrun the police cars, the helicopter can follow us."

He did not answer. They raced between a scrubby stand of piñon. The heat rose out of the earth, rode into the car on the wind. The trail twisted between the rise of a small range of hills. Beyond these hills, the earth was swollen and broken by higher ranges and over the tops of these, jagged peaks glistened bare and snow-stained.

The trail wound upward into the foothills. He had to slow for boulders, stands of fir, outcroppings of slate.

"I don't see the cars any more," Eve said. She was twisted on the seat, staring out the back window. "The 'copter is closer now, though. I can see two men in it."

The churning sound of the helicopter engine filled the car, drowning the sound of the Porsche motor. He did not glance upward. There was no need for that. He could watch the elongated shadow of the helicopter leaping and lunging across the rocks and up the sheer sides of the hills ahead of them.

He did not slow down. Eve was holding on to both sides of the seat and she was watching the twisted trail ahead. They were ascending deeper into the hills now. They struck a flat plateau and the trail was gone, lost on the slate surface.

The Porsche slid and twisted. The helicopter shadow hovered above them, the sound of its engine reverberating from the sides of the hills so the whole silent land was filled with it.

Ahead, Ric saw two boulders, sand-blasted like two pillars between close-set hills. He whipped the car between the boulders and took his foot off the gas. Ahead was the twisted bed of a dry canyon. The sides of it rose sheer and gray, less than thirty feet apart.

The shadow of the helicopter hesitated and then lunged upward and was lost. Ric laughed, an angered bitter sound of satisfaction.

The rocky canyon bed made talk impossible. Ric put his head out the car window, glanced upward. The helicopter had been forced to pull away, to climb the ranges and return.

He glanced around the canyon. Ahead was a rock shelf to the right in the canyon wall. He pulled the car upward, climbing the incline. He drove as close against the rock wall as possible, killed the engine.

He laughed, a cold, harsh sound. "This ought to give them a fit for a little while. We don't even cast a shadow."

Chapter Sixteen

They sat there in the shadow under the shelf. For a few moments it was quiet. He watched a dust devil race along the canyon floor. Then he heard the faint whimpering sound of the helicopter.

"They're circling around up there," he said. "They're trying to find us."

He sat there, waiting. The sound of the 'copter was loud. He saw its shadow slithering along the wall on the other side of the canyon. Then the sound was gone and the shadow was jerked out of the canyon.

"They think we've turned around," he said.

"They're giving us credit for good sense."

"If you say so."

"Do you hear the cars?"

"I don't think we will. We lost the trail somewhere back there. If they come in, it'll be on foot."

He got out of the car, closing the door softly. Whispers of sounds were picked up and hurled along these walls. He walked to the edge of the shelf, staying back so that he cast no shadow beyond its rim. The helicopter was nowhere that he could see.

He shook his head. There was nothing enviable about this position. It was good for only a little while. That whirlybird could check this canyon and these foothills in a few hours. They could pinpoint the Porsche somewhere in this area, even if they could no longer see it, and they could lead the police in by radio.

"If we could last until dark," he said aloud, "we could beat the 'copter."

He knew she'd heard him but she did not answer. He glanced over his shoulder. She was sitting as he had left her.

He walked back to the car. He saw that she had opened the rear compartment again. The green of the money winked at him. His jaw tightened.

"What's the matter? You never saw money before?"

She turned, staring at him. "Not like this."

"Thought you boasted about how rich you were."

"I have money."

"Enough so some guy tried to kill you for it."

"I keep my money in banks, Mr. Durazo."

"Well, that's where you and I are different."

She looked at her hands. "Yes. We are different. You take your money out of banks, don't you, Mr. Durazo?"

His eyes chilled. He opened the door, sat down with his legs outside the car. There was silence. He strained, listening for the helicopter.

"Think what you want."

"What should I think?"

"Nothing. You never asked to see my social register status when you jumped in this car."

"Oh, no. I thought I was clever. I thought you were good. All I could think was I had to run away from Martin and that you would help me. Oh, fine. Run away from a killer—with a thief and jailbird."

He gripped the steering wheel.

After a moment she said, "Where did you get this money?"

"What difference does it make?"

"You told me you were in jail. Why don't you tell me why you're afraid to talk to the police. Is it because you've stolen this money?"

"If it weren't for you, I wouldn't have to worry about talking to the police."

"Did you steal this money?"

"What difference does it make? I've got it, haven't I? We can't all inherit our fortunes, Mrs. Kimball. Some of us have to work for them."

"Work." Her mouth twisted and her voice made an angry bitter sound of the word.

He stared upward. From where he sat he could barely see the top of the far wall. It was a place of ragged rock croppings. He could no longer hear the 'copter. But just when he began to hope by some miracle that they'd been misled he heard the churning sound begin. It filled the canyon, rolling in like a flashflood.

Eve slapped down on the doorhandle. The door flew open and she jumped out. She slammed the door behind her and the sound was like the crack of gunfire.

"Damn you," he snarled at her.

She ran around the car.

"Where do you think you're going?"

Her voice was cold, raging. "I'm going to signal those people in that helicopter. I've had all the criminals I can stomach for one lifetime."

Chapter Seventeen

"Come back here."

He lunged upward from the car. She turned on her heel and ran toward the rim of sunlight.

He caught her just inside it, caught her with his arms about her middle and hurled her backwards. She slipped, lost her footing and went toppling back. She struck against the wall deep under the shelf. The breath was smashed out of her.

She crouched there, her arms at her sides, staring at him. Her eyes were distended and her pale face was pulled. She looked beyond him at the helicopter shadow leaping the stones on the canyon floor.

He walked toward her, watching her warily. She opened her mouth to scream and he leaped again, catching her and clasping his hand over her mouth.

She beat at him with both hands, scratching at his face and kicking at his shins.

He thrust her back hard against the wall, pressing his body against her body so she could not kick. He pinned her arms between them.

The sound of the helicopter filled the canyon now, reverberating against the walls and pounding upon them like the overwhelming raging of the surf in a storm.

She bit his hand. He felt her teeth sink into his palm. Rage burned through him, louder than the sound of the 'copter. He stared down into her eyes. She was staring up at him and what he saw in her eyes made his heart turn over inside him. It was a hot and pleasingly agonizing feeling. The blood throbbed in his temples and he could no longer hear the helicopter because of the blood in his temples and the rage pounding through him. He wanted to kill her. He wanted to close his hands on her throat and press until she could no longer breathe. He wanted to smash his mouth against her mouth until her mouth bled. Then suddenly he did not want to kill her at all, and knew that he had never wanted to kill her.

She writhed in his arms, her body fighting against his body. She bit down on his hand again and he felt the blood spurt into her mouth. But he closed his fingers on her cheeks, tightening his grasp.

She pulled away from him, and he wrestled her back beneath him so that abruptly she lost her balance and fell sideways along the wall, dragging him with her to the slate floor behind the car.

She tried to thrust him away from her but she could not. Her eyes were wild, but she could not speak because he held her mouth tightly in his grasp.

He pulled at her skirt, half tearing it away from her. His fingers caught the fabric of her pants and the ripping sound was lost in the thunder from the helicopter circling along the canyon like a lost child.

He heard his own voice, and realized he was talking breathlessly, the words spilling out of him. "Tell them. Yell at them. Damn you. Yell. Go on. Yell at them. Tell them about the money. All about the money. And tell them about the rape. Scream. Because you'll have something to scream about. Now you'll have something to tell them about."

She was writhing beneath him but she was no longer fighting him. Her arms had gone about him and her fingers clawed into his shoulders. The sound of the helicopter rose throbbing through them, and then it faded and then it was loud again. She was against the slate of the shelf floor and she did not care. She did not know.

He did not move his hand from over her mouth. Her teeth sunk into it until his blood leaked along the side of her face, making a red streak on her jaw and throat. He did not remove his hand and then she was chewing at it, kissing it wildly and sucking at his fingers and she was crying.

There was a silence, and he did not know how long the silence had existed. He lay there and listened for the 'copter but there was no sound of it. Its ugly shadow had stopped leaping along the canyon. He lay there and felt her arms holding him, and then she was kissing his hand.

"I hurt you," she whispered.

"Did I hurt you?"

"Oh God, no."

"This rock is rough. We must have been crazy."

"I don't know. I don't care." She kissed his hand, running her tongue gently over the place where she had bit him.

He laughed, baffled. "I could never rape any woman. Not me. Because she would have to want me or I wouldn't—"

"I wanted you, Ric. Only I didn't know it."

"I knew it. Last night I knew it."

"Yes. I knew it, too, then. But that was different. Last night was not the same. Last night it could have been anyone."

"Not for me."

"But for me. Because I didn't know."

"And now it's different?"

"For me. Because now I know what it's like. What it's truly like. I know what you're supposed to have, what you're supposed to do. I never knew. So how could I know I wanted you—or anyone? How could I know it? I never knew what it could be."

He rolled to the side of her and she burrowed close against him.

"Think," she said. "This huge world. And I never knew what it was all about. I never knew why. I never could figure what all the shouting was for. Why did anybody care? It wasn't much of a world. But now it is. Now it is much of a world."

"You talk a lot."

"I never talked before. Never. In all my life. There was never anyone so wonderful."

He laughed. "That's what a girl says when she doesn't know anything. A man knows when a girl knows nothing. She tells him he's the most wonderful thing in the world."

"Don't tease me. Not now. I don't want you to tease me. I want you to love me."

"Are you crazy? I'm dead."

"Hold me then, with your hand. Please. Hold me because I've never been loved before—never truly loved— and I can't stop wanting to be loved, yet. Maybe I'll never stop wanting to be loved again."

"You'll kill me."

She burrowed her head against his throat. Her mouth was warm, parted against his throat.

"I don't care. It's your fault. You started it."

"This rock is rough."

"I don't care. Hold me."

He moved his hand over her and felt her breath quicken against his throat. The excitement started in him again. She said nothing, loving him, and the silence rode along the canyon on the wind. Her fingers dug into him, and he smiled, whispering to her. "Aren't you going to scream?" he said.

"Only when you make me scream."

"What about the money?"

"What money?"

Chapter Eighteen

Ric sat with his back against the wall beneath the stone shelf. The sun had moved upward, cutting the shadows sharply in the canyon. He watched the mouth of the canyon. If they came on foot, they would come from there.

He licked his lips, thinking he was not as worried about those men as he was about water.

"Are you all right?" he said to Eve.

She pressed closer in his arms, pushing her face against his throat. "All right? What an empty way to express what I am right now."

"I'll try to find water. There may be some in this canyon somewhere."

"Don't leave me, Ric. Not right now."

"I don't want to leave you, but I'd like to keep you alive."

She laughed. "I never lived before. I'll be all right. And Ric—if anything happens, I won't mind, because of you."

He tightened his arm, closed his hand on her. "You say it so much better than any of the other girls."

"You never knew any other girls, did you?"

"What are girls?"

"That's better." She sighed. "Oh, I know. There must have been hundreds."

"Hundreds."

"But I wouldn't want you so terribly if you were different, would I? Would I?"

"Eve, there's something I ought to tell you."

"You don't have to tell me anything. I'm afraid for you to. It might be something I wouldn't want to hear."

"I owe it to you."

"You don't owe me anything. I owe you—because I never knew anything until you came along."

"Still. I better tell you. About the money."

She smoothed his face, trailing her fingers along his cheek. She pressed closer, and he stared across the top of her head toward the twist in the canyon. He listened for the sound of voices, of the helicopter, gunfire, or perhaps the clatter of a loosened stone. There was nothing but the silence. The heat reflected from the narrow floor of the canyon. He knew they were cooler under the shelf than they'd be out in the wastes.

"Ric, I cared about the money—before I cared about you. I don't care any more. It's that simple."

"Still, it's there—and you'll want to know."

She smiled. "You mean when I wake up?"

"Yes. When you wake up."

"That's what I'm afraid of. In a moment I'll wake up in a bed in Sherman Oaks, or back at La Pueblo. You don't know how horrible that would be for me—now."

"Are you going to listen?"

"Why? It's only money."

"Eve, there's one thing we don't know. That's what that helicopter and those police are doing. There's a chance they've pulled away, knowing we'll have to come out of here. But most likely they're moving in on foot. This canyon might be a cul-de-sac—"

"I'm with you."

"Yes. I want you with me—when they come. Any minute they might walk around that turn in the canyon, or they might come from the other way. When they come, I want you to trust me. I want you with me. You've enough things to doubt right now. I don't want to be one of them."

She laid her head back on his arm, brushed her hair from her face.

"You don't have to tell me, Ric, if you don't want to."

Remembering was a painful process, and yet all of it had been out of his conscious mind only since he'd pulled Eve out of her gas-filled cottage. Before that, in all the miles west from Manhattan, he had thought about nothing else, gone over it again and again, not because he wanted to, because he could not help it. Every hurting moment of it haunted him like the words of a song you couldn't escape.

It had been agony looking in the senator's face. Senator Ironfield was a man nearing sixty, a man who had given up even believing he'd have a son of his own. And they'd kidnaped his child. He looked as though the face he wore was not his face at all, but a mask to conceal his inner weeping, a mask to hide the hurt nobody could bear to look at. He had held himself erect, spoken stiffly, as though all the years of training in self-control were all that kept him from falling on his knees and crying out. His voice was cold. He could not express the mildest emotion. If he did, he would break down.

"I am convinced you can be trusted," the senator had said. "I am convinced you are the only one who can be trusted."

He'd wanted to laugh when the senator said that to him—a man just out of prison on parole, a man the senator himself had sentenced to prison. But when he thought it over, he did not laugh, and he knew the senator was right. He could be trusted.

Why not? The senator held aces, all the aces. Ric Durazo would not lift his hand to aid the senator, but Anne had told the senator all about herself and Ric. His smile was bitter when he thought about that. Had Anne told the senator everything? He tried to think how she might have told him—quietly, across his desk? in a car somewhere? over a dinner table? or lying beside him in bed, unable to sleep, talking about Ric, and the way she had loved him, and the way he had loved her before the senator sent Ric to prison for five years.

She must have told him everything. The senator did not doubt that Ric would deal with the kidnapers for him. The senator needed a man he could trust, a man who could meet with the kidnapers, a man who'd give his life to return that baby to its parents. No other man would possibly answer his desperate need. Ric was the answer. Would he give his life to return Anne's baby to her?

His hand tightened into a fist, aching. The senator held aces all right. Nothing in God's world would keep him from bringing Anne's baby back to her—if it lived.

He spoke softly to Eve now, his voice carrying the deadly hill that had ridden west with him. "Have you read about the Ironfield baby?"

He heard her catch her breath. "The kidnaped baby?"

"Yes."

She was tense, not breathing. "Oh, Ric—you're not one of the kidnapers?"

His laugh was mocking. "Thanks."

She caught him in her arms, pulling him against her and crying out, "I didn't mean that, Ric. Oh, God, I didn't mean that. It was just—"

"Sure. I know. I'm fresh out of prison. You're afraid to believe the best. Don't worry, everybody feels that way."

"No, Ric, please don't be mad. It's just that I was afraid. Try to understand me. If it was the worst about you, I wanted to know it. Right now. I wanted to know before I heard any more words."

"It's all right."

"Oh, Ric. You are mad."

"I'm not mad at anybody. If it makes you feel any better, I'm not a kidnaper. I've done a lot of other things, made a lot of mistakes. No. Senator Ironfield, the great Senator Gifford Ironfield hired me to deliver that quarter of a million dollars."

He heard her exhale, felt her hands tighten on him.

"So that's it," he said. "Contact man. It was nothing I wanted, or asked for, or would have taken—except I had to. You see, there's more in this kidnaping than just the money. The senator is a very hated man, some very old hates. It looks like whoever kidnaped his two-year-old boy did it for vengeance as well as the money. They've put Ironfield through hell. It doesn't help that he's fifty-six and this is his only child—his first. The kidnapers have made promises, broken them. They've accused him of double-crossing them with the police and the FBI. Finally, they gave him some new terms and that's where I came in."

He did not speak for a moment. A shadow flickered high against the rocks. It was a hawk.

"These terms were slick. Ironfield was warned to keep the police and the FBI out of it. He was told to call off the FBI or the child would be returned in small packages. Then they told him he could choose a man he trusted. The man was to drive to the La Pueblo in Los Solanos, New Mexico, and wait there, attracting as little attention as possible, until he was contacted."

"Oh my God."

"Yes. That's what I've been telling myself. And that was why, whether I was innocent of assaulting Martin Kimball or not, I couldn't afford to get mixed up with the police."

She shuddered, buried her face against his shoulder. "God, Ric. Have I cost that baby his life?"

He closed his fingers on her arm, held her away from him. "We had two days, and one of them is gone. They swear the child is alive. Of course we have no way of knowing whether it is alive or not. But they've agreed to contact me before they do anything. They're on the spot now. Delivering the baby to me is the only way they'll get this money."

"Do you know them, Ric? Do you know who they are?"

"No, I don't know them. All I can do is wait for the contact man. If we hold out here until night, we're going to try to get back to Los Solanos. I've got to do that."

"Of course you have to. You don't have to worry about me any more, Ric."

"Don't I?" He sighed, staring along the narrow strip of canyon. "No use turning you over to Kimball now, unless I have to."

"You've got the baby to think about. I wouldn't be able to live with myself if anything happened to it because I delayed you. Ric, we've got to get out of here."

"Sure. And what will you do?"

"It doesn't matter. Not any more. I'll do what you told me in the first place. I'll call Father. Truly I will."

He glanced at the patch of sky he could see from beneath the shelf. The faded dryness of the sky made him thirstier.

"It doesn't matter what we do—we've got to wait until dark."

"All right, Ric. I won't fight you any more."

"That's too bad. You fight so sexy."

"Yes. I'm a sexy fighter." She stared into his face. "Why you, Ric?"

"What?"

"Why you? Why did the senator choose you to contact these criminals?"

"Fight fire with fire."

"No, Ric. Tell me. Why did he trust you?"

How could he tell her, or anyone? It was Anne's baby, and somebody had to bring it back to her alive, or Anne herself could not go on living.

"Why not? I was born in the gutter, and I grew up there and know all the gutter tricks."

"How did he choose you?"

"Oh, he knows me. He hasn't always been a senator. Not Ironfield. No. A few years ago, he was a judge, and he sentenced me to prison."

"And he trusts you?"

His laugh was chilled. "Oh, he's convinced I can be trusted."

She tightened her arms. "So am I. But then, I know you so much better than he possibly could."

"It's not that, baby. You see, the senator—he holds aces."

Chapter Nineteen

Ric lifted Eve in his arms and carried her back to the car. He placed her gently in the reclined bucket seat. His hand lingered on her a moment. She looked up at him, eyes liquid.

"I don't like this little car. I can't do what I want us to do in it."

He laughed at her. "You just don't know this car. It's a sports car. That means it was made for sports. Why do you think this seat lets down?"

"Let's try it and find out."

"My God. What you are is a pig."

"I just never had anything so wonderful before."

"You want to convince me, don't you?"

"Stop being cruel. You don't know what it's like to live with a counterfeit, a phony, for three years—and then learn how badly you've been cheated all your life."

He kissed her cheek, brushing his lips along it. "It's just pretty hard to believe I could be that different, that much better."

"If you believe that, then you don't know very much, either."

"I'm pretty stupid, all right."

"You're wonderful."

He stood up. "Will you wait here for me? Will you be good and stay right here?"

She sat forward. "I'm afraid. What are you going to do?"

"I don't know if your husband and the cops are going to come in here or not. I've got to find out. It's not too long until dark. If I'm going to find out anything, I've got to look around."

"Suppose they see you?"

"That's just the gamble we've got to take. We may be bottled up in here. I've got to know that, too. You know, that might be the reason they pulled off the 'copter and left us in here. They know a lot more about this country than I do."

"Can't I go with you?"

"One of us can hide better than two. You're fixed right here."

"Will you love me when you come back?"

He smiled at her, as if exasperated. "If you insist."

"Then hurry."

She waited until he was at the rim of the shadowed shelf. She called after him. "You promise?"

He grinned at her across his shoulder. "Yes. I promise. As soon as I come back. You lie there and think about me."

"Oh, no. You want me to go nuts?"

He walked down the incline to the floor of the canyon. He moved along it, sensing the way the sheer walls closed in. Above him the shoulders of the canyon loomed gray against the sky. It was along these walls they had watched the skittering shadow of the 'copter earlier in the day.

He reached one of the many twists in the canyon and glanced back. Eve was watching him from the shelf. He waved to her and walked around the turn. The walls veered higher and the canyon floor narrowed. In places ahead the lower rocks were in shadow, but not cool. The deeper he walked the more breathless and hot it became.

He searched for some sign of water, but found none. He wished he could find water and carry some back to Eve. She would really think he was wonderful then. Funny, wasn't it, that was really all every man wanted—a woman who thought he was wonderful. It was such a simple lesson. It was odd more of them didn't learn it.

Ahead, he saw a narrow trail that made its tortuous way up the side of the canyon wall. Sunlight glanced off the rocks up there, glittering with fool's gold and quartz. A man would have to be part mountain goat to make it up there. Yet, from the top of this wall, he could see for twenty miles in every direction. It was worth it.

He moved up the wall, walking as long as he could. He placed his back against the rocks and slid upward along them. In places the ledge was so small that the toes of his shoes were hanging over the rim. Rocks dislodged, rattled all the way to the canyon floor. The sound echoed and reverberated. It seemed to him it would never cease.

He caught at the wind-flattened rocks for a grasp, found none. His knees wavered and the canyon seemed to pull at him, down, down. He did not look down again. It was better to watch the brink of the wall above him.

He climbed slowly, not daring to take a full breath, as though filling his lungs might push him off the ledge. He heard a loosened rock clatter down the wall.

He snagged at the broken places on top of the ridge, hung there a moment with his legs dangling from the ledge. He caught his footing and shoved himself upward. His hands clawed at the flat rocks, missed. He felt himself being borne outward. His hands caught and he clung there a moment and then slid upward on his belly until he sprawled on the flat wall top.

A buzzard circled high against the whitened sky. Ric lifted his head and peered around. West of him reared mountains, reaching upward into chilled snow flurries.

Stunted mesquite grew along this flat tableland. Out below him there was no movement and no sound.

He pulled his head around and then he saw the sun glint on glass. Pulling up to his knees, he shaded his eyes and stared downward. The glass was a windshield. Then he saw the two cars, and was certain one was Kimball's Cadillac. They were waiting for him down there. They knew this land: they had all the advantage.

He turned suddenly, searching the canyon. It narrowed, twisted into the rising wall of hills and then it disappeared. In this land without water, he and Eve could not last much longer. They had to come back from this canyon, and when they did, those men would be waiting.

Keeping low, in case one of them was searching with field glasses, Ric moved along, keeping close to the canyon rim. He found a boulder, slightly larger than a car. He leaned against it in the shadows, staring down at the four men.

He cursed aloud. That was the only satisfaction he would permit himself. He wanted to stand there and scream at them. They had set up some kind of umbrellas and were sprawled in the shade. He saw they were drinking from cans, something cool, perhaps beer, maybe even by some miracle, iced water.

He dragged his tongue across his parched lips. He wanted to yell out the building rage he felt. *Sit down there, damn you, so sure of yourselves—laugh and talk and wait.*

He walked, in a kind of insane and fruitless searching, around the tableland seeking any sign of water. He found none. He moved slowly, behind the juniper that fringed the canyon top, going downhill.

He came into the canyon the way he had driven in. He spent some time walking across the slate outcroppings, getting his bearings.

Eve came off the shelf and ran to meet him.

"They're out there, on the edge of the plain, waiting," he said. "They're out there drinking beer, sitting in the shade. The bastards."

"I'd rather be here," she said, "with you."

He put his arm around her, walked with her toward the Porsche, trying to think about her, trying to check some of the senseless rage against those men in the shade out there.

"They think they're going to stop us, the sons of bitches. They think they're going to stop us."

She looked up at him, eyes troubled. "Ric. Are you all right?"

His voice was savage. "Hell no, I'm not all right. I'm thirsty. So damned thirsty I couldn't drink if I had water. And those sons of bitches out there think we can't get out of here."

"Come back to the car, Ric. You'll be all right."

"I'll never be all right. Not as long as they sit out there laughing at me because I can't get out of here."

The canyon was almost fully dark, but Ric could see that the sky was lighted, streaked with orange and beige and purple. Eve lay on a blanket near the car. She was asleep. He was more exhausted than she was, but he had not slept. He had spent the whole afternoon, staring at the mouth of the canyon, thinking.

He waited until the purple welts across the face of the sky faded to blue, then he bent over Eve, shook her.

"Wake up. We've got to get out of here."

She opened her eyes slowly. Her lips were colorless and parched. She drew the back of her hand across her forehead. She tried to smile. There was more fever in her eyes than pleasure.

They tossed the blanket in the back of the Porsche, then got in. Ric started the car, not even daring to rev the motor. He let it idle, warming for a long time. He glanced at the fuel indicator, refused to admit what he saw there.

He put the car in reverse, felt it slip in the loose sand. He rolled out onto the canyon floor. There was just room enough to turn the car and head east.

He drove slowly, came out of the canyon, crossed the slate outcroppings. By now the sun was gone and darkness was moving in. A wind blew downward from the mesa-lands across from them.

He got out of the car.

"Move over and drive," he told Eve. "All you've got to do is watch me. I'm going to walk right in front of the car. You won't have any lights—and in the name of God, don't touch that brake pedal. No matter what happens, don't touch it. That red flare would light up everything between here and El Paso."

"All right, Ric."

"Give it just enough gas to keep it moving."

"I will. I want you to know how smart I can be for you."

"I'll pick the trail. All right, let's go."

He walked as swiftly as he dared, seeking a lane through the foothills, through the growth of piñon and the boulders.

They moved steadily downward. Suddenly he slowed, and kept slowing until Eve had to remove her foot from the accelerator. The car coughed, idled, slowed to a stop.

He walked back, knelt and looked in the window. He pointed across the flat sage country to a point of light.

"The bastards," he said with a wry laugh. "That's them. They've made a fire. They're settling down to wait us out. If I can find the roadway from here, we got it made."

"I told you, you're wonderful."

"You're not back in Daddy's arms yet."

"That's not where I want to be, either."

He kept walking east with the car boiling and coughing behind him. After a while it was not a matter of walking at all, he was simply putting one leg ahead of the other. The wind rose and the sand cut at him, but the wind was not cooling.

He stumbled, and then leaped around with a yelp.

"The road. Eve, it's the road!"

She was so startled, she stepped down on the brake. The taillights flashed so the sky was lighted with it.

She cried out and jerked her foot off the brake. The car lunged forward and stalled.

Ric ran back to her.

"Oh, Ric, I'm no good. I'm no damned good."

She moved over and he slid into the car. He started the engine, glancing through the rear window.

"It doesn't matter. Maybe they didn't see it. They should be watching the hills."

"They saw it."

He did not answer. There was nothing to say. Headlights had leaped into being out across the plain and were circling, turning toward them.

"We got the road, and once we cross the creek, it's pretty smooth all the way to the highway. I can outrun them." He did not add he could outrun them if the gas held out. He refused to allow himself to look again at the gas gauge.

He did not drive on the road now. He turned on the headlights, kept to the shoulders, plumes of dust arose behind them. The headlights bounced, danced, moving across the flat land.

At the river he got out again, found the tracks of the police car, led Eve across the creek bed and up the other embankment.

He was doing ninety when Highway 58 loomed suddenly ahead.

He whipped the car back toward Los Solanos, watching the spinning beacon on the airport tower.

For a moment it was as though he could not pull his gaze from the light spinning over the airport. It was as though he were drawn toward it. It was the center, the heart of everything. It had been the first thing he looked for when he hit Los Solanos.

Approaching the airport entrance, he stared at it, hating it because it reproached him with his own failure. "We'll meet you there, Ric," the senator had said last. One of the last things the senator had said. "Anne and I will meet you." Anne was going to be at this airport. He would see her again for the first time. God how long had it been? At that moment he had begun to dream the way it would be. He would stride in, bringing Anne's baby back to her, doing for her what nobody else could do.

His eyes ached. In his mind he could hear the senator planning, hoping without any hope. "Anne and I will meet you at the Los Solanos airport Friday, Ric. We'll give you the two days they asked for. Then we'll come. We'll wait for you at the airport." He had swallowed hard. "I pray to God you'll have good news for us, Ric. Somehow, I can't believe the baby is—still alive—but God help us, I hope we never have to tell Anne that it is dead."

Ric turned the Porsche into the filling station across the road from the airport entrance. Eve ran to the water cooler and let the water splash against her face and eyes before she drank. Ric paced the station apron watching the highway while the attendant filled the gas tank and checked under the hood. Even when Ric went to drink, he knelt over the water spout half-turned so that he could watch the road behind them.

It was ten-thirty when they entered the city limits of Los Solanos. Ric parked the Porsche on a side street beside a white stone hotel. He held Eve's arm and they walked in. He felt wary, watchful. He signed for a room. They followed the night clerk up the stairs to the second floor, waited while he opened windows, turned on lights. Ric tipped him and he went away.

"Call your father," he told her.

"I will, Ric." She was looking about the room. It was as though the dust had blown through these windows for twenty years and burned itself in so nothing could ever brush it out.

He moved toward the door. She caught his arm. "Ric."

"Yes."

"How will I get in touch with you?"

"You'll be all right now. Eve. Martin Kimball won't know where you are. Get your father here. Fast."

"Ric, I can't stand to lose you like this. And that's not all. I need you. I'm afraid without you."

"What would you do with a guy like me?"

"I'm too bashful to say it right out loud."

Suddenly she was in his arms again. He felt her hands digging into his shoulders. It was very pleasant, having her like this. He had forgotten how pleasant it could be when somebody truly cared.

"Take care," he whispered into her hair.

"Oh, Ric. I hope he's all right. I hope I haven't spoiled everything."

"If he was alive from the first day, they'll wait until they get in touch with me. Forget about it, Eve. You've got your own woes. You get on that phone."

"You've got to come back to me, Ric." Her voice was low, but it was frantic.

He pushed her away, held her at arms' length. His voice was a tense whisper. "Don't count on it. Eve. You hear me? Just don't count on it."

He turned, crossed the room, closed the door behind him. He paused for a moment in the hallway, the sense of desolation going all through him. He had thought he'd been lonely before.

Hell, he hadn't even known what loneliness was.

Chapter Twenty

Ric came down the stairs and paused looking around the hotel lobby. Except for the night clerk, the place was deserted. He walked to the desk and the clerk looked up, smiling sleepily.

"You have a private phone?"

The clerk nodded toward a booth near the front entrance. Ric went into it, closed the door. He found the number of La Pueblo. He dialed, listening to it ring. He hoped perversely that he was waking Peggy up. But when she answered, her voice did not sound sleepy.

"Mrs. Davis, this is Ric Durazo."

He heard her sharp laughter. "I got the word for you, Mr. Durazo. You better get out of the world."

"Any calls for me?"

She laughed again. "Any calls? Mr. Durazo, everybody is either calling for you, or looking for you."

"Sorry to cause you trouble, but I'd like to know if there were any messages?"

"Oh, there are messages. Even one from the police. I'm to let them know the moment you or that woman shows up around here."

"I don't mean the police—"

"I'm supposed to let them know if you call."

His voice hardened. "All right. You tell them I called."

"I will. I have to. We have to run a nice place. I'll have to tell them."

"Did I get any messages?"

"I just hope it was worth it, that's all. Looks like you got yourself in a lot of trouble over one woman. I'm sorry that you acted that way."

"Are you stalling so this call can be traced?"

She caught her breath.

"Why no. I was trying to be friendly. Even if I do have to report to the police, I hate to see you get in any more trouble."

"All right. Then you just tell me one thing—did I get any messages—any personal messages?"

"Yes. A Mr. Perriquey has called you three times."

Ric felt his nerves tighten, as though a fist had clenched his solar plexus. The name Perriquey meant nothing to him, but the three calls did. His hand gripped the receiver more tightly.

"What did he say!"

"Well, he was pretty upset. He sounded mad at you. Isn't it funny—everybody is mad at you, Mr. Durazo."

"The hell with that. What did he say?"

"Well, the last time he called, he said he was at the X-Bar Dude Ranch, and that he would wait for you until midnight—"

She went on talking, but Ric was not listening. He turned in the booth, glanced at the clock over the night clerk's head. He caught his breath, muttered, "Thanks," into the phone and slapped it back on its hook.

He returned to the desk. The clerk looked up again, yawning.

"Where could I rent a car?"

"At the bus station, down at the end of this block."

Ric drove to the all-night garage, parked the Porsche, locked it. He paid the attendant for a day and then strode out into the night. His footsteps sounded loud along the silent street.

The woman at the Rent-a-Car desk wanted a fifty-dollar deposit before she would rent Ric a car, seemed surprised when he paid it immediately. He decided he must resemble a desert prospector by now.

He glanced at the bus station clock again while the woman filled out the quadruplicate forms on the Plymouth. There was not time even for a shave. If Perriquey didn't like his looks it was too bad. He glanced at his reflection in a plate-glass mirror and shook his head. This wasn't the way they'd planned it.

He signed for the car, took the keys. The girl told him the car was parked at the rear door of the bus station.

"You know where the X-Bar Ranch is?" he asked her.

"About ten miles west on Highway 58. You can't miss it. There are signs all along the road."

It was six minutes to twelve when Ric turned the Plymouth into the stone-enclosed ranchyard at the X-Bar Dude Ranch. He slowed the car, letting it roll toward the main ranch house. This place had the look of money lavishly applied. It was all adobe and stone, with a carefully manufactured look of age. The cottages were lined together with slate roofs that almost met so the whole line of them resembled an old fashioned bunkhouse, with bridles tastefully hung along the front walls. Between the ranch house and the guests' bunkhouse were shuffleboard courts and a swimming pool that was lighted even at this hour. Inside the ranch house Ric saw a few couples dancing and others around card tables.

Ric parked the car in the area of swank cars. He walked up the steps, feeling the wind cold against his sweated face.

A cowhand in chaps and sombrero opened the door for him. The clerk was also in fancy western garb. Ric glanced at the guests, saw they were outfitted in expensive variations of cow-country dress. Even the women wore boots. Three cowpunchers played music softly and slowly from an alcove at the end of the community room. At the left of the desk was a bar made to resemble an early times saloon.

"Mr. Perriquey," Ric said to the clerk. "What cottage?"

"Mr. Perriquey is in cottage five, sir. He has been expecting a gentleman caller." The clerk called the cowboy from the door. "Would you show this gentleman to Mr. Perriquey's bunkhouse, Shorty?"

Shorty's accent was straight from Brooklyn. He chatted steadily as they crossed the shuffleboard courts, skirted the swimming pool. Ric did not say anything, but this did not discourage Shorty. He rapped on the door at cottage five. After a moment, Ric heard someone move inside. He felt that old tightening, the worry.

He handed Shorty a quarter and the boy went back across the courts, talking to himself.

Ric looked around. The music sifted across the area from the ranch house, tired and uninspired. His hands sweated. He rubbed them along his coat pockets.

The door opened wide, spilling light across Ric and out to the sodded grass. Ric stared, surprised at the looks of the man who stood there. He had not known what he expected, but it was not this type of man.

"You Ric Durazo?" the man said. He stared at Ric coldly.

"Yes."

Perriquey glanced at his wrist watch.

"You slice it thin, don't you, Durazo?"

"That's the way it rolls," Ric said. "May I come in?"

The man's sharp featured face pulled into a faint one-dimension grin. "Certainly. Please do."

Ric stepped into the room and Perriquey closed the door behind him. Again Ric was surprised to find they were alone. The bathroom door stood wide open. Ric looked around. The bed was untouched. Perriquey had been sitting in one of the chairs, waiting.

"Sit down," Perriquey said.

Ric sat down. Perriquey stood near the door. Looking at him, Ric had the odd sensation that in twenty-five years Martin Kimball might look like Perriquey, except for the look of intelligence about Perriquey. Here was an elderly Martin Kimball, but equipped with brains. Perriquey was tall, slender so that even in his expensive gray tweed suit he looked as though he would snap in two, like a brittle limb. His iron-gray hair was carefully brushed, waved, groomed.

Ric said, "Is the baby all right?"

Perriquey's chiseled features looked as if they would pull into a laugh, but instead his mouth twisted faintly and he pushed the palm of his hand across his temple, smoothing his already smooth hair.

"Aren't you rushing things, Durazo? We have a few things to talk about yet. You've wasted my time. Quite a lot of it. First, I don't know who you are—any more than you know who I am."

"All right. I'm Ric Durazo." He reached inside his pocket and removed an envelope. "This is from Senator Ironfield. You want to read it?"

"Of course."

Perriquey took the letter, slit it open with a manicured finger. He moved nearer a floor lamp, pince-nez on the bridge of his thin nose. He held the paper away from his face.

He read the brief note: "This will inform you that the bearer represents me in all matters, with full power of attorney." It was signed by Senator Gifford Ironfield.

Ric took the note back, placed it in his coat pocket. "All right Perriquey, who are you?"

Perriquey permitted himself a faint smile. "I'm Norton Perriquey. I am the man whom you have come so far to see, Durazo. But I'm also the man who holds all the aces and asks all the questions."

"Will you answer one?"

"I might. If it pleases me."

"The same one I asked before. Is the Ironfield child still alive?"

Perriquey lighted a cigarette, held its holder daintily. "You're a very direct man, Durazo. But I'm in an odd position. I cannot answer that question. Not just at this moment."

"Why not?"

"It's very simple. You're a direct man, as I said. You have a gun in your shoulder holster. You might kill me if I told you the baby was already dead."

Ric's fists knotted. "I might."

"You very well might. And there's more; if we bargain at all, we must have something to bargain over, mustn't we?"

"Get it said."

"I said it. You would not bargain for a dead child. So as long as it pleases me to say so, I'll tell you the child is alive—and as long as I say so, you'll have to accept that."

Ric wiped the back of his hand across his forehead, feeling the sweat. The sense of fatigue moved downward through his body. He wondered if he would ever again escape that pang of emptiness in his solar plexus. It seemed almost to be a part of him by now.

"I've got the money, Perriquey. What else is there for us to talk about?"

Perriquey gave Ric a smile that was almost sad. He drew deeply on his cigarette, exhaled in sharp straight plumes of white smoke.

"In many ways it is too bad that Ironfield chose a man like you to represent him, Durazo. You're a man of action, and I might add, even of primitive impulses. I can see the senator's reasoning." He stared at the bright tip of his cigarette. "In his distraught condition, it is quite easy to imagine he feels he is dealing with criminals and a man like you—a man who could beat their heads together seemed an ideal choice. Too bad we don't operate that way. Too bad Ironfield did not think the thing through more deeply. When I say it is too bad—what I mean is—it's too bad for Ironfield."

Ric sat forward on his chair. "When you say that Ironfield is in a distraught condition, Perriquey, you've hit it. I don't think he would have called on me if there had been any other way out that he could see. The man is suffering."

For the first time Perriquey betrayed some of the primitive emotion he accused Ric of displaying. He stared hard at Ric for a moment, the cigarette forgotten between his manicured fingers. His eyes tightened and a muscle worked along his sharp-hewn jaw line. He looked at the cigarette as if it offended him and ground it out in an ash tray. Ric thought he looked as if it gave him pleasure to smash it—as if he were smashing it in Gifford Ironfield's eyes.

There was the faintest quiver of exultance in Perriquey's tone. "Is he suffering, Durazo?"

"I don't know what kind of thing you are, Perriquey, to doubt it. Ironfield is in his late fifties. This baby was his first child. You wouldn't have to be with him more than five minutes to know he worships it. What kind of kick does it give you to know he's eating his insides out?"

"The kind of kick you wouldn't even understand, Durazo. Well, it was worth waiting for, worth waiting to meet you. You know, I fully planned to walk out of that door at midnight and let you howl at the moon. You really sliced it slim, considering you had no way of finding me if I didn't want you to do it."

"I cut it thin because I couldn't help it."

"That's because the Ironfield child is not your only interest in life, Durazo."

"If you don't think he is, you just keep fooling around with me."

"Violence. Ah, violence. That's something you understand, isn't it, Durazo? And now you're threatening me."

Ric stood up. "We might as well get one thing straightened out now, Perriquey. I'd snap you in my hands right now. I'd step on you like a cockroach out of that wall. You mean nothing to me. You and your kind are slime to me. I'm playing it your way because I want that kid safe."

Perriquey smiled. "That's what you would do. But get this straight, Durazo. You won't do anything. I'll walk out of this door and you won't stop me. You won't lift your voice to stop me, much less your fist. Get this clear. You try to lump me in with all kidnapers—"

"You're all alike to me."

"But we're not. I don't have to defend myself to you. But it pleases me to show you how wrong you are—how wrong Ironfield was to send you here."

"The poor bastard did what he could."

"Oh, it pleases me to hear you describe him as a bereaved parent. Ironfield. The son of a bitch. He's been so many other things in his life. He got married and became a human being almost at the last minute. You know? Almost as though he woke up one morning and realized the human race was enjoying itself and he was almost old enough to die and he hadn't even joined it, yet. So the son of a bitch married a girl thirty years younger than himself, had a brat and thought he was one of God's favored people. I wonder what he thinks now."

"I don't think he thinks anything. He just sits and stares and wonders if he'll get his kid back."

"Let him wonder. Let him pay. He never paid in his life for anything."

"You hate deep, don't you, Perriquey."

Perriquey inclined his head in a slight bow.

"And for a long time, Durazo. That's why I tell you that you don't have the Ironfield child driving you as I do. Gifford Ironfield gave me the dirty end of the stick—the chewed up part—a long time ago. When I got where I could, I wanted to hit back at him, the cold fish of a son of a bitch. But I never could. You know why? There was no way to touch him. He was just that. A cold fish. What can you do to a fish? There's no way you can touch him. But then, it was just as though he set it up himself. He got married. For a long time I used to lie awake nights thinking about his wife—thinking about the things that could happen to her, and what it would do to Cold Fish when it happened. But I was afraid it wouldn't hit deeply enough. I wanted him to hurt—in his guts—the way I had hurt, so he could live with it twenty years—the way I lived with it."

Ric stepped forward. His voice was hollow. "The baby is dead."

For a moment he and Perriquey stared at each other in the silent room. Ric's hand was shaking. He brought it upward toward the shoulder holster.

Perriquey's voice stopped him. "If the child were already dead it would defeat me, Durazo. You're thinking with your gun hand. I want Ironfield to suffer just as long as I can stretch it out."

Ric's hand dropped to his side. "You've run it all the way out, Perriquey. It may excite you to laughter to know that his wife has already tried to commit suicide. She blames herself because she turned her back on the sleeping baby for five minutes—long enough for it to be stolen. You've hurt them enough, Perriquey, even for your dirty rotten warped mind. You've left them nothing. They've sent the quarter of a million dollars—in cash. You deliver the baby to me and you can have it."

Now Perriquey did laugh in his face. "You make it sound so quaint and simple, Durazo. Pay the money. Get the baby back. It isn't that simple."

"That was the deal."

"That was the deal a week ago. Time changes things. People change them. You have changed it all. I only wish I could be there when you go back to Ironfield and his wife and tell them you have failed."

The fist tightened in Ric's stomach. They were tying him in knots so he wanted to double over with the sharp agony. He could see in Perriquey's face that all the deal was off. Perhaps it had never been on. Perhaps Perriquey only wanted to string out the torment and torture. He wanted to build up their hopes and then knock them dead.

"You never meant to accept the payment."

"Oh, but I did. I did until day before yesterday."

"I'll go along with you for another five minutes, Perriquey."

"That time is quite adequate for me, too, Durazo. And remember that you set the limit yourself. In five minutes our negotiations end."

"What happened day before yesterday to change your mind?"

"You happened, Durazo. You threw a kid out of your sports car—the only such vehicle in Los Solanos."

"A punk trying to pull a gun on me."

"Sure, and you smashed his gun, and broke his ribs. He had to tell the police he was attacked, and he described you. They are looking for you on that little matter."

"I have the money. We can close the deal and both of us get out of here."

"No, Durazo. It's all off. I told Ironfield I wanted a man who would attract no more attention in nice surroundings than I do. But in the first few hours you were at La Pueblo you made a pass at the owner's wife—"

"Did she tell you that?"

"I find out what I need to know. And you attracted other attention. Within an hour after you checked in at La Pueblo, an FBI agent checked in."

"I knew nothing of it. I swear that."

"Saul Rehan? I think you did know. You carried on a very guarded conversation with him in the La Pueblo Cafe. Oh, it looked so innocent. You thought you were going to pay me off and Saul Rehan would pick me up. Well, I've news for you and Rehan."

"My God, Perriquey, we've tried to do exactly as you ordered."

"Don't bother to lie about it. I can tell you Rehan will never find a dollar of that money on me, because I refuse to touch it. I wouldn't spit on it handed to me from you. And there's more you can tell Rehan. They'll never find the child or his body, and they'll never connect me with it because it's only your word against mine and I'm leaving this part of the country tonight."

"I know nothing about Rehan. Ironfield is on the spot. If the FBI was smart enough to keep him tailed even when he got in touch with me that's a rotten break. But get me the baby, and I'll see you get out of the country if I have to kill Rehan."

"You are determined to get that baby, aren't you. It's too bad. You should have thought of that when you were laying Kimball's wife and getting him so stirred up he's got the State Police looking for you."

"Perriquey, all that stuff happened to me, just as you tell it. Only not quite the way you tell it. I swear to you I'll protect you to the Mexican border if you'll take the money and turn the child over to me."

Perriquey's mouth twisted. "You're too hot, Durazo. I won't touch you or that money."

"It's a quarter of a million dollars, Perriquey."

Perriquey shrugged. "You know where you can stick that quarter of a million, Durazo. The deal has fallen through. You can go back and tell Ironfield that. The kid is as good as dead. You're too hot to deal with."

Durazo stepped forward. Agony worked in his face. He caught Perriquey's arms. They were like broomsticks in his hands.

Perriquey regarded him with distaste. "Take your hands off me."

"The money, Perriquey. I'll get you out of the country. If Rehan gets near you, I'll kill him. All I want is that baby. In the name of God, man, I'm begging you."

"You can stop." Perriquey smiled and picked up his hat from the bed table. He set it precisely on his gray curls. "What beats me, Durazo, is that you care at all. What's in it for you? I happen to know enough about you to know that five years ago when Ironfield was a circuit judge he sent you to prison on what later actually was proved to be a bum rap. You should hate the son of a bitch. I don't think much of you, Durazo. You forgive mighty easy."

He turned and walked, a rigid man, grown taut and brittle with middle-age, a man driven by hate under his urbane exterior. He paused at the door.

"Don't go out that door, Perriquey. If you do, I'll hunt you down. That's something I understand."

"It won't get you the baby."

"You won't live to see Ironfield suffer either, Perriquey."

"I am seeing that. And I will see it. I'm quite safe. You wouldn't touch me. You think as long as I'm alive there's a chance you'll get that baby back. As long as you think that, nothing's going to happen to me."

"You're wrong, Perriquey. I'm going to hunt you down. You'll never be able to run far enough, or hide in a rat hole deep enough. I'll find you and I'll kill you. It's going to kill that baby's mother when I tell her I failed. When that happens, God help you, Perriquey."

"You underestimate me, Durazo. If I were afraid of you, I'd have been afraid of the police, of the FBI. I would never have started this deal if I were afraid of anybody. But I'm not. Your threats fall somewhere on the floor, between you and me."

"All right, Perriquey. I came in this room thinking you were smart. I don't think that any more. I think you're insane, and that's all I think. So you walk out that door. Go on. And then you start running, and don't you ever stop, and don't forget to keep looking over your shoulder."

Perriquey laughed at him.

He turned the door knob. Sweat beaded Ric's forehead, ran along his temples.

"Your time has expired, my friend," Perriquey said. "Good-by. Before I go, I'll give you a little advice."

"Yeah?"

"Yes. You have in your possession a quarter of a million of Ironfield's money. You'll never buy the baby's life with that money. Take my advice. Get into Mexico with it while you can. Go, Durazo, and keep going."

Chapter Twenty-One

When Perriquey slammed the door behind him, Ric moved toward it in almost a reflex action. His hand was on the knob before he stopped, staring at the closed door. He stood there and forced himself to count to five, slowly. He hated standing there. It was against everything he was and had become in his way of existence. He decided he was one of those condemned to strike out, to move forward and keep moving. Against the quality of enemy he'd faced all his life this had been permissible, even smart. But he would not be smart to dash out there after Perriquey. That was what Perriquey expected him to do.

Perriquey was certain he had Ric Durazo pegged pretty definitely, too.

It seemed a long time counting to five. He stared at the furnishings of the room. Perriquey had been in here and seemed to have touched nothing. That would figure. If Norton Perriquey knew Saul Rehan was on Ric's trail, he could be sure the FBI would dust this room for fingerprints. Those gloves of Perriquey's had not been an affectation.

Ric snapped off the light, stepped out on the narrow veranda that ran the length of the simulated bunkhouses. For another moment he pressed against the wall with his eyes closed. The light out here was faint, and he wanted to be sure he saw what he needed to see.

From a curve in the parking area, Ric saw a car reversed slowly. The headlights were not on, but when the car was put in reverse the back-up lights glowed. He saw that the car was a Chrysler Windsor, last year's model in cream and green. For one instant when the car was turned, the brake lights glowed and the license plate was illumined. Ohio 1621. Ric could never remember license numbers; here was one he would never forget.

The car pulled all the way to the exit in the stone wall before the driver turned on the headlights. The car swung left on Highway 58, not moving swiftly. Perriquey was a man who never attracted attention to himself if he could avoid it. Right now, Perriquey was a man with a duodenum liquid-full of fear.

Ric ran across the plotted grass, struck the pavement of the parking area at a ran, his shoes sounding loudly in the quiet darkness.

Ric had his hand on the Plymouth door when he felt the gun bite into his kidney, thrust hard and cold.

He turned slowly. "Put your hands against the top of the car," the man ordered.

Sweating, Ric stared. "Rehan," he said.

"You were expecting maybe Doctor Livingston?"
"Wise guy. What the hell do you want?"
"You know my name—"
"It's no secret in this whole county—"
"You know my name, you must know what I want."
Ric stared past Rehan to the darkened highway.
"You don't want me, Rehan."
"Maybe not. What say we go into town?"
Ric's mouth twisted. He stared at the gun.
"Are you asking me?"
"Practically."

Ric sat across the blood-veneered desk from Rehan. A younger man, whom Rehan didn't bother to introduce, sat against the only window and stared at Ric as though he were a wanted poster on a post office wall.

The room was almost bare. Ric supposed it was an interrogation room used by the Los Solanos police department. Anyhow it was upstairs in headquarters.

Ric could not get a full breath of air in the musty room. The tautness that had built in Perriquey's room had him stretched like violin strings now. Through his mind raced the picture of Perriquey's cream and green Chrysler disappearing west on Highway 58.

"Now, I'm not going to fool around with you, Durazo. I know you. I know your record, and it dates back to the time you were twelve years old. A bad kid that grew up bad in all the best reformatories."

"You were lucky, Rehan. Maybe you were never hungry when you were twelve years old."

The youthful man stirred at the window as if offended that Durazo had answered Rehan at all.

Ric just looked at him.

"The hell with what you were. I know your record, so I know the last term you spent in prison was on a bum rap. Is that why you're bitter, Durazo?"

"Am I bitter?"

"A man doesn't get mixed up in kidnaping unless he is bitter or mentally warped."

"I'm all warped, Rehan."

"Trying to hit back at Senator Ironfield? Now, Durazo, we can save time. We know you met with Ironfield in a hotel room out in Wantaugh, Long Island. Oh, he went to a lot of trouble to meet with you out there. Unfortunately, the senator isn't a wealthy man—not so wealthy that he could get together a quarter of a million in cash without attracting attention."

"You were already on him, Rehan. Your whole office was. He told me about it. He even told me he had seen your supervisor and had gotten his promise to lay off until he could get his child back alive. Your supervisor promised."

"I'm the supervisor, Durazo. I'm the man the senator talked to."

"Then I've only one thing to say to you. You bastards are just as stupid as city cops. The only difference is you cover more territory."

The young man stood up, shrugging his coat up on his shoulders. His face had hardened, eyes narrowed.

"Sit down, boy," Ric said. "You've been seeing too many G-men movies."

Rehan smiled slightly, head turned from his assistant. He said, "Now, Durazo, you may not know it. Our function is public welfare. We have to protect the lives and property of our citizens, whether they want us to or not. Any oral promises I might have made to Senator Ironfield have to be predicated on that premise. This is kidnaping—a federal offense. Our job is to bring in the men behind it. We're going to do it."

"You're going to get the child killed."

"Don't you threaten me, Durazo."

Ric laughed coldly. "You've got it all figured out. I contacted Ironfield. He paid me and now I'm trying to deliver the loot to accomplices."

"That's it. Now, we're prepared to make a deal with you. You're on your way to the electric chair. That's the penalty for kidnaping. You turn state's witness, we'll work something out. We can get you off with life."

"I swear, Rehan, I don't know how to thank you."

"Keep a civil tongue in your face," the young man said.

Ric didn't even look at him.

"You met a man out at the dude ranch tonight. Is he one of your accomplices?"

"We talked golf."

"Be smart, Durazo. We've plenty of time. We're going to get it out of you. And don't worry about your friend. We've got an agent tailing him, too."

Ric leaped out of the chair, knocking it over. He moved so abruptly that both agents reacted, coming to their feet, poised and waiting for him.

Ric's voice was hoarse. "Call him off. Rehan, I beg you. Call that man off. You're going to get Ironfield's baby killed."

"We're going to break up that slime gang of yours."

"Your damned devotion to duty is costing the Ironfield baby its life."

"Is that your word to us?" the younger agent asked.

Ric kept his gaze locked against Rehan's. "You know what happens,

Rehan. This may be College Boy's first assignment. But you know. You crowd them and they'll kill the baby."

"If they haven't already. You can tell your people this for me, Durazo. We've been in this business a long time. We operate under the assumption that the baby was dead within a few hours after it was taken from its home. Why shouldn't they kill the baby? To keep it alive is just that much more trouble for them. They've got plenty of trouble, and it does not in any way assure they'll get the money."

Ric's fists clenched, unclenched. "But I'm working on a different idea, Rehan. And that one is that the baby may be alive—may have been alive until you put one of your slicked-up patrolmen on him."

The young agent spoke. "I've warned you for the last time about keeping a civil tongue, Durazo."

Ric glanced at him. "A law degree doesn't change a thing, boy. You're still a patrolman on a dirty job. You like it or not, that's the truth. You people have shown no intelligence on this thing." He heeled around, facing Rehan again. "God knows, if you know Senator Ironfield well enough that he would come to you to call off your boys, you know he would not deal with me if I were even remotely connected with kidnaping. He'd have turned me in back in Wantaugh, even if it meant his baby's death. He's that kind of man."

Rehan hesitated, and his gray face was paler. He exhaled.

"We're not questioning the senator's honesty, Durazo. But we do question yours. We think he was convinced you were not part of this operation. But we believe you are, and you're going to stay here until you name the rest of your gang—"

"Beat cops." Ric spat the words.

"You may well wish you were dealing with police at the precinct level, Durazo, before we're through with you. Our interrogation methods may be more refined, but they are more thorough. You've never been in trouble before. You'll be pleading with us to let you name the rest of your rat pack."

Ric stared around him helplessly. The young agent remained poised, standing just before the window. Through the blind Ric saw it was still night.

"Rehan, on this deal, I'm as honest as you are. But I'm in one hell of a better spot. You gave a United States senator your word that you'd give him the time he needed for one last attempt to deal with the kidnapers and save his child's life. Then he was to cooperate in every way with you. You can hold me here. Soon it's going to be too late anyhow. If the baby was alive, it'll be dead. But before you're through with me you're going to find out from Ironfield that I was brought in on this thing at his insistence. I didn't want it. I told him I didn't want it. I didn't think I could do him any good. Finally he convinced me I could try. And that's the truth."

The young agent gave a sharp laugh. "You were better able to track down the kidnapers than the Federal enforcement agency?"

"I never said it. Ironfield thought so because of some peculiar aspects of the case. There are a lot of your men, but sometimes that's about all you can say for them. And this was one of those times." He watched Rehan's scowling face. "So you go ahead, Rehan. You hold me. You get the baby killed. Oh, I admit he might already be dead. But there's one chance he isn't, and as long as there's that chance, his life depends on how smart you are. You get in touch with Ironfield. Oh, it's going to take time. Time we don't have. But you've got the government on your side—and it's just the life of one little baby. You want those kidnappers. I want that baby. By the time Ironfield chews you out for what you've done, the way you've screwed the works out here, the baby will be dead—and Junior here will be your superior."

Rehan walked around the desk. "Durazo, I'm twenty years older than you. This I know. You're tough. I'm tougher. You believe you're a smart character. I think I'm smarter. Threatening me with a demotion that might come if I've gambled wrong doesn't even touch me. I've got a duty I've sworn to uphold, and that's what I'm doing. I cannot believe that I could be wrong in this case. You've a bad record and I've a good one. However, there is one thing in your favor. Ironfield did tell me that there was one last chance he might get in direct contact with the kidnapers, and that the baby was alive when he talked with them. If he has put his faith in you, I'm deeply disappointed in him. I believe that I and my bureau could have done him a better job. But there's this I know. You can't escape me now. So I'm going to turn you loose. You're free, Durazo. You can walk out of that door. If I were you, I'd run to Chile and keep running. These may be your last free moments on earth. Get out of here."

They stood and their gazes locked levelly. The color moved slowly upward in Rehan's face.

"You're on your own, Durazo. We've got a man on the tail of the man you met at the dude ranch. You can't turn to the police. You try to leave this country and we'll shoot you down. You beg for help, Durazo. I want you to. I want to stand there and watch them gun you down while you beg for help. Now get out of here."

Chapter Twenty-Two

Ric crossed the walk before the police building and got in the Plymouth. Without close scrutiny, he saw the car had been minutely examined. His mouth twisted. No sense in keeping this car now.

He started the engine and then sat there a moment. He did not know how long until dawn, but it had been a long and miserable night. He was tired. He pressed his forehead against the steering wheel for a moment. What else could he do? There was not much chance of finding any trace of Perriquey's Chrysler by now. Even if he found it, very likely Perriquey had changed cars and names. He could not think how he could go back and tell them he had failed. Two people had advised him to get out of the country and keep running. Sitting there, that was what he wanted to do.

He laughed, a bitter sound, wondering if he could accomplish even that.

He glanced back at the window of the interrogation room. Yellow glowed up there. No sense thinking Rehan was letting up. Rehan wasn't trying to get off any hook by releasing him. Rehan considered him guilty, and believed that eventually he would lead them to the kidnapers. Ric was too tired even to laugh at that idea.

He put the car in reverse, moved to the silent street and drove to the bus station. He paid for the rented car, got back most of his deposit and walked out.

He went along the shadowed street, walking tiredly. The weariness was like a virus inside him. He no longer had any will to go forward. He wanted to sit on the curb and rest. It had been so long. He could not remember when he had rested. He thought about Eve Kimball in that hotel room. Briefly he wondered if she'd gotten in touch with her father. He was tired. It did not matter. *The hell with you, Eve Kimball. Hell with you, Ironfield. Hell.*

He entered the all-night storage garage, walked through the echoing tunnel past the parked cars to the Porsche. He fought in his pocket, found the keys. He would drive out of here. Maybe the State cops would get on his tail and chase him somewhere. Anywhere. That would make up his mind for him when he was too beat to make his own decisions. Maybe he'd run into Martin Kimball somewhere and he'd slap him around until he began to feel better.

"Ric."

He spun around. "Eve. What are you doing here?"

"I've been here, Ric. Most of the night."

"Where's your father? What happened to your hotel room?"

"I called him, Ric. I told him I was in trouble. I was afraid to tell him too much. I begged him to come help me. You know what he said, Ric?"

"Something charming, I'll bet."

"He said to take a couple aspirin and that he'd send one of his lawyers out here tomorrow. He wouldn't even call the lawyer tonight. Said he didn't want to disturb him. That's how urgent it was to Father."

"So you got scared and ran?"

She shook her head, moving close to him. He felt her shiver. "No, Ric. I was terrified. You were gone, and Father wasn't going to do anything, except notify his lawyer who might or might not fly here. I went downstairs. I went to the night clerk and asked him if you'd said anything about where you were going. At first, he couldn't remember. Then he said you'd asked about a car rental. That meant you were going to put the Porsche up for a while. This was the only all-night storage garage. I came here. I found the Porsche. I asked the attendant if I couldn't wait for you. I told him you were my husband. He let me sit in that car there."

"All very lovely. But why didn't you stay in the hotel?"

She pressed against him. Now she was trembling. "Ric, while I was talking to the night clerk I looked across the room. He was there."

"Who?"

"Martin."

"Kimball. He was there and didn't see you?"

"I don't think he did. He was in the phone booth. He was turned away. I was numb. First I thought he had seen me and was trying to keep me from recognizing him. Then I saw he was talking to someone on the phone. I took a chance that he hadn't seen me. I ran back up the stairs. I was afraid to go back to my room. Maybe it was my room that Martin was calling. Maybe he'd gotten the room number from the clerk, wanted to be sure I was alone. I don't know. I was too scared to think. I just ran. I went out the back way and came here."

Ric unlocked the Porsche. "Get in," he said.

"What about the baby?"

"I don't know. I've been stopped. I'm finished."

"Ric. No."

"There's nothing else I can do. I didn't want to start this thing, I never should have."

"Ric, what happened to you?"

He helped her in the Porsche, got in beside her. He started the engine, let it warm up. Briefly he told her what had happened. He put the car in reverse, changed gears and rolled out of the garage. She did not speak for a long time.

"I'm beat," he said. "I've got sense enough to know I'm beat."

"Ric. That man turned west. You can look for him."

"In this country? I couldn't if I had ten years, and I don't."

"But you know the make of his car, his license number, its color. We could drive. Somebody must have seen him."

"Sure. How long could we drive? Until the State Police pick us up?"

"Yes. That long. I want to be looking for that baby when we're stopped, Ric. It doesn't matter what else happens to us. As long as there's any chance that baby's alive, we've got to keep looking."

Ric stared at the quiet buildings as they rolled along the street. They moved through the residential section in the shadow of the cottonwoods. He glanced at the motel, La Pueblo. Its lights were out. He wondered if Peggy had slept well.

"Better than sitting around there waiting," he said half to himself.

"Better than anything, Ric. We can try. We can ask along the highway, because we've got to."

Ric watched the first rifts of daylight in the sky, long jagged ribbons of cerise and blue and faded yellow. He stepped hard on the gas. The little car leaped forward. They raced past the airport, but Ric didn't glance toward it.

"This is the dude ranch where I talked to Perriquey," he told her as they passed the stone gate and the entrance. Behind the cottages men were moving about in the corrals saddling horses for the morning canter. "Perriquey turned west here. Rehan stopped me. Perriquey's had all these hours and all the country between here and the Pacific ocean."

"Not quite," Eve said. "If they did intend to deliver the baby to you, they must have had it in this territory. They've been waiting for you. They've had to wait somewhere. Why would it be too far from the dude ranch?"

For a moment, hope glowed in Ric, and some of the weariness dissipated. Then he shook his head. "Even if that were true, they've had time to clear out."

"There's one more thing, Ric. You said the FBI agent had trailed Perriquey's car. That might have changed everything."

"Yes. It would have speeded the baby's death."

"Or it might have kept Perriquey pinned down wherever he was hiding." Her voice vibrated. "All we need is one break. Just one person who has seen that car along this highway in the past week. He's had to buy gas, groceries, something."

Ric nodded. He pulled into the first yard and stopped before an adobe house. Two Mexicans were working in the yard over a dilapidated car.

Ric carefully described the car, gave its license number. They looked at him, grinning, and shook their heads. He asked about the nearest filling station and they pointed west. "Five miles. At the crossroads."

Ric roared out of the yard and turned the Porsche toward the crossroads. He pulled into the station. The owner came out the screen door, let it slam.

Ric described the Chrysler, going over it slowly and carefully as he had with the Mexicans. The man just stood there watching him and scratching himself.

"Car like that stopped here a couple times. Gas. Groceries."

"They ever buy anything like—well, canned milk?"

"Yeah. Matter of fact they did. Once the young guy bought milk and nothing else. Nothing to me, mister. Lot of cows out here. Not many men know how to milk them."

"Which way did they come from? Did you ever notice? Down the highway?" Ric could feel the excitement building in him.

The man shook his head, jerked it toward the unpaved hardpacked side road.

"What's out there?" Ric said.

"Few families. Some people keep sheep. Some Mexicans. Not much."

Ric thanked him. He walked back to the car, wanting to run. Eve was sitting tensely. "They're down this road, Ric. They've got to be."

"We'll play it out," he said trying to conceal the hope inside him. "People along here must have seen that car."

Twenty miles later, Ric realized the grocer man had not said the houses were on the road, or even if there were houses. In the East, people built close to the roads, even poor side roads like this. Out here they looked for shade, for grass, for water—or concealment.

The hard-packed road trailed off through stones to a sand track. In the indeterminate distance loomed the hills. The silence and the heat had settled now. The hope Ric had had was fading now. Eve was silent, staring into the flat wasteland of boulders, cactus and sage.

"Ric. Look." Eve sat forward, pointing to the right across the silent country.

He slowed, staring. The top of a car gleamed out there. It was a dark car. Sunlight showed that.

Ahead was a rutted road leading to the right. Ric pulled the Porsche, heading toward the dark car.

He stopped behind him. Before he got out he saw the man sprawled on the ground beside the black coupe.

"Stay there," he told Eve. He walked warily forward.

The man was youthful, in a way reminding Ric of the stiff-backed young agent in Rehan's office. He did not need to look at the man's credentials to know he was an agent. He didn't need to touch him to see that he was dead and had been for the past few hours. There was a bullet hole in his forehead. They had suckered him out of the car and had gunned him down.

Ric walked ahead of the car. He saw tracks that did not match those of the black car. They led into the foothills. He returned to the Porsche. "He's dead. There's nothing we can do for him. They ambushed him right out here in the open. Unless they've cleared out on some other road, they're up there somewhere."

"Let's go, Ric."

She glanced back toward where the young agent was sprawled outside the open car door.

"Don't worry about him," Ric said. "Rehan will never let us get too far ahead of him. He'll find his boy. Not that it'll do either one of them any good."

The car tracks led past boulders, and upward along a winding hill road that wound upward through piñon and juniper and bald rocks.

"If they're up here," Ric said, "they'll have a lookout. You see anything, hear anything—anything—you hit the bottom of this floor and you stay there."

Eve nodded. The road wound deeper into the hills, carrying them downslope, and then upward again. The scorched earth appeared unchanged, unchanging. Suddenly, he saw that the road appeared to end up ahead.

He killed the engine. He got out, leaving the door open. He went ahead of the car to what appeared to be the brink of a precipice. He paused, leaning against the face of the rock. The road turned sharply, going downward on what appeared to be an ancient Indian sand trail. A car could descend, but it would be perilous.

He stared below. Perriquey's car had gone down this sand shelf. It was parked in the hollow below it. Ric saw another car near the Chrysler. Then he saw the ruins of an Indian rock dwelling. He moved his gaze over the ancient openings, the entrances, the ledges, the stones discolored and broken with age.

He turned, walked back to the Porsche.

"Eve, I'm going down there."

"Ric—"

"The cars are down there. They haven't gotten out of here yet. Maybe they think they're safe, maybe they think they're trapped. I've got to find out. You walk to the edge of this cliff where you can see down there, and watch the trail behind us. If nothing happens, you wait an hour."

"Ric—"

"An hour. No more than that, you hear? Don't panic, just start this car and get the hell out of here. You get back to Rehan. You tell him about this place."

"Oh, Ric." She writhed out of the car, caught him in her arms. "God help you, Ric. Please, God help you."

Chapter Twenty-Three

Ric returned to the sandslide. Pressed against the face of the hill, he stared down into the flat stone table and the solid rock from which the Indians had painfully hacked a dwelling.

He saw nothing move. But he figured that Perriquey, or someone with him, had killed the agent back on the desert. A lookout would be on guard. Unless they were deep inside the ruin they should have heard the engine as the Porsche climbed the narrow path.

He walked back along the road, found a path that led upward through the boulders. He moved along it, hurrying. He rounded the hill and when he started down he was on the far side of the ruins.

He let himself down cautiously. He did not even breathe until his feet touched the flat surface of the wind-smoothed rock.

He was on the blind side of the stone dwelling. He ran across the rock to the wall and then moved around it. He felt the sun blazing against his head, against the back of his neck. The stone was hot against his hands.

He stared at the cars. No one was in them. He stepped into the first arched opening. This corridor ran across the front of the dwelling. The other floors had been destroyed or eroded so that long shafts of sunlight poured through all through the ruin.

He pushed himself into a shadow, listening. The place was silent with the heavy silence of ancient tombs. Outside on the flat rock fine sand sifted in the breeze, but there was no whisper of it in here.

He moved along the corridor, warily. He removed the gun from its holster, pushed off the catch. He felt better with the heavy firearm in his hand. He passed other broken arches and saw they led like ant tunnels deeper into the ruin, but most were illumined because the whole roof of this place had been torn away except in small patches.

His foot slipped and he stopped, drawing back. Gasping, he stared down into a prospector's shaft. He heard a stone clatter down it and for a moment he did not move.

A shadow flickered ahead of him and he jerked his head up. From an arch thirty feet in front of him, a man leaped, shouting.

The man's yell sprang through the ruin, struck against the walls and trailed through the ruined corridors.

For a second he faced Ric, both standing in shadow with an oblong of sunlight like a forbidden rug between them.

The man brought up his gun and Ric shot him.

He pressed the trigger, hearing the sound of his gun going away from him with the speed of the bullet, smashing itself against the stone and the walls and the empty places, and then echoing through the hills as though it would never cease.

The man fired in the fraction of an instant after Ric pressed off his shot. The bullet from the man's gun struck the stone flooring and ricocheted into the wall. But its sound raced after the other sound, bouncing from hill and canyon.

Ric moved forward, watching the man. He dropped the gun as if moving in slow motion and clutched at his coat front with both hands. He sank to his knees with his head lowered and for an instant he looked as if he were praying to the ancient gods who had once inhabited this place. He sprawled forward then and was dead by the time Ric got to him.

Ric stepped through the arch through which the guard had come. The darkened corridor led deep into the heart of the dwelling, going downward.

Ahead, a man shouted. Ric pressed against the chilled stone, standing in the shadow and waiting. Someone answered, deeper. The sounds rode on the silence and echoed so that they were lost. Ric could not say just where they came from.

He was moving forward when he heard the wailing cry of a baby. Something happened to him. It was as though there were an upward thrust of hope and exultation. The baby was alive.

Suddenly Ric was running. The baby was alive. The baby was alive. He had no other thought. He forgot caution. He just whispered, praying the baby would keep crying like that. It would lead him to it like radar.

He ran, feeling the baby's wailing striking against him, bouncing off, pulling him forward.

The wall curved suddenly and Ric rounded it. He was breathing through his mouth. The baby was nearer, directly ahead of him.

He heard the sound of footsteps and they were like fists against the back of his neck. He leaped to the wall and turned around.

He felt something like the sting of a wasp. It drove him stumbling forward. He grasped at the wall, and did not even know he had been shot until the reverberating sound of gunfire beat its way through the pounding of blood in his temples, the fire of agony in his side.

He toppled to his knees, still clinging to the flat surface of the wall, dragging his splayed fingers along it.

The corridor spun around him. All he could think of was what a crazy damned fool thing to happen. He had found the baby and it was alive, and it was too late.

The footsteps grew louder and Ric turned. He felt his fingers loosen on his gun and knew if he dropped it he would never be able to pick it up again.

He sagged forward, using all his strength to hold the gun.

He struck on his side, watching the man run toward him.

He saw him pause and lift the gun to fire again.

Ric pressed the trigger. He pressed it again. He pressed it again. The man staggered backward and never fired his gun.

Ric moved forward on his knees. He could feel the blood hot and sticky down his side. He tried to hurry but it was as though he were crawling through mud.

He managed to get to his feet.

For a moment the baby had stopped crying. Either somebody had his hand over its mouth or the sound of gunfire had startled it into silence.

Ric closed his eyes so the corridor would not spin. He moved, then realized he was walking toward the man he had killed. He was going the wrong way. He turned around slowly, stumbling along the corridor.

The baby cried once and the sound was abruptly clapped off. Somebody was holding his hand over the baby's mouth.

Ric ran forward, holding his bleeding side. His head would not clear. This was one of those nightmares where you ran on rubbery legs along an endless corridor.

His shoulder bumped an arched wall. Lamplight flared from a circular room with a domed roof.

He saw Perriquey. The tall slender man was standing across the room. Ric saw he had the baby in his arms, his hand slapped across its mouth.

Perriquey threw the baby to the stone floor and grabbed out his gun from its shoulder holster. Perriquey was mouthing curses, and there was no suggestion of the suave guest of the dude ranch.

He leveled the gun at the baby.

"Perriquey." Ric spoke his name sharply. Perriquey cursed, not even hearing him. He said it again.

"Perriquey."

The tall man spun around, shooting. Ric stayed where he was, holding the deliberate aim he had fixed on Perriquey.

He pressed the trigger. For a moment he went on standing there against the arched wall. Perriquey was hit. He stumbled back, bending like a brittle limb that is snapped. He dropped the gun and it seemed to Ric he was taking two forevers to fall.

Painfully, Ric hefted the gun, lifting it to fire again. But he did not press the trigger. Perriquey sprawled forward on his face. For a moment the sense of release and the fire of fever flared through Ric. The domed room wheeled around as if spinning on a pin. He felt his knees give way and he almost fell.

Then he heard the baby crying and he held on tight until the room was still enough so that he could stagger across it toward the crying baby.

Chapter Twenty-Four

Ric was panting. He had not known it was so far across this room. They had set up a table near the wall. On it were opened milk cans, cigarette packs, bread, matches, a clutter of odds and ends, an ammunition cylinder from an automatic.

He paused, leaning heavily on the table, breathing through his mouth.

Perriquey was sprawled on the floor near his feet, but Ric did not look at him. The baby whimpered and as though driven by some force he didn't even understand, Ric stood straight, squinting his eyes, shaking his head, hoping it would clear.

He saw the baby move from the floor at the wall where Perriquey had hurled it. He stepped over Perriquey's body, a giant step and knelt.

Through the blur that obscured his vision he saw the baby withdraw from him. "Hell, kid," he said. "I won't hurt you. You're all right, kid. You're all right now."

He never knew what soothed the child, the tone of his voice, some instinct inside the baby, or perhaps the gentle way he lifted him. The baby whimpered once, but did not cry out again. Ric felt the baby arms go about his neck. He felt a tightness in his throat. It had been a long time. The kid needed somebody to cling to. *You picked a great one this time, kid,* he thought, *I don't even know if I can make it out of here. It's like wading knee-deep in alligators.*

"Mama," the child said.

Ric was moving toward the corridor.

"Yeah, kid, that's right," he said. "You're on your way. You hang on."

He stopped in the corridor, staring both ways along it. He could not remember the direction he should go. Shafts of sunlight illumined the tunnel, impossible distances from him. It had to be right the first shot. He didn't have the fuel for any dry runs over the field.

His gaze touched the body of the second man he'd shot. He walked toward him, biting down on his underlip, feeling the sweat work through the pores of his forehead.

"Oh, kid," he said. "I thought you weighed about twenty-two pounds. You're heavy, kid. Anybody ever tell you, you're heavy, kid? You want to carry Uncle Ric? How about that, kid, you want to carry Uncle Ric?"

He could hardly lift his leg high enough to go through the arch into the outer corridor. He tightened his grasp on the boy and staggered across it, stepped out into the sunlight. The two cars still baked in the stone forecourt.

He lifted his head, stared at the sandslide across the courtyard, the impossible distance.

"Eve."

There was no answer. He told himself he had not expected there would be any answer. That would be too easy. To walk across a sunblasted flat rock, one lifted one leg and placed it before the other. Ric did that again and again. The sun spun behind his eyeballs, boiling the liquid inside his head.

He started up the sandslide, feeling his shoes slip. Up the sandslide, Ric thought. The story of my life.

"Eve."

He heard the engine of the Porsche roar into life. She was starting the car. She had waited for him and now his time was up. She was getting out of there.

Laughter sobbed out of him. That was funny. Maybe the funniest thing that would ever happen to him. He was almost up the sandslide and Eve was going to drive away and leave him.

Suddenly he saw her. She was a blur there at the top of the chute. But she was there.

"Ric. Oh, Ric, I had to come back for one last look."

She ran the three steps down the incline to him, caught his arm. He felt the pressure of her fingers and he wanted to laugh again. He would never have made it if her fingers hadn't touched him just at that moment.

"Couldn't have made it, Eve. Not by myself. Couldn't have made it."

"The baby is alive. Oh, Ric. Thank God. It's alive."

"Yeah. Fine."

They were at the ridge above the sandslide and for a second Ric wavered. Eve removed her hand from his arm to smooth the baby's forehead and he almost fell.

She caught his arm, staring at him. Then her distended eyes saw the patch of blood on his shirt.

"Ric. You've been shot."

Her arm around him, she propelled him toward the car.

"It's all right," he said.

"I'll drive."

"I'm all right. Let me drive, Eve. I got to keep doing something. I'd pass out if I stopped. Let me drive."

Gently, Eve took the baby from his arms, laid it down on the Porsche seat. "You're all right, darling," she whispered to it, "you're going to be all right. Ric will take care of you. Long as you've got Ric to take care of you, you're all right. You're fine." All this time she was scratching through Ric's suitcase on the rear deck. She came up with undershirts.

Ric had toppled into the seat behind the steering wheel. Eve ran around the car, tore away his shirt. She chewed at her underlip. "I can't do anything about the bullet, Ric. Maybe we can stop the bleeding."

He laid his head back, did not protest.

She tied the bandage securely against the torn place in his side. She stepped away from him.

Ric lifted his arm, stared at his watch. "We got to get out of here."

She went around the car, took the child in her arms. She held its head against her shoulder, smoothed its soft hair, crooning to it.

Ric was thankful the engine was started; anything he didn't have to do put him that far ahead. He shifted into reverse on the narrow ledge, let the back wheels climb the incline and turned the steering wheel as far as it would go.

Eve closed her eyes. He let the clutch out slowly and the car inched forward, turning, its right front wheel touching the brink of the ledge.

Then they were rolling down the hill. Ric drove with the car in second gear. His hands were clenched on the steering wheel.

"You all right, Ric?"

"Yeah. The pain's not too bad now. There's only one road now and I'm on it. We got it made."

"The baby's asleep, Ric. Poor ragged little thing."

Ric said nothing, watching the road. He had stepped harder on the gas and they were winding downhill, wind whistling at the windows.

Eve stared downward at the lower levels of the road. At first she thought she saw a dust devil, then she realized it was a car climbing toward them. It disappeared around a turn and then showed again.

"It's my Cadillac," she said aloud.

"What?"

Ric slowed down and stared across the descending ridges to the far curve toward which Eve pointed. The Cadillac was racing upward, dust billowing.

"Martin," Eve said.

"What the hell does he want up here?"

"He's going over the side," Eve cried out. "He's driving like he's insane."

Ric watched the big car careening around the sharp curves in the mountain road.

"He's looking for us." Eve's voice was dead.

Ric nodded. "Sure. It figures. He was with the State Police. If Peggy told them I was back in town, or if they got with the FBI men when Rehan came out here looking for the agent, they must have trailed us out of town."

"There are no police with him."

"No. Probably they stopped down there where the agent was killed."

"How would Martin know we were up here?"

"Why not? If he was with the State Police as far as where they found the dead agent, he could sure as hell recognize the Porsche tire tracks in that sand."

"He came looking for us—alone."

"Sure as hell he did. By now he has had time to realize his story isn't going to stand up. He wants to find us—before the police do."

She gripped his arm, fingers taut.

"Ric. He's seen us."

Ric nodded. He set his jaw, holding the wheel. He rounded a curve and on the long stretch of straightaway he saw the Cadillac speeding toward him, hugging the inside of the narrow road. There was no doubt about it now in Ric's mind, if there ever had been. Martin was coming up that mountain looking for them. Martin had had time to think, and Martin was desperate. His plans for riches didn't include a stretch in jail, and as long as Ric and Eve lived, Martin stood a chance of losing. It was his word against theirs, and it would be a good idea if they never got to speak their pieces.

"He's going to force us off, Ric."

Ric stared at the sheer drop to his right, at the oncoming Cadillac, at the incline to his left, sheer and rock strewn. Almost any car would overturn attempting to go up it. And Kimball would never let him over there if he guessed his intent.

Ric hesitated, holding the Porsche at even speed and straight on the narrow roadway. The Cadillac was almost upon them, sun glittering in the windshield, the hood ornament growing large as a battering ram.

Ric swerved the Porsche hard to the left and at the last possible minute straightened the wheels. The little car had been climbing upward and when it was jerked back to the right it shivered, rocking.

For an interminable time the Porsche seemed to be standing on two wheels, teetering on its side.

Ric thrust the accelerator to the floor. He heard the screeching scream as metal grazed against metal, the little car scraping along the side of the Cadillac.

"Oh, God," Eve said.

Kimball had jerked the wheel of the Cadillac at the last moment, pulling to his right. In that second his face was turned toward them, eyes distended, mouth pulled down. Hatred and rage seemed to boil from the windows of his car, and then he had hurtled past them.

The Cadillac's left front tire crushed away the brink of the roadway. The big car shook as Kimball whipped the wheel trying to pull away from the edge. The back end whipped around but the front wheel had slipped too far down the steep roadside. The Caddy quivered for a moment, motor roaring as Kimball gunned it. Then abruptly it spun outward and went hurtling off the ledge.

Eve buried her face against the baby's head. But they could not escape the loud jolting crashes as the car struck below them, spun outward, struck again.

Ric slowed down. His hands were sweated, knuckles white where he gripped the steering wheel.

He looked back and saw the flames lunging upward. The car was still slowly sliding down an incline.

"Damn it," Ric said in agony. "Oh, God damn it."

"Ric. I'm sick. I don't know. I—"

"Hang on. For God's sake, just hang on."

"Can we help him, Ric?"

"The car's on fire. There's nothing we can do."

She moaned. He did not try to think what was going on inside her mind. Martin had tried to kill her at the motel, he had trailed them into the hills and had tried to kill them. But you couldn't know what she would be remembering. She did not look back. She was staring, but she was seeing something in her memory, in her life as it had been. She did not speak. They drove swiftly, going down the mountain.

Chapter Twenty-Five

The nearer they came to the flatlands the hotter it became. The air was dry and thin. Ric did not speak to Eve. Whatever was inside her, she needed to be left alone. He heard her muffled moans. Once she sobbed. She did not say anything. She held the baby tightly, rocking it in her arms.

Ric felt a strange sense of loneliness that he could not define or even understand. She was rid of Martin Kimball, well rid of him, and she would have a better life somewhere, no matter what she thought at the moment. Martin had tried twice to kill her. He had died trying. A man with one thing on his mind. But she'd meet a decent man. Time was going to help Eve.

Time. It was never on your side when you needed it. And time stretched ahead of him was a lonely empty space. He felt as if Eve were already gone from him, as though he were alone in the car, driving nowhere, no longer of any value to a living soul. What life and what time he had was leaking out the hole in his side.

Before they left the foothills, he could see the cluster of cars out there on the dirt road. State Police and Rehan's car, parked around the black auto. He saw the men standing around the agent's body. It was clear now. Martin had followed the State Police this far, seen the Porsche tire tracks and traced them upward into the mountains, driven frantic with the knowledge that he was about to lose everything.

He slowed. He could not get near those police cars. He had to take a chance on crossing that wasteland to the side road as far as possible from these men.

He removed his foot from the accelerator as they rolled down the last turn from the hills, searching. When he saw the sand trail leading to his left, he grinned. Perriquey and his men were smart rats, too smart ever to be bottled in anywhere with only one open exit.

He stepped on the gas. The Porsche sprang forward and he turned the wheel, sending it off to the left on the hard packed trail. He looked across his shoulder. The police cars were already moving in pursuit.

"The hell with you," he said aloud.

He looked back at them one more time—State Police cruisers and FBI cars racing after him. He felt a wave of dizziness, but shook it off and stepped harder on the accelerator.

Ric turned the Porsche off Highway 58 and entered the parking area of the Los Solanos Airport. He drove the car slowly, parked as near the administration building as possible.

It was breathlessly hot here on the treeless plain. Men sweated on the runways. Everyone who could be was in the air-conditioned administration building.

He got out of the car, walked around it. He tried to keep his gaze from those double glass doors of the building, could not do it. He was overdue, but they had said they would wait for him. They were in there.

He opened the door, lifted the sleeping child from Eve's arms.

She looked at him, worried. "You all right, Ric?"

He stared at her through the rising mist across his eyes. It was as though he had never seen her before, didn't know her. That was the way it had to be. Her father's lawyer ought to be around here somewhere. He'd take Eve back to her kind of life. That was the way it ought to be. He did not answer her.

"Ric!" Her voice was hollow, almost pleading.

He straightened up. The baby was heavier than ever. He stared toward the administration building, an impossible distance through the deepening haze.

He inhaled deeply, turned from the car and moved along the wide walk. It was as it had been on the Indian sandslide. You put one foot in front of the other. You bit down on your lip. You ignored the fire-hot pain in your side.

Suddenly the glass doors were thrust open. A woman ran through them, moving toward Ric and the baby, arms extended. Tears were streaming down her face. She was pallid, looked as though she'd been crying for a long time, but these tears were not the same.

Anne.

Her heels clicked on the pavement. Ric paused, watching her come toward him. The sun blazed against the back of his neck. A plane motor was revved up on the runway.

She was not looking at him. Her gaze was fixed on the baby in his arms.

The child stirred, wriggling. He cried out. "Mama."

Ric felt the sense of good well up in him. The pain in his side didn't matter, the loss was nothing. Whatever had happened, this moment was worth it.

Ric watched Anne's face. She was the loveliest woman in the world. He'd always said that, and it was no different now. The way she looked at her baby made her more lovely than ever. It was not a matter of physical beauty—it was everything about her. She was everything a man could want in one lifetime.

She lifted her face to Ric's, extending her arms and clutching the baby to her. For one instant, for the last time in this life, Ric knew, she stared into his eyes. In her eyes he saw everything, all the things they would never say, but the things that had always been between them, always and forever.

"Anne," he said.

"Ric. Oh, Ric."

"I brought your baby."

"Yes. Oh, yes." She was crushing the baby in her arms, crying over it, running her trembling hands through its hair. "Oh, Ric. I never doubted. I knew you would."

"Hello, Durazo."

Ric pulled his gaze from Anne's face. He looked at Senator Gifford Ironfield, hating him with a hatred that ripped at his insides, that burned far worse than the bullet in him. In that moment it was three years ago and he looked up at judge Ironfield, a man without human mercies, a man who believed you guilty even when he couldn't prove your guilt.

Ric shook the angry memory from his mind. Ironfield had been through hell himself in these past weeks. They belonged to the same club now.

The senator had his arm about Anne. Ric tried not to see it. *Hell, it's almost over now. It won't be long, not much longer.*

"You did it for me, Ric," Anne whispered.

"Yes."

Ironfield's voice was very low. "I won't try to say anything, Ric. There's nothing I can say." He extended his hand, clasped Ric's. "Better get the baby inside, Anne. The doctors are waiting."

Ric dropped the senator's hand. There were doctors inside. No. He would find his own doctor. He met Anne's gaze and then she turned, hurrying away.

"I've something for you, Ironfield," Ric said. "I'll get it out of the car."

He nodded curtly, watching Anne go through the door. He turned on his heel. The sun reflected from the Porsche was painful in his eyes.

When he got to the Porsche, Eve was gone.

He heard the swish of tires, the scream of brakes. Three police cars shivered to a stop near the Porsche. Ric ignored them. From the rear compartment he removed the suitcase containing the senator's ransom money.

When he got out of the car and straightened up, State troopers and Saul Rehan awaited him. He looked at them, moved along the walk. They fell in step beside him. None spoke.

Senator Ironfield awaited them just inside the glass doors. Ric saw Eve talking with some man near the reservation counter. His gaze lingered on her a moment.

"This is yours," he said to the senator. "I didn't have to use it."

He set the suitcase at the senator's feet.

"You better come along with me now, Durazo," Rehan said. "We got a lot of talking to do."

"Wait a minute, Rehan," Ironfield said. "If you've got to talk with someone, why not talk to me?"

Ric stood a moment, looking about the air-conditioned lobby. There seemed no place to go. At the reservation desk Eve was talking with the man, probably her father's lawyer. He didn't want to be near her, the sooner he got her out of his mind, the better. Across the room, two doctors and a trained nurse were huddled over Anne and her baby.

There was a Coca-Cola vending machine in what looked like neutral territory. Ric walked slowly toward it. Nothing was entirely clear, the room was shrouded in a misty red. He glanced toward the place where the senator was in deep conversation with the troopers and Saul Rehan.

He sat down in a waiting room chair beside the vending machine. He tried to sit straight. He let his head sink against the cool metal of the machine.

"Ric."

He straightened up, guiltily. When he saw it was Anne, he buttoned his coat, pulled his hand away from the agony in his side.

"Ric. I've never forgotten you."

"No."

"He was good to me, Ric. I was alone and afraid."

Suddenly he stared at her. She was alone and afraid. What a ball he'd had. Had he been out on somebody's yacht yakking it up? No sense being bitter. Not any more. He saw that Anne was what she was, and that she had what she needed. She could lie with him and sleep with him, but she needed the security the senator gave her. She had just what she had to have.

He smiled, feeling his mouth pull. He had thought it would hurt a hell of a lot more. But then he'd been living with the loss of her for almost three years. Time had helped him. He could look at her now and see her as she had become, see Mrs. Gifford Ironfield, and know that's what he wanted for her.

"Nobody could ever do for me, Ric, what you did."

"Sure."

She reached out to touch him. At that moment, her baby whimpered.

She heeled half around, biting her lip. She looked up at him, in agony. "Ric. The baby. I must go."

"Sure."

She hesitated one more moment. "God bless you, Ric."

He sat down again, feeling the room spin. He saw Gifford Ironfield come toward him. Beyond he saw Saul Rehan pause at the glass doors and then go out of them, walking away in the sun.

He hated the thought of having to stand up again. He was so tired. "Don't get up, Ric," Ironfield said. He slid into the chair beside Ric's. "I know you've been hurt. I know you're trying to keep it from Anne. I agree it's best. She's had shock enough."

"I'm all right."

Ironfield nodded. "You truly are, Ric. Whatever charges there were against you, with the State Police and with Rehan, they've been dropped."

"Thanks."

"My God, don't make me more in your debt by thanking me, Ric. I'll spend the rest of my life regretting the wrong I did you. But believe me, Ric, I believed I was right. I am what I am. Even, Ric, when we needed you so badly, when Anne was hysterically pleading with me to get in touch with you because you—you alone—would get her baby back for her, I had to know you were innocent of those old charges first. Forgive me, Ric. I know what I am. It's not for myself I ask you to forgive me, but for you. Don't poison the rest of your life with bitterness against me. I deserve it, but, God help me, I'm not worth it."

"I'm all right," Ric said again. He would have said more, but he was too tired. And it was true. He wasn't bitter any more. He just wanted to get away while he could still walk.

He got up, leaving Ironfield sitting there. His gaze raked across the room. Eve and the lawyer were gone from the reservation desk. Hell with it. He walked across the lobby, pushed open the doors, went through them.

Once he hesitated, sure he heard Anne call his name. His mouth twisted into a wry grin. That was imagination, that was the way it was in TV movies. That was the way he didn't need it to be any more. Thanks to Eve, he'd found out the truth. He'd grown away from Anne, and the memory of Anne. Funny, but that was God's truth.

He walked around the car. Now to the nearest bar, and he could drink Eve out of his system, find a doctor to probe out that bullet. Then he could start living again.

He slid into the car.

Eve was sitting there. She touched his arm.

"What do you want?" he said.

"I'm with you."

"Where do you want to go?"

"We've got to get you to a doctor, Ric."

"I'm all right. Where do I let you out?"

Eve's hand covered his on the steering wheel. "She's lovely, Ric. Worth getting shot for. You never got over her, did you?"

"I asked you. Where you want to go?"

"That's up to you, Ric."

"God knows I didn't adopt you."

"Stop being bitter, Ric. It's better this way. Inside I think you already know it. You'll be fine when it stops hurting."

"You're going to walk out," he said. "Why don't you go now?"

"Oh, Ric." She laughed. "Is that all? Oh, Ric, I'm nuts about you. I love you so much. I was afraid you were thinking about—about something else."

He was silent a moment. Suddenly he laughed. She buried her head against his shoulder.

"Come on, she said. Get this car started. I can't have what I want as long as you've got that bullet in your side."

"You think not?" he said. "You don't know me very well." He started the engine, shoved it in gear. They were doing sixty when they reached the highway.

THE END

HELL CAN WAIT
Harry Whittington

Chapter One

She was lying face down on a tan throw rug, wearing only a Bikini swim suit with bra untied, straps like two black threads lost on the bare gold of her back.

She lay flat with chin on folded arms, smiling oddly at the young man who stood over her. From the way she regarded him, you got the faint sensation that she was looking down at him.

They didn't hear me walk across the yard to this place where they were on the patio. It was a sun-stricken area of flagstones, set with a glass-topped, wrought-iron table and aluminum and nylon deck chairs. French doors to the house itself were closed a few feet beyond them.

I stood in the silent morning with the sun beating down on me, waiting for them to admit I existed, despising them without even knowing them and hating myself even more because this was what I had become.

Finally she turned her head casually and removed her sunglasses while looking at me. She was an unusually self-possessed young woman but for a moment, when she recognized me, her eyes widened slightly. She knew me instantly. I had the feeling I'd seen her somewhere before but just then I couldn't remember where or when.

"Angie, if you'd only please—" The pale young man said this much even after he'd realized I was there but before he could check himself. He looked miserable. He looked as if he might cry. He seemed to be in his middle twenties, about five eight, slender, with delicate hands and rounded shoulders. His clothes were cheap and sweated, better than rummage-sale items, but not much. I was sure I'd never seen him before, but then he was that sort of colorless soul you might see one moment and forget in the next.

She shrugged a lotion-slicked shoulder, dismissing him.

He slouched, more miserable than ever. He stared at me in a defiant way and then faced her one more time.

"Please, Angie—"

She did not bother to look at him again. She lay with her upper body quivering on the foam-rubbery cushioning of her breasts, watching me. After that first startled moment, her face regained its composure and she was very casual. She seemed to have forgotten the pale young man except for one throw-away epitaph. "Don't mind Walter," she said to me, and these words put him out of her mind.

"Not a bit," I said. "Any friend of yours—"

"Angie—"

Walter glanced from one to the other of us, miserable and frustrated. Then he shook his head as if something—something unsettled and untenable—were left dangling, and he walked away across the weed-patched lawn toward a seven-year-old Ford coupe parked in the shaded driveway.

I waited for her to say, "Poor Walter" or something, but she had forgotten him. She watched me with a faint smile pulling at the corner of her mouth, her eyes slightly narrowed as if I were something she saw but still didn't believe.

"What do you want?" she said.

"I'm looking for Saul Koons," I told her. The car started out on the drive, the engine purred a moment as if waiting for something that wasn't ever going to happen, and then it roared and the car sped along the drive toward the highway. I glanced around, seeing the bay windows, the cupolas, the cypress wood roofing, the new paint baking on the ancient walls. "This is his house, isn't it?"

She nodded, and there was something in the intensity of her expression that reminded me where I'd seen her. She was Saul Koons' wife and I had seen her at the trial. I remembered her well now.

Every day she'd been there at the trial, sitting rigidly and quietly in the second row, wearing sedate clothes that concealed all this satin and gold body, in hats that hid the soft red-gold of her hair. She hadn't even resembled a dowdy cousin of this doll on the tan rug.

No wonder I hadn't recognized her here now, like this.

But during the trial I had noticed her all right, because day after day she sat in that same spot among the spectators, silent and watchful, never glancing right or left and never talking to anyone else. You noticed something like this because every time a point was made in the trial, the spectators leaned heads together, chewing it over until the judge banged with his gavel. But not her. She was withdrawn even from the people brushing her on each side.

I'd leaned across the defense table and asked Bartley Whitman who she was. He glanced over his shoulder, finding her after a moment in the crowd. "His wife. Saul Koons' wife," he told me.

Now I remembered her testimony.

She had testified, briefly. She'd spoken in a halting, hesitant way—almost as if reluctant to say the things that would brand me—a stranger to her—negligent, drunk, culpable. Yes. All the testimony her husband had given was true, exact. Yes. I was guilty. Bartley Whitman had tried to discredit her. He asked if she'd been drinking that night. She said no, speaking in that sad quiet way. He asked her if she drank habitually and both Koons' lawyers were on their feet before the judge could wipe the look of horror from his face. "Objection, your honor. This question is irrelevant. Immaterial. Without bearing on this case. Further, it is insulting to a woman like Mrs. Koons. An uncalled-for allegation. Mrs. Koons is not on trial here." The judge sustained the objection without hesitation and Bartley Whitman capitulated. He had no further questions. But the woman on that stand bore no resemblance to this lush beauty.

"You like emasculation?" she said.

I stepped forward, looking down at her.

"What?"

"Self-inflicted, of course."

"What are you talking about?"

"You."

She slid her crossed arms down expertly over her breasts and under her arms, catching the two bra straps and securing them between her shoulder blades.

She sat up then, wiping at the thin beads of sweat under her gray eyes in the tinged shadow of her glasses.

She studied my face again with that odd intensity. "You like to suffer? Is that it? What's the word? Are you a masochist?"

"I don't go to any church at all."

"You know what I'm talking about."

"Do I?"

"You know all right. You don't even smile when you make with the smart answers."

This seemed to intrigue her and she chewed on the temple of her sunglasses and looked me over. One thing I could say for her now, here on this patio, she looked like something Saul Koons would own. Saul Koons' lovely young wife.

She'd make him a lovely young widow.

I moved my own gaze over her: the red-gold hair almost shoulder length, the knowing gray eyes, the large mouth, the uptilt of squared chin.

Lovely, she was lovely, not that it mattered to me. You might as well know I didn't regard her as a woman I could ever want or covet. There was no place in me anymore where I could feel such emotions. She was lovely. She was young. But I could look at her, aware she was startlingly beautiful, but unable to feel any other response.

I couldn't see that being Saul Koons' widow would impair her happiness in any way at all, either. I couldn't force myself to believe she could care anything about a man like Koons. I hated him with such bitter intensity that I couldn't believe his own mother would ever give him more than a snarl and a bark.

"Greg Morris." The way she spoke my name almost made a joke of it.

"Yes," I said. "Here I am."

I stood there over her and glanced around at this monstrous old colonial-style house set among cypress trees beside a pear-shaped lake. Perhaps it was the flow of bile in my system discoloring everything I saw, but I found nothing beautiful about this fifteen-room antique. It was placed on a lawn too huge and too sun-baked for a six-man gardening crew to save. Hedges were clipped within an inch of their lives, there were guest houses, a cottage of a boat house, and a grove out behind the house, but it all added up to ugliness.

It was the pride of the community. People in the town of Koons Mills—three miles east on the highway—called it the House, as if it were the only human habitation in the county. Somebody—maybe Bartley Whitman—had told me that Koons himself called the fifteen-acre estate Cedar Hill, and this figured. There were no cedars, and no hill. The house was situated in a cypress grove beside a lake on flat hot soil.

It was an ancient house, built in the late nineties and constantly repaired and restored since then. There was nothing but the look of money wastefully squandered here—a smell of money even in the flower beds where roses smelled like sweaty fifty-cent pieces instead of roses, and the jasmine had the scent of a disinfectant used in banks.

Everything smelled of money, even the twenty-six-year-old wife sunning herself in the Bikini, and even the pale frightened young man who went scurrying off across the yard when I appeared. I didn't have any notion as to whether this Walter was her lover or not, but I hoped he was. Anything that would discomfit Saul Koons offered me a bitter kind of pleasure.

"Never thought it," she said.

"What now?"

"Never thought I'd see you here," she said, shaking her head.

She glanced around the tan rug, found a pack of filter-tipped cigarettes, extended the pack toward me. I shook my head.

"A drink?" she said. "A last hearty meal?"

"I'm looking for your husband, Mrs. Koons."

"What makes you think you'd find him here?"

"Won't I?"

"This time of day?"

"Doesn't he live here?"

"Whenever he can make it," she said.

"They told me I could find him here."

"Who told you that?"

I shrugged. Nobody had told me. I'd assumed it, I'd asked only where Saul Koons lived. A man I stopped on Main Street in Koons Mills had said, "Ever'body knows the Koons' place. The House. Out on the highway. Three mile. Maybe three and a half." A worn, leathery-faced man in coveralls, he had nodded in this general direction, too depleted by the heat to lift his arm high enough to point.

"He's not here," she said. I got the feeling that she was getting a charge out of this, the same kind of pleasure she'd get from keeping an ant from returning into its hill.

"Where is he?"

"The mills. He's at the mills."

I felt the sudden rush of new anger. Nobody in the town had mentioned the mills. I hadn't asked, but I hadn't known to ask, and nobody had volunteered that much information. They knew me in town, too; even the ones who had never seen me before, they knew me.

"How far?" I asked her.

She adjusted the bra. "You got a car?"

"How far?"

"I just wondered if you had a car."

"Don't do me any favors, Mrs. Koons."

She smiled again, scraping a red fingernail along the inside of her leg. "Certainly not."

"How far?"

She shrugged and the shrug indicated distance meant nothing to her. She didn't even fill the gas tanks of her cars. She paid someone to do that for her.

"About eight miles. Straight across town. You can't miss it. You can smell it. Even when you're upwind. A pulp mill. You can't miss it."

"Thanks."

I turned to walk away. Her voice reached out after me, in a casual, taunting tone.

"Morris?"

I stopped.

"Tell me something?"

I glanced over my shoulder. "All right."

"Why the mills?"

"I told you. I want to see your husband."

"That's what I mean," she said. "Haven't you had enough?"

Chapter Two

I had walked almost half of those eight miles from the House to the mills when I heard the sirens screaming along the road behind me.

I jerked my head around, looking back over my shoulder, feeling the muscles tighten like a cramp in my stomach. Why was I afraid? What was I afraid of? There wasn't any quick answer to this. All I could think was, this was Saul Koons' town. It was named for him, wasn't it?

What else did I need to fear?

I saw the cars behind me, and they grew larger at ninety miles an hour, and their sirens wailed.

They raced past me, the wind from them hot and sharp as a blow across the face.

I recognized the man in the green-and-white cruiser. It was Sheriff Harley Baskins himself, a hulking blob of a man even behind the steering wheel of his car.

I felt my fists knot at my sides. Just this fleeting glimpse of Harley Baskins was enough to churn it all up in my mind.

I shook my head, refusing to think about it. What was the profit in thinking about it? What did I gain by torturing myself with the perjury, the lies, the purchased testimony? How did it help any to remember the way he had sat there on that stand, looking as though he pitied me all the time as he piled one lie on top of another, saying over and over that he was a man doing his duty, as he had always done it for sixteen years, without fear or favor. He had to tell the truth, no matter whom he hurt. And he went on lying.

I walked faster on the shoulder of the highway. The two cruisers and the ambulance passed me in the space of one breath. Yet it seemed to take a long time, a long, slow time. Then they were gone and I was alone on the hot road again.

I wiped at my face with a handkerchief. It was silent on the highway again. The heat came down from the sun and up in waves from the asphalt. It was the hot kind of day that would sweat anything out except the hate inside me, hate that was tamped down so tight that I felt as though I would burst with it.

I walked faster, hurrying.

The ambulance was turned around, headed back toward town, when I got to the scene of the accident. They were carrying a woman and a man on stretchers from the overturned car to the ambulance. Near the truck, I saw this man in overalls. He was on his knees, sobbing with his hands covering his face. The sheriff and his deputies were standing in a circle around him. They were watching him but they did not speak to him.

Nobody paid any attention to me and I did not stop walking. I stayed on the shoulder across the highway from where the pickup truck had plowed into the sedan.

My gaze struck against the sign painted on the door of the pickup truck. KOONS MILLS. INSTANT DELIVERIES.

I thought I was going to be ill. For a moment I could not keep walking. I couldn't do anything but stare at that sign painted on the truck door. It was as though if there were a God in heaven at all, He could not get enough pleasure from tormenting me. Greg Morris. Greg Morris, it's been almost a year now, there's a scab over the old wound, it's almost healing, let's rip it away, let's expose it. Let's rub some salt in it. Why did I have to get here just at this instant in time to see this particular truck, that overturned car, and the victims, bloody and inert on stretchers borne toward an ambulance?

The ambulance started up and sped toward town with its siren screaming.

The scream of the siren pulled me out of it and I walked away from the cars parked along the highway. I didn't want to look back, but I couldn't help it. And when I did, all I could see was the sign on that truck door.

The Koons pulpwood mills were about a dozen corrugated-tin-roofed buildings a mile or so off the highway between the Seaboard Railroad tracks and the Koons River. The first thing I saw when I walked down the narrow secondary road to the mills was the string of flatcars loaded with sawed lengths of soft pine pulpwoods. I had begun to smell the place before I left the highway. In one of those sheds sodium sulphate was chewing up the pine logs to pulp that would make wrapping paper and paper board.

There was a man sitting in a small crib sentry house at the entrance of the mill yard. He did not glance up as I walked past. But when I was inside the yard, I heard movement and looked back. He was standing in the doorway of the crib watching me.

He wore a gun in a holster at his belt.

Men were leaning in the doorways of all the sheds along the road. Halfway down this string of buildings I saw a new white two-storied structure that looked like an administration building and I felt the tension in me as I walked toward it.

Nobody spoke to me as I walked down the paved road. There were side alleyways between the sheds, leading on one side to the railroad, and on the other to the river. None of the men seemed to be working in the middle of the afternoon. But none of them talked to each other, either. They all seemed to be watching me. They were silent, their faces set and rigid, unblinking eyes like marbles in their sockets.

I had the crazy feeling that they were watching me because they were expecting me. This didn't make sense. How would they know I was coming out here?

I shrugged my shirt up on my shoulders, thinking about Angie Koons. Would Koons' wife have called ahead to say that Greg Morris was on his way out to the mills?

I couldn't buy that one. I couldn't make myself believe she would care enough where I went to bother calling anyone.

I heard the sound of a car speeding behind me and I moved from the center of the road.

Sheriff Harley Baskins' green-and-white cruiser sped past me. He didn't glance toward me. He parked outside the new white office building, radio aerial snapping.

He got out from under the steering wheel, stepped out of the cruiser. He was a thick-shouldered man, six feet tall, weighing over two hundred pounds in his denim shirt, khaki trousers and sweat-stained Stetson. He was forty but there was the look about him of the man who had once been very handsome and was now gone to lard. His nose sat small and straight in his overfed face. There was a spoiled twist to his mouth. I remembered that I had even thought during the trial, seeing him in the courtroom, that here was a man who'd been elected best-looking in high school and hadn't realized yet that his black curls were receding at his temples and his chest had sagged.

There were half a dozen men sitting in the shaft of shade outside the office door. Baskins spoke to them and each of them smiled and spoke his name as he passed them, going through the screen door.

It slammed behind him and he was gone before I got to the office. The men sitting in the shade stared up at me. The expression in their faces did not alter. Across the street three men whispered together. One of them laughed, and it was as though I could feel the impact of their whispers and their laughter all the way across the hot company street.

I let the screen door slam behind me.

There were fifteen or twenty desks in this wide front room. A receptionist sat at a telephone switchboard inside the doorway. The women and the men at the desks stopped working, stopped talking, and stared at me. It seemed to me they even stopped breathing while I was in the room.

I asked the receptionist for Saul Koons' office. She didn't speak, only inclined her head toward a stairway at my left.

I turned my back on the silent, staring faces and climbed the stairs. I could hear the distant throb of motors that seemed to vibrate from the earth itself. This building was air conditioned but heat seemed to have followed me through the front door.

I came off the stairs into an office much like the one below except that this one was smaller and at its rear were doors, closed and marked PRIVATE.

A woman looked up from one of the desks. Folders were stacked before her, she worked with a pencil caught between her fingers and there was a pencil smudge across her nose. She was in her early thirties and wore a white shirtwaist tightly buttoned at her throat.

"I'd like to see Saul Koons."

"Do you have an appointment with *Mister* Koons?"

"No. But what I want won't take long."

What did I want? I had come to this place with my plans made, I knew what I wanted, what I was going to do, but maybe right now I'd accept an admission from him that everything he'd done to me was based on lies. I had come here looking for justice. Justice? I felt a sudden urge to wild laughter at this thought. Yet justice was all I wanted. Justice. The one impossible quality. And this was what I wanted.

"I'm sorry, you can't see Mr. Koons without an appointment."

"I am going to see him."

My voice rose slightly whether I willed it or not. The silent people at the silent desks sat straighter. Their gazes became more focused, fixed harder upon me. "You want to tell him I'm here, or do I just walk in?"

"Please, sir. Don't cause a disturbance."

"I'm not causing a disturbance. I want to see Saul Koons. If you'll tell him I'm here, there'll be no disturbance at all."

"I'm sorry, sir. I can't do that."

"Then I'll go on in—"

I moved to go past her. She jumped up from her desk. Her face was colorless.

"Please, sir—"

A young man had moved from one of the desks. He came up quickly behind me and caught my arm.

I shook his hand from my arm so violently that for an instant he lost his balance.

He caught himself. "Shall I call the police, sir?"

I stared at him. He was somewhere in his twenties, overwhelmed with his own sense of importance. And clearest of all was the fact that he knew me, recognized me, and looked along his nose at me.

"You want to call the police, sonny, you do it," I said. "You do whatever you want to."

When I didn't wilt at his first attack, he became nonplused, looking around helplessly. Somebody snickered.

"You better go," he said. "You better get out of here while you can."

"No," I said. "I came out here to see old man Koons. And I'm going to see him."

"You're going to end up in jail."

"You've made that threat once, sonny," I said. "I told you. Go ahead. Just don't try to stop me."

He stared at me, and then his gaze fell away. He looked around the room but nobody moved.

Then the door at the rear of the outer office opened, and there was a faint sound as every employee in the room inhaled sharply.

Saul Koons stepped through the doorway and there was deadly silence. Here was the man I had come to see. Nobody breathed. Our gazes met and held across that room, and now all they were waiting for was to see which one of us would back down first.

Chapter Three

He was a big man, standing well over six feet tall with wide, raw-boned shoulders. But there was a sense of bigness about him more than a reality. He was somewhere between fifty-five and sixty, probably nearer sixty, though he didn't even admit to being fifty-five. In the past few years it was as though something had been devouring the fleshy fat from his body. He'd always worn a size seventeen collar and he still wore it though it was loose on his neck. His suits were tailored for him but the expensive fabrics hung on his spare frame now. Like an old buzzard, time had been chewing away at the strings of his flesh. His weather-beaten face was rutted with lines down across his cheeks, around his mouth, and one wrinkle cut across his chin like a cleft.

I stared at him and I could feel this helpless sense of outrage. His gaze struck against mine and I saw he wasn't even surprised to find me here.

When he had stepped through his private doorway he paused, turned slightly and Sheriff Harley Baskins minced past him into the outer office.

Baskins had his five-gallon Stetson in his hands now, and though he was grossly huge, he looked comparatively small beside Koons—he looked like an average man gone to lard, while no matter how you hated Koons you had to admit he had the look of a giant waging a losing battle against the years.

Baskins still didn't bother looking at me. He was giving Koons a big smile. "Now about that boy, Saul. You better do something about him."

"I told you, Harley. My personnel people handle these matters—"

"It won't work this time, Saul. He was likkered up—"

"Then you take care of it." Saul Koons' voice was a throaty baritone, edged with that sharp impatience of a man who hates ever to say the same thing twice.

"He was likkered, Saul—"

"You heard me, Harley. You heard what I said. Take care of it."

"Suppose I can't?"

Saul Koons laughed abruptly at this, and the laughter pulled at those ruts in his leather-colored face.

"That'll be what I'll have to see, Harley. Anything you can't handle—"

Baskins would have spoken again, but Saul knew how to handle him too well. He laughed again, put his arm about the sheriff's shoulders and moved him across the office toward me.

They were almost to the railing when Baskins saw me.

He stopped walking. His gaze struck against mine. I saw the blood mount behind the sunbaked flesh of his face.

"Morris. What are you doing here?"

"I came to see Koons," I said.

Saul Koons laughed again, slapping Baskin on the shoulder. "It's all right, Baskins. You take care of this other little matter for me and everything will be fine."

Baskins looked me over again. He said to Koons, "You sure you're O.K.?"

Koons laughed. "Why wouldn't I be all right? You go ahead." The slap he gave Baskins' shoulder dismissed him. For another moment Baskins stared straight into my face and then he walked past me.

Koons looked me over. Although we were almost of equal height, I got that same old feeling that he was looking down at me. I had gotten that feeling the first time I saw him and that wasn't even here in this part of the country where they named even rivers after his family.

"I want to talk to you," I said. There was more belligerence in my tone than I'd intended but that was because the way he looked at me put me on the offensive.

"Why, any time," he said. "Come right in. Come right in."

It was easy to believe he didn't have the faintest memory of all the things he had done to me, or the reasons I had for hating him, wanting even to see him dead. He stepped back and motioned me ahead of him into his office.

I could feel myself trembling as I walked past him.

He closed the office door behind me. The office was about twenty by twenty with a picture window overlooking the other buildings and roads of the mill. There were large framed pictures of other Koons males and a photo of Angie Koons on his wide flat desk. The desk itself was highly polished with only a small stack of papers on the blotter in front of a judge's-type office chair. The office furniture was heavy leather and the wall-to-wall carpeting was thick and tan.

He motioned me to a chair beside his desk. As he went around to his own chair he said, "You find me a little upset, Morris. This business with the sheriff. Of course you remember Harley Baskins—from the little trial." He appeared not to notice the way I tightened up at those words. "One of my trucks was involved in an accident on the highway. Car swerved, ran into my driver. You have to watch these things. These bastards pull these tricks, then try to take me for a big settlement—"

By now I was poised on the edge of that chair, ready to lunge across the desk and throttle him. He glanced at me and smiled. "I don't mean you, Morris, of course—"

"Why not?" My voice shook.

"Come now. It's not the same thing at all. You and I were involved in an accident. I know that you don't feel at fault in any sense—"

"You know bastardly well I wasn't at—"

His voice rode over mine, but smoothly—very smooth. "But with these people it's different. It's almost a racket, a business. Some of them get to needing money and it's almost as if they say, We'll get tangled up with a Koons Mill truck and sue them—well, an occupational hazard, I suppose."

I stood up. "It must be wonderful. Sit up here protected, and tell yourself you're right, no matter what you do."

"Oh, no. No. I never tell myself I'm right. I never consider that. I do what I have to do, Morris. You'd have to be in my place to understand a thing like this. Hundreds of employees—millions of dollars invested. Why, I've only a small pulp-process plant out there, but it cost over a million to install it alone. I've all these responsibilities—and if you don't think there are coyotes yapping at my heels all the time, you were never so wrong."

"Well, it must be nice to tell yourself that."

He shook his head. "Morris, I'm truly sorry to see a man like you let himself take such an attitude. You've got to realize, man, that our very civilization is based upon law—and the obedience to it. Now, I've got every kind of pity for you—you lost your wife, your young, lovely wife—and on top of that you were subjected to a long recovery in a hospital and then faced with an unpleasant ordeal in court. I can see by your attitude that you blame me for what happened to you."

I could barely speak. "You know a better man I could blame?"

"Oh, I understand the way you feel. I know how you must have loved your wife—this was in everything you said or did. But I'm afraid you've let your grief blind you to the true facts."

"The true facts? The true facts are that you ran into my car and killed my wife. The true facts are that you bought witnesses, you lied, you made a joke out of a courtroom, you ruined me and you sit here untouched—and so damned sure you are untouchable."

He exhaled heavily. He pushed his hand along his head. "Will you listen to me a moment?"

"I listened to you. In that courtroom. I listened to your perjured witnesses, your lies, your lawyers—"

"I'm sorry about all that. I'm sorry for everything that happened to you, Morris, whether you believe me or not."

"I don't believe you're sorry at all. Not yet."

He shook his head. "I'm trying to help you, Morris. The best way I can. I know that you have suffered a great loss, but make up your mind to one thing: the case in court went entirely against you. But face up to this. It was in a court of law."

I laughed at that, a sound that tore out of me. "Law? Damn few law courts are places of law any more. Lawyers and judges have made a game out of it, with certain moves allowed, and certain moves prohibited so that truth and justice have nothing to do with a case. But that courtroom was no more a place of law than this office is. That's all it was—an extension of this office where people did just what you told them to do."

"Naturally, you're bitter."

"Oh, naturally. But save your phony sympathy—"

"I am truly sorry for what happened."

"Are you? And yet you set it all up. A judge that made subtle prejudicial instructions to the jury. Witnesses that lied. Facts suppressed—"

He stood up suddenly. His face was hard and his eyes were cold. We faced each other across that desk.

"I'm sorry about your bitterness, Morris. About your loss. But I cannot spend any more time listening to you. You faced the due processes of law and you lost. I can give you just one bit of advice. You had a bad time. I'm sorry about that. But you were in the wrong. The best thing you can do is accept it. Live with it. It's a sad thing. I don't deny that. But you've got to get it out of your mind and start over again."

I stared at him. "God knows why I wasted my time coming here—"

"God knows."

"I came to give you one last chance to undo some of the wrong—"

"I've done no wrong, Morris. You were tried in a court of law. I didn't try you. You were found guilty. I didn't find you guilty. You were ordered to pay. It was out of my hands."

"It was your organized plan, Koons. Every step of the way. And I can't live with that. When I came in here I had some fool idea that you were human enough to undo some of the wrong. No matter what I wanted to do, I had to give you this last chance, Koons. And I can tell you this. It's not over."

He shrugged. He turned his wide back on me and walked to the window. His deep voice was very low. "Then I am sorry for you, Morris. Sorry about what happened—sorrier about what is ahead for you."

"What's that supposed to mean?"

He didn't turn from the window. He went on staring out into the sun-blasted yard of his pulp mill.

"Just this. Stop beating your head against stone walls, boy."

"No. I'm here, Koons. Here in your town. I'm going to stay here.... You're going to pay for what you've done."

He turned then from the window. His lined face looked gray and he winced. But his mouth was taut and there was no look of weakness about him.

"You're smarter than this, Morris."

"No. I *was* smarter than this."

"You better get smart again. Not for me. I can take care of myself."

"Yes. You sure proved that."

"Right. Then forget it, Morris. You got sense enough to realize nobody wanted any of this to happen. None of it. But sometimes we're caught in something we didn't make, boy."

He stood tall and there was something almost like anguish in his face. I frowned, feeling empty, staring at him. It didn't balance. It was all out of plumb. It was so alien to what I knew about him, I couldn't believe it. I wouldn't believe it. He sounded almost human, but I knew better.

I said, "But you came out of it fine. I didn't, and that's the difference."

He walked away from the window, went across the deep carpeting to his gleaming bar. He opened a paneled door and removed two glasses, a tray of ice. He glanced over his shoulder.

"I want you to drink with me, Morris.... I've an idea you'll come to your senses, and you'll regret all this. Will you drink to that?"

I shook my head. That anguish I'd seen in his eyes troubled me, but this was no time to be misled by him, or to feel pity for him.

"I don't want to drink with you, Koons."

He studied me a moment and then calmly replaced the glasses and the ice. He closed the paneled door and stood straight again. His face was chilled, the hated face I remembered.

"Well," he said. "Then, goodbye, Morris."

"I'll see you," I replied. "I'll be here."

"Well, there you are," he said. His face was lined, gray. He shook his head. "But on the other hand, I wouldn't drink to that."

Chapter Four

The mill hands leaned against the stacks of pulpwood, against the doors of the tin-roofed sheds, the uprights. The sun was still a white blister, and the shadows were narrow and tight in the company street but it was as if a whistle had blown ending the work period.

The men grinned. It was the odd mirthless kind of grin you might see on faces of vigilantes watching a hanging. There was nothing to share in it. As I walked away from the white administration building it was as if I were seeing the same grin on every face. Each face was leathery and brown and drawn by sun and smell of wood pulp churning in the sulphate baths. All the faces were thin and hard, and the eyes were narrow and chilled with this soulless grin. It was as if they were all one man, one ugly grinning face.

As I walked between them they nudged each other, nodding toward me and grinning as if they had never seen anything quite like me outside a circus sideshow. One man stepped away from a woodshed wall.

"You lost, friend?" the man said. His voice carried in the hot silence along the hot company street.

I didn't read anything hilarious about this line but all the mill hands laughed. Maybe it was the delivery.

I didn't say anything. I kept walking in the middle of the asphalt paved road. I didn't need a Ouija board to tell me trouble was brewing here.

"Maybe you're looking for work?" another one called. He was even a finer comedian than the first. The loungers really laughed at this.

They took it up, making a slow chorus of it as I walked.

"You looking for work?"

"What kind of work do you do?"

"What you want around here?"

One of the men walked out into the road. He wore a narrow-brimmed felt hat, a denim shirt buttoned tight at his throat. His trousers were speckled with pine sawdust.

"Hey there, fellow. We'uns ast you a question. What's the matter? You can't answer a question?"

"Maybe he's too good to answer a question."

This was the best laugh-line any of them had heard. It registered high on their laugh meter.

A man called from the street ahead.

"Hey, you city bastard. Why can't you talk when a man asks you a question?"

Another man called from behind me. "Now wait. Wait a minute. He ain't no bastard."

"You think not?"

"I got the certain feeling he ain't. No, sir. More a son of a bitch. You look at him—way the light strikes him now—don't you reckon he's more a son of a bitch?"

Four men stepped out into the street, peering at me as if trying to decide. They formed a line across the narrow company road at the end of a saw shed. They stood there, staring at me, grinning.

I paused. It was plain enough in their faces, I was going to have to fight my way past them on the company street. I glanced around. The sentry house was still a block away. The guard stood there, watching. The mill hands lined both sides of the street, grinning, waiting. Behind me was the white administration building, the pulp plant, to the left was the river. At my right a small clay lane, ankle-deep in sawdust, led to the railroad tracks where the flatcars were strung out a mile long and stacked with pine logs.

I looked at the four men ranged across the company road. I saw nothing in their faces except the sweat, the heat, and an unexplained hatred for me. Their faces begged me to try to pass between them on the company road.

The hell with them. I could look at them and see the ignorance in their faces. I was a man somebody had told them to hate and they hated me. But my battle was not with them, only with Saul Koons who owned them. At least this was what I thought then. I didn't want any trouble with them. I paused and then I turned to my right, going between the two sheds along the lane toward the railroad.

There was a sound behind me that was like nothing more than a pleased sigh. I had done just what they wanted. The men along the company street moved away from the buildings, hurrying along the street to the lane.

The four who had barred the company street now followed me down the lane.

I didn't walk faster or slower, only kept moving through the sawdust toward the railroad.

The lane behind me was filled with men.

Others came around the sheds, watching as I walked away from the buildings toward the railroad cars.

I could hear them talking behind me and I could feel the movement of them toward me and the anger and hatred began to build up. At first I didn't feel it, I was already so full of hatred—for Saul Koons, for the law courts he controlled, for the people who had perjured themselves for him, and the sudden rage I felt toward these stupid men was almost that same hatred.

I felt the tension drawing me taut and I looked around, wondering what I would do, what I would be able to do against them. I knew only one thing: it would be good to return some of the hatred I had been living with all these months.

I was almost to the tracks. I looked both ways trying to decide which way to walk, what to do. The stacked flatcars were linked together as far as I could see.

Suddenly a short piece of pinewood struck me in the middle of the back. I was drawn tense, waiting for them to make some move, but I hadn't expected this.

The breath exploded out of me and I staggered, losing my balance.

The laughter erupted behind me, suddenly loud, and suddenly ceasing.

A man's laughing voice said in mock anger, "Goddamn, Earl. You do that, Earl? Goddamn, you shouldn't've done that."

Another called, laughing, "You want to make him mad?"

I had walked up close to the railroad cars before the hatred exploded in me and I heeled around, staring at them. My stomach was twisted with the hatred, tied up in knots. I was aware of everything, those faces, railcars stacked high with pulpwood, sawdust thick under my feet from the wood grinders. Both ways along the tracks the cars were piled high. Before me these men were ringed, tense and waiting, faces pulled with that meaningless grin.

I pressed my back against one of the cars.

I stared back at them. I didn't try to count them. It didn't matter how many grinning cracker faces were there in front of me. I had walked through them, trying to walk away from a senseless fight, trying to avoid trouble. Hell, why walk away from it? Wasn't this the reason I had come here? What was the matter with me? Wasn't this what I wanted? I was nothing any more except hatred, I was sick with the way I hated, and until this moment it had all been bottled up in me—and anything that would relieve that hatred was good. I was through walking away from them.

"Lost, mister?" One of the four men stepped closer.

Behind him they laughed, spurring him forward. Somebody had to start it, and he was elected. The other three stayed a step behind him but moved slowly forward, too.

"You lost?" he said. "We'll show you how to get out of here."

Somebody in the crowd called, "Let's show him how to get out of here."

"Way out, so he won't never get lost in here again." They all laughed at this.

By now the joker was near to me. I could smell him. I couldn't see his face though, except as a red blur with a grin spinning in it.

I held myself as loosely as possible, trying not to telegraph any of the contempt I felt for him, or the way I was setting myself to hit him in the middle of that grin. All I wanted suddenly was to smash one grin from one of those faces.

I stared at the nearest man, at the crowding knot of men behind him, the grinning faces in the lane that led down from the company road and the faces along the sheds. But they seemed to be only one face: it belonged to Saul Koons.

Then I saw Sheriff Harley Baskins standing near one of the pay shacks about forty yards away from the tracks. He was with two men in white shirts and this meant they were office workers, and they had come down from the white administration building to watch. They were not speaking, and they were not grinning, they were merely watching in a detached way as though none of this remotely concerned them.

I pulled my head upward and across the glittering tin sheds I could see the big picture window of Saul Koons' office. The sun glinted, reflected on that window from the sheds. It was easy to imagine the old man was standing there behind that sun-glinting window. I told myself his face was pulled in the same grin these mill workers wore and the rage gorged up and I struck out, driving my fist into the nearest face.

I put everything I had into that blow. I didn't fool myself. I wasn't going to last long. I brought my fist upward, not trying for the jaw. I smashed my fist between his eyes and when I hit him there was the sharp splatting sound of my knuckles against his nose structure.

Joker staggered and went sagging backward against the man behind him.

You might have thought there would be a yell from the crowd. But there was not a sound. Only one thing happened in that moment: they stopped grinning. As one man they stopped grinning. I wondered if old

Saul up behind that window had stopped grinning. Because it was his nose I broke, his face I smashed.

Something hit me on the left side of the head.

I swung around, saw only a blur as a short piece of wood struck me. I stumbled back against the flatcar and they surged forward on me.

I began swinging wildly. There were too many of them and they came upon me too fast but I swung as hard as I could, as long as I could.

I wanted to yell with the fury I felt. I know I growled, making the only sound beside those tracks. I was a savage animal. For the first time in a year I was able to strike back at the people I despised. I let them crowd in as close as they could and I hit them low, under the belt, in the groin as I went down to my knees. I was still hitting them with my elbow and the back of my fist when I could wrench it free.

I was down on my knees, still swinging, and I came up swinging and I felt my fist dig into bodies, smash against faces and then for one instant I was on my feet again, standing in a small cleared place beside that flatcar.

Then the wood knots came flying at me. The men along the side of the saw shed were hurling them like bricks and they ran forward throwing them.

I threw up my arms to cover my head and they brought their clubs down on my shoulders and my head and the back of my neck as I fell. They used them on my kidneys, my spine and the backs of my legs.

I staggered and fell under their clubs. I struck on my knees and the clubs came down, harder. I crouched on the ground with my knees up and my head under my arms like a Moslem at prayer. But that wasn't good enough for them. They crowded in, bringing down those pine clubs until I was sprawled out on the ground and my face was pressed in it and they used those clubs over my body until I no longer knew it, until I no longer felt it at all.

I don't know how long it lasted.

I heard their voices but it was as if from a great distance. Nearer there was only the thunder of agony inside me, a rushing sound in my ears.

I felt myself being lifted. At first I knew it only because my face was pulled away from the sweet coolness of the dirt under the sawdust.

I was lifted the way a sack of feed is hoisted and I was thrown upward. Then I struck at the top of the stacked pine logs and I felt the rough bark against my face, but there was no longer any sensation of pain. It was very soft up there and very fragrant and then suddenly I didn't remember anything else.

The laughter and the talk was distant, and then it ceased and went away and I didn't hear it anymore.

I did not move. The pine logs were like feathers under my body. As long as I lay still I was all right but the agony was inexpressible when I moved at all.

I don't know how many hours I stayed there on top of the logs. I knew it grew dark because when I opened my eyes I no longer saw the blood-red blur before my eyes. Now I saw only the blackness, and then there was the distant sound of an engine, and the train was moving, slowly picking up speed. I could not care. The flatcar rocked, and then moved more smoothly as the train moved faster.

My body was on fire as if I had a high fever. The night wind was strong and chilled against my fevered flesh. For a long time I lay there on the stacked logs feeling the jolt of the car as the train raced faster.

I lifted my head. The lights of the mill receded from me, blown away on the wind, growing smaller until they were only a glow and then I was whipped around a curve and the lights were gone. There was only the darkness, the smell of the pine, the jolting of the train.

Finally I was able to sit erect. Now I began to watch for the town. Koons Mills. The train slowed and I saw the lights of the town ahead of me.

I moved painfully over to the edge of the logs.

I set myself and shoved, leaping outward, but I was already so full of pain that I felt nothing when I struck the roadbed. When I rolled down into the ditch it was as though I were turning over on a soft bed.

Chapter Five

The night was still and hot, the ground was stony, and finally I no longer liked lying there in the ditch. I sat up, struck a match and checked my wrist watch. It was almost eight.

I got up in the darkness and silence that had settled along the tracks. In the distance I could see the glow from the town lights. I couldn't tell how far the town was. In my condition anything more than three steps was too far.

I took a deep breath, bit down on my bottom lip and moved out of the ditch to a dirt road that ran through palmettos and jack oaks to the highway. Distantly I could hear the cars racing past, whispering on the asphalt. It took me three years to walk to the highway but when I made it and looked at my watch again, it was only ten after eight.

I stood very straight and tall to keep from staggering and walked toward the lights of Koons Mills. A few cars went past, but none slowed down. I stayed in the shadows far out on the highway shoulder.

I kept lifting my feet in a kind of slow and painful rhythm. When I reached Main Street in Koons Mills the town was almost deserted. A few cars were parked before the drug store and near the movie theatre. A Western picture was playing and the cashier was buffing her fingernails in the ticket office. She glanced up and shook her head when I went by. I guess she thought I was another drunk.

I had to stop outside the hotel and lean against the building until the trembling stopped. Reaction set in and I was shaking all over. For a moment I couldn't stop trembling. Even my teeth chattered.

The desk clerk looked up when I crossed the lobby. I had stopped shaking and now all the pain was localized behind my eyeballs.

When the clerk saw me he winced. It was like looking in a mirror. I could see what a wreck I was.

"Mr. Morris."

I managed to walk as far as the desk. I leaned against it and stood there looking at him, tasting the blood in my mouth while I waited.

"Mr. Morris. I have your bag here. I packed it. It's waiting for you."

I had to clench my teeth tight and hang on to the desk to keep from yelling at him. I could feel the shaking starting deep inside me. I held on, staring at him.

He pushed my suitcase around the side of the desk with his foot. He was a mild-appearing man in his middle thirties, almost bald and wearing a hearing aid with lines leading from his ear into his wilted collar. He looked unhappy about the whole thing.

"What's the idea?" I was finally able to speak. "What the hell's the idea?"

"I was trying to help."

"Who asked for favors? Did I pay for my room?"

"Yes. You did, sir. But—well, there were some changes. You see we had to take your room back." His hands shook. He opened the drawer behind his desk, took out some bills. "Naturally, we'll refund—"

"I don't want a refund. I want a room."

"I'm sorry, sir."

"I'm not going anywhere." The room was spinning, and he whirled past my head. "I couldn't—go anywhere. All want is a room. I've got to lie down—"

"I'm sorry, sir—"

"Damn it. You hear me. I want a room."

"I'm sorry. I'm trying to tell you. Nothing available Mr. Morris. We have nothing available."

I half sprawled across the desk, reaching for the telephone. A calendar and a glass container of paper clips toppled over. He leaped forward. "What's the matter?" he said. "What are you trying to do?"

"I'm calling Whitman. Bartley Whitman. Know him?" My hands shook on the telephone.

"Yes, sir, your lawyer—"

"Right. Lawyer. There might be some reason you can refuse me a room, but I'm going to know it. I'm going to know it—" My hands were swollen and it was hard to dial even the three numbers of Whitman's local telephone.

He touched my hand with his, stopping me. "Never mind," he said.

I looked up at him. He was still whirling.

"Never mind making that call. It may cause a little trouble—but—I can let you have a room—for tonight."

"All right. Where is it?"

He found a key. "I packed your bags, sir. Myself."

"Why?"

"Why? Well, we—thought you'd be taking the first bus out of town and—"

"Why?"

"Well, sir, since what happened to you—today—"

"You've heard about that?"

He nodded, picking up my bag and moving toward the small self-service elevator. "Everybody's heard about it," he said.

I didn't bother unpacking my bag. When the clerk set it down in my room, I took one look at it and then fell face down across my bed.

I reached around, hardly knowing what I did, and pulled a blanket over my shoulders. After a while the shaking stopped and I sank into a kind of warm oblivion.

For a long time I didn't know where I was. I was nowhere. I was in a school, staring out a window, wishing I was in the open. I was in night school studying accounting, still staring out of a window, still wishing I was somewhere else. Maybe that was the story of my life. Greg Morris. Born wishing he was in some better place. I remember I did feel that way most of my life until I met Cora. And the funny part of that was, we were not for each other. She loved fishing and hunting, camping— and I got miserable the first time I heard the song of a mosquito. People used to laugh—in that strange dream world where I once lived where people did laugh—and say that Cora and I were made for somebody else. I liked to dance. I liked music. I liked one drink and a really good band somewhere. For Cora this was wasting your life. So we fell in love like nobody ever loved before. Nobody ever tried to keep us apart and yet it was as though we could not be together enough, not close enough, not often enough. For the first time I was Greg Morris, the guy contented to be where he was.

The old desire for the greener pastures, the slicker dame, the faraway places didn't even die a lingering death. I just held Cora close, smelling the warm good smell of her hair, and I would have died just to stay all the time right there where I was.

Nothing I had was good enough for her. That was me speaking. She didn't want much. She liked to fish, but if she couldn't afford a fancy rod and reel set, why she'd settle for a cane pole, line and earthworms. It was her idea that people spent too much time trying to accumulate a lot of things they could never use or take with them. She wanted just enough in the bank so I wouldn't worry, and some quiet place where we could be alone together and she could get in a little fishing.

God, she was wonderful.

Where were we going on our honeymoon? Where else? Cora had read about the bass fishing at a place called Rainbow Lake. I tried to tell her every mud hole was called Rainbow Lake, but I knew all the time that if Rainbow Lake was what she wanted that was what she was going to have.

We were driving along peaceful and silly, talking about stupid things that don't mean anything to anybody else, and not much to you, just the warm noises you make when you're too much in love to be quiet about it. What were we talking about? About how much farther it was to Rainbow Lake than we had planned, or else we'd spent too much time in that motel last night. We were married one whole day and she was pressed close against me in the warm car and the quiet night and it was as though we had this whole road to ourselves. And we talked, about the accounting firm I was opening, the income tax work I'd get that would put us on our feet that first year—and she was saying I was silly to worry about too much, because we didn't need too much—not until we began to have babies. "Though we might have begun last night," she said, smiling up at me.

I grinned at her. "I tried hard enough."

She laughed. "You tried often enough, anyway."

"I hope they got a bed at Rainbow Lake."

"It's fun on the floor," she said.

"Oh? Do you like it on the floor?"

She laughed at me. "My God I never knew you were suspicious."

"Answer me. Do you?"

"No," she said. "It gives me the hiccoughs."

I held her closer. God, she was wonderful.

I don't know where that car came from, maybe from hell itself. First I saw the lights racing out of a side road. It all happened terribly swiftly and yet with an interminable, sickening slowness. There was the car in front, and behind it another car as though they were racing.

The car ahead swerved out onto the highway blasting toward us, the other car racing along behind it. Neither Cora nor I spoke. There was no time for words. There wasn't even a chance to say goodbye to her.

The car in front came directly at us, on the wrong side of the road, swerving and bouncing as though it had gone out of control on the turn.

I slammed on brakes. I tried to turn the car to the right to go off the highway. I wanted no argument with this insane man, whoever he was. If he wanted the highway, he could have it. Only I never even got a chance to finish that thought. The big black car struck us at an angle across the front left fender, plowing us ahead of it across the shoulder and down the embankment.

I don't even remember when the car stopped turning over.

I woke up in a hospital. For two weeks they fed me through a tube.

One week, I don't even remember which one it was, they told me I was luckier than Cora. I was alive. Cora was dead.

God, was I lucky....

I was in a wheelchair when a nurse told me I had a visitor. I told her to tell him to go to hell. I didn't want to see anybody. It was a hell of a thing. I'd be sitting there and all of a sudden I would start to cry. The tears would well up in my eyes and spill, and my throat would choke up.

I didn't want anybody to see me like that.

He kept coming back, every day, sending in his card: *Bartley Whitman, Attorney at Law.*

I said all right, I would see him.

Whitman was a slender man with deep-set gray eyes deeply ringed. He was in his early forties with light brown hair that he parted low on one side and combed straight back. His hair was gray over his temples.

"It was a terrible thing," he said. Another time, he said, "You've got to start living again." And then he said, "You can't bring your wife back. Nothing can bring your wife back. But you can sue. You can make these people pay."

How could you make people pay for a wife that nothing could bring back?

The way you made people pay was you hit them in the pocketbook.

Bartley Whitman said he would handle everything. There was something odd about his desire to start making these people pay. You'd have thought it was his wife they had killed.

"The way it was was like this," Bartley Whitman said to me one week. I don't know which week. There were so many weeks, all in the hospital, all alike. "A man named Koons was driving his Rolls Royce—"

"His what?"

"That's right. It cost him eighteen thousand five hundred dollars and had five thousand miles on it when he bought it."

"You sound as though you know him."

"I know him. Everybody in my part of the country knows him. Anyhow, Koons and his wife were driving on this road, coming from their fish camp at Rainbow Lake—"

I felt something grab at me. I closed my eyes hard. I clenched my teeth. Nothing could ever bring her back? Hell, everything brought her back.

When we could talk about it again, Bartley Whitman told me the rest of it. Evidently Koons had been drinking, but this was going to be hard to prove. The Rolls Royce had smashed into my car, turning it over four times so it rolled down the embankment, killing my wife and injuring me. The big Rolls had plowed into the soft shoulder and settled there on the brink of the ditch. Koons and his wife had been shaken up slightly, but there were no other wounds. The car behind them was a sheriff's cruiser, and oddly enough had been driven by Sheriff Harley Baskins himself.

He would have had to witness the whole accident. "We can throw the book at them," Whitman said. "We can really make them pay."

The next time I saw Whitman the circles beneath his eyes were a deeper black. His face looked ashen. He sat beside my wheelchair for a long time.

"A hell of a thing," he kept saying over and over. It was as if he were speaking to himself. "Koons and his wife are suing you. They are suing you for a hundred thousand dollars."

He tried to explain it to me, but he was almost incoherent. According to Koons' complaint, I had been driving on the wrong side of the road. Koons said he had swerved to miss me and at the last minute I had turned back into his path, causing him to crash into me.

"But the sheriff," I said, beginning to feel the first wild outrage. "He must have seen it—"

"Yes." Whitman nodded, looking ready to retch. "He's signed a deposition swearing Koons' version is right, and that he was the first one to reach you in the ditch—you were drunk, he swears—he could smell whiskey over everything else."

We were both incoherent. I began to see what I was up against.

There was more. This was just the opening gun. It now seemed that expert bone specialists had made X rays of Saul Koons.

He had been injured in such a way, said his complaint, that he was doomed to remain a semi-invalid for life. For one thing, an operation in that delicate area, and upon a man of his age, would prove fatal. The expert word of the specialist nailed that one down.

The bill stated that the injury caused him continual severe pain and distress and rendered him unable to enjoy the privileges and pleasures of matrimony. He was made so uncomfortable that his work had suffered, would continue to suffer, and his loss would be incalculable. He was suing me for a hundred thousand dollars to repay a small portion of business losses and as punitive repayment for the loss of his wife's comfort and companionship.

I was cold, lying on this hotel bed, cold and in pain. I tried to turn over but the pain was too sharp, paralyzing. I couldn't do it. I pulled the cover closer about my neck and after a long time I sank back into this state of nowhere—this place where it was all with me still, screaming at me, where I couldn't escape any hurting memory of it.

I sat in that courtroom and the back pains were still bad, especially when I sat too long in the hard chairs.

I heard the judge give the jury its first instructions. They were to take into consideration the way a man behaved on the witness stand, the way he answered questions, the way he did not answer them; they were to understand that this was a civil suit brought before circuit court and the fact that there were or were not insurance monies involved should not enter into their consideration of the facts of the case. They were to consider first the character of the plaintiff and that of the defendant, and to remember that everything a man might say in his defense might not be true, and should be borne out by evidence. At first I didn't believe it, but it was on the court reporter's tape and I read it later.

The parade of witnesses began. Lying there I could see their faces. There was the orderly from the hospital. He said that my clothing reeked of whiskey the night I was brought to the hospital out-ward by the ambulance.

Koons was put on the stand. Almost a whole morning was spent by his attorneys impressing the jury with just who he was: the owner of the Koons paper mills, grove owner, bank director, church deacon, third-generation landowner in Koons County, a man with an impeccable record, a man known for his charitable works.

The judge finally laughed and said, "I reckon we all know who Saul Koons is."

The attorney for Koons did not join the court and jury in their laughter. He remained very dignified. He said, "I am trying to show that this man has a record for honesty."

The judge laughed again, "I reckon we all know him to be an honest man. Let's proceed."

"Very well, your honor. I simply want it clear to the jury the character of the man giving this testimony. He has advised me that he gives it reluctantly—that the defendant suffered the loss of his wife. Only the fact that obviously the defendant was negligent, careless and intoxicated caused Mr. Koons to come into this courtroom at all."

Nobody mentioned the hundred thousand dollars. After all, Koons had millions. What was a hundred grand to him?

"It is only in the interest of justice that I am here at all," was the first thing Saul Koons said on that stand, and I began to hate him that moment, and that hate grew, through the lies he told, that his witnesses told. The judgment against me no longer mattered. It took all the insurance I had, it took everything I owned. It still didn't approach the hundred-thousand-dollar judgment he was awarded in that court.

I hated Saul Koons and I knew just one thing. He was going to pay.

I was on the stand. It was clear in my mind, as clear as though it were happening. I could feel nothing except the pain and the loss and the outrage.

Bartley Whitman had warned me repeatedly that I was a poor witness. My voice shook, my hands shook. I looked at that judge, and that jury, and those witnesses, and my whole body shook and all I'd believed in about justice and law was smashed. And there was only one thing left.

Saul Koons was going to pay.

"How fast were you driving?" It was Koons' attorney.

"I told you. Slowly. Very slowly."

"I thought you testified you were in a hurry to get to a fish camp. Isn't that what you testified?"

I looked down at my trembling hands. "Yes."

"Then why do you persist in saying you were driving slowly?"

"Because. If you don't understand, I can't make you understand it—"

He smiled, "Well, I certainly must confess to this court that I don't understand it, Mr. Morris."

"We weren't in that kind of a hurry—not the kind that makes you speed."

"And why not?"

"Because we were together. Because we were happy as two people could be happy. It didn't matter—where we were." I felt the ache across the bridge of my nose, the burn of tears, the way my voice shook.

Did the jury believe I was sick with grief?

Oh, hell, they probably thought I was lying.

"Were you drinking. Mr. Morris?"

"No. I wasn't. Not all day. I—we didn't even have any whiskey with us. We didn't need it—"

"Yet, isn't it true that the hospital reported your clothing saturated with whiskey when you were admitted to the out-ward?"

"I don't know."

"Isn't it true?"

"I don't know. I was unconscious."

"It has been testified here—"

I struggled in that chair. I wanted to get out of there.

"I don't know!" I yelled at him.

I was a hell of a witness.

I was a hell of a witness but I was all I had and the case went against me. As I said, Koons was awarded his judgment.

How could a case like that go against me, even in the home county of a man who operated a multi-million dollar business, manipulated political offices, directly and indirectly supported its inhabitants? I don't know. I spent almost a year in a hospital, Cora was dead. Koons got his Rolls repaired and was still driving it. How could he get a judgment against me? Ask God. Ask the judge. Ask the jury. Ask Bartley Whitman.

The outcome of that trial hit me hard enough, but it seemed to destroy Bartley Whitman. His eyes refused to focus, he hardly heard when you spoke to him, he went on chain-smoking but seemed not even to know what he was doing. That defeat ruined him; you could see he was ruined.

I tried to pry something coherent out of him about what was to become of my suit against Koons. He looked as if he would have laughed except he was afraid he'd cry instead. With all that testimony against me? Would I go into that court again? Into any court? Did I think I had a chance against Koons now? It was established in the court record that I was drunk, sodden, on the wrong side of the road, criminally negligent, and Koons had come out of it with a permanent spine injury.

I yelled at him. "But he was lying. They were all lying."

"But the jury believed them."

"He lied about that back injury—"

"What difference does it make?"

"What difference? He lied. There's nothing wrong with his back. It's as good as yours, better."

"I don't doubt that. But he had specialist testimony. Juries love that. They eat it up. As far as a jury is concerned, no specialist will lie, not even when two of them come into the same courtroom and give diametrically opposing testimony. They believe any expert witness, and a medical specialist is above suspicion. I tell you they believed that Koons' back was injured."

Maybe someone more removed than I was from that trial in Koons' home county could believe it was less than rigged. Maybe the jury had believed that its most outstanding citizen had made every effort to avoid a collision, that its sheriff was telling the truth, that I, the stranger, lied every time I opened my mouth. Maybe they even regretted that my wife was dead, but you could see in their faces that they didn't pity me: I was guilty.

Bartley Whitman couldn't think about me or what was to become of me. He was an attorney practicing in Koons Mills—the town that was named for Saul Koons' family. Maybe I had come out of that trial with troubles, but Bartley Whitman couldn't see them for the mountain of woes that awaited him back home.

I tried drinking, I tried working, I tried moving around. Nothing helped. I was raw and hurting inside; I was savage. I devised one plan, simple and terrible. I could not live again until I had made Saul Koons pay for the evil injustice he'd done me. I worked long enough to get a stake that would carry me to Koons Mills, sustain me until I executed my project. I made no plans beyond the one simple operation for dealing with Saul Koons. Nothing seemed to matter beyond that moment.

I sank deeper and deeper into this lost place of time and space. Now there were no more white stark hurting scenes and it became warm and I sank deeper and I slept.

I don't know how long I slept. A chambermaid knocked at my door until I came up out of it. I lay there agonized and chilled.

"I'd like to get in to clean up, sir. It's after four o'clock."

"Go away," I said. "It's all right. Go away."

After a long time I was able to sit up on the side of the bed. Pain lanced through me, shot through me, nerve ends writhed and twisted, and I shivered all over with the pain.

I dragged the back of my hand across my mouth and looked around the room.

There was an untouched fifth of Haig and Haig on the table beside the bed, and it hadn't been there when I'd come into this room.

Chapter Six

I shuddered.

Who had put that fifth of whiskey there?

I rubbed my hands across my eyes. I stared at that unopened fifth of Haig and Haig. The trembling started deep in my stomach and mixed well with the burn of pain.

"Damn."

I didn't look around. I had said it. It was the only word I knew any more. Somebody had been in my room while I slept. When? How many times? How many people?

What did they want? Wasn't it enough that they had beat me into insensibility? Obviously it wasn't.

I glanced toward my suitcase. It was where I'd left it when I fell across the bed last night. It did not look as though it had been touched.

I couldn't buy much reassurance from this. Anyway, it didn't matter if they went through my possessions: my clean shirts, tooth brush, shaver. What the hell, anything they wanted to know about me they could find out by asking me. If they didn't know yet who I was, I could tell them that, too. I was the wrath of God, come to be visited upon Saul Koons. I was the handwriting on the wall, vengeance, a loaded gun. I was what they had made of an ordinary character named Greg Morris who once loved a girl named Cora.

I got off the bed and walked slowly to the window. It was an endless, painful way. I stared into the street. The town seemed to be heat-stunned, the sun was reflected in the pavement, dust stood on the leaves of the big oaks, and there was no breeze. I turned around, staring at that bottle of whiskey, wanting a drink, desperately needing it, but hating whoever had put it there too terribly to touch it.

I walked into the bathroom, pulling off my grimy, sweated clothing as I walked, letting it fall on the floor behind me. I stepped into the tub, turned on the hot and cold water full force. I began to come alive under the burning needles of water. I stayed there until the water began to run cool from both taps.

I came out of the bathroom, able to walk steadier now. I hoisted the suitcase to the rumpled bed, snapped it open and found a fresh pair of underwear. I pulled them on, deciding that I was going to live, after all.

Which was great news.

I glanced again at that bottle of whiskey. I don't know why I didn't pick it up, tear off the tax stamp and take the slug I needed. I can't say why, except that doing it seemed an admission of weakness. I knew inwardly how weak and how helpless I was; I didn't need a drink of somebody's whiskey to prove it. It seemed to me that whoever had put that bottle of Haig and Haig there had laughed to himself, knowing how badly I was going to need it—and maybe I'd take a drink of it and get wise enough to catch the first bus out of town.

"The hell with you," I said aloud.

I walked slowly through the business district of Koons Mills. There was a sluggish sense of mid-afternoon silence over the four blocks of sun-blistered stores and office buildings. The movie theatre was closed in the afternoon. I walked past the drug store and a breath of air-conditioned chill came out thick with the smell of perfumes and chocolate. The shades were drawn at the Koons Mills National Bank. I crossed the street against the traffic light. There wasn't a moving car within two blocks.

I went into the county building and walked along the corridor until I found a door marked, SHERIFF, KOONS COUNTY. I opened the door and went in.

A woman homely enough to be any wife's conception of an ideal secretary looked up from a roll-top desk just inside the door.

I told her I wanted to see Sheriff Baskins.

She didn't bother asking my name. She went to an inner door marked PRIVATE, opened it and spoke through the slit.

"That man Morris. Out here. Says he wants to talk to you. Wanta see him?" she said in a mannish voice. She had nice hips and legs, which was too bad—they were wasted. By the time a man got that far he was discouraged, or if he started there, he was abruptly startled when he lifted his gaze. She'd have had a big career as a WAC sergeant.

"Sure. Tell him to come in."

She turned slightly, motioning me to her with her head. I glanced into her face trying to find some response. But I saw nothing—nothing except a small mole with two short hairs sprouting from it.

Harley Baskins was seated behind another roll-top desk pushed against a wall in a small hot room. Three windows opened upon the county building lawn and the street beyond. Lazy sounds floated in. There was no breeze.

He did not get up, but motioned me to a chair beside his desk. It was cluttered with Wanted posters, opened and unopened letters and a few stuffed filing folders. There were a few pictures on the wall.

I sat there a moment as he looked me over with a faint smile.

"There were some things—during the trial," I said.

He lifted his hand. "That's all past, Morris. Why don't you forget it?"

"Would you forget it, Sheriff, if it happened to you?"

"But it didn't. It happened to you. It's tough. But that's the way it is. I don't get it. I don't see why you wanted to come here and try to stir up something."

"People lied in that court. I want to prove they lied."

"Why?"

"My God. I've got to live with this."

"No. You could forget it. You're only asking for more trouble."

"That's what you don't seem to understand. These people can't hurt me. Not anymore. But I can prove they lied—I can make them pay for what they did—if I can get just the least help."

"Why did you come to me?"

"Who would I go to? You're the sheriff, aren't you?"

"I'm the sheriff."

"You know what the truth is. There was no truth told in that court. But I'm going to get the truth."

"You got it, mister. In that court. And you better make up your mind you got it."

"No. There were tire tracks, skid marks on that highway. There had to be. Those skid marks would show where I put on my brakes—how long my skid marks were—and they would show where I was, where my car was—and where that other car was."

He shrugged. "You know that Whitman tried to show all that in court. But there were no such tracks. You already know the county topped that stretch of the highway the next day after the wreck, before we could make any real estimate of where those tracks were."

"But you were there. You testified in court that you were out at Rainbow Lake on another case—and you were behind Koons in that Rolls when it happened. You had to see how it really happened."

"I testified, mister. As far as I'm concerned, that ends it."

I stood up. "He really owns you, doesn't he?"

His overfed, over-handsome face turned beet red. He was half out of that swivel chair before he stopped, caught himself and sank back into the deep padding of his own fatty hips.

He grinned tightly. "Nobody owns me. Nobody. And I don't take talk like that, mister. Not more than once. I testified to what I believed the God's truth. I was under oath. I'm a sheriff. I do my duty. As I see it."

"Like yesterday. Out at the mill. You really performed your duty there, didn't you?"

He looked up at me, his face dispassionate. "I look at it different, that's all, mister," he said. "I been a law officer in this territory for a considerable spell. Right here in this county. I know what the law is. Nobody has to tell me. I know what the good people of this here county expect of me. And if I do say so, I know what's best for them."

He got up from the swivel chair then, walked slowly to the water cooler near the windows, thick-set, pork-hipped in cheap khaki pants and denim shirt. He pulled a paper cup from a container, blew into it, and put it under the water tap. Then he pressed the button, letting perhaps three tablespoons of water run into the paper cup.

He straightened up, watching me, then. He had the arrogant look that proclaimed him a hell of a man with women, and one who dominated most men.

He tipped up the cup, watching me still over the top, let the water trickle into his mouth. He washed it around, gargling it and sloshing it between his teeth. Then he walked to the brass spittoon, stood over it and let the water run out of his mouth into the spittoon.

"Heat," he said. "Never drink iced water in heat. Makes you sweat like a goat. Just wash your mouth out once in a while. That's all you need."

He wadded the cup in his fist and threw it into a wire waste basket. He walked back to his desk then, licking at his teeth with his tongue.

"So you admit a man needn't expect any aid from you?" I said.

"Aid?"

"You stood there in the mill yard. You watched them beat hell out of me."

"So?"

"For God's sake. You are the sheriff, aren't you?"

"Yep. From where I stood, it looked to me as though I did the best for you that I could."

"You nuts? You didn't do a damned thing."

"That's right. You see, mister, when you been a law official long enough, like I have, that's what you learn. And like I say, I been a law official for a considerable spell. I learned a lot about it. Sometimes now you can aid a man by helping him out of a scrape. Other times this might just be the worst possible thing you could do for him."

"I hope you make more sense than this when you talk to your voters."

He managed a thin smile. "I'm making real good sense right now, mister. Only sometimes a man can be so blinded by anger and hatred and just plain cussedness that he don't understand—because he don't want to understand."

"Oh boy. I'd like to understand you right now."

"Then you listen quick. Because I haven't got a lot of time to waste explaining this here thing to you. Why, first place, it's plain as the nose on your face.... You're a stranger here in Koons Mills. Right?"

"What's that got to do with it?"

"You're poking around here when nobody around here wants you in town at all."

"And what's that got to do with it?"

"Ever'thin'. If I had stepped forward yestiddy and clouted a few of them boys—nice, clean-cut fellows when you git to know them—maybe out of line yestiddy a little—"

"Yeah. Just a little."

"All right. So for the sake of argument, they were out of line—"

"For the sake of argument, for God's sake—"

"But, if'n I stepped in there and stopped them, you'd think I was offering you assistance—"

"Hell, I might even get the crazy idea you were doing your job—"

"Same difference. You would think you could count on my assistance then. You would believe you could stay around here, threatening people like Mr. Saul Koons, digging around, stirring up people—and you might even decide to stay because you'd think Mr. Harley Baskins is such a fine noble law official that he will protect you no matter where you stick your nose. If I'd help you yestiddy, that's what you might o' thought—"

"But now I won't think that?"

"Right. Now you begin to read me loud and clear. You know better than to stick your nose around until some dark night somebody kills you. You know better than that, now. You know that as far as I'm concerned you get no aid whatever from this office."

"That's pretty clear."

"On the face of it, you might call this pretty bad. A bad thing. But when you calm down, when you get out of this town and think it over—rational-like—you'll know that Sheriff Harley Baskins was your real friend, doing you the best favor he could possibly do for you."

"Thank God I don't have many friends like you."

He shrugged. "Well, that's it. You're the kind of man don't make friends easy."

Chapter Seven

The look on Bartley Whitman's face really bugged me.

"Morris." His eyes widened in their deep black pockets as if I were the last person in the world he expected to see, and more than that, the very last he wanted to see.

"I'm thrilled to see you, too." I couldn't help the bitterness and sarcasm in my voice. By now I was brimming with it. Sure, I had no reason to expect to be greeted with any warmth here in Saul Koons' town, but after all, this character was my lawyer.

"What are you doing here?" He found a pack of cigarettes, offered me one, didn't even glance up to see whether I shook my head or not. He stuck a cigarette in his mouth, lit it and then looked around in a panic for an ash tray to park it. His desk tray was piled high with butts. He emptied it into his waste basket, got ashes on his suit and then for a few moments sat there slapping at the dead gray ashes on his trousers.

"I came to see you," I said, and even I was beginning to wonder why.

"I don't mean that. Of course you came to see me. But here—why are you still here in Koons Mills?"

"Didn't you know I was going to be?"

He jerked up the cigarette and took a long draw on it, holding it between thumb and forefinger, ready to replace it in the ash tray at once. This boy might get cancer of the lungs, but not skin cancer between his fingers from tobacco stains.

"No." He shook his head, lost for a moment in a cloud of smoke. "No. I didn't. The best advice I can give you, Greg, is that this case is closed. Of course I'm terribly disappointed. It was a bitter miscarriage of justice—"

"If you want to make an understatement—"

"But it is closed. There isn't anything else I can do for you. Nothing anybody here in Koons Mills can do for you."

"I don't know. I'll have to see about that."

"Please, Greg. Try to understand my position. You are my client—" he paused for another long drag on his cigarette—"and I hope you are my friend. But try to understand. I took your case in good faith. It was my honest belief we had a good, supportable claim against Koons. As I saw it, he drove a car wildly, using it as he might a deadly weapon with intent to kill. It didn't turn out that way. I'm sorry, but this is as far as I can go."

"I suppose you want to tell me what that means?"

"If I can. Maybe you've never lived in a town this size, Morris, in a community dominated by one man, one family. It's an old town. It is not a tourist town. The people who live here have lived here for generations. People who have lived here as long as fifteen years are still spoken of as 'that new family.' I—don't exaggerate. People in towns like this have strong allegiances, loyalties. And it's a strange thing: power is right in a community like this more than in any other spot on earth. When I took your case, I thought I would win. I had an airtight case—and I would have emerged stronger in this community. Much stronger. It was what I wanted. What I needed. But when the case backfired on us, took a turn for the worse, and then went entirely against us, I did not back out. I stayed with you. It has cost me a lot. If I had won, I would have been stronger—Koons weakened by that much. It didn't work that way. I can tell you this, if I want to go on living in this community, I can't represent you any further. Is that clear?"

"Not even for money?"

"You haven't that kind of money. I am losing clients all the time. Koons uses every kind of subtle and crude pressure against me. I gambled that I would win against him. And I lost—but unfortunately, I'm having to give up the gamble. I can't afford it anymore."

"You know of any other lawyers who might represent me?"

"In this town?" He shook his head, started to speak, changed his mind, took a long drag on his cigarette instead. "No. But as a matter of fact, why do you need a lawyer?"

"I want a warrant."

"Warrant?" He looked green with the illness that boiled up inside him. "A warrant for what?"

"You heard about what happened at the mills yesterday?"

"Of course. Everybody has heard that. That's why I was surprised you were still in town."

"Should I have run?"

He stubbed out the cigarette, lit another. He took a long drag. "Shouldn't you, Greg?"

"I'm not going to. But I do want a warrant sworn—"

"Against the people at the mill? Are you going to arrest them all?"

"I don't know."

"And what will you charge? Technically you were trespassing, Greg. What happened to you is regrettable—"

"It's slightly worse. It was assault—incited—"

"You'd have to prove it."

"In court I would. But I don't have to prove it to swear out a warrant."

He licked his lips. "Are you going to swear out a warrant against Saul Koons?"

"That's what I want."

"Will you listen to me? You don't believe that Saul Koons told those men to attack you?"

"You mean did he pick up a phone and tell them that Greg Morris was annoying him and he wanted him worked over? No. He probably didn't—"

"You know he didn't. He kept clear of anything like that."

"But he knew it was happening. He knew it was going to happen. He knew I was on my way to that mill yard, they were waiting for me when I got there—"

"Saul Koons has spies—he knows anything he wants to know in this county. But that doesn't prove that he told that gang of men to work you over. It was payday, maybe they had something to drink, you were trespassing, they decided to teach you a little lesson—"

"With pine clubs? You know better than that."

"That's what Koons would say—or his lawyers would—if they said anything at all."

"I still want that warrant served."

"Why? It will get you nowhere."

"It'll harass the bastard. He won't forget I'm here. That's good enough for a start."

"And where do you expect it to end?"

"I don't know. I'll kill him if I have to. When I get the chance, I'll kill him—"

"Greg. Listen to me. You're an embittered, hurt and angry man. You have every reason to be that. You are justified. But you won't kill Saul Koons—or anybody else. I've known you only a year—but I know that."

I looked at my trembling hands. I got up. "Stick around," I said. "You'll see."

He exhaled heavily. "I'll stick around, Greg. But not as your attorney. That's like a reserved seat section. Too rich for my blood. I can't afford that."

I walked back to the hotel in a kind of wild and bitter void. The sun had dropped slightly but there still wasn't a touch of a breeze the length of Main Street. I walked swiftly, moving fast in the heat. The one hope of help I had had in this dirty little town was gone, sick with fear, running white and scared.

Damn him. Why had he ever taken my case in the first place?

I went into the hotel and crossed the lobby, looking neither left nor right. I think the desk clerk spoke my name but I didn't turn or pause. I went up in the elevator, got out, walked along the hall, went into my room.

The chambermaid had cleaned up my room, made up the bed. That bottle of Haig and Haig was sitting on the table beside the bed.

It was stifling hot in the room. I shoved up the window, waiting for a breeze that didn't come. Then I walked back across the room. I looked at the bottle of whiskey, picked it up. I twisted off the cap and took a long, raw drink.

I hoisted the bottle in a toast to whoever had left it here. "Thanks," I said. "Thanks, you son of a bitch, whoever you are."

I took another drink, walking around the room. I fell down on the bed, hearing it squeal under me, still holding the bottle. I lay there with the bottle in my fist.

So Whitman and the sheriff were troubled, were they? So they wanted to know why I was staying here, what I thought I was going to accomplish.

It seemed to me Bartley Whitman would know. He had put it in words. As I lay there I heard the words that Bartley Whitman had spoken to me in the hospital: *make them pay.*

I was going to make them pay. No matter what Bartley Whitman thought of my chances now, I was going to make them pay.

My throat felt taut. It had all been cold and clear in my mind when I arrived in Koons Mills. I had come to this town with a plan that was simple and direct. I would stay in this stupid village until somehow, sometime I got Saul Koons alone. Saul could live happily but his days were numbered. I figured I had them numbered. It was up to me. I sweated, thinking how it would be. I would beat him until he confessed he had murdered my wife, had lied in that court, bought perjured witnesses. I would get it all out of him before I killed him, slowly and agonizingly.

I sat up and took a drink. Sure it was savage and wild. I was savage and wild. But all my life I had been an ordinary kind of guy and when I arrived here, it seemed to me I had to give Saul Koons one last chance to admit his wrongs, undo some of his evil.

I didn't feel that way anymore. I had arrived in town with hatred like a virus, like a fever, driving me. I had tried to talk to Koons, and that was no good. His mill hands had attempted to kill me, and I still didn't know how they'd failed. The sheriff had warned me I could expect no help from the law. Bartley Whitman had scurried, scared and sick, for cover.

And that brought me right back to where I was when I got here. I had had a plan when I came to this town and no matter how savage it was, it was up to me—and it was time now—to put it to work.

I tipped up the bottle and took another long swig, feeling the painful burn and gagging sensation purging its way slowly into my stomach.

I sat there, holding the bottle by its neck, pressing it against the top of my knee. There were weak links in Koons' case against me, if I could break them. There was the hospital orderly who had testified I was whiskey-soaked when he saw me at the hospital the night of the wreck.

I'd thought about him a lot, for a long time. Had somebody paid him to lie? Or had somebody poured whiskey all over me? This would have been a hell of a lot cheaper, a hell of a lot safer. Only this brought me to that same tired old road. I had been down that road plenty. Who? Who would pour whiskey all over me? Koons might have. But with the sheriff standing there? And he must have been dazed after slamming his big car into mine at seventy miles an hour. Would even he have been thinking that clearly? Who? Why?

I jumped up and walked across to the window, breathing in deeply, trying to get a full breath of air.

I stared down across that sun-stricken town, red brick streets, dusty oak leaves, parched lawns, the few cars baking along the curbs. The truth was down there, all dirtied and slimy and covered with garbage, but it was down there—and it was the only thing I could use to hit back at Saul Koons. And I was helpless without it. God knew, it looked as though I was helpless to find it.

And that meant I was back to my first mad plan. The whole thing would end when I got Saul Koons' throat in my hands.

I must have stood there for half an hour or more, and then I noticed the car, or rather it crossed my vision so repeatedly that it worked its way into my conscious mind. I had seen it somewhere before. It was a Ford coupe. It was gray, about seven years old. It had moved along the street below me at least six times in the past half-hour. It was like a mosquito that keeps singing around your head until finally you notice it and then you can't think of anything else.

A Ford coupe. Gray. About seven years old.

It parked directly across Main Street from the hotel. A man sat alone in it. He stayed there with the engine cut off for perhaps five minutes. Then he started the car again and backed out of the parking place. He drove away slowly, going around the block.

A Ford coupe. Gray. About seven years old.

In a few minutes he was back, parked in that same place across the street. I stared down at him, wishing I had a pair of field glasses. But even at that distance there was something familiar about him. He was young, slender, pale.

He turned slightly in the car as if watching the street for somebody, something.

A Ford coupe. Gray. About seven years old.

And then I recognized him. It was Walter, that pale young Romeo who'd been standing miserably over Saul Koons' wife yesterday morning out at the House.

Our boy Walter was waiting for somebody and that was for sure. I stayed there, without moving, watching him. He stayed another five minutes, started his car, backed out, drove to the end of the block, made a left turn.

I counted, knowing almost precisely to the moment when he would appear again on Main Street down there in front of the hotel.

But before he made it another car rolled into view and parked over there in his parking place. The car was a new Cad and I recognized its driver immediately. Angie Koons.

By now the gray Ford coupe had rolled back into a parking place beside the Caddy. I went back across the room, put the Haig and Haig on the bedside table, and carefully capped it. Then I went downstairs and out to the street.

Chapter Eight

"Mr. Morris!"

The desk clerk was leaning so far across the desk that he looked as though he was going to fall over it.

He was reaching out his arm toward me. Whatever it was, it was certainly an urgent matter to him.

I shook my head at him but didn't slow down. I didn't want either Walter or Angie Koons to leave those parking places across the street. And if this was one of those innocent-looking assignations, they might let it look as though they met accidentally in town and then would strike for the pig-track country immediately.

"Later," I said, and kept moving.

"But—"

"Later."

He was coming around the desk but I was already at the hotel doorway. He stopped there and stared after me as I hit the street.

Walter was already backing his gray Ford out of the parking place when I reached the curb.

I stood there a moment watching Angie in the Caddy. Then I moved quickly. I got across the street fast, going behind Walter's rear bumper as he pulled away.

I slowed then, making it look casual.

I stopped beside the left front door of the Cad, looking surprised.

"Well, hello there."

Her eyes widened slightly. "Hi."

"What are you doing in town?"

"Oh, I'm doing the weekly shopping. You'd be surprised. Sometimes I come in as often as three times a month."

I gave a meaningful glance after the gray Ford. "Maybe I wouldn't be so surprised."

She stared at me a moment, then followed the direction of my gaze, brought her eyes back to my face. "You're just going to have to part your hair differently, sweetie—the point of your head shows."

"Does it? Poor Walter ... Like you say, poor Walter. He waited a long time, round and round this block."

She frowned slightly, watching me, and then the frown was gone, and the look was very casual.

"I could ask you the same question," she said.

"Yes? What question is that?"

"What are you doing in town?" She stared straight into my face. "Still using that sharp-pointed knife on yourself, aren't you?"

"It feels so good when I stop."

"I hear they asked you to leave the mill yesterday."

"Very polite. Clubs."

"You're still walking around."

"I'm hard to kill. Remember?"

"It can probably be accomplished, though. But then you act like that's what you want. I suppose you think Saul was behind that beating?"

"I think so."

"And what do you plan to do?"

I shrugged. "I'm just putting it on his account."

"You hate hard, don't you, Morris?"

"I don't know. This is my first experience with it. It didn't come easy. Maybe I just got a bad case the first time."

"I do hope it isn't fatal."

I stared into her eyes. "Well, there are worse things than dying."

Her eyes held mine a moment, then they fell away. "Yes. I suppose so."

I stepped back, glanced again down Main Street. Walter's Ford had disappeared. I felt my mouth pull, twisting. "Don't let me keep you," I said.

"I'm in no hurry. It's nice to have someone to talk to."

"Someone you don't have to be nice to."

"I don't have to be nice to anyone."

"Well, even being Mrs. Saul Koons must have its compensations," I said.

Her eyes chilled. She put her hand on the window of the car. The sun glittered on a diamond.

"We can get one thing straight. I like being Mrs. Saul Koons. Make no mistake about that."

"I'm sure you must. A lot like using the sharp-pointed knife on yourself."

"Not at all."

"Don't protest too much, honey. Remember, I'm the guy you don't have to be nice to. You can tell me the truth."

Her voice lowered. "You have such a lovely mind, Morris, along with all your other endearing qualities. Sure. All you can see is that I'm twenty-six and that Saul is fifty-six. What do you know about it?"

I shook my head. "That's all. Just what you tell me."

Her head jerked up. "And just what do I tell you?"

"How happy you are. How deliriously, wildly happy you are."

She stirred slightly in the car. She looked around as though the richly appointed interior was a trap of some kind. She spoke sharply. "There are other things, Morris, besides being wild. Delirious."

"Whatever you say."

"There's security—"

"Sure. A. T. & T., General Motors—and then there's always Walter, isn't there?"

Now she laughed, relaxed once more. "Oh, you're so wise. So sure you have all the answers. You're so sure I'm a slut, aren't you? I married Saul for his money, and I chase after boys like Walter like a fat cat."

"If you say so."

She stared up at me and there was a kind of panic in her face.

"Oh, God," she said. "Just to meet one person who didn't believe that about me."

"Believe me. It doesn't matter. If you say you're happy with Saul, fine. If you say Walter was driving around this block all afternoon testing his brakes, that's good enough for me. I'm happy that you even talk to me. A friendly face in this town. It gets to me. Right here. Like a gentle heartburn. I'm even surprised you're not afraid to talk to me."

"I'm not afraid to talk to anyone."

"Saul might not approve."

"This will shake you up, but Saul trusts me."

"Sure he does. But then I'm not in the Koons Mills social register."

"Do you think I am?"

"Offhand, I'd say you were its editor."

"You're not bright, boy. You've so much to learn.... And you've so little time."

"I love the way you threaten me."

"I'm not threatening you. If I thought about you at all I'd be sorry for you."

"But you've got your own woes?"

"A run in my stocking. Company for dinner. Always problems. I can't worry about you, Morris. I can't even feel sorry for you. You think what happened to you at the mill yesterday was bad, you should live through a Ladies Aid meeting in this town."

"You never went to one."

"Oh, yes I did. One."

Oddly enough, we were both smiling. And it was a strange thing. The smile was as unnatural in her face as it was in mine. She could lie, she could play it slick all she liked, but it was in her eyes, that incredible hunger. I'd seen that same kind of look in the eyes of a Korean orphan.

I had one answer I wanted. Angie Koons might be the richest woman in this state, but she was also something else. She was one of the unhappiest.

I nodded toward the cocktail lounge in the hotel across the street.

"You brave beyond the call of duty?"

She shrugged. "Brave?"

"Come have a drink with me."

She laughed at me.

"You are afraid," I said. "You're afraid of Saul Koons."

She laughed again. "It might be that I don't want a drink with you, Morris. This will astound you, but I don't find you irresistible."

"That's too bad. I'm clever with a couple Martinis in me."

She laughed again. "I'm sure you must be."

And then in the middle of her laughter she did an odd thing. She shivered. Her whole body shook suddenly as though she were chilled.

She reached out, turned the ignition key. The Caddy purred to life. She slapped the car into reverse. I stood there and watched her drive away. She was doing sixty before she reached the first corner.

I walked slowly back across the street. The desk clerk called to me as I crossed the lobby. I went to the desk. He chewed on his lip, white and apologetic.

"I'm sorry, sir. The management. They asked me to inquire. How long do you plan—to be with us?"

I glanced toward the street, remembering that car, that woman, the way she had laughed and the way she had shivered, and the look in her eyes.

"Tell them I don't know," I said. "Tell them I love it here—I may just stay here the rest of my life."

He looked as though he'd just lost the Irish Sweepstakes by one digit.

I went into my hotel room, closed the door behind me. I felt better. I uncapped the bottle of Haig and Haig. I walked back to the window with the bottle in my hand.

I hoisted it in a toast to that unseen, fleeing Cadillac and the woman who couldn't run fast enough to escape herself.

"To you, Angie," I said. "To you, you bitch."

I took a deep drink. I didn't even feel the way it burned.

I walked back to the bed, sat down on the edge of it. I looked at the whiskey bottle, at the window, at the buildings I could see beyond it. Koons Mills was beginning to look one hell of a lot better to me.

I took another deep drink. It felt warm in my stomach; it soothed the tendons bruised by those clubs. I didn't know a lot of things and among them was whether I was any smarter than before, whether I was smart enough to do what I vowed in that moment to do. But one thing I knew that I hadn't known before. Saul Koons wasn't untouchable. He had a weakness. Our backwoods Achilles had his vulnerable heel.

Its name was Angie.

Chapter Nine

The next morning I could slide the shaver over my jaws without wincing. I stared at myself in the mirror, thinking that I felt better than I had in a year and feeling this new tension building inside me.

Dressing, I glanced at the bottle of Haig and Haig, picked it up and finished it off. Still holding the bottle, I had the sudden urge to hurl it through the window. But I resisted the impulse—senseless to be carried away by high spirits just because my plan, no matter how crazy it had looked before, might work after all. I had known I had to get Saul Koons alone, and this had seemed impossible. But now it looked as if I could manage it through his lovely little Angie, his sexy little weak spot, his red-haired Achilles' heel.

Angie could be had, and once you got her alone, Saul would come running like an enraged bull.

I went out of the room, admitting I didn't have it set up yet. But I had something. I knew how I could work it. It was more than I'd had when I arrived in Koons Mills three days ago.

The town was beginning to suffer from the heat at nine in the morning. There had been a breeze earlier, but walking along Main Street, I could feel it dissipate, evaporating in the blaze of the sun. The leaves hung thick with dust on the oaks, and the townspeople moved past me on the walk, already moving more slowly, without spirit.

I paused outside the Townhouse Restaurant. There were a few people at the long counter inside, and some at the tables. I pushed open the door and walked in; it smelled hotly of bacon grease and eggs frying.

The men at the counter glanced up when I walked in and stared for a moment before they turned back to their plates.

I walked past them and sat on a stool. A man near me pointedly put an extra stool between us, moving his plate, water glass, coffee cup. The other men grinned but made nothing more of it. The boy who'd moved glanced toward me, waiting to see what I'd make of it.

I didn't look at him. The waitress brought a menu.

"What'll you have?" She smiled, not sharing the community hostility, or perhaps wanting a tip more than she wanted to get along with her neighbors. Anyhow, she smiled in a friendly manner, and I accepted this as a good omen. It was the first friendly smile I'd encountered in a long time.

"Coffee," I said. "And I'd like a small steak, hashed brown potatoes, rye toast, orange juice."

She wrote this down and smiled again, a slender blonde girl with blue eyes. Somebody said something down the counter. She glanced toward him and walked to the kitchen.

After a few moments the waitress returned. She was no longer smiling. "The cook says a steak is too much trouble in the morning like this. Nobody eats steaks around here for breakfast."

The men along the counter grinned. In what they felt was a subtle way, I was being told my patronage wasn't wanted.

I looked up at the waitress, keeping my gaze as friendly as I could make it. "You tell them I'm in no hurry. I'd like a steak. I feel fine. There's a big day ahead. I'll wait for it."

She held my gaze a moment, grinned, and then walked away to the kitchen. After a few moments she returned, bringing me a cup of steaming coffee and a cloth napkin. Some of the men along the counter made disgusted noises and dropped their money loudly beside their plates as they got up and left.

Someone walked along the aisle between the counter and the tables and sat down beside me as the waitress brought my steak.

I glanced around. It was Sheriff Harley Baskins.

He checked my steak. "A hearty breakfast," he said.

"A big day," I told him.

He gave me an odd smile—odd only in that it never touched his eyes. His eyes had that faded, sun-hardened look that most men's eyes got around here when they stayed in the open a lot.

"Seems to me you have a lot of big days," he said.

"Always something doing when you're on the side of the angels," I told him.

He laughed at this, and it was almost an honest sound; the nearest thing to an honest sound I'd ever heard from him until this moment. And this time the amusement nearly reached his eyes.

He looked up at the waitress and motioned toward my plate.

"I'll have a steak, like his," he said.

The waitress laughed. "Ho boy," she said. "The cook is going to love this." She went away, smiling to herself.

The sheriff watched me eat my steak. I was truly hungry; for the first time in a year I felt hunger more than anything else.

"So you've decided to stick around, Morris?"

"Oh, yes."

"What do you expect to accomplish?"

"I'll think of something."

"You're making a mistake."

"Maybe," I said. "Or maybe you people made it when you decided to give me the finger."

He didn't like this. It sat sharply and painfully with him. His hand tightened on his water glass. But he managed to go on smiling.

"Sort of a conscience for the town, eh?" He made a fine joke out of it, the way he said it.

I shrugged. "It could use one."

The old man was standing outside the front entrance of his hardware store. He wore an apron, the way storekeepers did forty years ago. Inside the double doors his shop looked ancient and smelled of oil and harness. He was staring up at the oak tree that grew in the parkway before his store.

"Squirrels," he said.

"What?"

"I say, them damned squirrels. I swear they beat all. They used to jump from that oak to the roof and get in the attic. Sounded like they rolled pecans from one end of the store to the other."

"I see."

"I cut off them oak limbs. Cut 'em flush with the trunk. Damned squirrels run back and forth on the tree trying to figure what happened to their limb. Damnedest thing I ever saw."

"You stop 'em?"

"Hell, no. Now they jump all the way from the trunk to the roof. *Kerblam!* Like an explosion ever' time. Make more damned noise now than they ever did." He laughed, and looked up at me for the first time. "What can I do you for?"

"I need a job."

He stopped smiling. "What do you do?"

"Get hungry, mostly. Thought you might need some help."

"No."

"Anything at all. Drive a truck. Sell. Anything."

"No."

He turned around and walked into his store.

The fifth place I asked for a job that day was a Texaco station at the edge of town. It was a modern building with three sets of bright gas pumps, freshly painted, smelling of new tires, gas fumes and grease drippings. There was a hand-painted sign in the front window: HELPER WANTED.

A man in his middle thirties came out of the front door when he saw me. He stopped, looking around for my car. The sun glittered whitely, reflected in his front window.

"What can I do for you?"

I nodded toward his sign in the window. This was the kind of job I wanted; I was trained as an accountant, but I was too full of hatred, and my mind was too sick with the anguish in me for any kind of mental work. What the hell, all I needed anymore was enough to exist on.

"I'd like a job," I said.

"No."

"Your sign—"

"No." He pulled a cotton rag from his back pocket, wiped his hands on it. After a moment, he said, "I'm sorry."

He was the first one who'd expressed this sentiment. I said, "You mind telling me why?"

He frowned. "Your name's Morris, ain't it? Greg Morris?"

"That's right."

He made a sound in his throat, clearing it. "Well, that's the best reason I can give you, mister."

"I've tried five places today—"

"Here in Koons Mills?"

"That's right."

"Why don't you save your breath?" He scrubbed his hands on that cotton cloth. He rubbed them faster, harder than ever. "You ain't likely to get a job in this town."

"Why not? You need help."

He shook his head.

"But not you, mister. I need to stay in business. Three kids. A wife. A big appetite. I like it here. I don't need you."

"And that's the way the whole town feels?"

He nodded. "What else? Face it, mister. Nobody works in this town who's got Saul Koons for an enemy."

I was walking back along Main Street. Cars moved by me, stirring the dry breathless heat. People walked past me but if they looked at me, I didn't catch them at it.

Did Koons think he could stop me by keeping people in Koons Mills from hiring me? I had enough money to last me a while, and hatred enough to keep me here until they buried me.

"Greg!"

The sound startled me. It was as though I'd been here so long I'd forgotten my own name.

I stopped in the middle of the walk. Bartley Whitman loped toward me, sweated and scarecrow thin in the heat. He was getting the last two puffs from a cigarette and he tossed it into the gutter from between thumb and forefinger.

Seeing Whitman didn't fill me with any tingle of warmth. I figured he had walked out on me, and I also figured that capped it. The hell with him.

"May I talk to you, Greg?" he said. He took my arm. Whatever it was, it was urgent to Bartley Whitman.

"Go ahead." My voice had a chill I didn't attempt to hide.

"Not here." He glanced around. A man like Bartley could make a host of enemies in his own province by bucking its biggest man. Whom Saul Koons hated the town despised. By now I knew that all that saved Bartley Whitman in this area was the fact that his family had been here before it was Koons Mills.

"Where?"

"How about up in my office?" He saw I was reluctant to have any more to do with him. "As a favor, Greg?"

He was heated up about this business. He didn't even wait to light a cigarette when we were in his office. Nerves were twitching in his face.

He leaned across his desk. "You want to really get at Saul Koons, don't you?"

"This is news?"

"I think I've got it fixed this time."

I was interested. "All right, I'm listening."

Now he lit a cigarette. "One of Saul's trucks was involved in an accident on the highway." He brushed the smoke away from before his face.

"So?"

"So, the driver was a kid whose license had been lifted for traffic violations. Saul let him drive anyway. The kid had been drinking moonshine. It was right there on the seat beside him—what was left of a pint bottle of bootleg. He was on the wrong side of the road. He laid down skid marks more than forty feet long. I don't have to tell you what kind of speed this means, according to the police manuals. They have it figured from two-foot skid marks up. He crashed into some people named Cowley."

"And now they want to sue Saul," I said.

He looked up at the lack of enthusiasm in my voice. "That's right. But that's just part of it. Saul has been trying to fix this thing. He has been getting witnesses to swear the kid was sober, that Cowley was drunk and on the wrong side of the road."

"Sounds familiar."

"Sure. But they're going too far this time. There were too many witnesses. If they go into the courtroom with the lies they've hatched up, we can break them down. We can show it is a pattern of falsifying evidence, bribing witnesses."

"And where do I come in?"

He was really sweating now. "You were out there—"

"It was over when I got there."

"That makes no difference. You saw the position of the cars. You can testify about what condition that kid was in, where the Cowleys were."

"Sure." I shrugged. "The truck had smashed into the car."

He looked as if anxiety were wrecking his kidneys. He couldn't sit still. "You'd swear to that?"

"Where?" I just stared at him, remembering how he had left me hanging when I needed him, and right here m this office.

"In court."

"No."

"You were there. You saw it."

"I'm not going into court again. Not against Koons."

"Why not? You want to get him for what he did to you, don't you?"

"In my own way."

"Listen to me. You can't hit at a man like that outside the law. Don't be fool enough to try it. He's too powerful. You can't touch him."

"Maybe I can. Sure his hide is tough. You think it would stop a bullet?"

"I told you. You couldn't kill anybody. And you'll try some fool stunt, born in unthinking hatred, and get hurt a lot worse than you have been. No! Greg, the only way you're ever going to strike Saul Koons down is by process of law—"

"Sure. We did swell—"
"But now here is another chance."
"Thanks. But no thanks. You better count me out."
"Greg, this is the only way."
"No. This is your way. You hate the big man. You buzz around his head like a mosquito, picking at him on little cases like this Cowley thing—go ahead, until he gets tired listening to you buzz and slaps you down. You go ahead, but don't try to drag me in on it."

Whitman sank back in his chair and exhaled heavily. He looked deflated, but this didn't change his external appearance appreciably. He just looked as though his spine had finally dissolved into gray tobacco smoke and left him limp in that big chair.

The next morning I was back in the Townhouse Restaurant. I didn't feel as well as I had the morning before. I knew that Bartley Whitman—whatever he was, however weak—was the only friend I had in Koons Mills—and he was gone now. The tension was building worse than ever.

The waitress smiled at me as if we were in some kind of pleasant conspiracy together. I grinned back at her and ordered a steak. "Medium," I told her. "See that it's just right."

Baskins sat down on the stool beside me before my steak was served. I stirred my coffee, not looking at him.

"Man," he said. "I'm tired seeing you in town."
"So?"
"A man like you. No visible means of support."
"I'm looking for a job."

He couldn't help smiling at that.

"I could like you, Morris. You're not a bad guy. But you cause trouble. I don't like trouble—and you're nothing but trouble in this town. So—I think if you don't get a job in the next day or so—you best look in some other town. Right?"

Chapter Ten

The ringing of the phone woke me. I sat up in bed, not even knowing where I was. I felt groggy, and the phone rang two more times before I realized I was in my hotel room. The night sky beyond the window was thickly dark.

Still sleep-drugged, I reached over and lifted the receiver.
"Morris?"

The voice was familiar. I frowned in the darkened room.

"What? Who is this?"

"Don't you recognize my voice?" It was wide awake, full of savage life. I began to tremble as I recognized it. I reached over, snapped on the bedside light. I grabbed up my watch and checked the time. It was five A.M.

"Morris. Don't you recognize my voice?"

"What the hell you want, Koons?"

He laughed. "Did I wake you up?"

"I'm up. What you want?"

"This is a friendly call, boy."

"At five in the morning?"

"Is it that late? I've been up for hours. Man like me—doesn't need much sleep—"

"Or are you afraid to sleep?"

"Why be nasty, boy? I'm friendly. Hell, I'm always up before this. Don't need much sleep. A few hours and I'm ready to go again. Lots better than you young bucks, eh? Better than you young bucks that think you're so much better than the old man, eh?"

"Are you drunk?"

He laughed again. "You mean, sloppy drunk? Why no. I admit I had a shot, with my morning orange juice. But I always do that. A shot of whiskey, a half ounce of orange juice, and a glass of raw liver blood. Keeps you fit."

"Is that what you called to tell me?"

"Young calf's liver. Calf's liver. Has to be blood from calf's liver. Best thing in this world to build you up."

"Good night."

"Hold on, now. Wait a minute. I called you for a reason. I want to see you."

The tension was really getting me now. My hand gripped the phone tighter. "When?"

"Why, right now. That's why I called you like this. Tell you the truth, boy—a man like me, only time he really has that he can call his own is early like this—before the rest of the world is awake. Once they're awake, I'm pushed. Always somebody wanting something."

"It's like that with me at five in the morning," I said. "What do you want?"

"Want you to come out here to the House, boy. Come out and have breakfast with me."

"Listen to me. Last time I talked to you, it took me two days to recover."

"Boy, I'm deeply sorry about that. By God, I am. If those men of mine thought they were acting in my behalf—well, it won't never happen again, boy. Nothing like that. You listen to me. I want to talk to you. Come out here and have breakfast with me."

"What are you after?"

"Boy, I'm just being friendly. Maybe I don't rightly know how to go about it with a man like you—but that's my sole intention at this here moment—I want you to come out for a friendly breakfast. Tell you what, you be ready in fifteen minutes, I'll have a car in there to pick you up. Right?"

"Well, I'm not afraid of you, if that's what you're trying to find out."

"Sure, you're not." His voice rose. "That's the only kind of attitude to have in this world. Hear you like steak for breakfast. I'll have you the best-tasting steak cooking you ever set your teeth into when you get here.... Like yours medium. Is that right? Fine. Fifteen minutes, eh?"

Fifteen minutes later I went downstairs and crossed the hotel lobby. A night clerk was asleep with his head down on the telephone switchboard.

A high breeze was tumbling leaves and trash the length of Main Street when I stepped through the hotel doorway.

I stopped on the walk. A Negro chauffeur tipped his hat to me and opened a door of the car at the curb. For a moment I could not move. It was as though I were paralyzed with outrage.

The son of a bitch had sent his Rolls Royce to pick me up.

I didn't speak all the way out to the House. But by the time we rolled into the drive and stopped at the side of the big Colonial-style mansion, some of the trembling had stopped inside me.

I got out of the car. Large lights played on the terrace where I'd seen Angie Koons the first day I was here.

I moved away from the car toward the terrace. The chauffeur drove the Rolls Royce along the drive to the stables which had been converted into garages. An old-fashioned stable light burned above the doors, and I saw it reflected, glittering in the freshly waxed surface of Angie's Caddy. There were other cars parked out there, a jeep, a Buick, a station wagon. There had been nothing but cruelty behind his sending that Rolls into Koons Mills to pick me up.

I lifted my head, staring at him as I crossed the dry, sun-crisped lawn to the terrace. He was lolling back in a nylon-and-aluminum terrace chair with a 20-gauge shotgun across his legs. He wore high boots, khaki hunting trousers, a pale green corduroy shirt with a brown scarf around his throat. At his feet were four or five bird dogs that glanced up sniffing as I came near, but he spoke quietly to them and they did not move.

"Morning," he called.

I nodded, but didn't speak. I saw that the glass-topped, wrought-iron terrace table had been covered by an expensive linen cloth and was set with two places for breakfast with fine china and silverware that gleamed in the lights. A full pitcher of iced orange juice sweated on the table; in the center of the table was a small bowl of flowers, as well as a pitcher of milk and a smaller one of cream.

"You made good time," he said. "Fine." He sat forward and spoke to the Negro man working over a metal grill that glowed with bright red coals. "You got them steaks about eatin' ready, Henry?"

Henry nodded. "They're ready, any time you-all is, Mistah Saul."

I stood there looking down at him. Saul Koons turned and looked up at me. "Sit down. Sit down."

When his gaze struck against mine, his smile ceased. He scowled. "What's the matter?"

"Nothing. Not a goddamned thing. Let's get on with it. What do you want?"

He frowned a moment, looking at me, at the elaborately set table, at the steaks on the grill. Then he picked up the gun and set it carefully on the terrace stones. He spoke to the cook, "Henry, you call Spades in here."

"I mighty busy, Mist' Saul. These here steaks, they don't wait for me to run no errands to the barn."

"I don't mean run back there. You call him. You yell for him."

Henry grinned. As he tenderly lifted the steaks from the grill without puncturing them with his fork tines, he yelled, his voice carrying deep and mellow. The chauffeur came running across the yard.

Saul spoke to him. "Spades, who told you to use the Rolls?"

The chauffeur shook his head. "Why, nobody told me, Mist' Saul. Nobody. But I thought—you sending in for company and all—you'd want I should use the fine car, that's all."

Saul nodded, then jerked his head, dismissing the chauffeur. "A hell of a thing," he said to me. "I'm sorry. I wouldn't have had it happen."

"It doesn't matter."

"No. It don't matter. But at least it's settled."

Saul cut himself a thick triangle of steak almost two inches thick. He chewed it, talking. "I like things nice, Morris. A good breakfast. Anybody will tell you I was born with a lot handed to me, but I never sat on my ass and used it up. I got right now three hundred times what my old man left me. Three hundred times. I'm never satisfied with what other men have, or other men can't get...." He laughed. "That reminds me of a little story. You know I make a lot of trips. A lot of trips. Business. And football games. I never miss a good football game, I don't give a damn what part of the country it's played in. I like football because a man has to clip and fight to stay alive. I can feel like I'm right down there on that field, with them—"

"Gouging and cutting," I said.

"Sure. I don't like things easy. I never asked 'em to be easy. I play rough. I fight rough. But that's not telling you my story. I like it, because I've had men tell me it shows just what kind of man Saul Koons is. I mean, I tell it on myself, but it expresses the way I feel. It happened in Chicago, I was up there on business and pleasure. Few paper-mill men with me—and we were drinking it up. A really beautiful doll in the Hilton there and one of the men tried to pick her up. She gave him a tongue lashing that I thought would bring the house detective. This guy—one of the biggest men in paper in this country, I can tell you that—the poor son of a bitch slunk back to the table like he'd been crisped. So we got to talking and I bet them fifty grand apiece that I could pick her up. Might as well tell you I was pretty loaded—"

"Blood from the calf's liver," I said.

"Some tonic!" He laughed and slapped his leg. "Well, I went over. She was sitting at the bar. I sat beside her, ordered a drink, never gave her a glance. She didn't look my way. But when the bartender came back, I told him to refill both our glasses. She still didn't speak. But she didn't refuse the drink. Now, my friend had been as gentlemanly as he could be, matter of fact all he said to get her stirred up was that Chicago weather was rough, and she accused him of trying to pick her up.

"So I let her graze on that drink I bought her for a couple minutes, then I looked at her and asked her if she'd like to go out and do Chicago up right with me. She said in a chilled voice that she didn't know me, but I told her that was all right, that if she went with me, she could have all the steak she wanted to eat, all the liquor she could drink and the best goddamn lay she had ever had in her life. For a whole half a minute she just looked at me, and then she began to laugh, and she said she liked me from the first minute because I was her kind of man."

I ate my steak in silence. It was a fine steak; that Henry could cook as nobody I'd ever met. He had baked rolls that were so light you could hardly butter them—or you couldn't have except Henry had warmed the butter to just the perfect temperature. His yams dripped a honey that was delicious. All of this—plus all this charm—for me?

"I don't get it," I said.

"What's the matter?"

"What do you want from me?"

"Nothing. I hear you been looking for work around Koons Mills."

"You hear everything, don't you?"

"That's right. Down to what a man likes for breakfast, down to how a man likes his steak cooked."

"Then you must have heard that nobody would hire me."

"They were afraid of me."

"That's practically what they said."

"I'll give you a job."

"Why?"

"Because it looks like you're going to try to stay around this town—"

"That's right. There's got to be justice. I'm going to try to find it."

"Well, like I say, in that case you might be here a long time. So, if you're going to be around, you might as well work for me—that way I don't have to keep getting reports about you—you'll be where I can watch you."

"You'll never watch me close enough."

"You let me worry about that. Maybe you'll see you got less reason to hate me than you think."

"No. I get new ones every day. My lawyer quit me. Or did you know that?"

"Bartley Whitman? Hell, man, you were better off without him. Look, he never was with you. All he ever was was against me. You see, Bartley comes from a family a hell of a lot older in this area than mine, but with one hell of a lot less money. And they keep getting less all the time. Bartley hates me, and he wants to see me defeated. He thought he had something in you. But when he lost, you see how quickly he dropped you, don't you?"

"I guess you've had plenty men buckle under when you used enough pressure."

"Frankly, I have. Don't try to criticize me for using the weapons I have. You'd do the same. Any man would. But what about that job? You want it?"

"Where would I work?"

"Why, at the mill. I happen to know you're one fine CPA. What the hell, we can always use another one."

"Working for you won't keep me from doing what I'm going to do to you."

"Maybe. Maybe not. That's what we got to live with. You want the job?"

"No."

"I pay top wages."

I put down my steak knife and fork. "You might as well know this. I'm so full of bitterness that I couldn't do accounting work. It calls for brain work, and I couldn't force my brain to concentrate on any work like that."

"What kind of work you want to do?"

"I'll drive a truck."

"We don't pay top wages for that."

"I don't need much."

He shook his head, watching me. "I never saw a man like you before, Morris. Never met one. Does me good. You want a job driving one of my trucks, you got it. It'll be waiting for you when you show up at the mill."

"Free beatings go with it?"

"You got nothing to fear at that mill, Morris. It was a bad mistake, but it won't happen again." He stood up. "Well, you want a job, it's yours. Meantime, finish your steak and Spades will drive you back to town. If you'll excuse me, I got to take these dogs for a run in the quail fields."

He bent down, picked up his 20-gauge Winchester. "I got some fine quail fields, Morris. Have to keep them for big-shot visitors. They like to shoot tame birds. So I bring them in, feed 'em, and have them waiting."

"You're making a mistake if you think you can do that to me," I said.

He laughed, and spoke to the dogs. They leaped up, trembling with anxiety. They raced off across the lawn. He let them run about thirty yards, then he whistled sharply. They all stopped in their tracks, turning and looking over their shoulders, trembling as they waited for him.

He laughed again, nodded at me and walked away across the terrace.

I sat there scowling, troubled, watching him go across the yard.

He made no pretense that he was suffering from an injured back. Either he had forgotten it, or he was laughing at the whole idea.

But this wasn't what was bothering me. Everything was out of focus again, just off-center. I remembered the way he had caught me off balance that first day in his office. He had seemed anguished, troubled about what he had done to me. It was a quick thing, fleeting, but it had been there, like something that changed everything. Only I didn't know how it changed it.

And now, it was happening again. He seemed to have no motive except the pleasure of my company for inviting me out here to breakfast. Why? Why the interest in me? And damn it, why the charm? What did he care what happened to me? Why offer me a job?

I tried to tell myself it had a simple explanation. He had won the trial, won everything, hadn't he? Wasn't it easy to be friendly under those conditions? But I couldn't buy that. The whole thing just didn't ring true. It puzzled me. It beat me. You could look at Saul Koons, listen to him, sink under the spell of his charm, and you could believe he was a good guy—a man you'd like to know well under any other circumstances.

I stared around at this place, trying to regain that feeling of hatred that had sustained me for a year. I had hated him when I believed he'd sent that Rolls into the hotel to pick me up. I knew he had faked that back injury and I could hate him for that. And then I could remember that but for him Cora would be alive ... and then it was easy.

I could detest him then. The hell with him. I wasn't falling for his charm. I shivered there in the predawn chill. But the shudder had nothing to do with the wind riffling leaves across the wide flat lawn.

Chapter Eleven

"Anything else, sir, Mr. Morris? You want anything else to eat?"

Henry stood beside the table when I finished my steak. He looked actually afraid that I had not been pleased. "You're a fine cook, Henry."

"Yes, suh. Yes. I is."

"Best breakfast I ever ate."

"Thank you, Mr. Morris. Only, is you sure they ain't something I can get for you? Mist' Saul said to be sure you got ever'thing you wanted."

"It was fine, Henry. Thanks. If you'll just tell Spades I'm ready to go back to town."

Before Henry could move, the French doors were thrown open and Angie stormed through them. She wore a filmy pale green gown under a loosely tied negligee. Her hair was wild, and her eyes were puffed with sleep.

She was beautiful though, in a wildly raging way.

"Goddamn it," she yelled. "Goddamn it, Henry, who is making all that noise down here? How in hell does he expect me to sleep when he's yelling and laughing and whistling for those stupid dogs at this time of day—"

Henry sounded mournful. "He's done just this minute gone off, Miss Angie. Gone huntin'—"

She stopped walking, staring at me.

"Goddamn," was all she said. "What are you doing here?"

"Came to breakfast with Saul," I said.

She shook her head, unable to believe it. She pulled her negligee closer, knotted it.

"Henry, get me some coffee," she said.

He nodded, moving quickly.

"How about a steak?" I asked her.

"Are you nuts?" She flopped into the chair where Saul had sat. "But of course you are. If you weren't nuts, you wouldn't be out here in the first place."

She flung her arm toward the soiled dishes on the table before her. "Move this goddamn stuff away from here, Henry. Makes me ill to look at it. And put on a clean table cloth."

"You're in even a better mood early, like this, aren't you?" I said.

"Don't try to talk to me until I've had my coffee."

I shrugged, sat back in the chair. "I was just leaving," I said.

"I don't blame you." She didn't say anything else then until Henry had removed everything from the table, replacing on the clean linen cloth only two fresh cups of coffee, the cream pitcher, the sugar and the bowl of flowers. She yelped at that. "Take those damned flowers away," she said. "They give me hay fever."

"Yes, Miss Angie." Henry removed them hurriedly.

She took a long drink of the black coffee, draining her cup before she set it down. She waited, her hands shaking slightly, while Henry refilled her cup.

"I'm damned if I can see what anybody finds to be cheerful about this time of the morning," she said. Now she bent forward and put cream and sugar in her second cup of coffee. When she saw me smiling at this, she said, "Hell, no sense wasting cream and sugar in the first one. I never taste the first one, anyhow."

I took a drink of the coffee, watching her. There was a great deal to watch, even this time of the morning, or perhaps especially at this time of the morning. She still had the warmth of the rumpled bed about her.

She glanced up, her gaze struck against mine.

"All right," she said, her voice defiant, "so I look like the wrath of God."

I shook my head. "No. That wasn't what I was thinking at all."

Her mouth pulled with a bitter-tinged smile. She didn't speak to me. She glanced up. "Henry, go somewhere. You're too young for talk like this."

"Yes, Miss Angie."

"You might ask Spades to bring a car around," I said.

Henry paused, nodded. "Yes, sir. I will." We watched him walk away.

"You look exciting," I said, keeping my voice low. "Like beds weren't made to sleep in at all." I hoped there was no quality of calculation in my tone. I wanted her to believe the sight of her body like this really excited me.

"Well, aren't you nice?" She said it casually, not as though it meant anything, but only as though she were still too sleepy to protest.

"I could be nice," I said. I leaned forward, dampening my lips with my tongue, letting her watch me lick my lips. "You make me want to be."

She smiled in that sleepy, casual way. "You think if you got me in bed you'd be hurting Saul, don't you?"

I exhaled. "Do you really think I'm thinking about Saul at all right now?"

Her laugh was lazy. "Oh, I suppose you do think I'd be interesting, exciting. You probably think I know a lot more than I do. Most men do think that about most women. But mostly you hate Saul."

"No. Mostly, I want you. When you came through that door—you were all warm, rumpled. I haven't thought once about Saul since you walked out here."

"You have a nice voice."

"I have good hands, too. You'd like my hands."

"Your voice makes me all warm. I like voices that can do that. Sometimes I think maybe I'm nuts, but a voice can do a lot more to me—than touching me."

She pushed her hand through her tousled hair, pushing it away from her face. Her lips parted and her tongue darted out, moistening them.

I got up, moved to her chair. I sank beside it, touching her thigh with my hand, closing my hand on her. She gasped, caught her breath.

"Don't do that."

She didn't move away and I didn't move my hand away. For a moment she stayed poised, leaning forward slightly. I let my hand move, gently, touching her, slipping down the warm inside of her thigh, loving her with my hand.

Almost as though in a hypnotic spell she sank back against the chair, her breath rapid and short across her parted lips.

I moved my hand, faster.

"Oh, don't," she whispered, the words barely sounding at all above her rapid breathing. "Oh, no, please don't."

"You want me to." I spoke against her ear. "You want me to, as terribly as I want to. You want it, and you need it."

She writhed away suddenly and stood up. She pulled her negligee tightly about her. She shook her hair back from her face.

I stood up, too, slowly, across the chair from her. Her voice was cold, and very sharp. "You better get out of here."

"But I'll come back."

"No."

"You want me to."

"I never want to see you. I never did. I never will."

"Maybe you never did, Angie. But you will."

"I don't. Now, leave me alone. If you want to stay alive, you'll leave me alone."

"Maybe I want you more than I want that."

"You're a fool. But you're not that big a fool."

"Angie—"

"Go on. Get out of here. And just remember one thing. I'm Saul Koons' wife. That's all I want to be."

Then she looked at me and laughed.

The station wagon rolled up the drive. Spades sat there behind the steering wheel, waiting.

"There's your car," she said. "Goodbye."

"I'll be back."

She met my gaze and laughed again. "Sure. Any time. Not all Saul's guns are loaded with bird shot."

I had turned. Now I stopped and looked back at her. "No," I said evenly, "some of Saul's guns aren't even loaded at all, are they?"

She drew in a deep breath and stood tall, the breeze from the lake riffling the soft hair about her forehead. Her face was white with rage.

"Goddamn you," she said. She whispered it, but it followed me clearly all the way out to the station wagon.

It wasn't even time to get up when I got back to my room in the hotel. The sun was up now and the town was beginning to broil. It was breathless in the room, but I didn't have time to think about that.

There were a lot of angles to figure, but it seemed to me that it was falling into my hands. Angie had responded to my hands on that terrace, right there on that terrace. This girl was suffering from her own brand of malnutrition.

And Saul Koons was playing the magnanimous victor, offering me a job. Hell, a job was what I needed, wasn't it? I had to get around. There were things I had to do if I hoped to catch Koons off guard long enough to do what I had come here to do. It would be easier if I worked for Koons, in one of Koons' own trucks. And when I got to his wife, it would be that much easier.

I went over it in my mind, the things I was going to need. I made a list of them. Then I went down to the ten-cent store. I bought a roll of clothesline, two rolls of friction tape and a Boy Scout knife. I don't know why I chose a Boy Scout knife, any penknife would serve my purpose, but somehow a Boy Scout knife seemed appropriate as hell.

I walked along Main Street with my packages, feeling the sting of the sun but not the heat of it. I was chilled all the way through.

At the hardware and appliance store I checked the small tape recorders. They had several makes, but not what I wanted. The kind I wanted had to operate on battery as well as electricity. I was taking no chances this time on failing to get what I wanted.

Disappointed, I went into the drug store. Like any other drug store, they had everything for sale. They had just the kind of recorder I wanted. It operated on electric power or battery. If you had to, you could plug it into the cigarette lighter of your car. It didn't have much pickup range, not much volume, but it was surprisingly free of distortion. The sounds it recorded it played back, true and recognizable.

I was sweating when I went back into the hotel, but I was taking long steps, and I felt as though for the first time I was going somewhere, taking long, long steps.

Chapter Twelve

"My name is Morris," I told the man at the mill yard gate. "Greg Morris."

He nodded, looking at me as though he'd been expecting me. He didn't bother to smile. "Report to the personnel office," he said. He pointed it out to me.

I walked through the mill yard. The mill hands were busy now, the saws were screaming at one end of the yard and the wood grinders were working at the other. Men passed me on both sides but they only glanced at me. They had been told I was going to work here; anyhow, the word had gone around the yard. Whether they liked it or not, they didn't protest. In fact they passed me almost as though I didn't exist any more than their squat shadows in the blistering sun.

The man at the personnel office had me fill out a government work form and withholding statement. Then he told me I would be driving a pickup truck in the parts replacement department. He pointed out that shed to me along the company street.

Then he said, "But before you go to work, here's a note for you. From upstairs."

He handed me a folded sheet of paper. I opened it. It was an office memo. On it was scribbled, "Before you start to work, see me. Saul Koons."

His handwriting was slightly less legible than an over-worked general practitioner's.

I entered the air-conditioned administration building, climbed the stairs, feeling the unaccountable tightening and tension inside me.

When I stopped at the first desk on the second floor, the woman looked up. "Mr. Morris?" she said. I nodded. She pressed an intercom button and said, "You may go right in."

"Things have really changed around here, haven't they?" I said.

She didn't even bother to look up.

Saul Koons was standing at his big window looking out on his mill yard.

"You decided to go to work here," he said. He still didn't turn around.

"Why not? It's a job, isn't it?"

"Yes."

"Didn't you think I would?" I went on talking to his back. The hell with him.

"I didn't know. After what happened at the house this morning."

I laughed at him. "You mean Angie?"

He spun around as though I'd thrown something at him.

His eyes were cold. "Yes. That's what I mean. Maybe I underestimated you, Morris."

"Maybe you did."

"If you ever see her again, you'll do well to remember that Angie is my wife."

"You offered me a job. I never told you I'd take it and promise to be a good little boy."

"No. But I don't want to have to rip the flesh off your body—"

"You mean a second time, don't you?" My voice was as cold as his.

This stopped him for less than a second. "For God's sake, don't think I won't do it if I have to."

"That's your choice. Anyhow it's only a matter of which one of us does it first."

He shook his head. His hands were clenched at his sides.

"No," he said. "It won't last that long. Not if you try to mess around with my woman—at my house."

I laughed at him again. "You better talk to her."

That really twisted the knife. His face went white.

"No. I'm not talking to her, Morris. I'm talking to you. I'm not saying anything to Angie about this. And I better not have to—"

"Oh, you mean she didn't tell you what happened?"

His voice was very low. "She didn't have to tell me, boy. And that ought to be warning enough to you."

I shrugged. "Is that all?"

"I'll kill you, Morris. If I have to." That was spoken softly, quieter than ever.

I shrugged again, struggled to keep my voice in that same level pitch.

"Is that all?"

"Yes, goddamn you, that's all."

"Well. Sorry about that job."

He looked up. He exhaled sharply. "Take the job. It has nothing to do with the job. Just stay away from that house. That woman. That's all."

"I can't promise that."

He stared at me, almost took a step forward. Then he stopped, almost as if he saw I was giving him the shaft. He turned and walked back to the window.

He stood there staring out of the window. After a moment I turned, opened the door to the outer office. I waited for the chatter of typewriters to subside. I spoke clearly and loudly. "I want to thank you for giving me this job—sir."

He heeled around at the window. His face was gray. His eyes were wide, blazing. He whispered at me, "You son of a bitch."

"Yes, sir," I said, keeping my voice clear and guileless. "Yes, sir. Now we begin to understand each other."

In less than an hour I was out in one of their trucks on a delivery. I did not spend any time worrying that someone at Cedar Hill had reported my little love scene with Angie on the terrace. This didn't spoil anything. It was better. It was like waving that old red flag in front of the bull's nose. It stirred him up. The more aroused he was, the more likely he was to come charging when I wanted him to.

I spent a long time that afternoon driving the back roads around Koons Mills. I knew they'd bitch at the plant, but I'd tell them I was new in the area, I got lost. What the hell could they do? Koons himself had hired me, hadn't he?

It wasn't hard finding the isolated place I wanted. Maybe I'd better tell you first that the whole county out there was sparsely populated, with unpaved roads wandering snake-like through the pine hills and flat lake country.

A small lake three or four miles off the nearest paved secondary road stopped me. A rusted wire fence enclosed it along the sand lane. A gate had fallen down, rotted, but I left the truck outside, stepped through the break in the fence and walked down to a sagging shack overlooking the black water.

It was what I wanted. There was no sign of any other habitation around the lake, in fact the shack was on a pine-slicked incline, but the rest of the shoreline was thickly matted swamp growth.

The shack door wasn't locked but hard to open because it was warped. Inside the single room was dusty, cobwebbed, with a wood stove, an old table and a cot without a mattress. Plainly it was used for fishing trips, but it had been a long time since it had been occupied.

On the door I found a card: "For Rent. See Ben Keller. Keller's Hardware. Koons Mills."

Ben Keller wasn't thrilled that I wanted to rent his fishing shack. He had nothing against renting it to me. It was just that I had been in there earlier looking for a tape recorder. Now I had forgotten the tape recorder and was looking for a fish camp.

In Ben Keller's mind, this made a man flighty and unreliable. And I already had two strikes against me in Koons Mills.

"You won't rent it to me?" I said.

"Sure. You can rent it. Ain't nobody been out there in most a year. Fishing is poorly. How long you reckon to need it?"

"Let me rent it for a week," I said.

I saw his eyes widen slightly. "You figure to be in town that long?" Then he bit his lip. He had said more than he intended.

"I don't know," I said. "Anyway, I might get in some fishing before I leave."

That night I sat in my hotel room with the things I'd bought: clothesline, tape, knife, tape recorder, and a rent receipt on that fishing shack for a week. I sat there, going over them in my mind, looking at them, and I felt an emptiness in my solar plexus. I felt like a miser with his possessions.

Chapter Thirteen

Next morning the first job I went out on was to deliver some equipment to the Seaboard freight office in Koons Mills. I drove the truck into town, made the delivery. I didn't turn the truck back toward the mill yard. Instead I rode out toward Koons' place, Cedar Hill, driving slowly, watchfully.

I drove by the house once. It squatted silent and sun-broiled, even the lake beyond it looked like a bowl of steaming stew. From the road I could see her Cad parked in the shade near the side of the house.

I found a side road where I could watch that driveway. I parked the truck, killed the engine, and sat slumped under the wheel with my head against the seat rest.

I didn't wait long. Hell, I didn't think I would. I hadn't misread what I saw in that gal's eyes. She could fight me off, maybe—but she had to get that strength to fight somewhere, didn't she?

She rolled the Caddy out of the drive almost to the highway. She paused there a moment, looking both ways, like a careful little driver, or like a dame who is looking for somebody.

By the time she'd stepped on the gas and turned toward town, I had the truck started and in gear.

I hit the highway, going fast.

It was easy, like shooting the tame quail in Saul Koons' feeding fields.

She was in no hurry, cruising, pretty obviously waiting for somebody, something.

She wasn't even suspicious of the pickup truck racing up behind her. She didn't react until I turned abruptly in front of her, forcing her to step on the brake and pull her car sharply off the road.

When she was parked on the shoulder of the highway, I stopped the truck, killed the engine and jumped out.

She started her engine and tried to shove the car in reverse as I walked up beside her. I reached in, yanked the gear stick upward to park. She tried to reach the power window button, but I caught her wrist.

I held it, twisted, until I'd opened the door.

I released her then, stepped around the door and slid into the seat beside her.

Her mouth twisted. "What do you want?"

"We're past that category, honey," I told her. "Besides, we both know this is a rigged quiz. You know all the answers long before I get to the questions."

"I'm in a hurry."

"You've got time for me." I looked at her, at the way the red-gold hair shone, the way her anger lighted that face, the way her body pressed against her swank clothing as though the bare knit dress were fetters.

"Get out of here, and let me alone."

"No."

She drew in a sharp breath. "Listen to me. If you think because I let you touch me that morning on that terrace that I'm some sex-crazy slut, you're wrong—"

"I never said anything, except that you're beautiful, and soft and lovely—and that you need me as badly as I need you."

"I don't need you—"

"You need me. You weren't fighting just me that morning. You were fighting yourself—"

"I've got everything I want—and you're just messing it up. Can't you believe that?"

I shook my head. "No, sweetheart. I can't. Because I've seen Saul

Koons—and I've seen Walter Youngblood—and all I can say is, baby, you can't pick them."

She laughed in a frustrated, angered way. "You can get off that Walter Youngblood kick. Poor Walter. He's nothing to me—"

"He's nothing to you, and you're too much for Saul—and that's where I come in."

I slid my arm around her. I felt her tremble when my hand closed on her bare shoulder. She writhed away.

"Let me alone. If you don't, I'll tell Saul. I didn't say anything about this morning—but don't get the wrong idea. You push me and I will tell him."

"You don't have to tell him, baby. He told me."

Her face went white. Now she did thrust at me. "You've got to get out of here. You've got to leave me alone."

"I thought you weren't afraid of Saul. I thought he trusted you—"

She cried out wildly, "Stop it. Are you trying to drive me crazy? I want you to leave me alone."

"I can't—"

"You've got to. Saul will kill you!"

"Do you care?"

"No. No. I don't care. And I will tell him."

"In fact, if he suspects, you've got to tell him."

She shook her head, staring at me in a wild, tormented way. "What's the matter with you? Are you trying to get us both killed?"

"Saul wouldn't kill you, would he?"

She covered her face with both hands; trembling. "Oh, please, let me alone. Let me alone, will you?"

I put my arm around her, drew her close against me. She was really trembling. When I touched her hands to pull them from her face they were like ice.

I pressed her face back and kissed her. "I don't want to let you alone. You know I don't. You're the most beautiful thing I've ever seen—"

"Let me alone! Oh, please let me alone!"

I kissed her, gently at first, pressing my mouth harder against hers until her lips parted and our tongues met, hot, hot inside her mouth.

She writhed away, rolling her head away.

"Oh, my God! Let me alone."

She turned her head and stared at me. Her hands were still in mine and her nails were digging into me. Her eyes were wide.

"I want to see you."

"Let me go."

"Will you meet me?"

"No. I can't. You know I can't."

"You want to. Don't you?" When she didn't answer, I caught her shoulders, pulled her against me again, until our faces were only inches apart. "Don't you?"

"Are you crazy?" Her voice rose and she rolled her face back and forth on the seat rest. "Are you insane? I can't see you. Ever. He'd kill me. He'd kill both of us. You know that."

I moved my hands down from her shoulders, moving them over her body, touching her, loving her with my hands and my fingers. She tried to writhe away from me, and then after a moment she stopped writhing and lay there panting, her lips parted, her eyes wide, fixed on the top of the car, as if in a trance.

"Damn you," she whispered. "Damn you. Damn you. Damn you."

I whispered to her, telling her how lovely she was, telling her how much I wanted her. It was like Saul himself, trapping wild quail and then bringing them in to his game preserve. The same thing; it's like that with all wild things. You trap them by feeding them; you find out what they're starving for, and that's what you feed them.

"Oh, Greg ... oh, Greg, please don't. Not here ... not like this. Please don't."

"Will you come see me?" I kept my hands on her, kept moving them.

She swallowed at the pulse throbbing in her throat. "He'll ... kill me ... us ..."

"Will you meet me?"

"All right.... All right. Oh, God ... all right."

"When?"

"I don't know—"

"When?"

"I don't know.... You know I don't know—he heard—about that morning—he'll kill us—"

"When?"

"I don't know. As soon as I can ... as soon as I can get away...."

"Swear it." I couldn't think of anything for her to swear by. I couldn't think of anything that might be holy to her. "Swear it."

"I do ... I swear it. Will ... I will come, Greg. As soon as I can ... only, please, let me go now. Please."

She pushed away from me and rolled hard against the far side of the seat. Her knit dress was twisted high up over her thighs. She no longer cared. She didn't care what she looked like. The little quail was following the trail of food right into the trap.

A car raced by on the highway. She tried to pull her head down as though anybody in this county wouldn't recognize her Cad.

She turned her head, her face flushed with blood, her hair tousled and those eyes stricken. "You've got to get out of here. You were crazy to stop me here like this."

"If I'm crazy," I said, "it's your fault."

I tried to make that sound as though it was her body that was driving me crazy.

"Please, Greg, don't be such a fool—"

"Are you coming? You promised."

"I'll call you."

"Where?"

"At your hotel, Greg. I swear it. Now let me go. Get out of here and let me go."

"Call me," I said. "You've got to call me. You hear? I won't stay away unless you do.... I can't...."

She nodded, turning back on the seat as I got out of the car. Her eyes were a little less wild, and she managed a faint smile. She could believe I was wildly and passionately in love with her. That's easy for any woman to believe about any man. It was no chore at all for Angie Koons. Men had been standing in line for her since she was thirteen.

I stepped back, watching her. Sure, she believed me. I had to be nuts for Angie Koons, and it added to the excitement for her that I was fool enough to buck Saul Koons in his own town for her.

She started the car, straightened her dress, and gave me a faint smile. "You mess me up," she said. "I never saw anybody go so crazy, Greg, the way you do."

"You ought to see horses," I said. "A horse will rip himself to pieces on a barbed-wire fence for a hell of a lot less."

She laughed and shook her head. "I don't understand you, Greg. I really don't."

I stood there on the shoulder of the highway, watching her drive away, and I thought, You sure don't, baby. You sure as hell don't.

Bartley Whitman was waiting for me in the lobby of the hotel when I got there at six that afternoon.

He was dragging on a cigarette held between thumb and index finger. He had piled up a respectable stack of butts in the ashtray beside his chair.

He gave me a sick smile and jerked his head toward the elevator. He was ill about something, but neither of us spoke until we were in my room.

I nodded toward the only chair but he shook his head. "I'm not staying that long," he said. His voice had that ulcer-rasp in it.

"Is this a friendly call?" I said. "Or are you back about the Cowley woes?"

He shook his head. "I don't know why I'm here," he said. "I don't know why I bother. You're trying to get yourself killed, it's none of my business."

"No. You walked out on me a long time ago."

"I ran out on you. It's the only thing I've done lately that I'm proud of. You're dangerous, Greg. Not only to yourself, but to anybody who gets near you."

"Koons has really thrown a scare into you, hasn't he?"

"The hell with Koons. You scare me."

"What have I done?"

He held up his hand. "I don't know. I don't want to know." He paused to light a cigarette and this seemed to calm his nerves for a few seconds. He walked to the window and turned. He stood there, drawing on that cigarette as though he pulled his hope for life from it. His hand was shaking.

He stared at the small tape recorder I had bought. He shook his head, lifting his gaze. The illness was in his face now. "Oh my God," he said.

His gaze fell on the things I'd bought at the ten-cent store. He checked off the clothesline, the tape, the stubby little knife.

He looked sicker than ever.

At last he said, "In a way I feel responsible, Greg. I took your case against Koons. I lost it."

"Forget it. We never had a chance."

"I'd like to forget it. But I better tell you, Greg. If you didn't win in court, stop this." He gestured sharply toward the tape recorder, the other things on the dresser top.

"Stop what?"

"My God, Greg. Do you really think you can come into a small town like this and pull a trick that isn't even smart?"

"I don't know what you're talking about."

He stubbed out his cigarette, lit another. He walked to the door, puffing on it. He opened the door, checked the hall. He closed the door, returned to the window.

"I could give you your damn fool plan, chapter and verse. But I don't want to put it in words. You're a fool, Greg. A damned fool. You rented that shack on Loon Lake from Ben Keller. Isolated, isn't it?"

"How did you find that out?"

"Oh God, man. Everybody in town knows it. If you went out there— and attempted the stupid thing you plan—you'd have Sheriff Baskins and two deputies out there in twenty minutes. They know short cuts to

Loon Lake you've never even heard of."

I felt my face sting, felt the emptiness in my stomach. I stared at the recorder, the rope, the knife, the tape. Sure. My plan was raw, but that was the way I was inside. Maybe I was too full of hatred to think at all. Simple and savage. Get that sex-cat wife to meet me, force Saul to come for her, work him over with fists and knife, and listen to him spill his guts on a tape recorder.

I stared at Bartley Whitman, standing there smoking a cigarette, ash-gray with the sickness. He had known what I planned without even talking to me. Who else had guessed? Saul Koons? Baskins? Ben Keller? The cashier at the corner drug store?

Bartley's voice was soft. "Why don't you give it up, Greg? You can still leave town. You're a young man. You've got a life."

"Life? He killed my wife. Have you forgotten that?"

"No. That's why I came over here. First, I said to hell with you. You wanted to get killed, it was none of my business. But then I knew how torn up you are. I knew the kind of thing you would plan. Something brutal, direct. Maybe I don't even blame you. But that's what every man does, Greg, when he goes outside the law. He plans the same fool thing: to get the truth by force. Don't you think they're waiting for you to pull something like that, Greg? It's what they expect, and you're playing right into their hands."

He stubbed out the cigarette, lit another one. "When I heard that you had rented Ben Keller's fishing shack, I could have gone over the rest of your plan, step by step. Don't you think everybody heard you rented that shack? Don't you think Baskins is at least smart enough to add one and one? No matter what you think of these people, you've got to give them credit for minimum intelligence. You think Ben Keller believed for one minute you had fishing on your mind? Then I came over here, and here are all the other toys—the knife—oh, Koons would talk rather than be emasculated, wouldn't he? The rope. The tape. And the recorder."

"All right," I said. "So thanks. Maybe I'm doing everything wrong by now."

"You're all torn apart inside, Greg. I understand that. But I better warn you. You might someday get back at Saul Koons. I doubt it. But you might. But there's this you've got to get in your head—if you ever do get him, you'll have to be one hell of a lot smarter than you've been up until this moment."

He was gone and I was alone in that hotel room. Alone with the mirror, my own bitter hatred of myself, and with those trinkets I'd bought—like playthings to amuse myself with on the fast hot run to the nearest electric chair.

I stripped down and went into the bathroom. I turned on the shower full force, standing under it trying to wash out the bitterness and frustration.

It occurred to me to admit I was beat, to walk out, and let Saul Koons go on taking everything, owning everything.

I went back and sprawled naked across the bed. I had to be smarter, I had to realize that every time anybody went slugging into a fight, with nothing but rage, he got his brains beat out.

The first thing I had to do was to stop thinking and hating at the same time. Was there any way I could hit at a man like Saul Koons? Did he have a weakness?

I thought about her. She was his only weakness. You got at him, you got at him through her. He was crazy about her, and where she was concerned he thought with his viscera.

I had charged into this town with a plan as simple and as savage as my hatred, and now I had to change all my thinking, do a fast reverse or I didn't have a chance. And I wasn't going to stop for the simple reason that I couldn't stop. Maybe my only chance was that they would be thinking about that fishing shack of Ben Keller's, while from this minute I was going to concentrate on Angie Koons.

I lay there naked, and concentrated.

Chapter Fourteen

That night at seven-thirty I went into the air-conditioned drug store on Main Street in Koons Mills.

I got a dollar's worth of dimes from the druggist and went back to the public phone booth. A teenage girl was curled up in there and I sweated a few moments, waiting. Finally, she came out scowling at me and wriggled her little behind, going to the front counter.

I stepped inside the booth, closed the door. I pressed the first dime into the slot and dialed the number of the House. In my mind I could see them, Angie and Saul, at home, as nearly a picture of contentment as one would ever find out at Cedar Hill. Well, I was soon going to fix that little picture.

I felt myself being wound tighter and tighter as I listened to each separate ring of that bell across the lines.

And then the receiver was picked up. I heard Angie's voice, as light and unburdened as a bird.

I said, speaking in a breathless way, "I thought you were going to call."

I heard her gasp and then she slapped the receiver down.

I sat there in the booth, thinking about what was happening out there now. Had Saul asked her who had called? What had she said? Wrong number?

I counted to ten, inserted another dime and dialed that same number again.

It rang longer this time—fifteen, maybe twenty times. She wasn't going to answer it again.

Saul answered at last. "Hello," he said. There was anger in his voice. Whatever it was he had been doing he hadn't wanted to stop to answer this phone.

I waited a few moments, without breathing to let him know without any doubt that the line was open. Then I carefully replaced the receiver.

It was very pleasant in the booth. It was very comfortable there. I sat there until the teenager finished her banana split up at the fountain, then I counted an extra twenty and dialed the House again.

I counted and this time it rang twenty-two times and then Angie answered. She sounded ill.

"Hello," she said.

"Angie," I said. "I waited. You didn't call—"

"Hello," she said again. Her voice practically shook. "Hello." She stood there saying hello as though no one had answered at all.

"You promised, Angie. You promised you'd call me—"

She said hello one more time and then the line went dead. I sat there for a longer time, wishing I'd picked up a pocket book to read—one of those detective stories in which one man tortures another man cruelly. When I dialed this time, the line was busy.

Probably it was Saul raising hell with the phone company. If something wasn't done to improve his service, he'd buy the damned company and rip those goddamn trunk lines out by the roots....

I went out on Main Street and walked up and down the four blocks of it for a while. The movie wasn't much, but I decided to see it anyway. I bought a ticket, went inside and sat staring at the screen for two hours. I don't know what I saw, it would never win an Academy Award anyhow. A few people laughed out loud. Once in a while I chuckled, but I was thinking of something else, and was laughing in all the wrong places.

The drug store was closed when I came out of the show. I walked down to the Seaboard railway station and stepped into a public phone booth. I dialed the number of the Koons place at Cedar Hill. I sat there and listened to the telephone ringing across that line. I counted thirty times and finally I just laid the receiver on the book rest and sat there yawning. When I picked it up again, it had stopped ringing. Somebody had picked up the phone at the other end of the line and then replaced it.

It was quite a game we were playing. I wondered what Saul Koons was thinking about now.

I walked back to the hotel wondering if Saul ever thought much about the old Mosaic Law: an eye for an eye....

In my room, I fell across my bed and slept better than I'd slept for a year.

The next morning the phone rang as I was shaving. I took my time, finished shaving, went back in the bedroom and then lifted the receiver.

"Greg?" It was Angie. She was breathless.

"I waited," I said. "I—"

"Stop it. I can't talk. Not now. You know I would have called you. But I couldn't get away."

"I waited—"

"You've got to stop calling here. Do you hear me?"

"You said you'd come see me—"

"I will. I'll call you. There. As soon as I can. But don't call here again like that. He's wild—"

She dropped the telephone as though it were hot, or as though someone had come suddenly and unexpectedly into her room.

When I was returning the truck to the mill yard that afternoon after my last delivery about four, I saw Saul and four strangers in clothing even more fashionable than his boiling out of the administration building. They were laughing and talking. Their faces were flushed. They looked as if they'd been hitting the bottle up in Saul's office.

I drove the truck into the shed. I walked back to the dispatcher's desk.

"Old Saul looks like he's heading for a party."

"On his way to a football game at the university."

"Probably be gone overnight," I said.

"That's his business, Morris. Not ours."

I shrugged and walked out. In town I bought a fifth of whiskey and took it to my room. I wasn't hungry. I couldn't have kept food in my stomach if I'd eaten it. I sat on the bed. I stood at the window watching it grow dark. I waited for that phone to ring.

I waited until it was dark. I stood in that room and watched the gray night boil in along Main Street, deepening the shadows, ringing the early lights. The movie theatre stood like a patch of gaudy yellow in the falling darkness.

I glanced toward the silent phone. She wasn't going to call. I was not too disappointed, not too surprised; I hadn't really believed she would call. She had no way of knowing I'd learned that Saul had roared off to one of his football games. Besides he'd been going to a lot of football games for a long time. There must be a heavy two-way traffic out there every time he left home.

I took one more drink, gave her another ten minutes. I went downstairs, left the hotel and walked out the highway. I kept on the right side of the road down in the slope of the shoulder. Cars passed me, hurrying, but none slowed down and of course I had no way of knowing if I were recognized.

For a few minutes I stood at the gate entrance at Cedar Hill looking at the house. It was quiet. There were no lights on upstairs at all. Far in the rear there were lights in the servants' cottages, and in the darkness I could hear the baying of Saul's hounds, the yelping of his bird dogs.

I stayed off the driveway, walking slowly toward the glow of yellow spilling from the big sun room beyond the terrace.

I paused outside the French doors.

She was in the sun room, alone. She had a magazine in front of her face but it may as well have been upside down for all the attention she gave it. She sat poised there, as if listening for something, waiting. She wore a sheer gown and negligee, as if she were ready for bed—or as if she were a woman who hated to waste a lot of time with clothing.

I held my breath, listening for any sounds from the rest of the house. I moved as quietly as I could across the flagstones to the door, but she must have heard the scrape of my shoe against the stones. She laid the book down in her lap, listening.

I rapped at the door and she jumped up and hurried across the room. She grabbed the door, pulling it open, saying, "It isn't locked—"

And then when she recognized me, she almost fell.

She staggered back, reaching for something to support her. She leaned against a chair, her fingers pressing hard at the base of her throat, her eyes wide.

"What are you doing here?"

"Weren't you expecting me?"

"No. Are you trying to get killed?"

I stepped inside, closed the doors. She looked around as if the whole room were suddenly a trap.

"Saul bowled out to a football game," I said. "I waited. I thought you would call."

"I couldn't. Someone might see you come here—the servants."

I stepped toward her. "You were expecting somebody."

"Don't be a fool, I—"

"You ran across to that door—"

"I expected Henry. He—he went in town to get me a refill on my sleeping pills, that's all. You've got to go. He'll be back any moment."

The telephone rang and we both froze there in the center of the room. Angie looked around, miserable and white. She looked as if she wished the telephone had never been invented; worse, as if she devoutly wished Alexander Graham Bell had been stillborn.

It rang again, shrilling at us. She walked across the room, picked it up. She listened a moment and then I saw her sigh, sinking against the table.

"Oh, hello, darling," she said. "Why nothing, dear.... I was just—brushing my hair, that's all. Why, I'm going to bed, Saul, that's all.... I'm ready for bed right now.... I will. I will, dear. You have a good time. Goodnight, sweet."

She replaced the receiver and heeled around to face me, her face white and drawn.

Her voice was low, tense. "You know who that was? That was Saul. Said he called to tell me goodnight—he was calling to check up on me. That's the first time he's ever done that."

"I thought you said he trusted you—"

"He did—until you started this calling me, and trying to see me.... It got him all upset—it's got us both upset."

"I'm not the first one, Angie."

"Don't talk to me like that. You're such a fool.... Did you ever live in a hick town like this? Who in this town would dare to come near me?"

"I don't know."

"Nobody. They know what Saul would do. To them. To me. You've got to let me alone. I can't see you. I won't see you. You've got to let me alone."

"That's not the way you talked when I was holding you."

"It's the way I'm talking now—all right, I was excited.... Maybe it is exciting for any woman—for a man to act so wild wanting her—but I've had time to think. When I got away from you—when you called up here last night—you don't act like you care anything about me.... You act like you want Saul to kill you."

"You know better than that. You know it's because I want you so terribly. I can't think about anything else."

"Well, I can. I've got to. You must go. Right now. If you don't, Greg, I'll tell Saul—"

"There have been those other times, you haven't told him—"

"That's because I am not as crazy as you are. I don't want to stir up trouble. I thought you'd let me alone.... But if you keep coming around like this, you'll ruin everything I want. I'll tell him. I swear I'll tell him if you don't get out of here right now."

I could see she meant it. It didn't matter whether she was worried about Saul or the man she was expecting when she opened those doors for me.

It was in her eyes. If I moved near her she was going to start screaming for the servants. It was all she could do. She was really on a spot. Not only with Saul, but with that other guy, whoever he was, standing outside waiting his turn.

Chapter Fifteen

I walked out of there because for the moment that was it. She was not only scared, she was on the verge of hysterics.

I closed the French doors quietly behind me and looked back. She was standing as if paralyzed beside that telephone table. She couldn't believe yet that I was gone. Maybe she was afraid to move for fear I'd come back.

The last thing I said to her in that room was that I would come back. I tried to make it sound good by saying maybe it wouldn't be because I wanted to come back, but because I couldn't help myself. I couldn't stay away from her.

She only nodded. She was so relieved to get me out of there that she would have agreed to anything.

I walked as far as the first ring of dark trees. I stood there in the shadows and waited. I was certain I could not be wrong. She had been waiting for somebody. I wanted to see who it was. Knowing the identity of her lover seemed the most important thing I could accomplish at the moment.

I had a long wait. I leaned against the bole of a tree, staring at the glow in that sun room.

That didn't last long. After a moment a light went on in an upstairs bedroom. I saw her come to the window and close the venetian blinds tightly.

After a few minutes the light in the sun room was cut off. The whole downstairs of the big house was in darkness. In less than three more minutes that light upstairs winked out.

I stayed there in the loud night: the frogs croaked from the lake shallows, a loon screamed far across it, and the dogs yelped in the kennels. Nothing moved in the darkness. Cars went past on the highway, but none slowed to under forty miles an hour.

I stared up at that darkened bedroom window, thinking about Angie lying wide-eyed and restless on that bed. If the light in the sun room had been the invitation for her lover, the darkened house was certainly a warning for him to stay away. Whatever it was Angie had planned for tonight, I had messed it up.

A car slowed at the drive. It didn't turn in but it did pause there long enough for its occupant to check for lights in that darkened house. He even paused as though he didn't believe what he saw.

The car was too far away, and in the darkness I could not recognize it. I ran through the shadows toward the gateway trying to get a better look.

I wasn't fast enough. Suddenly that car raced away on the highway, rocks and pebbles spurting out from beneath its rear tires.

It looked as if it was going to be a quiet night at Cedar Hill. I waited another twenty minutes but the house grew quieter and the night louder. There were fewer cars on the highway now, and none slowed down at the front gate at all.

I walked slowly back to town. I wasn't convinced anymore that Angie Koons was a faithful wife. I was certain she wasn't. But she did have a lover and that kept her from starving for what she needed so badly—and she needed it. Angie wasn't only human, she was human as hell. I love these people who insist that only men want sex, and that women only endure it. All they prove is that they never met a woman like Angie. Here was a girl with all the money in the world. She had everything. She could buy anything—except what she needed most.

I glanced back over my shoulder. I'll be back, Angie. The hungrier you get, the better I'll look, and unless you decide to picnic with me, you're going to get hellish hungry in the next few weeks. But don't you fret, don't you cry, baby, because I'll be here. I'll be here. Waiting....

I paused at the hotel entrance. I don't know why I did. Instinct, the sense that something was wrong. Hell, this night everything was wrong.

A car moved past on Main Street. It rolled around a corner, moving slowly, but as I turned my head to glance at it, it picked up speed, racing.

All I could see was that there was a man in the car, alone.

I went to work the next morning carrying the tension like a knot in my solar plexus.

Why kid myself? The man in that car last night had been watching me. I didn't need a lot of gray matter to realize that this was an insurance of sorts that Saul Koons had left behind for himself while he howled at the football game last night.

I checked out my pickup, waiting for the lightning to strike. I saw Saul come into the administration building about noon. He looked haggard after a big night, a long plane flight. I supposed it would be only a matter of time until he collected all his reports from his operatives. He hired somebody to watch his house, watch the people he suspected for any reason. This was the boy I'd like to know.

I was sitting in the truck waiting for a load of equipment. I saw these three men coming along the company street from the saw shed. They weren't speaking and they seemed to be staring at me.

I sat there, waiting. Here it comes, another beating by Saul's boys, and maybe this time Saul won't pretend he knew nothing about it.

They walked right by me. They didn't even glance at me. I had been accepted as a part of this plant, but nobody bothered to be friendly.

I exhaled. What a hell of a thing a bad conscience can be. If atomic scientists would spend less time perfecting destructive machinery and more discovering a pill that would calm bad consciences, the threat of war might almost disappear.

I wiped the sweat from my forehead. Still, this sweated fear didn't mean I was going to stay away from Angie. I was just going to have to be a little more careful.

"Morris!"

It was the equipment shed boss. He stuck his head out of the double doorway, yelling for me. My first thought was that I'd been fired.

I got out of the truck, leaped up on the platform. "Yeah?"

"That equipment we wanta ship won't be ready for a while. You better get lunch while you got a chance."

I stared at him. "Is that all?"

He scowled. "What the hell? Sure that's all. What else?"

As I stepped off the platform I was telling myself I might as well stay on guard. I didn't fool myself that the man watching me last night hadn't seen me going out to the House. He must have seen me leave. He could have driven past me twenty times on that highway and I'd never have noticed him. By now Saul knew I had been out there. He'd know how long I'd stayed inside those grounds. What he wouldn't know was how little time I'd spent inside the house, how much of it I'd spent alone in the darkness.

I exhaled heavily, walking toward the commissary lunch room. Maybe Saul wouldn't let his underlings handle this; maybe he had something personal and special planned for me.

"Morris."

I stopped walking, turned. It was Sheriff Harley Baskins. He was parked near the white administration building. I hadn't even noticed his cruiser.

I paused, waiting for him.

He squinted against the sun, nodded his head to indicate the mill yard. "How you liking it around here?"

"Fine," I said. "I like it better every day."

"No," he said. His voice was cold, but very level. "I don't think you like it at all."

"Why not?"

"Do we need to go into all that?" he said. He looked pained. "I been trying all along to be friendly with you, Morris. You won't let me. Why don't we just say you ain't no truck driver, and let it go at that."

"Because I like driving a truck. It's about all I'm fit for right now. It keeps me in the open. I like it."

He cleared his throat. "We got to have the words, eh? Plain?"

"I guess so."

"This is the word, then. You don't like it here. You're moving on, Morris. You can collect your pay any time and move on."

"You mind saying why?"

"Got to have all the words, eh?"

"Looks like it."

He wiped the back of his hand across his mouth and glanced around. We were alone in the middle of the company street.

"This here is a small town, Morris. People notice things. Everything. Quick. It don't take much to start talk."

"Angie?" I said.

"Mrs. Koons." He said it sharply, his face hard.

"What are they saying?"

"What difference does it make? How long you think it'll take talk to get back to Saul in a town this size?"

"I don't know. But why does it fret you?"

"Because like I told you from the first, I don't like trouble. You're trouble. I told you at first that if you hung around here somebody would kill you. I don't want it to be Saul Koons. He's got trouble enough."

I went on to the commissary lunch room. But I wasn't hungry anymore and I didn't eat anything. I pushed a sandwich around on my plate, drank half a cup of coffee.

When I got near the administration building I saw Saul. There was another group of out-of-town visitors. More of those VIPs that he kept the quail fields for. They were laughing and talking around a dust-filmed Chrysler with a New York license. Saul didn't even glance my way as

I walked past.

But the man who really interested me in that group was Harley Baskins. The sheriff was there, smiling, bowing. He practically jumped to light cigars for the visitors. He even ran inside the administration building and fetched paper cups when Saul gave him the word.

My truck was loaded for me when I got back to the shed. I got the manifest sheet and drove out of the yard. Sheriff Baskins was still running and fetching and smiling as I rode past.

I delivered the equipment to a logging camp about ten miles on the other side of Koons Mills. I had to pass the House on the way out, and coming back I began to get that old feeling of tension. I wanted to see her. The only way to make it look good was to drive right into the yard in the truck and pretend it was business.

I parked out on the drive but I didn't even have to go into the house. Spades was out raking up some leaves near the converted stables.

I yelled at him, "I got a message to deliver to Miss Angie."

He shook his head. "She ain't here. She left. Drove away in the Caddy about an hour ago."

Chapter Sixteen

A town policeman pulled up to the curb beside me. It was about five-thirty and I was on my way to the hotel.

"Come here," he said.

I stopped walking, looked at him. "What do you want?"

"Don't give me any trouble. I'll take you in for resisting an officer."

"For God's sake—"

"That's the way it is. That's the word. You spit on the sidewalk in this town and we throw the book at you."

"You get those orders from the sheriff?"

He just stared at me. "I didn't say where I got the word. I just said that was the word. Don't make any trouble while you're here."

I watched him pull away, feeling completely tired. I was glad it was only a few steps to the hotel. I walked past the Townhouse Restaurant. I wasn't hungry. I was too tired to eat.

The hotel clerk called to me as I crossed the lobby. "Mr. Morris."

He had my hotel bill in his hand, extended toward me when I reached the desk. There were two people in the lobby, silently watching across the tops of newspapers.

"All right," I said. "I'll pay it."

"It isn't that," he said. He kept his face expressionless. "We'll have to have your room. After tonight. We can't have you here anymore."

"What's the matter?"

"Don't make it difficult for me, Mr. Morris. I just work here."

I paid the bill, tossing the money on the desk top in front of him. "The old pressure, eh?" I said.

"I don't know, sir."

He marked the bill as paid and I crossed the lobby to the elevator. I was more tired than I had ever been in my life, emotionally, mentally, physically exhausted.

I closed my hotel door behind me. The first thing I did was look for the fifth of whiskey. But when I found it, I didn't want it.

I fell across the bed. Why did I go on staying here? What was I trying to prove? By now I could admit one thing. Saul was too much for me. He was too well heeled, too secure. I couldn't touch him.

But right now I had a more immediate problem. He was squeezing, putting on the pressure. They would hound me out of Koons Mills now for sure. First the sheriff, then the cop on Main Street, and now the hotel.

Somehow I had to stay in this town. I had no friends to help me—and then I remembered Bartley Whitman. I couldn't call him a friend. We had taken turns walking out on each other. But he was an attorney, and he could help me.

I even knew how I could enlist his aid without even asking for it.

I got out of there, hurrying. There wasn't any more than a chance that I could catch Bartley in his office at this hour. When I stepped out on the street, the place was beginning to be shrouded in shadows. The stores were closed for the night. Townspeople had gone home for dinner. Everybody had somewhere to go except me.

A man was in one hell of a spot when Bartley Whitman was the only friend he could turn to.

I glanced up at his office building, checking on the off chance that there was still a light in his window. There was. It occurred to me that Bartley would be up there working on all the angles in the Cowley case. The poor silly clown had one more chance to peck away at Saul Koons.

Funny he couldn't see himself how much he resembled a Pekinese yapping at a Great Dane.

I walked up there, thinking the Pekinese would be all the aid I needed at the moment. He could fix it so I had to remain in Koons Mills as a witness in the Cowley case. It was that simple. In exchange for his aid, I'd agree to testify for Cowley in his suit against Koons. This ought to make Whitman happy—and he was a man who found little joy in life.

The outer office was empty. His secretary had gone, but the lights were burning in his office. His door was ajar.

I rapped on it and slowly it swung open, whining faintly on dry hinges.

Bartley Whitman was sprawled back in his chair. His head was twisted at an odd angle. He looked as if he had lain back to rest his eyes and fallen asleep like that.

I moved across the room, slowly, and I ground down to a full stop by the time I reached his desk.

I stood there, staring at him across it.

His eyes were wide open, distended. But they weren't seeing anything. He was dead.

I looked around the room, feeling my heart slugging against my ribs. Papers were spread out on his desk before him.

I didn't need anything but the quickest glance to see it was the Cowley brief he had been preparing. It had become his whole life—and as far as I could see, it had become his death, too.

I brought my gaze back to him. That was when I saw the bullet hole in his forehead. Somebody had stood across this desk from him and shot him with a small calibre gun. Whoever it was had stood just about where I was.

I shuddered and stepped away from the desk.

Then I heard something. It was the heavy tread of someone hurrying in the corridor, coming along it, almost running.

I didn't know who had killed Bartley, or why. All I knew was that if I were caught here in this office, it was all Harley Baskins needed to put me away.

I looked around the room for another exit. There was none. I ran to the window at the rear of Bartley's office. His suite looked down on Main Street. There was a fire escape at the rear window, but it was only ten or fifteen feet around the corner of the building from Main Street. Anybody glancing up from out there would see me going down it.

The man in the corridor was running now. He was at the outer door of Bartley's office. I had no choice. I didn't know if that man were coming in or not. But I couldn't wait to find out. If somebody wanted to fit me in a perfect frame for murder.... He was coming through that outer door and into Bartley's office.

I was already going across that sill and out to the iron fire escape as I thought this. My heels hit the ladder and I was moving down it in the darkness. I tried to move quietly, but every step was like sharp small blasts of thunder in the silent supper hour.

I kept my head down. I didn't glance toward Main Street. Even if somebody saw me up here, I didn't want them to recognize me. I hit the alley in the deepest shadows, stayed close to the building, running.

By the time I got back to the hotel, coming in from the opposite direction from Bartley Whitman's office, I had calmed down a little. Whoever had killed Bartley hadn't planned on my being up there; I hadn't even planned to go there. Maybe he had seen me go in, and hoped to frame me for that murder. I didn't know.

All I knew was that my last chance for help was gone now that somebody had killed Bartley Whitman.

The clerk barely glanced at me as I crossed the lobby. I got back in my room, closed the door, locked it, secured the extra lock. I sprawled across the bed. It looked like I would never even any score with Saul Koons now.

That killing had stopped me cold. Saul was out of my reach.

What could I do now? I hated him for what he'd done to me. He had killed my wife as surely as if he'd held a gun to her head. And it looked as if somebody had killed Bartley Whitman in his name, too. God knew, if there were justice on this earth, Saul ought to pay.

But I was beat. What could I do against him? I'd had one hope that I could wreck that phony marriage: sure, Angie was a sexy little alley cat and if I could hit at him at all now, it would be through her. But she had her own little playmates, and I couldn't even get at her.

What was left? A gun. It had worked on Bartley. It would stop Koons, too. I could get a gun somewhere, walk up to Saul Koons, press the trigger and that would end it. He would know why. There wouldn't be any need for words. He would know.

I rolled my head back and forth on the bed. But even if I got the gun, I didn't know if I could get near Koons again.

If somebody had seen me near Whitman's office tonight, I wasn't going to have another peaceful moment in this town. I'd thought the pressure was on before. And I began to see what hellish things could befall a guy who persisted in staying in a town where they didn't want him.

Baskins had played gently with me so far. Now he could accuse me of murdering Bartley Whitman, and arrest me. It was that easy. He could lose me in any one of his county jails. I could rot in one of them before I'd come to trial, if I ever did. I could yell my head off and nobody would hear me.

And I wouldn't be the first man this had happened to.

My eyes burned. I scrubbed my hands across them. I had vowed I would get justice where there simply wasn't any justice.

The phone rang. At first the sound came from a great distance. It sounded far away. I must have fallen asleep, completely exhausted, running away from truths I couldn't endure to face.

The ringing was louder and I sat up, chilled. It was very dark in the room. A few sounds drifted up from the streets.

I lifted the receiver.

"Greg." She whispered it. I caught my breath. It was Angie.

"Yes."

"I can't talk. Listen to me. I want to see you."

"Where?"

"At the House. Saul is away. He'll be gone all night. I can't talk anymore. The lights will be out. I'll be waiting for you. In the sun room."

There was the sound of a click; she had hung up. The line hummed. I sat there for a long time holding the receiver gripped tightly in my fist. I didn't know why she suddenly wanted me out there, but she said she did, and I wanted to be out there. And now that Bartley Whitman had been killed, it was even more urgent that I spend this evening with Angie. I needed an alibi for tonight. Who would be a more impeccable witness than Saul Koons' wife?

I stood there, pulled both ways. I wanted to be with her tonight and yet it was as though the wrong in this thing threw the whole world just out of balance.

Why had she chosen this moment to invite me out there?

It didn't make sense that she knew that Bartley Whitman had been killed. But did it make sense that she was suddenly wildly anxious to have me out there?

It looked like coincidence that the night Bartley Whitman was killed Angie Koons did a complete reversal and decided I was the man she wanted to spend a lonely evening with, after she'd sworn to tell Saul if I didn't stay away from her.

But it had all happened so abruptly and at the same moment in time, and I couldn't keep the two incidents separated in my thinking, not even when it didn't make any sense trying to tie them together.

I was conscious of nothing and everything, standing there. Vague sounds penetrated from the street. Somebody's radio or TV blared in the building. The hum of the phone line was vibrant. I was waiting for the tread of police feet in that corridor out there. Then it occurred to me how funny it would be if they came to arrest me for Bartley Whitman's murder, and found me with Saul's wife. Still, I could not escape the terrible twisted feeling inside me that something was wrong—dead wrong—in her inviting me out there tonight.

Slowly I replaced the receiver. It was easy to tell myself she'd been thinking about me—the morning on the terrace, my hands on her, loving her in that car beside the highway—and she'd gotten excited and called me. But it wasn't that simple. It wasn't ever that simple.

I didn't move. Something was so wrong that I could feel it all about me in that hotel room. I was suddenly very cold and I shivered from the chill.

Chapter Seventeen

Just before I stepped out of the hotel doorway I paused in the inside shadows, far enough back so I couldn't be seen from the street and yet could see both ways along it. I stood there and waited. I saw nothing unusual out there, but I was taking no chances until I saw who was checking up on me. Moments dragged by, infrequently people passed on the sidewalk, or cars moved by on the street. It occurred to me then that I might have done a foolish thing. Whoever was watching me might very well be sitting in the lobby behind me.

I shrugged my jacket up on my shoulders and stepped out into the street. I turned to the left, walking rapidly until I came to the deep shadows of a closed store. I stepped into the shadows and waited again, watching the hotel entrance. I waited five minutes. Nothing happened. The only odd occurrence was that a man I hadn't noticed across the street stepped from a shadowed doorway and walked rapidly away from me on Main Street. I waited deliberately to see if he came back. But it was quiet.

About a block and a half away, down near the theatre, I saw Walter Youngblood's gray Ford. Anyhow, it resembled his. This didn't mean anything except that at least he wouldn't be out at Cedar Hill tonight.

I moved across the shadows, stepped out into the street and kept as close as I could to the buildings. I left Main at the first side street, going in the opposite direction from Koons' big house. I walked about three blocks in the night along residential streets. When I hit the railroad, I walked left along it.

I saw no one else in the night. There was no sound except the pad of my feet on the crossties and the rocky road bed. After about a mile there were unexplained noises from the dark, skittering sounds, the sudden call of an animal, a cry of panic, a whistle, and there were the mosquitoes.

There was a faded slice of a moon and a few stars by the time I came up behind the big house. I left the tracks, walking through the orange groves. She had not lied about one thing. There were no lights on in the house. In the servants' cottage the TV was blaring and there were many lights. I crossed the yard, almost running, and then stopped in the shadows and watched the darkened house for a long time, unable to escape that persistent sense of terrible wrong. Nothing was as it was supposed to be—and that was all I knew for sure.

At last I stepped out of the shadows, feeling the pounding of my heart. I crossed the drive and went up on the terrace. I don't know what I expected. I only know that I moved cautiously, set for anything. From far away in the night a loon cried and I shivered again, chilled in the warm night.

She must have been watching for me. As I reached out toward the French doors, they opened carefully, making a whisper of sound that was a fearful noise in the night.

I stepped through the doorway and she stepped in close against me.

The first thing I noticed was that she was wearing that filmy gown. Only this time she'd left off the negligee. Her body was full and resilient against mine.

"I might have been Henry this time," I whispered, trying to keep my voice light. But something had happened to me when she pressed her almost naked body against mine in the darkness, something I would have sworn could not happen, something that had not even been in my mind for over a year. For the first time since Cora had been killed, I wanted a woman. I wanted this woman, this woman's full breasts, her rounded stomach and the way her body rose against me, pressed against me. I wanted her breathlessly and instantly.

"I've been watching for you," she whispered.

"Do we—have to whisper like this?"

"No." Her own voice rasped slightly in the same breathless way mine did.

But we went on whispering. We stood there, pressed against each other, moving gently as though in rhythm to some unheard-of music. My hands moved along her throat, loosening her hair, moving through it, feeling the warmth of it.

I didn't have to lie to her now when I told her I wanted her. But I didn't have to tell her, either. She could feel that as well as I could.

She turned her body against mine so I could feel the heat from her body, and I could feel its outline as she moved, swaying slightly against me.

"My God," I whispered.

"I've wanted you," she said. And I felt the first chill of wrong. Her body felt like she wanted me, her breath was hot against me. But she didn't sound like it. Her voice sounded as though she were acting, consciously acting.

I felt myself withdrawing slightly; some of the terrible and frantic need went out of what was happening to us. I began to be watchful, waiting for the sound as the jaws of the trap snapped on me.

"Why didn't you come to me?" I whispered. I went on loving her, moving my hands over her lovely, fiery-hot body, but I was listening now for what lies she would tell me. We were that quickly back where we started.

"I couldn't, Greg. You know I couldn't. He watches me all the time."

"Saul?"

She nodded, moving her parted lips along my throat. "Sometimes he'll tell me in detail the least things I've done all day—anything—just to let me know that he keeps up with everything I do—everywhere I go."

"You told me he trusted you."

Her laugh was bitter in the darkness. "No wife likes to boast of the kind of life she's forced to live."

"Last night I thought you hated me."

"You're a fool. Why would I hate you?"

"I don't know. But I got that distinct impression."

She moved herself in a wanton, urgent way under my hands. "Do I feel that way now?"

I closed my hands on her, feeling the throb of her heart hard against mine Maybe she didn't hate me. Maybe it was Saul she hated.

"I want you," she whispered. If only she wouldn't talk. Her voice called everything her body did lies. Even through the heat of her body I got the horrible sense of chill, the chilling feeling that she was moved much more by hatred right now than by desire. "You drive me so crazy, Greg. Your hands. Your voice. I want you.... want you...."

We had moved until our legs bumped the big divan.

"Here?" I whispered against her face.

Her voice was shaky and she tried to laugh. "Well, I don't think either one of us will make it to the bedroom."

Chapter Eighteen

We lay close together on the divan. It was no longer dark in the room; it was faintly gray. The wonder was that what we had done hadn't lighted the place up like a carnival. I could see her body plainly in the gray light. What had happened to us had been savage, as though we'd wanted to destroy each other, with sledge hammers. And I still felt, even now, that there was less heat than hatred in what she had done.

But it was a lovely body, and suddenly I was the starving one. I could not touch her enough. If this were bait, I was deep inside the trap.

I felt weak all the way through, but I couldn't forget the sensation that she was watchful, on edge, and only giving half her attention to me.

"You liked it. You really liked that." There was sarcasm in my whispered voice, but it was lost on her.

"Loved it." She moved her hands on me: sensations of delightful agony, delicious pain and the chilled thought she might move her hand away.

"You really love it," I persisted.

"Oh ... I really love it."

"You need it." I was pressing, but this was lost on her too.

"Is that bad?"

"Not for me."

"You think a woman ought to act coy? You think she ought to act like she hates it?"

"I'm tired but I'm not crazy."

"You're sweet.... Did you like it? Did you like me? Do you like the way I'm built?"

"Yes." I whispered in her ear, and in this moment I was deadly honest. "Yes. Because you're different—than I thought you'd be—there's more of you than it looks like there'll be—more of everything and still not enough."

I stared at her in the grayness of the room wondering what she would do if I told her the truth, that her body responded but her mind wasn't even with it. But I said, "You really wanted it."

She sat up. "Why wouldn't I want it?"

I felt cold when she moved that far from me. I pulled her back against me. "Don't misunderstand me. I'm not fighting it."

Her voice chilled. "Why wouldn't I want it?" Her eyes were wide, fixed on the distant ceiling. "Why wouldn't I all to hell want it? Sure, you guessed it, right from the first. Didn't you? And I hated you for knowing, for guessing.... But I can't help it. Do you think it's any fun being Mrs. Saul Koons? You know what he can do to me? He can't do anything at all to me. Oh, God. You know how long he can last? Well, he can't last at all, that's how long he can last."

"You married him."

"Sure. I married him. It was different before we were married. He was crazy about me. Wild crazy. He would do anything for me, anything I told him to do. Any crazy thing. And I wouldn't let him have me then.... Because I learned one thing—the hard way." Her eyes grew misted and she turned her head on the divan, staring through the window for a long time, seeing something beyond the window, beyond the night, something lost, gone, forever lost and gone, and forever damned. She exhaled sharply. "Oh, I found out. There's just one true way to get a man helpless for you. Any man. You can drive him crazy and he'll chase you like a hound dog. That's the way it was with Saul. It was a lot of fun then, teasing him. He was always so crazy for me. All the time. He was well over fifty, even then—and he was always—ready for me when he was around me. He used to tell me that when I walked near him he got like that and he stayed like that, and I was driving him crazy and he was following me around like a hound dog. So I never let him do anything until we got married. Oh, sometime I'd let him touch me, maybe look at me for a minute, naked, if he gave me a present—a diamond or a bracelet or something. But I wouldn't let him do anything really—and the little samples I let him have made him crazier for me than ever. He knew what I was like. And he knew he couldn't have me. Except one way. I kept him crazy. All the time, crazy. Until he had to marry me...." She laughed, a long bitter sound that wracked her body. "He just had to marry me. There just wasn't anything else.... Only it gets kind of ironic. Because all this time I had been keeping him away from me, I was building up, too—and I didn't know what he was like until we were married. And then I was caught—oh, a lot worse than he was. The damned old fool. The first time—that very first time after the wedding party and we were alone in a hotel room—in a bridal suite in a hotel in Houston, Texas. And I took off all my clothes for him because he got down sobbing and begged me to because we were married now and I belonged to him—and he begged me to let him look at me—and it—it happened, he was suddenly impotent, before he even touched me, when he just stood there looking at me, it happened, like he was a very young boy seeing a naked girl for the first time, and then he was no good, all the rest of the night, no matter what I did, no matter how crazy I was, he was no good, he was dead and ugly and no good—and he's never been any good—"

"The poor son of a bitch—"

"And I've hated him."

"You hid it pretty well."

"What else could I do? What was I supposed to do? Advertise to the world that what they snickered about and what they whispered about behind my back was true—that he was a shriveled old man, no good, and that I had married him for his money, and I was no better than a whore. Oh, no. Nobody ever found out—nobody until you came along. I couldn't help it. I could look in your eyes and I could see that you knew the truth and I couldn't help it—I tried to stay away from you—you know I did—"

"Sure."

"But I couldn't. What am I supposed to do? Go crazy? Go on until I'm in a nut house, rubbing against the furniture?"

"You ever think about divorce?"

She laughed in my face. "What chance do you think I'd have in his courts, with his lawyers? You were against him in a court once—how far did you get?"

"You got another point there."

"Another point?"

I smoothed my palms across her breasts. "With all these other lovely points, you got another one."

"You're damned right I have. He'd crucify me in a court room."

"How could he? You've been faithful—"

"You think he couldn't hire men to swear they'd bedded me down? You think he wouldn't?"

"I think he would."

"You think I'm going to give all this up?" She swung her arm above us on the divan. "You got any idea just how much there is to all this? You got any fool idea in this world just what there is in that pulp mill—even the small paper mill he runs cost him over a million dollars just to install the machinery. You know how much land Saul owns in this state? Businesses? Orange groves? Packing plants? Stocks? You got any idea how much money that rotten, evil man has got?"

"I get the idea you're not giving any of it up."

"Not without a fight. Oh, he's had plenty of dames since that first wife of his died. But I was no dame, and I am his legal wife. That's why you were crazy to think I'd jeopardize it running out to meet you. Sure, Saul runs around, drinking with sluts, goes to his football games in his private plane or his Rolls Royce, and he drinks and he cheats—or he would cheat if he could stand up like a man long enough. And then he staggers back home here and wants to know what in hell I've been doing while he was gone, who I've been bedding down with."

"Whatever you get from him, you've earned."

"That's God's truth. Whatever I get, I've earned—I've already earned. And I'm going to have it. I've stood it all this long—and I'll go right on. Let him have his sluts, and his whiskey, and everything else—let him suspect me, let him beat hell out of me, but every time he comes home, I'm going to be here, I'll still be here when they bring him in on his back."

"He thinks you cheat?"

"He doesn't know what he thinks. You've got to be a man with a guilty conscience, a man that's drank his guts rotten and his brain soft—before you'll ever know what he thinks. He doesn't think at all. He uses money instead of brains. Don't worry. You got enough money, you don't need brains."

"Maybe he thinks he has reason to suspect you."

"Well, he's crazy. Oh, I know what you think, all right. You've told me plain enough. I'm young, I'd have to see some young guy around here and fall in love with him—but you're wrong. I want just one thing—I want to be loved—just for me. Some young guy ... you're wrong. You just don't know how wrong. I've been there. I been all through that. I was married when I was fifteen. To a rotten, selfish, beautiful, muscle-bound hunk of no-good—oh, I know what they are, young and selfish. They don't want to give you anything. They want to take. That's all they want. I could walk through a field of them barefoot and never feel a thing. Oh, no. That's what Saul yells at me. The young men, the handsome young men—I must get the hots for them. How crazy wrong he is."

"You never wanted anybody else?"

She looked at me, her mouth twisted in a faint smile. "No matter what I wanted, I wanted all this one hell of a lot more.... Oh, I know. I'm here. Like this. With you.... But I want just one man to want me crazy wild—for the one man who wanted me like that I could do anything.... I was wild for you, Greg, wasn't I?"

She sounded almost frantic.

"I think you'd have had more fun if you'd have had a good cry."

"What are you talking about?"

"You. First I thought it was passion, wild crazy need. But what I thought was sex was pure hatred—you hate Saul so badly you have to burn it out of you—like this."

"Oh, you're wrong."

"Am I?"

"You wanted me. I could see you wanted me. It had nothing to do with him."

"Hasn't it? You hate him—one hell of a lot more than you wanted me."

"I've hated before."

"Sure. That first one. The beautiful hunk of no-good. You really loved that one, didn't you?"

"Didn't I though?" She cried out, laughing through the agonized sound. "Didn't I love him, from the hairs on top of his toes up I loved him. I'd have done anything in God's world for him. But don't worry—I hated him, finally, more than I ever loved him."

"You haven't had a lot of luck with men, have you?"

"Does any woman?"

"I don't know. I'm only thinking about you. About how you could love—only you can't anymore because there's nothing left, a new hate piled on top of an old hate."

"A man who really wanted me could change that."

"Could he?"

She moved those fingers on me. "You could change that, couldn't you?"

"No."

"You could try."

"Could I?"

"Couldn't you? You are a man, aren't you? You think I'm pretty. You want me. If you wanted me again, you could take me again, couldn't you?"

She could rouse me, wild and quick, no sense pretending she couldn't. "I could try."

"No. You could do it. I can feel you and I know you could do it."

"But I'm not going to."

Her hand closed on me, frantic. Her nails dug into me. "Why? Why not?"

"Let's just say you've vented enough hatred for one night."

"And you don't believe I want you?"

"I don't know."

"What don't you know?"

"Whether you wanted me at all, or just wanted to do anything that might hurt Saul Koons—and that other one, the pretty one."

"What have they got to do with it?"

"Looks like they've got everything to do with it."

"You mean you can't make me forget them?"

"Looks like I didn't."

"Looks like that's up to you. Looks like if you were man enough, you could."

"Looks like it. If that was what you wanted. But you don't. All you want is to hate Saul Koons."

She laughed. "All right. Come back to me. Now. Let's hate Saul some more. Only harder this time. Harder. Harder."

Chapter Nineteen

We hated Saul together like that until almost daybreak.

She insisted on getting a car out of the converted stables and driving me back into Koons Mills. I told her she was crazy. But she seemed happy, almost gentle, and in no phony sense of pretending, contented, satisfied. She laughed and said none of the servants would think anything about her taking a car from the garage at four-thirty A.M.; one of the only rewards in being a Koons was that any unusual act was accepted by lesser souls as perfectly natural.

It was warm in the car and I almost fell asleep on the short drive into town. For those few moments, Angie was tender and gentle and without pretenses. She held my hand all the way into town, tightly, warmly.

She parked on a dark back street and I stepped quickly from her car. The courtesy light flashed on when I opened the door and I jerked my head, staring around in the night. But there was no movement in the darkness. I closed the door hurriedly.

Angie whispered something toward me but the sound was lost in the rising purr of the engine and she moved away, racing around a corner.

I stayed in the shadows returning to the hotel. Main Street was cemetery-silent. That gray Ford was still parked down near the theatre. I couldn't be sure if it belonged to Walter Youngblood or not. But I was too tired to care.

When I walked into the hotel lobby, fear grabbed at me and for a moment I forgot how tired I was.

A uniformed cop was talking to the night clerk at the desk lobby.

I looked around wildly, wanting to run. I was sure he was here to arrest me on suspicion of murder. Bartley Whitman was dead, and though I had gotten out of his office before I could be trapped there, I could still be arrested on suspicion.

I poised on the balls of my feet. Sure, they'd wait for me here. If Bartley Whitman was dead, those people were somewhere behind it—Koons and the people he controlled. Why would they look for me in Saul's house when it was so much cleaner and neater to pick me up in the hotel?

I moved forward across the lobby, waiting. The night clerk glanced up at me with a look of distaste about his prim mouth, but he didn't speak. The cop didn't even bother looking at me.

Bartley was dead, and now the waiting was getting at me worse than an accusation or arrest would have. At least if they arrested me, I'd know what they were up to, wouldn't I?

I didn't sleep that night. I was bone-tired, weary in every muscle and every tendon in my body, but I didn't sleep. I kept remembering the way Bartley Whitman had looked slumped behind that desk, the way those footsteps had sounded like the approach of doom in the corridor outside his office, coming toward me, not hurrying but steady and certain.

When it was time to get up and go to work I moved like an anemic zombie.

I showered, shaved and got out of there. I bought a newspaper in the lobby and sat in one of the dusty chairs to read it.

The story was there about Bartley Whitman's death.

His body had been discovered by a building janitor. The gun that had killed him had not been found. Police had tested his hand with paraffin, had found that Bartley had fired a gun. There were powder burns on his face and forehead, the kind of burns that would show when a gun was held within inches of his head—the kind of powder burns present in suicide.

According to the newspaper story, the police were closing the case, calling it suicide. The reasons they gave were rather thin, it seemed to me. Bartley Whitman was depressed—he was a man who'd been born depressed. He was known to be in debt. Maybe. But this was nothing new with him.

I felt sick. Suicide? I couldn't make myself buy that. Whitman had been living for that Cowley trial. On his desk were the briefs he'd been working on when he was killed—or as the police insisted, killed himself.

There was only one ray of good in the whole ugly mess. It looked as if they were off my tail for the moment.

I managed to load my pickup. As I left the loading platform I saw Sheriff Harley Baskins.

He had parked his car outside the loading shed and was standing beside it, leaning against the left window. His thick-jowled face was freshly scrubbed; he looked as though he'd had ten hours of restful sleep. I hated him for this if nothing else.

He called me over. I got out of the pickup thinking, Here it comes. But I was too exhausted from the night with Angie, and the worry about Bartley's being killed. I couldn't care if he had come to arrest me.

I stopped in the sun, waiting. "Yeah?" I said.

He squinted in the metallic glare from the tin sheds. I waited for him to speak Bartley Whitman's name and take out his cuffs. But he didn't act as if he'd heard about Bartley's death, or if he had heard that he was affected at all, or in any way felt I might be involved. There was even a smile on his smooth-shaven face, a smile that almost reached his eyes.

It occurred to me that I could wipe that smile off by inquiring about Bartley's murder. It was public knowledge. It was in the newspaper. And to me it looked like the kind of murder that would profit Saul Koons more than anybody.

But I knew I couldn't stay healthy in Harley Baskins' county by mentioning murder and Saul Koons in the same breath. Anyhow, could even a man like Saul Koons hope to get away with murder? Oh, of course Saul had an alibi. He hadn't even been in town last night. Nobody knew that better than I—I and my aching back. He'd been away with VIP friends when Bartley was killed. Saul Koons probably never even spoke directly to whoever actually pulled the trigger that had ended Bartley Whitman's smoking habit forever, but it looked to me as if sooner or later the unexplained, unexplainable corpses would pile up by Koons' door like forgotten milk bottles.

But I didn't say any of this aloud, and though both of us may have been thinking about Bartley's death, neither of us spoke of it. He seemed to mistake my weariness for hostility—or perhaps both were in my face. He smiled. "Look. I just want to say—maybe I stepped out of line a little—"

I stared at him. "What are you talking about?"

Smiling was an effort for him, but he managed to hold it. "Don't make it tough, Morris. Like I said, I'm trying to be a white man where you're concerned. I said—more than I had any right to say—about you and Mrs. Koons."

I frowned, waking up fast. I felt my heart slugging against my ribs.

He went on talking slowly. "I mean, a hick town like this. You hear a rumor. Gossip even, and you get upset. Especially where a man like you is concerned. I got worried about what might happen if you fooled around with Saul Koons' wife.... I went overboard. I had no right to order you out of town. Forget it."

I had the same unexplained sense of wrong I got when Angie had called me suddenly last night. It didn't add up.

"It's all right," I said. "I might have to leave anyhow. Somebody has put the pressure on the hotel. They asked me to move out."

He gave a big, hearty, false laugh. "Oh, that. If somebody used some pressure on the hotel people, why, you just forget it. I'll tell you what. I'll stop by there today and tell those people that you're just all right—for as long as you want to stay."

"And that'll take the pressure off?"

He smiled. "That ought to do it."

I liked him better when he was filled with hatred. I said, "Well, that will be real neighborly of you."

"Right. I like to be neighborly. You ask anybody who knows Sheriff Harley Baskins, he'll tell you that."

I was too exhausted to eat anything all that day, and I was too full of confused thoughts to be able to think very straight. By five-thirty that afternoon I was ready to drop from fatigue.

I didn't even listen to the hotel clerk's stupid apology—a terrible mistake, they were pleased to have me—and I went up to my room. Inside, I shoved the door closed and fell across the bed fully dressed.

I was like that when the ringing of the telephone woke me up.

I sat up, sleep-drugged, and snapped on the bed light. The phone rang again, and I checked my watch. It was five A.M.

I reached for the phone, thinking it was Angie. Not quite. It was Saul.

"Well," he said. "What you going to do, sleep your life away?"

"Not as long as I'm within telephone reach of you, I'm not."

He laughed. "I want to see you."

"Right now?"

"What else? Like I told you, early in the morning. Only time I have for myself—and for my friends." There was something ominous in that pause and those last words. I could feel it, and it was more than a guilty conscience this time. I was pretty sure Saul was ready for me this morning. "I'd like you to come out and have breakfast with me. I've already sent Spades into town to pick you up."

I took a warm shower and then a cold shower and I began to feel human. As I shaved I tried to remember when was the last time I'd eaten. I couldn't remember, but something in the tone of Saul's voice had dulled my appetite anyhow. Food just didn't seem important. Saul was full of rage.

I was positive of it when I walked out of the hotel a few minutes later and saw the car at the curb. He had sent the Rolls for me. And this time I knew he had done it purposely.

Spades stopped the big car at the front door of the mansion. I got out and went up the wide steps to the veranda. As I reached the top step lights came on across the veranda and Henry held the front door open for me.

He led me through the foyer, across a formal dining room to a second dining room, brightly lighted and set for breakfast. Saul and Angie were at the table, awaiting me.

"Sit down," Saul said. He nodded toward a chair directly across from him. This put Angie between us. She gave me the briefest nod, lowering her head quickly.

And I saw why. She had a black eye, fat, swollen and purple.

I sat down, feeling some sense of satisfaction. I had no desire to see Angie beaten, but I couldn't stifle the sense of elation I got from knowing what I had done to Saul, in his own house.

Saul made pointless conversation until after Henry had served me with coffee, eggs and bacon. There was no foolishness about two-inch steaks this morning. Henry returned to the kitchen, closing the service door between us.

Saul watched me as I stirred my coffee.

"I won't waste any time," he said. "Angie says you were riding with her yesterday in her Cadillac."

There was a deep, early-morning silence in that dining room after Saul had said this.

I stared across the table at him, wondering what had happened to his private snoop service. Anybody watching me even casually would have known I staggered through a full day's work at the mill, or at least in the pick-up truck.

He kept his gaze on me and his face was expressionless.

I moved my eyes from Saul's immobile face to Angie. I played it cool. I admit I didn't feel as self-possessed as I acted, but I wasn't caught completely off-guard. I had known something was wrong when Saul ordered me out here to breakfast. The bruises on Angie showed that the Koonses had had a quiet evening of hell at home here all night. So I was able not to display any panic.

Angie was staring straight ahead. She did not look at me. Both her eyes were closed. Her chin was tilted. She did not need words. It was all clearer than any words could have made it anyhow; she was silently pleading with me to back her up in her lie.

I exhaled heavily and took a deep drink of coffee. I searched my brain for some clever repartee, but it was too early in the morning.

Saul went on, speaking slowly, full of agony, full of anger. The same thought went through my mind that had crossed it that night when Angie had been deriding him: the poor son of a bitch.

"Angie says you stopped her car and forced her to ride with you to—that place near Rainbow Lake where the accident happened."

"What?" The word burst out of me. From the corner of my eye I saw Angie sitting up straighter, rigid.

"That's what she told me." His voice sounded dead. "You can look at her and see I didn't believe her...." He shuddered, shaking his head. "She won't believe I'd rather die than lay a hand on her in anger—I can't help it. My God. She drives me to it with her lies."

By now, I had gotten over the shock. I said, very coldly—and this was easy because that's the way I felt inside—"Why did you think she lied?"

His head jerked up.

For a full half minute none of us spoke, and this can be an eternity. At last he said, "You did it? You took her back there?" He replaced his fork on the table because his hand was trembling so it looked as though he might drop it.

"What if I did?"

I ignored the gentle exhalation of breath from Angie. Saul was too wrought up to notice it.

"You took her back there. Why? Why don't you get that whole business out of your mind? Why do you go on torturing yourself with it?"

I leaned forward. "Or don't you mean, why don't I quit torturing you—and your wife—with it?"

His voice shook. "No. No, boy.... If you did that—I mean you. You're only torturing yourself."

"Am I?" I stood up. "Is there anything else you want?"

He shook his head, numb.

"I'm not very hungry," I said. "If you don't mind, I'll go on back to town."

"All right, boy. All right. I'll have Spades drive you in."

"Never mind. I've ridden in your Rolls enough."

He looked up. His eyes showed an almost human anguish. "This time I did it deliberately, boy. It was done in cruelty. It won't happen again."

"Just the same, I'd rather walk."

I went around the table without looking at either of them again. But by the time I had reached the doorway to the formal dining room, some instinct made me slow my steps, and when I was in this next room, I paused. There was a tension in that room like the silence before a storm.

It burst suddenly. Saul's voice was sharp. "I don't believe him," he said. "He wasn't with you.'

Angie's voice sounded weary, but cold. She had the upper hand now and she knew it. "Why would he lie?"

"God knows why. Why does he come back here like this? Maybe because he could see I had beaten you and he felt some misguided chivalry—a lot of men are such fools."

"Maybe. But maybe he was telling the truth. As I am."

"You're lying. Just as he lied to protect you. I was told that the man with you was Harley Baskins. He was recognized. He was seen with you. What more do I need?"

"You need a doctor. You're sick."

"If I can prove Morris was lying to aid you, Angie, God help you. God help you."

Angie's voice was sharp and full of cold hatred, "For God's sake, Saul, shut up and eat your breakfast. You're senile. You're even crazier this morning than usual."

I walked out, leaving them there. The beginning of another lovely day at Cedar Hill.

I walked back toward Koons Mills, keeping on the left side of the highway, facing traffic, the way the safety rules advise.

I was suddenly alive. I had stirred up something there between Saul and his little alley kitten. Maybe, as Bartley Whitman had warned me,

I had been unsubtle, crudely thinking I could beat a confession out of Saul before I left him dead in some lonely place. Maybe if I had trapped Angie and held her in that fish shack, Saul wouldn't even have come himself; he would have sent the sheriff.

But now it was fixed in Saul's mind that Angie was doubling him with somebody. His reports had named Sheriff Baskins, and I had confused the issue by lying to him. If I had been with Angie yesterday his operative had failed.

Saul was getting sick, and he was going to get a hell of a lot sicker before I was through with him. I want to make one thing clear: I wasn't trying to seduce his wife because it was the exciting thing to do, or because in itself seducing her would tear Saul down. I wanted to rip them apart, and stand back and watch when the pieces began to fly. If Saul Koons got enraged enough he would do something that not even his team of lawyers could fix.

I don't know where it came from. There was a whisper of sound behind me.

At first it didn't sound like a car at all. The nearest thing it sounded like was a hornet, a nest of hornets.

I had been walking along so deep in thought I hardly knew where I was. I don't know how far along the highway I had gotten from the house. It was still shadowy and cool early in the morning, and I don't remember anything passing me except maybe a milk truck.

At that buzz of sound something coiled up in me and I leaped off the road as far as I could, turning around at the same time.

A car was speeding toward me. It was on the wrong side of the road. There were no lights on it, and then abruptly the driver switched them on and the white gleam pinned me there on the shoulder.

I blinked my eyes against the blinding light, and in that flash of time the car was upon me, skimming along the rim of the pavement and at the last minute swerving out on the shoulder, coming at me like a metal monster from nowhere.

I yelled. The sound ripped from the bottom of my lungs. They should have heard me in downtown Koons Mills.

I lunged for the ditch, hitting on my stomach and rolling down.

At the very last second the driver jerked the wheels of the car to the right.

He was going so fast and his left wheels had chewed so deeply into the soft shoulder that he almost overturned. The car shuddered there a moment, swaying and nearly going over.

It plowed its way along the shoulder with the driver fighting it as hard as he could. At the last minute he was able to pull it out on the highway again. Then he stepped on the gas, streaking for the right side of the road and heading toward town at eighty miles an hour.

I lay there in that ditch, shaking all over.

Somebody had really wanted to kill me.

He had approached behind me with his lights off as quietly as he could, and then at the last minute he had poured on the speed like a maniac, hoping to run me down before I could react, and when I'd spun around he'd switched on those headlights thinking he could blind me.

For a couple of minutes I didn't move, I didn't even want to. I was too weak anyhow.

I just sprawled there, thinking about that somebody who had tried to kill me.

Somebody in a gray Ford. About seven years old. A coupe.

Somebody named Walter Youngblood.

Suddenly all the fear in me boiled up into something else—a fury that I couldn't contain.

I got up from there and brushed the sand and dirt off my clothes. I was already walking up the incline to the highway. Far down the road and heading in toward Koons Mills I saw headlights.

They were moving fast.

I ran across the road and stood on the rim of it, waving my arms. With a sense of relief and justice, I saw the car slowing. It was a new Buick. The man at the wheel was smoking a big cigar.

I got in and he was moving again all in one motion....

Three minutes later I was stepping out of that Buick on Main Street. I remembered to thank the man politely. He was a salesman and he'd talked steadily all the way into town. I hadn't heard a word he said. He didn't give a damn. He just liked to talk.

I moved along, knowing I was going to look for Walter Youngblood. That was all that was on my mind in that moment. I looked about for some place with a phone booth where I could look up his address.

I was almost to the hotel. The street was deserted at this hour. A bread truck was parked before a grocery store five blocks away. The sun was beginning to glint weakly in store display windows.

I saw that gray Ford coupe. It was parked on the side street around the corner from the hotel entrance.

At the instant I recognized Walter's car, I side-stepped hard, going against the wall and back out of his sight.

I hadn't moved fast enough. I heard that old Ford roar into life around that corner.

I sprinted. I went around the corner, off the curb and out into the street. I ran straight for the front of his car. I was there before he could thrust it into low. It didn't matter anyway. I didn't think Walter would run over me in downtown Koons Mills.

How screwy can lovers get?

My hunch paid off. Walter wanted to run over me all right. He slammed his foot on the accelerator, but he wasn't quite nuts enough to do it. He hit the brake so hard the little car bucked and stalled.

I was already going around the fender. I heard Walter moaning as he tried to start it. I slapped the door open.

He was still fighting that ignition key, but he didn't have a prayer. He was so mixed-up he'd left the car in low gear, but had forgotten to engage the clutch. He was getting nowhere trying to start it.

The door swung open and Walter yelled. It was an odd, swallowed sound. I caught him by the collar and yanked with all my strength. He came loose from that car and half fell out into the street at my feet.

I snagged his shirt front and pulled him up to his feet. He was shaking all over, convulsive shivers were going through him like tremors. He was even more frightened than I had been out in that ditch beside the highway.

My fist was so taut my nails were chewing my palms. All I could think was I was going to bust that pretty weak face into a lot of unrelated pretty weak parts.

He was babbling, sniffling, and I shook my head, sick of looking at him. My voice was so hoarse I hardly recognized it myself.

"Why? Talk to me. Why'd you try to kill me?"

He tried to talk, but it wasn't easy. He swallowed back his fear, worked his mouth, mewled some and I tightened my fist on his shirt, waiting.

"You—got to stay—away from her." The fear and hatred in his pretty face made him ugly to look at. "I—kill you...." His stomach was shaking now with his sobs of frustration. "They beat you—but you won't get out of here. You won't stay away from her.... If I run over you, you'll stay away from her—if I kill you, you'll stay away from her!"

It was one hell of a brave speech. The only thing was it was the last ounce of bravery in Walter Youngblood for the day. His knees crumpled and he sank to the gutter, retching up his insides. He was so afraid I was going to kill him that he couldn't even talk anymore.

There were plenty of things I'd wanted to say to him. I wanted to warn him to stay out of my sight, but I looked at him and knew it was no good.

He wouldn't even hear me....

Chapter Twenty

It was almost five o'clock that afternoon when I returned to the mill in the pickup truck.

On every trip all day I had watched for Angie, looked for her. I drove on the highway past Cedar Hills half a dozen times that day. I knew better than to go into that yard. Saul would have his little spies out everywhere. I was careful. I was too careful. I didn't get a glimpse of Angie.

When I turned in the truck there was a note for me. Saul Koons wanted to see me in his office at once.

"Big shot," the straw boss said. "Brown-nosing with the boss. There are hundreds of guys in this mill, been here ten–fifteen years, never set foot in Koons' office."

I didn't say anything. There were a lot of cheap answers. But I walked away along the street thinking that Saul had had twelve hours to probe into his miseries and the cause of them.

The office workers were leaving when I reached the second floor of the administration building. The receptionist told me to go on in. She was gathering up her purse and personal things as I passed her.

Saul wasn't alone when I entered his office.

Walter Youngblood sat lost in a leather chair near the picture window. He was pale. He had a highball in his hand but hadn't taken more than a sip from it. The drink looked too big for Walter, and the chair looked too big, and so did this office—and so did the world and all its problems. He didn't look at me.

I remembered the first time I'd seen Walter, standing over Angie on that terrace out at the House, begging her for something. He looked like the kind who is forever begging for something. And at the moment he looked as if he may have gotten it, and it didn't agree with him. And I remembered the last time I'd seen him, too.

"You know Mr. Youngblood?" Saul said when I came in. He nodded toward Walter in the oversized chair and I pretended that I didn't know him. I nodded, but neither of us made a move to shake hands.

Saul was standing at his bar. On a tray on its smooth cabinet surface were ice, soda water, highball glasses and a bottle of Haig and Haig.

I looked longer at the bottle of Haig and Haig than I did at either Walter or Saul. I supposed I must have known all along that it had been Saul who had sent in the fifth of Haig and Haig the night after I was beaten by the mill hands.

"You want a drink?" Saul said. He was already pouring it.

"No," I said.

He dropped in ice cubes, using a glittering pair of tongs. "Come on. Have a drink. Don't tell me you don't drink."

"I'm not telling you anything. I just don't want a drink. I haven't eaten. I'll get looped."

"Lot of things worse than hanging on a good drunk once in a while, eh, Walter?" Saul said. He stood before me with drink in his outthrust hand.

Our gazes struck, clashed. His face was gray. I took the drink. He exhaled heavily, went around his desk to where a highball awaited him. He sat in his judge's chair, a very tired-looking man.

"You lied to me this morning, didn't you?" he said.

"About what?"

"Let's don't waste time. You said you were with Angie. But you weren't. You lied."

"If you know I lied, why do we have to go through this?"

"I want to hear you say it."

"I'm afraid I can't help you there."

Saul replaced the highball glass on his desk and stood up. He stared at me, shaking his head. His voice rose, "Why do you lie to me? She wasn't with you. You know she wasn't with you."

His face was rutted, those lines and wrinkles had deepened in his face, pulling it and twisting it with the agony in him. I thought again, the poor son of a bitch, the poor rich son of a bitch. He was a man in hell, and not all the money and the AT&T stock in the world could help him.

None of this moved me to pity.

Suddenly I decided I would have a drink after all.

While I was drinking, the door behind me opened and we had our next guest.

I stepped aside, turning slightly. Sheriff Harley Baskins breezed in, walking on the balls of his feet, a big handsome man whose features were melting in fat.

He greeted everybody warmly, even me, a man with a lot of zest. It seemed sacrilegious in this room of agony. It was like laughter in a funeral home.

"Got out here soon as I could, Saul." His voice boomed. "Minute I got back to the office, got word, I came running."

Saul's voice was bitter, sarcastic. "You always come running, the minute I call, don't you, Harley?"

Harley's smile faded slightly, but reappeared fuller than ever. "You know I do, Saul. What's a friend for?"

"God knows," Saul said.

Harley began to feel the edge of the knife, but he looked around smiling. "What goes on here? Hell, how about a drink for a man, Saul, you old bastard."

"Fix it," Saul said from across the desk. "Fix it, Harley, you old bastard." He used Baskins' precise tone.

Baskins was moving toward the bar. He stopped, looking over his shoulder. "What gives, Saul? Something wrong I don't know about?"

"I don't think so, Harley. Nothing you don't know about."

Harley laughed and went to the bar. Saul let him get there, then he finished off his drink and extended his glass. "Here, Harley, freshen mine up, will you?"

"Surest thing." Harley bounded across the room, took the glass.

Saul's voice was cutting. "Two jiggers, Harley. And not too much ice."

Harley flushed slightly, but went on smiling. "Anything you want, fellow."

Saul stared at Harley across the room. "You deliver almost anything I ask, eh, Harley?"

Harley was preparing Saul's drink. He glanced up. "I guess we do each other favors," he said.

"You don't do me any favors," Saul said. He said it sharply, flicking the words like a whip. "You get paid for everything you do for me."

Baskins set the glass down on the bar. "I guess you can just fix your own drink, Saul. I don't know what you're trying to pull here, but I don't like it."

"Walk out," Saul said. He said it so softly that I wasn't even sure I'd heard it.

But Harley Baskins heard it. He heeled around and now his face was as gray as Saul's. "What's bugging you, Saul? What's the matter?"

"I'm waiting for my drink."

Harley flushed, he glanced at me and then at Walter. After a moment, he laughed and fixed the drink.

"What the hell," he said, with a forced laugh. "If you want to act like a child, it's nothing to me."

"It had better be," Saul said, taking the drink. "The way I act had better mean a lot to you. I thought I knew you, Harley. I thought I knew a man smart enough to know where his bread is buttered."

Baskins was fixing his own drink now. He heeled around.

"Drop it, Saul. I don't take that kind of talk from you—not from anybody."

"Don't you?" Saul looked ten feet tall behind that desk, his face gray, the light from the window red behind him. He loomed larger than the devil himself. "Well, maybe I've made a mistake about you, Harley."

He strode around the desk, went past me. He opened the outer office door. There were half a dozen workers still out there. He spoke to them, his voice rasping. "You people. Come here."

When they had come to the door and were standing in it, waiting, he turned, facing the sheriff.

Harley had prepared his drink and took a long slug of it straight. He stood there with an odd smile pulling at his fat face.

"I called these people as witnesses, Sheriff—"

"Take it easy, Saul—"

"Oh, no. I'm telling you, in front of all these people, Baskins. My house is closed to you." For a moment his voice shook, but it was instantly cold with rage again. He did not mention Angie's name.

Baskins said, "What the hell?"

"Do you understand me? You are not to come into my house, into this office ever again—unless you are personally invited by me."

"Saul, for hell's sake, Saul, you don't have to do anything like this."

"But I am doing it. You're tired of getting along with me, that's fine—"

"Who said that, Saul?"

Saul's voice rose. "Oh, didn't you? Well, maybe then I'm tired trying to get along with you. So now you don't have to jump when I tell you to jump. You can just stay to hell out of my sight—and away from my house."

He stood there a moment, his face muscles rigid in his gray cheeks. His hands shook when he waved the people away from the door without even looking at them. He had told Baskins clearly what he thought of him, had warned him away from his house before witnesses, but still I got the hellish feeling that this whole picture was upside down.

I couldn't escape the feeling that it was Saul who was deathly afraid of the sheriff, and that this shook Saul worse than anything else, because for the first time in his life he was afraid of something that he could no longer overcome by paying out some money.

Chapter Twenty-one

The phone was ringing when I walked into my hotel room about an hour later.

It wasn't any surprise to me that it was Angie. All hell was boiling with her and Saul. But I still didn't know all Saul had heard about her and the sheriff. I did not know what I could do to help her.

"I've got to see you. Now. As soon as it is dark."

"Where?"

"There's a road behind our groves. It leads from the highway across the railroad. It's a dirt logging road. I'll meet you there. Please. As quickly as you can."

I was empty-stomached from lack of food, but as soon as I could I left the hotel. I didn't take time to check much. But I was damned sure I saw Walter Youngblood's Ford parked a couple of blocks down Main.

I took the same circuitous route through the residential section and along the railroad track. Through the darkness I could see the black spread of the Koons' orange grove. And then on the other side of the tracks I saw Angie's Cad.

I ran down the embankment.

"Don't you know he'll be watching you now more than ever?" I said.

Her face showed the bruises of his beating. "What more can he do to me?" Her voice was bitter.

"I don't know. I think we're about to find out."

"He wasn't home yet. I left a note for him. By the time he checks up to find out if I was lying, I'll be back home."

"You sound like you've had practice—"

"You try being married to the devil for five years and see what you learn."

"No thanks."

I got into the car beside her. She grabbed my hands. Her fingers were ice-cold, trembling.

"I can't stand it anymore, Greg. I've taken all I can take."

I stared at her in the gray darkness. Wasn't this what I had wanted to happen? Wasn't this what I had wanted? Why then, couldn't I shake the feeling of wrong, of everything being just out of balance?

"What about Harley?" I said.

She caught her breath. "What? Who?"

"Oh, come on now. You can't make me believe you don't know Harley. Saul beat hell out of you trying to make you admit you were with him yesterday. Saul just warned Harley to stay to hell away from you—before witnesses."

"The damned fool."

"Harley?"

"Stop it. Don't make me hate you, Greg. You're all I've got."

"Saul seems to think Harley is all you've got."

"My God! You can't be that stupid. Not you. Only Saul could be that dumb. You ought to be able to see what is happening. Somebody is lying—about me and the sheriff—"

"Why would they want to lie—about you and the sheriff?"

"Oh, please, Greg. Be smarter than that. Isn't it clear? Somebody that hates me—but somebody who hates the sheriff more.... All they had to do was tell Saul that Harley Baskins is my secret lover. Don't you see what they could do to the sheriff if they could make Saul believe that?"

I didn't waste much time thinking that angle over. I bought it. I had been in Saul's office when Saul cut Baskins down. I saw what they'd already done to him.

It was an economical way for somebody to fix the sheriff but good, and forever.

"All right," I said. "All right."

She sighed and pressed her cold hands against me again. There was a raging excitement inside that car when she wanted to spark it.

"You're still in trouble," I said. "What are you going to do?"

"I'm going to kill Saul."

She said it quietly. She flatly stated it. As bland as though she might be asking me to kiss her. Even more calmly—just as she might have announced that there were a thousand sticks of dynamite tied under this car.

"You don't have troubles enough?"

"I'm going to get rid of him. I'm going to kill him. I'm going to get away with it."

"You mind saying how?"

"No. I want you to know. We've been robbed. At the house. Four or five times in the past five years. What if we were robbed again—and Saul was killed—during the robbery?"

"Looks like you'd be the richest widow in the state."

"Yes. I'd have everything. And it would be mine. Because I've earned it. And we can do it—"

"We?"

"I've got to have help."

"Goodbye, Angie. It's been swell—"

"Greg! Listen to me. Millions of dollars. Everything we could ever want. We wouldn't have to live here. We could travel. All over the world—"

"All that stands in the way is Saul—"

"I need help, Greg. I can't stand living with him anymore. I'll get everything when he's dead. You can share it with me. Isn't that worth some kind of gamble?"

"Why me?"

"Don't you know? Don't you really know?"

"Maybe it's all moving too fast for me. I've been driving a truck, suddenly we're talking about millions—"

"I told you. You know what I want—all I want—a man who wants me, for myself—who'll love me for myself…. You, Greg. I'd do anything in the world for you."

"You're asking me to kill a man—"

"To help me kill him. A man you have every reason to hate. A man who killed your wife, ruined you. Only now it won't be just for revenge—you can have all the money in the world…." She rushed on, breathless. "Listen to me. You've got to help me, Greg. You and me. We can do it. Tomorrow, you quit your job. You leave town—"

"That won't be hard. I don't think I'm loved out there."

"It'll be perfect. Nobody will suspect anything. You can even tell Saul you're quitting. Make it clear. You are quits with him. You go to Tampa, and in a day or two, I'll take a trip and I'll meet you there…. At the Astor Hotel on Florida Avenue. All you have to do is wait for me."

"And somebody sees us together?"

"They won't. Nobody will know you're going to Tampa. Don't buy a ticket out of town. Hitchhike to another town. Get on the bus after it leaves a station—"

"You've really got it figured out—"

"I'm in hell, and I've got to get out."

"Go ahead."

"I'll buy a cheap car in Tampa, for cash, under a false name. You and I will drive it back to Koons Mills at night. I have a key to let us into the house late. Saul will be there alone." Her hands pressed mine. "I don't ask you to kill Saul—I don't want you to. I will kill him. I've been in his hell and I'll kill him. I only want you to be there, Greg, with me, drive me and the car away. We'll abandon it, and I'll come home when they send for me with the news that Saul has been killed during a robbery."

I sat there, almost in a state of shock. It was hard to believe I was listening to a woman calmly plotting to kill her husband. But what was harder to believe was that a plan could be so simple, and so perfect.

And it was even harder to believe that she'd figured all those angles by herself.

I looked at her, shivering beside me, her eye black and swollen. Maybe it wasn't too hard to believe at that. If you live in hell long enough, maybe you begin to think like the devil himself.

Anyhow, it was a hell of a plan. I had to admit that.

"Greg." Her voice shook. "Will you help me? I've got to go. I've stayed too long now. Please. Quit your job. Tomorrow. I'll meet you. The Astor Hotel in Tampa."

After a long time a cold voice said from somewhere, "I'll be there."

It didn't even sound like my voice.

"You better go," she said. "I've got to get out of here."

"All right."

"Wait a minute." She flung herself into my arms, pressing that body against mine, that body that was so much more than you expected it could be, the hot body with all its hot memories. She covered my mouth with moist kisses. She was whispering something, but it didn't make sense. Maybe it wasn't words at all, just noises.

She pulled away at last and reached down, turning on the ignition. When she started the motor lights exploded in our faces, blindingly bright.

"Greg!"

For an instant she went all to pieces. She grabbed me with both hands, her body shaking crazily. In the moment that I had to straighten her out, I saw that it was a car that had rolled almost to us on the narrow dirt road. We had been too lost in our plotting, and in each other, to notice a car that had crept along the road without lights.

"Drive around it," I said in her ear, keeping my voice as level as I could. "Let's get out of here."

She was still shaking, but she was a girl with God only knew how many millions riding at stake. She was equal to any risk.

She thrust the big car into low gear, and stepped hard on the gas. The other car was only a few feet in front of us.

The driver slammed on brakes and at the last instant, Angie pulled the Caddy out of the ruts, hitting the weeds and undergrowth, plowing around the stopped car.

As we passed it, somebody yelled, "Please, Angie—"

I stared at the car parked in the narrow roadway. It was a gray Ford. And then I recognized the pale man at the wheel and I saw that he was alone. It was Walter Youngblood.

"Stop the car," I told Angie.

Her voice was frantic. She was pulling the car back into the ruts. "I've got to get out of here."

"It's Walter Youngblood," I said. "We better talk to him."

The very sound of that name had a tranquilizing effect on Angie. She straightened the car in the road and stepped on the brakes. She cut the engine and both of us got out, closing the doors.

Walter was already running back toward us.

Her voice lashed at him as though it were a whip across his face. "What in hell are you doing here?"

"Angie, please—"

"You're following me! I'll kill you, damn you."

"Please, Angie, listen to me. I'm only worried about you, that's all—"

"Liar! Why don't you run to Saul? Tell him."

He cried out as if in anguish. "Oh, no, Angie. I wouldn't ever do that. You know I wouldn't."

"I don't know anything about you. Except that you follow me around—"

"Angie! I'm afraid you're going to get hurt. Saul's ready to kill somebody. You know that."

I reached out and caught Walter's shirt-front in my fist. "Maybe Saul's not the only one ready to kill somebody, Walter. You listen to me. If I ever see you near me or Angie again, I'll beat you until you'll wish to God you were dead."

He was aware I was shaking him, but he wasn't even looking at me, he was staring at Angie, eyes wild. He cried out, "I'd never hurt you, Angie. I never have. I'm only trying to help you. I swear it."

Angie put her hand on my arm. "Let him go," she said.

I released him. "I'll take care of her now. She won't need you."

He looked at me a moment, tears standing in his eyes, and then he began to laugh and cry at the same time, wild insane tears pouring out of him, as though he was never going to stop. He sank down on the ground and covered his head with his arms, still laughing and crying and unable to get up.

Chapter Twenty-two

It was raining when I got off the bus in Tampa, a wet soggy day that matched the way I felt inside. I left the station and walked over to the Astor Hotel on Florida Avenue. It seemed a perfectly inconspicuous hotel, in fact it seemed almost too good, all of it too well-planned.

I got a room and a bottle and wandered around the room, drinking from the bottle. I was full of the tensions that had been stretching me tighter and tighter for the past three days since I'd left Koons Mills.

I took a drink, standing at the slick, wet window. At first when I got out of Koons Mills it had been as though some terrible weight had been lifted off me, but the nearer I got to Tampa, the more I thought about what was ahead and the more I needed another drink just to stay in the same room with myself.

I stared through the window, the rain like a silver netting between me and the street. I didn't really want to see what was out there. I didn't even really want to see what was in myself.

Saul had looked pretty relieved when I quit the mill. He wished me good luck when I told him I was quits with him, that I was leaving. Then he spoke in a cryptic way as though he'd been doing a lot of thinking about me. "I think it's best, boy," he said. "Best for all of us."

I took another drink. I'll be back, Saul, we're not really quits, but we will be.

I wondered what Bartley Whitman would think of his ex-client whom he'd been so sure could never kill anybody. And I had one more drink, to Bartley Whitman, wherever he was.

I shivered in that room. The rain made it dismal, gray. I wished I'd never thought of Bartley's name. Suddenly I was scared. In my guts, I felt the fear twisting at me. Maybe it was the thought association, maybe it was being cramped, waiting in that chilled room, but I couldn't get Bartley Whitman's death out of my mind. I didn't for a minute believe he'd committed suicide.

Bartley Whitman had gotten in somebody's way and they'd removed him.

They'd done it almost casually.

If Koons had been behind it, maybe he'd been glad to see me run. Was Koons behind it? Somebody had killed him, and then very calmly the police announced it was suicide, and the whole town accepted it. It was as though the town itself was as afraid as I was suddenly—as if they'd been afraid to question that announcement of suicide.

I didn't know who was behind that death, but I knew I had put myself in a defenseless position. I had run. Bartley was dead, and the police had called it suicide, but they could rename it in one hell of a hurry if they wanted to. Admittedly there was no connection between my leaving Koons Mills and Bartley Whitman's death; I'd hung around almost a week after he'd died. But if those people really wanted a fall guy, all they had to do now was to put out a Wanted poster on me.

The room looked smaller than it had when I entered it. It was as if the walls were pressing in on me.

When I heard the knock I felt a flood of relief, and knew it was she. Why in hell not? Hadn't I heard it a thousand times in my imagination waiting here?

I jumped up from the bed, opened the door. She came through it, and kicked it closed with her heel.

She pressed herself tightly in my arms, and I forgot everything else and remembered that night we'd had together; only one night, yet it had been so much—and so little. Her mouth was hot on mine and the chilled room was warmer.

I caught her hand and drew her toward the bed. I was all clotted up inside, the bottle didn't help me anymore, but I knew what would help.

God's best remedy for any ill that ever plagued a man.

She laughed and kissed me. "Darling. No. We can't. We'll have plenty of time for that. We'll have all the time in the world ... later."

So I had another drink. It tasted only slightly flatter than stale water.

I stood across the street from Lucky John's Auto Emporium on Florida Avenue. The street was alive with used-car lots.

I watched Angie over there, checking the cheap late models. I watched the salesmen lounging around checking Angie. Her dress looked as if she had fought her way into it and was still struggling against it. It was a dark green material and it did something for her hair, which was brighter than all the neons strung for six blocks.

She was making every effort to talk with the salesman about the car she wanted, a pale blue two-year-old, but he had the hots for her. He was a sharp character anyhow, with a tie choking him, hat back on blonde curls. He felt he was doing her an eternal favor by trying to channel her mind from the highway into the bedroom.

After an interminable time she drove the blue car off the lot. She waited for a string of cars to make way for her, then she pulled out on Florida and up to the curb for me.

She drove carefully, taking no chances. You'd have thought she had those millions riding in the car with her.

"You think that salesman will ever forget you?" I said.

"The hell with him."

"That's easy to say, but if they ever trace this car back here—"

"They won't."

"When he started making a play, why in hell didn't you walk out?"

"Darling, you're jealous."

"Like hell I am. I'm trying to be smart. You don't want to be remembered."

"You are jealous. How sweet."

"Saul Koons is jealous. You think that's sweet?"

"That's different. It's pleasant having a *man* jealous of you. You're a man, darling."

"Thanks for reminding me."

She laughed and removed her hand from the steering wheel long enough to pat my arm. "I'll remind you plenty, darling. All the rest of our lives. When this is over."

I looked up. We were already out on the highway, headed north back toward Koons Mills.

We passed a bar just at dark. "I need a drink," I said.

"We can't stop now. We can't be seen together."

"I need a drink."

Her voice got an edge. "You need a clear head a lot more than you need a drink."

"I need a drink so I can stand what my clear head is thinking," I said.

"All you need to think about," she said, "is what Saul has done to you, to both of us, all the money we're going to have. All the things we're going to do together."

"Gee," I said. "You make it sound so easy."

"It is easy," she said. "When you hate the way I do, it's real easy."

About ten o'clock we reached the outskirts of Koons Mills. I was driving. I felt a little better with something to do. I glanced at Angie, sitting with her handbag in her lap. I tried not to think about that handbag and the small blue gun she carried inside it. It was all so terribly businesslike. Like some terrible, businesslike nightmare.

"Turn right up here," she said. "We'll go around town. A back road I know. We'll miss the town."

"You know all the back roads."

"Be glad I do."

She was right. We came into the highway less than a quarter of a mile from Cedar Hill, and we didn't pass a car or see a living soul.

There were no cars on the highway now.

"Drive into the yard," Angie said.

"Are you nuts?"

"Look." There was a sharp edge to her voice now. "Can't you trust me at all? People drive in there all the time—by mistake. Nobody is going to think anything about it. Cut off your lights and go into the drive. Get as near to the house as possible. I'll tell you where to stop."

I cut the engine. Where we were in the darkness, we could see the lighted study beyond the terrace. It was on that terrace where I'd seen Angie that day—a thousand light years ago. And now we were back here together, and I could see Saul sitting alone in the study.

I couldn't help thinking that now he resembled one of those fat, overfed quails in his own feeding fields, a sitting target.

I had removed the courtesy light that flashed on when the car doors opened. Now we opened only one door and slid across the nylon seat fabric and stepped out to the ground.

I felt as though the ground were swelling and falling away from me. I knew one thing for true: I couldn't go through with it. You were right, Bartley Whitman, I couldn't kill. You were wrong about everything else, but you were right about that. I guess the law of averages made you hit it right just once. But you were dead sure right, I couldn't kill, not even that man in there.

The funny part of it was that I felt suddenly at peace. I had known for a long time I couldn't go through with this. Maybe I'd known it from the lonely moments I sat with myself in that hotel room in Tampa. The tension flooded out of me. It was gone. All I had to do was admit the truth to myself, and I was cured.

I turned toward Angie to speak, but she grabbed my arm, jerking her head toward the hedges in the shadows.

I heard the whisper of sound, too, the movement of a man caught for an instant by a twig, and then the pound of his feet as he ran away in the dark.

"Somebody," I whispered. "He saw us."

"It doesn't matter. He ran. Listen. He's still running." She turned and moved along the drive toward the house. I took a long step, caught her arm.

"It doesn't matter anyway," I said. "I'm not going through with it."

She spun around, her face rigid and eyes bright in the darkness. For an instant I thought she was going to use that little gun on me.

Her voice lashed at me.

"What's the matter with you?"

I shook my head. I stared toward that study. Saul was standing up in there, a tall, raw-boned man with gray hair and a gray, anguished face. I hated him, but I couldn't kill him. He took a drink from a glass, then picked up a handful of darts and began tossing them at a target he'd set up on the wall.

"It's all over," I said. "It's finished. I can't do it."

"Don't be a fool. You can't quit now." Her voice was above a whisper. In her rage she seemed not to care. She twisted away and dropped her handbag on the drive.

She knelt to pick it up, making noises in her throat.

"We're quits, Angie. I can't do it. I'm getting out."

She stared up at me, her face twisted with hatred. Her mouth was pulled and her voice rasped, "Go on. Go on. Do it."

Or maybe she wasn't talking to me. I was aware of movement behind me and I swung around. But I was too late. Whoever hit me behind the ear was expert, practiced. I folded like a wet shirt. I don't even remember hitting the driveway—and if I did somebody had paved it with feathers.

Chapter Twenty-three

In this dream I was being carried, bouncing like a pig tied to a litter pole. At first there was the sound of distant thunder that didn't really disturb me where I was: it barely reached me. Then I was thrown—and it was as though I landed on top of a pile of pulpwood logs. And then there was another crash of thunder, close, reverberating and bringing me slowly and painfully up out of this oblivion.

First I heard Angie's voice. She was in anguish, almost screaming: "His face! Oh, my God, Harley. You didn't have to do that."

And then Harley Baskins' voice, savage, riding over hers: "He won't need a face where he's going." Then he laughed in a brutal way. "If he does, maybe he can buy one. He could buy everything else."

She sounded as though on the verge of shock: "You didn't have to kill him like that."

"What the hell difference it make, how I killed him?"

"His face—his face—"

"Oh, shut up. You go to pieces now, you'll blast this whole deal—"

"I can't help it. I can't help it—"

"The hell you can't, baby. It didn't matter to you how he died that first time we tried to kill him—"

"He was drunk. He was unconscious—drunk, on the seat of the car. He wouldn't have known what was happening—"

"All right. So I let you handle it. Sure, you knew how to handle that big Rolls. Head it toward the bluff with Saul under the wheel and jump at the last minute—you fouled that whole deal. Well, I didn't foul this one."

I lay there and felt the horror creep upward from the backs of my legs, like a poisonous liquid that seemed to paralyze me as it flooded upward. I didn't open my eyes yet because I couldn't stand to look at them yet. It took a long time for that horror to reach my brain. She had been driving the Rolls when Cora was killed. She. Not old Saul at all. He had been unconscious, drunk, and never even knew that she and Harley had been planning to kill him when the big car plowed into mine and messed up all their careful planning. Saul had lied in court, had set up all that perjury and false testimony, not to save himself at all, but to save this woman he loved in his own strange crazy way.

It was like the sudden glare of floodlights in the darkness. Saul hadn't even suspected that his wife and the sheriff were planning to kill him. Maybe he had begun to suspect—that would explain why he had seemed afraid of Harley when he ordered him never to enter the House again. Sure. He learned they were meeting—and he suspected, he feared, and tried to do what he could to save himself.

Carefully, I opened my eyes. I could not stay there where I was any longer, knowing what I did about these two lovely characters.

When I opened my eyes the first thing I saw was Saul Koons, or what was left of him.

He was sprawled out across a shaggy white rug on the library floor. The rug wasn't white anymore; it was brown, streaked, discolored with Saul's blood. As a matter of fact you could only guess it was Saul. His face was blown away.

The poor son of a bitch. All the money in the world and this was what it bought him.

"He's coming out of it," I heard Angie say somewhere above me.

I shook my head, coming out of the daze slowly. I was only a few feet from where Koons lay dead.

I moved my arm, pressing my hand against the back of my head to keep it from flying off. My skull felt as though it were held together with Scotch tape.

I heard Baskins laugh and then I saw him sitting in a chair with a police special resting on his leg, the mouth of the barrel trained on me.

I sat up and moved my head slowly, painfully looking around. The library was a wreck. It looked precisely as it should look after a battle in which Saul Koons had lost his life during a robbery.

Everything so carefully planned. I looked at them, Baskins waiting in the easy chair and Angie, standing, white-faced and almost hysterical in the midst of all the blood and hell she'd concocted. So much was clear now when you realized they had been planning this for such a long time; they'd already tried to kill Saul once before and failed when my car got in their way.

"Let's go," Angie said, almost wailing. "I want to get out of here, Harley. Let's take him to jail—let's go."

"Take it easy," Harley said, "I'm running things."

Her head came up. She stared at him and I wondered if she knew yet what she'd traded Saul for. No wonder she'd never had any luck with men. This girl just couldn't pick 'em at all.

I sat there a moment trying to straighten out my thoughts; I was so full of horror that thinking rationally wasn't easy. She'd said they were taking me to jail—that part was clear: I was being framed for this murder. They had planned it this way—for how long? Since the night Angie had called, begging me to come to see her? Quail in the baited field.

I remembered the way she'd dropped that purse out on the drive. An accident? Or a carefully rehearsed signal to Baskins, waiting in the dark, that I had chickened out and that he was going to have to take over?

This made something else very clear. If I had come in here with her, aided her in killing Saul, I still would have been caught when I tried to run away—by Sheriff Baskins who happened to arrive on time. What a lovely, tight, beautiful frame.

It was so good that Baskins was willing to arrest me, go into court, because it was only my word against theirs. What could he lose?

I thought of one thing and I said, "Don't you think the servants heard the shot when you killed Saul?"

"What servants?" Baskins said. "Saul always sends the servants on vacations when Angie leaves here. Didn't she tell you that little detail?" He stood up, motioning with the gun. "On your feet. We haven't got all night."

Angie was already moving toward the French windows, clasping her handbag against her stomach, almost frantic to get out of this room.

I got up slowly. "How about—that man hiding out in the hedge?"

Baskins laughed, really pleased with himself. "Let me handle the details, friend. Don't worry about Walter."

"Walter?" The word was forced from me. I jerked my head around, staring at Angie. Pain almost blacked me out. "Your boyfriend, Angie? Out there? Watching?"

"Boyfriend?" Baskins laughed in a brutal way. "He was one of Saul's hired spies. Hired by the old man to watch Angie, and report. Only reason he never told Saul about Angie and me was he thought he could use the pressure on Angie to get a little loving himself."

"Let's go, Harley," Angie wailed, almost at the doors.

"You're smart enough to know you're caught," I said to Baskins. "He saw us. All of us. You and Angie."

"Don't fret about it. I saw him, too. And as soon as I took care of you, I ran him down. Unfortunately, he talked back and I had to shoot him."

"God, Harley. Let's go." Angie's voice was shaking.

I rubbed my hands across my eyes. "How many people do you think you can get away with killing?"

"As many as get in my way." His voice was cold. "I warn you. Bartley Whitman thought he could stop me. He caught on to what really happened that night at Rainbow Lake to you and your wife. Threatened to go to Koons. So I stopped him—with that little gun Angie's carrying—so at the trial we tie up this killing and Whitman's, to you and that gun.... I fixed Whitman and I'll fix you. Come on. Let's go."

He shoved me and I stumbled ahead of him, almost falling. I caught myself against the divan and turned, looking at him. This boy had all the angles figured. He had to have if he were willing to arrest me.

"There may be one more," I said over my shoulder. He paused, watching me. "As long as that guy in Tampa that sold Angie that car is alive, I don't think you're going to get away with it."

It was silent in the room. I straightened up, waiting. Baskins stared at me, and then at Angie, watching from the door, her face ill. She could not meet his gaze.

"Oh, he went for her big, Baskins. They were in that office together a long time—I don't think he'll ever forget Angie—even when she follows you to the electric chair."

The silence pressed in on us. He was a boy who never made a move until he was sure of all the angles. And here was one that stopped him. He kept his gaze fixed on Angie for a long time. Then slowly he began to shake his head, and it was as if I could read his thoughts. He wasn't going to be able to arrest me after all. His frame was perfect, but it wouldn't stand up, not as long as I was alive, not as long as a defense attorney could bring a car salesman from Tampa. He stood there, shaking his head.

Chapter Twenty-four

"Run."

Baskins said it to me between clenched teeth and at first I wasn't even sure he'd said it.

I was staring at Angie. Here was the girl who thought she'd earned all Saul's millions, and she hadn't even begun to earn them, yet. I turned around fast, so fast that he brought that big gun up in his hand.

"You heard me, Morris. Run."

"Not going to wait to get me in court?"

He laughed in my face. "I'm giving you a chance. Run."

Angie's voice rose hysterically, "Harley, no!"

I met Baskins' gaze. "I don't want to get shot in the back."

He snarled. "What you care how you get it? In the back, in the electric chair—"

"I want you and Angie to have to explain how you stood facing me in this room and shot me when I didn't even have a gun."

His voice was very low. "I'm telling you. You got one chance. You run—you got one chance."

Angie wailed. "Harley, no more killing."

"Keep out of this."

"You've killed enough!" Her voice shook.

"I'll handle this." His voice was hard, with the brutal coarseness that was in it when he shouted at his road gangs, only now he was shouting at her.

She opened her mouth, but was unable to speak.

"It's still the way I planned it," he raged at her. "We'll get rid of that car." He stepped toward me. "I told you, Morris. Run. You got one chance. I might miss you."

Angie ran back toward him. "You've got to take him to jail, Harley. You promised."

"Sure. Take me to jail. I want to hear you in court telling how you just happened to be out here and caught me—when Saul had warned you off the place—told you to stay off."

Baskins calmed down slightly. "I don't have to account to a killer. I got to protect the people of this county. Whether they want me to or not."

I moved just slightly and that gun came up again.

"Maybe," I said. "Only maybe more people than Walter saw you with Angie—hiding to meet her. Maybe they'll remember that other time when you just happened to be there—the time they ran Saul's car into mine and killed my wife. You're always around, Sheriff.... Only now it's one time too many."

"Harley—" the life was gone out of Angie's voice.

"Shut up," he snarled at her.

"You promised me," she said in that lifeless way. "I'm sick of killing—"

"What in hell's the matter with you?" He shouted. "You fallen for this guy?"

She stood there, staring at him, shaking her head as if she'd never seen him before.

"Harley. It's not going to work. We've got to run. We have to get away."

"Run? I just got what I wanted. Nobody's going to stop me now. You. Nobody."

I said, speaking straight at her, "The girl that wanted a man to love just her. And look what she got."

She shook her head, refusing to listen to me, eyes anguished.

"Harley. It won't work. We've got to get out of here."

He stared at her, eyes wild with rage. "You want to get out. Go ahead. Run."

"You loved me," she whispered, shaking her head, eyes fixed on nothing. "You swore you loved me."

He jerked his head up, snarling at that. "You were hot to believe that, baby. You never stopped once to ask yourself what in hell I'd want with you when I could buy your kind for seventy-five cents at the Crossroads any Saturday night."

She sprang at him, lunging forward, hands like claws. He brought his arm up, backhanding her across the face.

She went staggering back, fell on the floor against the divan a few feet from me. She lay there, gagging, sickened by the truth.

She shook her head and she was trembling all over.

Baskins stepped toward me and I set myself, ready to tackle him. But then I saw this was what he wanted—he was trying to sucker me into making any move at all. He could never take me into a court now. He was primed, ready to kill me. He just wanted to be sure of all the angles.

When I stood steady, he glanced at Angie. She was staring up at him.

"I hate you," she said between taut lips. Her underlip was broken and blood trickled across her chin. She didn't even know it.

"Go ahead, hate me. See what it buys you. I run things now. Harley Baskins. Saul Koons—the stupid bastard. Made me lick his boots. We'll see now who drinks the ten-buck rotgut and runs this county."

"You got nothing," I said. "It doesn't matter if you kill me—or Angie. You'll never make this frame stick."

He stared at me, wild-eyed. The gun came up. My hands trembled at my sides. I looked around hopelessly for something to hurl at him but I couldn't stop him, couldn't even deflect his aim. He couldn't miss this close to me.

There was a blur of movement. One moment Angie was sprawled on the floor and the next she was screeching, clawing at him, her hands like talons.

Baskins staggered under the impact of her body, but he was already pressing that trigger.

The sound was muffled against her body, and the bullet stopped her the way a stone wall would stop her and for a moment she stayed, stretched tall, before him.

He shook his head, staring at her. His world would really cave in if she died, and this was all he was capable of thinking in that moment.

I dived for that handbag of Angie's on the floor beside the couch. All I wanted was to get my hands on that small blue gun.

I grabbed the handbag, rolling beyond the divan, ripping the bag open, tearing at it and coming up with the small cold gun.

On my knees I saw her still wavering there between us. He was looking around for me, swinging his gun in his hand.

She toppled then, slowly, falling against him. She clung to him, dying, and he tried to writhe free of her and he swung around, trying to get free of her body.

And when he was half around, still swinging that gun in a crazy arc, I shot him. I shot him as coldly and deliberately as I could.

Something happened to Baskins' face. It was abruptly very rigid and white, deathly white.

I stood up, coming around the divan, watching to see if he would try to fire again. Baskins shoved at Angie's body as though she were something out of a nightmare he couldn't free himself from.

When he was free of her, he turned, trying to bring the gun up. I waited. But the gun was too heavy for him. He took an awkward step forward as though he had tripped. He staggered to his knees and then fell face down on the carpeting.

Angie toppled against the side of the divan and paused there a moment, wavering. I caught her as she fell and held her in my arms. There was nothing I could do; she was already dead. I went on holding her body in my arms and waited for Baskins to move. But he did not move. And I looked down at Angie, and her face was clear and young, and it was hard to believe she was what she was, what hurts and greed and more hurts had made of her, and when I looked at her, all I could feel was pity. I should have hated her, but she didn't look the same anymore, lying there in my arms. You could not look at her now and see what she had been at all.

After a long time I laid her gently down on the floor, without even knowing why I was gentle. Then I stood and looked around that room and the hell they had made in it, and then I dropped the little gun beside her on the floor. I turned then and walked out of the house and across the flagstone terrace into the night.

THE END

Harry Whittington Bibliography (1915-1989)

NOVELS

Vengeance Valley (1946)
Her Sin (1947)
Slay Ride for a Lady (1950)
The Brass Monkey (1951)
Call Me Killer (1951)
Fires That Destroy (1951)
The Lady Was a Tramp (1951)
Satan's Widow (1951)
Forever Evil (1952)
Married to Murder (1951; reprinted 1959)
Murder is My Mistress (1951)
Drawn to Evil (1952)
Mourn the Hangman (1952)
Prime Sucker (1952)
Cracker Girl (1953)
So Dead My Love! (1953; reprinted in Australia as *Let's Count Our Dead*, 1954)
Vengeful Sinner (1953; reprinted as *Nightclub Sinner*, 1954; abridged as *Die, Lover*, 1960)
Saddle the Storm (1954)
Wild Oats (1954)
The Woman is Mine (1954)
You'll Die Next! (1954)
The Naked Jungle (1955)
One Got Away (1955)
Across That River (1956)
Desire in the Dust (1956)
Brute in Brass (1956; reprinted as *Forgive Me, Killer*, 1987)
The Humming Box (1956)
Saturday Night Town (1956)
Sinner's Club (1956; reprint as by Hallam Whitney, 1953; reprinted as *Teenage Jungle*, 1958)
A Woman on the Place (1956)
Man in the Shadow (1957; screenplay novelization)
T'as des Visions! (1957, France; rewritten as *Passion Hangover*, 1965, as by J. X. Williams)
One Deadly Dawn (1957)
Play for Keeps (1957)
Temptations of Valerie (1957; screenplay novelization)
Trouble Rides Tall (1958)
Web of Murder (1958)
Backwoods Tramp (1959; reprinted as *A Moment to Prey*, 1987)
Halfway to Hell (1959)
Lust for Love (1959)
Native Girl (1959; reprint of *Savage Love*, 1952, as by Whit Harrison)
Strictly for the Boys (1959)
Strange Bargain (1959)
Strangers on Friday (1959)
A Ticket to Hell (1959)
Connolly's Woman (1960)
The Devil Wears Wings (1960)
Heat of Night (1960)
Hell Can Wait (1960)
A Night for Screaming (1960)
Nita's Place (1960)
Rebel Woman (1960)
Vengeance is the Spur (1960)
Desert Stake-Out (1961; reprinted in UK as by Hondo Wells, 1976)
God's Back Was Turned (1961)
Guerilla Girls (1961)
Journey Into Violence (1961)
The Searching Rider (1961)
A Trap for Sam Dodge (1961)
The Young Nurses (1961)
A Haven for the Damned (1962)
Hot as Fire Cold as Ice (1962)
69 Babylon Park (1962)
Wild Sky (1962)
Cora is a Nympho (1963)
Don't Speak to Strange Girls (1963)
Drygulch Town (1963)
Prairie Raiders (1963; reprinted in UK as by Hondo Wells, 1977)
Cross the Red Creek (1964)
The Fall of the Roman Empire (1964; screenplay novelization)
High Fury (1964)
Hangrope Town (1964)
The Man from U.N.C.L.E #2: The Doomsday Affair (1965)
Valley of Savage Men (1965)

Wild Lonesome (1965)
Doomsday Mission (1967)
Bonanza: Treachery Trail (1968; pub
  in Germany as *Ponderosa in
  Gefahr*)
Burden's Mission (1968)
Charro! (1969)
Rampage (1978)
Sicilian Woman (1979)

As Ashley Carter

Master of Blackoaks (1976)
Sword of the Golden Stud (1977)
Panama (1978)
Secret of Blackoaks (1978)
Taproots of Falconhurst (1978)
Scandal of Falconhurst (1980)
Heritage of Blackoaks (1981)
Rogue of Falconhurst (1983)
Against All Gods (1983, UK)
Road to Falconhurst (1984, UK)
A Darkling Moon (1985, UK)
Embrace the Wind (1985, UK; pub in
  the US as by Blaine Stevens)
A Farewell to Blackoaks (1986, UK)
Miz Lucretia of Falconhurst (1986)
Mandingo Mansa (1986, UK; pub in
  the US as *Mandingo Master*)
Strange Harvest (1986, UK)
Falconhurst Fugitive (1988)

As Curt Colman

Flesh Mother (1965)
Flamingo Terrace (1965)
Hell Bait (1966)
Sinsurance (1966)
The Taste of Desire (1966; revised &
  reprinted as *Winter Girl*, 2012, as
  by Harry Whittington)
Sin Deep (1966)
The Latent Lovers (1966)
Sinners After Six (1966)
Balcony of Shame (1967)
Mask of Lust (1967)
The Grim Peeper (1967)

As John Dexter

Saddle Sinners (1964)
Lust Dupe (1964)
Pushover (1964)
Sin Psycho (1964)
Flesh Curse (1964)
Sharing Sharon (1965)
Shame Union (1965)
The Wedding Affair (1965)
Baptism in Shame (1965)
Passion Burned (1965)
Remembered Sin (1965)
The Sin Fishers (1966)
The Sinning Room (1966)
Blood Lust Orgy (1966)
The Abortionists (1966)

As Tabor Evans

Longarm on the Humboldt (1981)
Longarm and the Golden Lady
  (1981)
Longarm and the Blue Norther
  (1981)
Longarm in Silver City (1982)
Longarm in Boulder Canyon (1982)
Longarm in the Big Thicket (1982)

As Whit Harrison

Body and Passion (1952)
Girl on Parole (1952; reprinted as
  Man Crazy, 1960)
Sailor's Weekend (1952)
Savage Love (1952; reprinted as by
  Harry Whittington as *Native Girl*,
  1956)
Swamp Kill (1952)
Violent Night (1952)
Army Girl (1953)
Rapture Alley (1953)
Shanty Road (1956)
Man Crazy (1960; originally
  published as *Girl on Parole*)
Strip the Town Naked (1960)
Any Woman He Wanted (1961)
A Woman Possessed (1961)

As Kel Holland

The Strange Young Wife (1963)
The Tempted (1964)

As Lance Horner

Golden Stud (1975)

As Harriet Kathryn Meyers

Small Town Nurse (1962)
Prodigal Nurse (1963)

As Blaine Stevens

The Outlanders (1979)
Embrace the Wind (1982)
Island of Kings (1988)

As Clay Stuart

His Brother's Wife (1964)

As Harry White

Shadow at Noon (1955; reprinted in UK as by Hondo Wells, 1977)

As Hallam Whitney

Backwoods Hussy (1952; reprinted as *Lisa*, 1965)
Shack Road (1953)
Sinner's Club (1953; reprinted as by Harry Whittington, 1956)
Backwoods Shack (1954)
City Girl (1954)
The Wild Seed (1956)
Lisa (1965; originally published as *Backwoods Hussy*, 1952)

As Henry Whittier/Henri Whittier

Nightmare Alibi (1972)
Another Man's Claim (1973)

As J. X. Williams

Lust Farm (1964)
Flesh Avenger (1964)
The Shame Hiders (1964)
Lust Buyer (1965)
Passion Flayed (1965)
Man Hater (1965)
Passion Hangover (1965; revised & reprinted as *Like Mink, Like Murder*, 2009, as by Harry Whittington)
Passion Cache (1965)
Baby Face (1966)
Flesh Snare (1966)

As Howard Winslow

The Mexican Connection (1972)

SHORT WORKS

The Man from U.N.C.L.E. novelettes as by Robert Hart Davis

The Beauty and the Beast Affair (March 1966, V1 #2)
The Ghost Riders Affair (July 1966, V1 #6)
The Brainwash Affair (September 1966, V2 #2)
The Light-Kill Affair (January 1967, V2 #6)

Classic hardboiled fiction from the King of the Paperbacks...

Harry Whittington

A Night for Screaming / Any Woman He Wanted $19.95
"[*A Night for Screaming*] is pure Harry. The damned thing is almost on fire, it reads so fast." –Ed Gorman, *Gormania*

To Find Cora / Like Mink Like Murder / Body and Passion $21.95
"Harry Whittington was the king of plot and pace, and he could write anything well. He's 100 percent perfect entertainment." —Joe R. Lansdale

Rapture Alley / Winter Girl / Strictly for the Boys $21.95
"Whittington was an innovator, often turning archetypical characters and plots on their head, and finding wild new ways to tell stories from unusual angles." —Cullen Gallagher, *Pulp Serenade*

A Haven for the Damned $9.99
"A wild, savage romp and pure Whittington: raw noir that has the feel of a Jim Thompson novel crossed with a Russ Meyer film."
—Brian Greene, *The Life Sentence*. Black Gat #1.

Trouble Rides Tall / Cross the Red Creek / Desert Stake-Out $21.95
"If these three Whittington novels are the only westerns crime fiction fans ever read, they will have experienced some of the best the genre has to offer." —Alan Cranis, *Bookgasm*

"**Harry Whittington delivers every time.**" –Bill Crider

Stark House Press

1315 H Street, Eureka, CA 95501
griffinskye3@sbcglobal.net / www.StarkHousePress.com
Available from your local bookstore, or order direct via our website.